TWICE LUCKY

Visit us at www.boldstrokesbooks.com

TWICE LUCKY

by

Mardi Alexander

2015

ISBN 13: 978-1-62639-325-7

This Trade Paperback Original Is Published By
Bold Strokes Books, Inc.
P.O. Box 249
Valley Falls, NY 12185

First Edition: March 2015

CREDITS
EDITOR: RUTH STERNGLANTZ
PRODUCTION DESIGN: SUSAN RAMUNDO
COVER DESIGN BY SHERI (GRAPHICARTIST2020@HOTMAIL.COM)

Acknowledgments

To all at BSB, a most sincere thank you for your welcome, support, and bravery at throwing a newbie writer a most wonderful chance. Receiving the e-mail from Sandy and Rad, accepting the rough manuscript with the offer of a contract, was one of the most stunning and exciting days ever.

To Sheri for nailing the cover, thank you.

To Ruth, editor of much awesomeness. Words fail me…which will surprise you, as you know my penchant for waffle. Your patience and guidance for this incredibly naïve and ignorant fledgling author has been unwavering and unparalleled. Thank you for taking me under your wing. I look forward to more adventures and paper cuts together.

To my wonderful friends, near and far—your excitement and support has been a treasure, providing much needed courage and energy with which to keep striving and moving forward, even when I had no idea what I was doing (which was most of the time). A special nod and wink to Cari who was partially responsible (albeit unintentionally) for getting me started on this writing gig, so if you don't like the book, blame me; if you do like the book, send her Tim Tams.

To my brothers and sisters who chew smoke—your selflessness and generosity of community spirit is the brightest flame of all. I dip my helmet in salute to each and every one of you.

Last, but never least, to Michelle, my very patient writer's widow, who lets me go off and do what I need to do, whether it be jumping on a red truck, or typing away long into the wee small hours. Thank you, sweetheart. My first ever dead body is dedicated to you. xxx

Dedication

For all the professional and volunteer firefighters
the world over and the families who support them.

CHAPTER ONE

Toowoomba, Queensland

The call came at 1:43 a.m. It took three rings to register in her sleep-befuddled brain—this was the third late call-out this week. She groaned as she rolled out of bed. Moving down the hall, she lengthened her strides to get the blood flowing to help speed up the wake-up process. Moving past the coat rack, she swiftly pulled off the fire pants and coat without breaking stride. This was a well-rehearsed and seamless routine. Next, she pulled a clean shirt on, then bent over and put on socks and pulled up shorts and fire pants. Boots were slid into and zipped up, helmet collected and jammed onto her head.

Without breaking stride, she locked the door behind her. Running to the truck, she wove her way into her fire coat, pausing briefly to toss her helmet onto the dash and slide fluidly into the driver's seat of the truck. She was already halfway through a mental check list: engine on, radio on, operational log out on the passenger seat, glance at the clock to check the time. She picked up the two-way radio's microphone handset and brought it to life.

"Bettsy, this is Mouse. Do you copy?"

Static applause competed with the gruff purr of the truck's engine and filled the silence of the night. No response, she tried again. "Bettsy, this is Mouse, do you copy?" She waited, hoping Bettsy was awake.

John Anthony Bettford had introduced her to the fire service nine years ago. They had shared much over the time, good and bad. She knew that no matter when, no matter the circumstance, they would always be joined by the strong tendons of mateship forged over those years.

"Copy ya, Mouse. Ready for a drive-by pickup. Bettsy, out."

"Gotcha, Betts. See you in one. Mouse, clear."

Leaning over, she replaced the two-way handset and picked up the fire-communications radio. "Firecom, Firecom, this is Turnout Rescue Nine. Do you copy, over?

She pulled the log onto her lap and logged the time: 1:45 a.m. She reversed the truck out of the shed and headed out the gate.

"Turnout Rescue Nine, this is Firecom. Respond to MVA, Middle Ridge, seven kilometres south of Freyling Park on A3. Single vehicle accident, person trapped. What's your status, Turnout Rescue Nine, over?"

She was approaching the outskirts of Middle Ridge, lights flashing blood-red patterns into an eerie, silent darkness. She could just make out Bettsy standing at the roadside, all kitted out, ready for a pickup. She eased the truck over and slowed to let Bettsy in. Betts opened the door and slid his six-foot-three bear-like frame into the passenger seat, then winked in greeting.

"Firecom, Turnout Rescue Nine has a crew of two to attend MVA. ETA four minutes. Any support on scene, over?"

Bettsy leaned forward and turned on the truck's heater. Funny, she hadn't really registered the chill until she saw him turn the heat up.

"Turnout Rescue Nine, police on scene. Ambulance called, still waiting on an ETA from them, over."

"Thanks, Firecom, will advise when on scene. Turnout Rescue Nine, clear."

"Acknowledge, Turnout Rescue Nine, zero one forty-six. Firecom, clear."

Their friendship didn't need words, and they sat in an easily shared silence as they made their way to the accident scene. She was still waking up, and she knew Bettsy was too, as their bodies began to embrace the rising adrenaline levels.

She gripped the steering wheel firmly as images of the possibilities of what might lie ahead for them at the scene of the accident crept uninvited. *Don't go there,* she mentally berated herself as she consciously shook her head as if physically trying to shuck off the what-ifs. Being fireys meant the list of what could possibly await them was almost daunting.

Bettsy must have noticed the shake of her head and reached over to pat her outstretched arm on the steering wheel. "Let's deal with it when we get there, huh?"

She turned to him and smiled wryly in acknowledgement. "I know, I'm just overtired Betts. My head's on overdrive."

"Yup, I hear ya."

She slowed the truck as she crept into the flashing spill of police lights. One officer, wearing a reflective jacket, was out on the road with a fluorescent baton of light, directing traffic that approached. She pulled up next to him.

The officer leaned into the truck's open window. "Car's off to the side. Male driver is out of the car, with a lady still pinned inside, front passenger side."

"Okay," said Betts. "We'll pull off on the opposite side to you guys and leave the lights on."

She picked up the comms mike. "Firecom, Firecom, this is Turnout Rescue Nine, blue, code two." Mac waited for the response, having acknowledged that they had arrived on the scene of the incident.

"Turnout Rescue Nine, this is Firecom, go ahead."

"Firecom, arrived on scene at A3, single car MVA. Confirm that police in attendance. We'll do a sit rep and update shortly. Turnout Rescue Nine, clear."

"Copy that, Turnout Rescue Nine, on scene zero one fifty-eight. We'll hear from you shortly. Firecom, clear."

She and Bettsy exchanged glances as she killed the engine. Each took a bracing breath.

"Showtime, Betts."

"Let's do it."

Simultaneously they opened their doors, pulled on their helmets, clipped their portable radios into position, turned their helmet lights on, donned their gloves, and stepped into the night. As they approached the station wagon, Bettsy turned to her. "I'll do a reccie, you check on the trapped person. I'll come back and we can work out a plan."

She nodded in acknowledgement. Glancing over her shoulder she quickly noticed that the driver was conscious, if not a little dazed, talking to the policeman. The officer looked up and gave her the silent thumbs up. She nodded at the officer in appreciation. Bettsy would check on him as a part of the size-up he was doing. Her priority was to look in on the trapped passenger.

As Bettsy turned left to circle the vehicle, she veered right to walk around the front of the car to get to the passenger's front door. She carefully negotiated the embankment, where the car had slid off the road and come to a halt, snugged in close to a tree. The front passenger side of the wagon had absorbed the impact, resulting in the female victim being stuck in the car, while the male driver was able to get free of the vehicle.

There was fuel leaking from under the bonnet. She could smell the crisp distinctive cutting smell of it. Small amounts of steam crept free from the engine as it cooled in the chill of the night air, but there didn't appear to be any immediate risk. She continued to make her way to the side door, confident that Bettsy would warn her to pull the victim out if the situation changed and turned nasty.

The car was tilted half on its side and resting in a drainage ditch which held water from the rain that had fallen only hours earlier. The rain might have contributed to the accident, but there was no time to think of that just yet, and anyway, not her job. She'd leave the investigative work to the police.

She had to get down on her hands and knees to see if there was a way in. "Great," she murmured. She was tired, cold, and now wet. She could just make out the woman lying against the door and window, softly moaning. The trapped woman was quite still, but moaning was good, meant she was still breathing. Mac walked to the front of the vehicle where her partner was taking a closer look at the engine and the tilted position of the car.

"What's the go, Betts?"

"Driver's name is Rob and he's okay. Few cuts and bruises and he's had his bell rung a bit, but for the most part he's good. The cops will keep an eye on him and let me know if things change. The lady's name is Bella. As for the car, we've got fuel leaking, the engine seems to be okay, I've disconnected all that I can, but I'll keep an eye on it.

I'd like to try and rope off the vehicle to stabilize it a bit, in case we get a bit more rain." Bettsy shrugged casually and grinned. "Don't want it to slip away when they've gone to so much trouble to park it here. Then I'll put up a containment line for the fuel. You?"

"The front is pretty squashed, so we might need to cut her out. Not sure how bad yet—I'll pop in from the top and get a closer look. I'll go to the truck and get the first-aid kit, spreaders, and blanket, and I'll radio Firecom and give them an update."

She pulled the equipment they needed off the truck, then grabbed her shoulder mike. "Firecom, Firecom, this is Turnout Rescue Nine."

"Turnout Rescue Nine, this is Firecom, go ahead."

"Firecom, confirm code nine, alpha two. Single vehicle, white Holden Calais 2010 model station wagon that has left the road. It's resting on the passenger side in a drainage ditch. Male driver free and conscious, appears to have minor superficial injuries, female passenger is still trapped in the vehicle, semiconscious. There's a small amount of fuel leaking from the vehicle, no danger at this stage. We will secure the vehicle and contain the spill to keep it from the table drain. Any ETA on the ambos? Over."

"Turnout Rescue Nine, nearest ambulance is finishing off on another call and could be twenty minutes away."

"Copy that, Firecom. We'll do our best 'til the cavalry arrive. Any developments and we'll let you know. Turnout Rescue Nine, clear."

"Copy that Turnout Rescue Nine. Keep in touch. Firecom, clear."

Straightening up, she shut the door, picked up the gear, and headed back to the accident scene. She stopped shy of the car to put on a double pair of latex medical gloves and threw the blanket to the top side of the car. She looked over to where Bettsy was tying off a security line on the car to some adjacent trees. "Stable enough for a crawl in?"

"Yeah, I'll tie off another line to be sure, but it should be okay for the minute. Just go steady in there. Holler if you need me."

She waved in acknowledgement. "No worries. I'm going in."

She grabbed the top side of the driver's window and tested the stability of the car. It held. She picked up the kit and placed it against the driver's door window which was still rolled up. She leaned over to the back window and popped the glass.

Carefully she lowered herself into the vehicle. "Hey, Bella, my name is Mac, but my friends call me Mouse. I'm with the fire brigade. You and Rob have been in an accident. Rob's okay, and I'm here to see if we can help you. Can you hear me, Bella? Can you open your eyes, sweetie?"

Bella moaned briefly, but her eyes remained closed.

Mac's helmet light lit up the cabin. Bella appeared to be in her early twenties. She had a decent three-inch head laceration and a shoulder that looked out of line. It was probably dislocated from the impact when the car hit the ditch, bodily slamming her into the side door and window.

Leaning forward over the seat to get a better view, Mac could see the dash and seat were jammed up, with Bella's legs hemmed in the middle. They were definitely going to need the spreaders to get her out. Worse still, Bella was very definitely pregnant, and about eight months along by the guess. "Shit."

Mac reached behind to where she stowed her kit and grabbed the stabilizing neck collar.

"Bella, I'm going to put this neck collar on. It's going to feel a little strange, but it'll help to keep your neck and head safe, honey. Okay?" Mac wasn't really expecting an answer as Bella appeared to be fairly out of it, but experience taught her that talking to people, even when they were unconscious, helped keep them calm, in addition to letting them know that somebody was there for them.

Mac felt for a pulse on Bella's neck—it was weak, but steady. Next she did a quick overall check. Bella's breathing was shallow, but regular. A quick check of her pupils showed them to be equal and responsive to the light on her helmet. Bella was pale and clammy from shock, but apart from some bruising starting to colour up in places, the shoulder and head wound seemed to be the initial obvious extent of Bella's injuries.

Bettsy stuck his head in the top window. "How's it going in there?"

"Not too bad. She's still out to it, but doing okay. Looks like a busted shoulder, head lac, bruising, and entrapment. Gonna need help with the spreaders. You might want to radio Firecom and get them to give the hospital a heads-up. Bella here is pregnant, looks like third trimester—they might want to call the OB team for a standby. I'll get some fluids started. Can you grab the O2 from the truck?"

"Gotcha—onto it." Bettsy slid off the car and set about calling in the details.

Mac opened the first-aid kit, retrieving an IV kit and a bag of saline. Being first response medi trained, she could start IV fluids without having to wait for the ambos to arrive in order to help combat shock and fluid loss. A line would also provide a quick site for any medications that might need administering by the ambos en route to the hospital. She tied off the band, tapped the vein at the wrist. "Hey, Bella? I'm going to put an IV line in your arm, honey. You'll feel a bit of a sharp scratch here." The needle went in quickly, the flash of blood showing she had hit pay dirt with a good vein. "Nearly there..." She flushed the line, attached the tube, and opened the gate on the bag, regulating the flow, then finished with taping the cannula down on her wrist. "Good girl, all done."

Bella opened her eyes slightly, trying to focus on her surroundings.

"Hey, sweetie. Can you hear me?"

Bella groaned and tried to nod her head. Mac watched as Bella's eyes changed from confusion at hearing a stranger's voice to surprise and apprehension as she felt the restriction around her throat from the neck brace, finally sliding to fear as she realized what had happened to her.

"Can you tell me your name?"

"Bella, Bella Larsen."

"Hi, Bella, my friends call me Mouse and I'm with the fire brigade. You and Rob have been in a car accident. Rob's okay and is outside with my friend, Bettsy. Your head and neck might feel a little weird because I've put a neck collar on you. It's just for precaution to keep your head and neck nice and safe and still. I'm going to ask you some questions, so try not to nod or shake your head when you answer them. Is that okay?"

"Yes," she whispered.

"Good girl." Mac had one hand on Bella's arm and with her other she reached around into her breast pocket, pulling out a small notebook and pen to take notes.

"Bella, how old are you?"

Bella whispered, "I'm twenty-four."

"Do you know your date of birth?"

"Yes, twenty-fourth of May, 1989."

"Are you on any medications?"

"No, only vitamin supplements."

"Are you allergic to anything?"

"No."

"Can you take a deep breath for me? Does that hurt anywhere?"

Bella took a breath. "No."

"Does your neck or back hurt?"

"No. They're okay."

"How many weeks pregnant are you, honey?"

"Thirty-six weeks."

"And everything going okay with the pregnancy? No high blood pressure or sugar issues?

"No, everything's fine."

"Any spotting?"

"No, so far it's all been good. I haven't had any problems, apart from morning sickness…Do you think my baby will be okay?" Bella's eyes were pools of fear.

Mac had always exercised a policy of trying to be honest where she could. The trick was finding a gentle middle ground. She held Bella's hand in hers and looked into Bella's eyes. "Well, we won't know for sure until we get you both checked out at the hospital, which shouldn't be too much longer now. In the meantime, you and baby bubble here are the most important people, so we are going to look after you with top VIP priority, how's that sound?"

Bella clutched her hand tightly and hoarsely said, "Thank you."

"That's okay, sweetie. Can you tell me when you last had something to eat and drink tonight?"

"Um, we had dinner around half six, before the show, and a couple of soft drinks during the concert, so my last was probably around eleven."

"Okay, great. Do you remember what happened tonight?"

Bella closed her eyes. "We were trying to get home. We'd been to a concert"—she smiled ruefully—"and we figured it would be the last chance to see a band for a while. We were going steady, because of the rain, talking and laughing…and then we started skidding. Rob tried to wrestle the car on the road, but we were spinning. I remember a loud noise…" She started to sniffle and tear up, and she looked up at Mac with tears rolling down her face. "I don't remember anything after that. I'm sorry".

"Shh, it's okay, sweetie. You've done a great job. Can you tell me where it hurts?"

"My shoulder's sore and my head hurts. I can't move my legs. They're stuck."

"Uh-huh. You got thrown about a bit and the dashboard has folded in and is pressing on your legs. We'll have you out in a little bit. You're doing a great job. You let me know if anything else starts to hurt. Okay?"

"Okay."

There was some rustling overhead. Bettsy popped his head over the top. "Here's the O2."

"Thanks, Betts. Any ETA on the ambos?"

"Yeah, they're en route and about five away. How's things in here?"

"All good. Thanks for the tank."

"No worries. I'll get the spreaders ready for when they get here."

"Cheers, buddy."

Bettsy climbed down and she could hear the rustle and clank of items being set up, ready for the extrication.

"I'm going to put this oxygen mask on you, Bella. It will help you and the baby with shock. Okay?"

Bella murmured her agreement and the mask was quickly put on her face and the elastic over her head.

"I know it's not easy, but just try and breathe deeply and relax as best you can." Bella took a deep couple of breaths. "Thatta girl, you're doing great. The paramedics are on their way and we'll have you out in a jiffy." Mac wrote some more notes in her pocket book, ready for handover.

Bella didn't respond. Mac looked up from her notes—Bella's face was covered in a fine sheen of sweat. "Bella? You okay?"

Just then Bella gasped and clutched her belly with her uninjured arm. Both women looked down at the same time and noticed a damp blood-tinged stain start to blossom and spread on Bella's dress.

"Talk to me, Bella. What's happening, sweetie?"

"Oh! Cramps...oh God! The baby, it's too early. Please help me. Get me out."

"Okay, Bella, I need you to take some deep breaths for me now...That's it, slow your breathing down. I know it hurts, honey, but we need to slow your heart rate down for the baby. Okay, breathe with me." She took in a deep breath. "That's it...now let it out. Okay, another deep breath." They both breathed in deeply. "Good girl, and out again. Okay, keep doing that for me. Close your eyes and just try and think about your breathing for me." Bella inhaled and exhaled obediently.

"Betts?"

"Yo." Bettsy's head appeared over the top.

Mac stood so that she could talk quietly. "Bring the ambos straight over. Looks like Bella's going into labour. Her waters have broken and there's a fair bit of blood in it. We need to get her out as soon as they get here."

"Gotcha."

Mac knelt and took Bella's pulse. Her heart rate was picking up with the pain, and she was taking short, sharp, shallow breaths. "That's it, Bella, nice deep breaths for me." Mac talked her through the breathing. "That's super. Deep breath in, and out...in, and out. That's great, keep going." She opened the IV a little more and noted that she had used a bit over a quarter of the bag. It would do until the ambos arrived.

She heard an engine approach and Bettsy called out, "The bus is here."

"Bella? The ambulance has arrived—not long now, sweetheart. Just keep breathing for me, nice and deep. You're doing a great job." She could hear Bettsy offering up a brief on the accident and those involved and then heard footsteps approaching. A face appeared over the top.

"Hey, my name's Trev. Who do we have here?"

Mac looked at her notes briefly and gave Trev Bella's details and history in the handover. She stood. "I'll swap places with you, Trev, and help Bettsy get the gear ready for release."

Trev nodded. "Goodo. I'll call you when we're ready."

Bella grabbed Mac's leg as she was getting ready to climb out, looking at her with frightened eyes. Mac squatted down again and brushed Bella's cheek with the back of her fingers. "Hey, Bella, it's okay. My friend Trevor here is going to stay with you. I'll be just outside getting some gear ready to help get you out. I'll be back before you know it, and we can work on getting you and baby bubble both out of here, okay?"

Bella smiled weakly in acknowledgement before another spasm hit her and her face crumpled with the cramp.

Mac climbed out and was swiftly replaced by Trevor. She could hear him murmuring reassurances to Bella while she worked with Bettsy and waited for Trevor's call. A stretcher had been wheeled over in readiness with a spine board resting alongside the car. There wasn't long to wait before Trevor gave the signal that it was time.

Mac climbed into the top of the car and spreadeagled down either side of Bella. She had left her helmet and coat outside as there was little room inside the vehicle. "Okay, Bella. I'm going to slide the wedge in near your legs and see if we can't make enough room to slide you out."

Mac looked up at Trevor who nodded. They were good to go.

She positioned the small wedge spreaders in the tiny space on the right of Bella's knee and cranked it open. She just needed to make a space big enough to get the bigger spreaders in. Little by little, she cranked it open. When she had enough space, she locked the jaws open, slid the small unit out, and replaced it with the bigger spreading unit.

"Here we go, Bella, take some nice deep breaths for me…"

She cranked the spreaders and slowly, with groaning, creaking, and crunching reluctance, the car began to relinquish its grip on Bella. As the pressure was released, the circulation returned to Bella's legs and she screamed at the assault of pain.

Trevor leaned over her. "Hang in there, Bella, nearly there."

A couple more cranks and Bella's legs were free.

Trevor nodded. "Okay, we've got space. Spine board."

Bettsy was atop the car and wordlessly passed down the board. Between them, Trevor and Mac slid the board under Bella, secured her in place, and raised her up to where Bettsy was waiting to balance the board on the top side of the car. Mac scrambled out, followed by Trevor. The three of them lifted Bella off the car and onto the stretcher where Trevor was able to undertake a more thorough head-to-toe assessment.

Trevor turned to Bettsy and Mac. "My partner is still at the hospital with the last call-out we were on—would one of you guys mind driving?"

Bettsy looked over and nodded. "You go. I'll clean up here and pick you up when I'm done."

Mac climbed in the ambulance's driver's seat and looked over her shoulder at Trevor. He gave the thumbs up that he was good to go. The injured driver, Rob, was bundled into the passenger seat.

With no traffic on the road, the trip to the hospital went swiftly as they sliced their way through the dark night and into town. The bright streetlights seemed harsh and garish after the embracing dark drive.

Arriving at the hospital, she backed the ambulance into the bay where hospital staff were at the door, waiting for their arrival. The ambulance doors swung open and Bella was whisked away by Trevor, whilst a nurse came to wrap Rob in a blanket, then walked him in through to Emergency.

Mac put her head down on the steering wheel and closed her eyes, letting out an enormous sigh of relief. Then she raised her head, took a deep breath, and wearily peeled herself out of the ambulance to head inside and make a start on the paperwork while she waited for Bettsy to arrive.

Chapter Two

Sarah Macarthur had always wanted to be a doctor, right from when she had watched a movie as a child, with a lady doctor calling the shots in a major trauma scene. The character was calm and in control, and even as a child, Sarah had admired the respect the character commanded from the people around her who followed her lead. Growing up, that was the vision that inspired Sarah as she aspired to finding and becoming that controlled person, just like her childhood hero.

As a young girl growing up, she was very shy, frequently turning to books to escape. She'd been a bit of a nerd at school, which only further ostracized her from her outgoing peers. But what had started off as a social escape quickly turned to a rabid thirst for knowledge. She'd read whatever she could get her hands on, but her passion was science—the need to find how and why things worked—driving her closer and closer to the world of medicine. With knowledge, came confidence, and at university she'd blossomed into a confident capable adult who had found herself and her place in the world.

And now, after years practising in big cities, she was head of Emergency in Toowoomba Hospital. Here, she had the opportunity to share her years of expertise with the Darling Downs community, yet still be in an environment and in a hospital that was well funded and provided more than enough challenges to keep her enthused and excited about her work.

The area itself boasted a population of approximately a hundred and fifty thousand, supporting a number of industries, whilst still remaining a largely rural agriculture-oriented centre. The slower, more relaxed pace of country life suited Sarah after years of being constantly on the move. There was still plenty of medical drama and variety to keep her challenged, but the lifestyle and the people were what attracted Sarah the most.

The night had been fairly steady for Sarah and the team. There had been a chef, who had somehow managed to use a filleting knife to slice his hand open, instead of the venison; a teenager, who had sustained several facial fractures and lost a couple of teeth after coming off a bike from a three-metre jump, landing face first in the dirt; and a child with a bead stuck firmly up his nose.

Sarah and her team of several nurses and a fourth-year resident were just cleaning up after sending the child and his bead home, having successfully separated them, when the call came in from the emergency services radio line for a single-vehicle, two-person MVA en route, one male with minor injuries, one female approximately eight months pregnant reported to have sustained several fractures. The team was briefed and awaiting the ambulance's arrival. Sarah called upstairs to Obstetrics to a colleague and long-time friend from university days.

"Dr. Colleen Baker, Obstetrics."

"Hey, Colly, it's Sarah in Emergency."

"Hey, Sare, what's up?"

"We just got a call—MVA, two people, one eight months pregnant. Report is her waters have broken and there's concern of possible internal bleeding. Contractions seven minutes apart. ETA is about four minutes."

"Okay, can you organize bloods for standby, and I'll ring theatre to see what's available, just in case. See you in a couple."

"'Kay, thanks. Bye."

By the time Sarah and her team had made the necessary preparations, Colleen walked in through the doors. "Hey, there."

"Hey, Col."

"I can't believe you're still working nights, Sare. People will start thinking you're a vampire. Do you even come out in the day any more?"

Sarah just chuckled and shrugged. "I don't mind nights."

"Other than running into you in the corridor here, God, I haven't seen you in like…forever. What are you doing in a couple of weekends' time? Brian and I are having a barbecue at the end of the month. Nothing fancy, just some friends. Tell me you'll come. Please?"

"I'll have a look at the roster and see what I can do. Okay, Miss Pushy?"

"I'll hold you to that."

They were both chuckling when the nurse, Alice, stuck her head around the doorway. "Ambulance has just pulled in."

Sarah was instantly in doctor-in-charge mode. "Bring them on through."

Alice nodded and headed out, only to return a few minutes later with Trevor, wheeling a pregnant woman on a gurney, and a young man walking behind the gurney, wrapped in a blanket.

Trevor gave a rundown of what had happened, occasionally referring to points on a piece of paper as well as his own clipboard notes. Alice noticed the two sets of notes. "Hey, Trev—since when do you have time to take multiple notes in the field? Weren't you solo for this run?"

"I got lucky tonight. One of the fireys took the details down. Did a good job. Saved me some time on the tar tonight, let me tell you."

Sarah walked over to Bella and held her hand. "Hi, Bella, my name is Dr. Sarah Macarthur. I'm the doctor in charge of Emergency tonight. My colleague here is Dr. Colleen Baker and she's an obstetrician. I'm going to have a quick look over you and see how you're doing, and Dr. Baker, here, is going to take a look at your baby. Is that okay with you?"

Bella looked up with tear-filled, frightened eyes and nodded. "Don't worry about me, please, just look after my baby."

"It's okay, Bella, we'll do our best to look after *both* of you. I need you to just lie back and relax as best you can while we check you out."

Alice was working around the head of the bed. She had a fresh bag of saline running, and the obs monitor on Bella's finger measured heart rate and oxygen efficiency levels. "BP is ninety over fifty five, sats at ninety five percent."

Both Colleen and Sarah were looking over Bella and listening to Alice's status report. Sarah could see some superficial bruising over several places on Bella's body. Her left patella was most certainly displaced, sticking out at a bizarre left-of-centre position. Bella was also guarding her shoulder closely. It too was out of alignment and looking odd, with more than enough bruising around it to make it obvious that it had taken a decent blow. She would need to get some X-rays of that. Alice, meanwhile, was busy beside her, positioning the fetal monitor and ultrasound ready for Colleen.

A nice bump to the side of Bella's temple was evident, as reflected by Trevor's report that Bella had been unconscious for several minutes after the first emergency responders had attended the scene. A quick series of neural tests revealed that Bella's pupils were equal and reactive and she was alert and responsive to time and place. Sarah made some notes on the chart. She would order some head X-rays too, just to be on the safe side.

"When you're finished there, Alice, can you bring over the portable X-ray please?"

Alice had just finished laying out the equipment for Colleen. "Sure thing."

"Thanks."

They were a good team in Emergency. There was a lot of mutual respect within the team for the varying layers of skills and expertise they each possessed. More than that, they all genuinely liked each other. This in turn made for a well-oiled and efficient unit, even in the midst of the worst possible traumas that could be thrown at them.

While the X-rays were being taken, Sarah assessed Rob. He had seat belt bruising, some bruised ribs, and a slight concussion, with a black eye starting to colour up nicely, but other than that, Sarah was happy with Rob's condition. Given that it was fairly quiet now in Emergency, Sarah was happy to let Rob stay and give moral support to Bella.

She walked back over to where Colleen was watching the fetal heart rate read out. "I'll do an ultrasound next and see what the story is."

Bella looked up at Sarah, and then over at Trevor, who was packing up his gurney. "Is Mouse, the fireman that helped us tonight, still here?"

Puzzled, Sarah looked over at Trevor. Was Bella's head injury worsening? A fireman mouse?

"I haven't seen her since we pulled in. How about I—" Trevor's comment was abruptly cut short as his radio mike went off, advising him to pick up his partner as they were needed on another call. He looked apologetically at Bella. "Sorry, Bella, I gotta go."

Bella gave a weak smile. "That's okay."

Sarah saw the disappointment in her eyes and knew Bella was trying to be brave. "How about I stick my head around outside and take a quick look while Dr. Baker here is doing the ultrasound?" Besides, Sarah was intrigued—what *was* a fireman mouse?

"Thank you."

Sarah headed off through the plastic swing doors to the nurses' reception area. Over in the corner there was a body in a uniform hunched over a notebook. Sarah's feet were soundless in her rubber-soled shoes. It wasn't her intention to sneak up, but she did have an opportunity to study the profile in front of her. She subtly cleared her throat to get the fireman's attention. When the fireman looked up, she was caught off guard and briefly froze in place, as surprised eyes looked up at her. It seemed a stupid thing to think, but her mind was reeling and the best it could come up with was: *Who knew a mouse could have such stunning blue eyes?*

❖

Making her way through the ambulance entrance, Mac slipped inside the hospital's inner sanctum to the nurses' station. The nurse on duty looked up with a smile, recognizing her uniform. "You come in with these guys?" Mac nodded. "The doctor's in with them now. Why don't you go and grab yourself a cuppa and bring it on back here. We should have some news by then. Cafeteria's third corridor on your left, down that way." She pointed down the hallway.

"Thanks. Do you want anything from the caff while I'm there?"

"If you could grab me a latte, I would love you forever." she beamed.

"No worries." She sauntered off in search of caffeine.

She got herself a hot chocolate, a jam doughnut for Bettsy, and the promised latte for the nurse. When she gave the nurse her steaming hot cup she was greeted with smiles and cries of being an angel. It had obviously been a busy night for everyone.

After her hot chocolate, Mac used the opportunity to seek out some fresh stocks of fluid to replace what she had used that night and decided to make a start on the report. She had her head bent over her notebook, writing up the details, when she heard a gentle yet subtle clearing of a throat. She jumped a little as she hadn't heard anyone approach, then noticed the feet in front of her. Mac looked up to see the warmest, brownest eyes looking down at her. A beautiful face, softly framed by loose waves of sandy-coloured curls, smiled gently down at her.

"Did you come in with the pregnant lady and her partner from the MVA?"

For a brief moment she had no voice. In fact, she had no thoughts. She was mesmerized by the warm chocolate eyes looking at her. She recovered enough to nod and stand up. *Breathe, Mac, breathe. Say something. You look like an idiot.* "Um, yes, sorry. I did." She held out her hand and found it enveloped by a soft, firm hand in return.

"Hello, I'm Dr. Macarthur. I thought you might like an update on the young couple you helped bring in tonight."

Suddenly her hands felt sweaty with nervousness for the mother and child. She nodded again, fingers silently crossed for them both.

"Rob has predominantly superficial wounds and a slight concussion. We'll keep him in overnight for observation. Bella looks to have dislocated her shoulder and she has a displaced patella, along with some bruised ribs. On top of that, she's had a pretty solid knock to her head, which we're keeping an eye on. The obstetrician is in with her now. There's a possibility the umbilical cord has partially come away from the lining of the womb, which might account for some of the bleeding. An ultrasound will tell us more about what's happening inside. Once we have a bit more information, we can work out a plan of care for her and the baby. But all things considered, she and the baby appear to be relatively stable at this stage."

She let out a breath she didn't realize she had been holding and smiled tiredly with relief. "That's great news. Thanks for coming to tell me, I really appreciate it."

"Bella has been asking about a fireman called Mouse—and as you are the only one here, and in the giveaway uniform, I figured it had to be you." The doctor smiled openly as Mac nodded and felt herself blush a little. "I'll go and check to see if the OB has finished the assessment. If you've got five minutes, I think Bella would like to see you."

"Sure."

"Okay, I'll be back in a minute." Just as quietly as she arrived, she turned and disappeared through the heavy plastic swing doors.

Mac was left standing there, rather like a mute statue. What was that? More importantly, who was that?

Before she had time to think any more, a nurse's head popped through the swing doors. "You can come in if you like."

Mac smiled in acknowledgement and entered through the doors. Rob was in one bed sitting up watching over at the next bed, where Bella was half reclining with an oxygen mask on, IV tubes, and a heart monitor on her and the baby. The captivating Dr. Macarthur was beside her bed quietly talking to another doctor in scrubs who was busy making notes on a chart.

Mac walked towards the beds. First she went to Rob who held his arms out for a hug. Mac stepped into his arms. "Thank you, thank you for everything," he whispered in her ear. "I don't know what I would do without Bella. I can't thank you enough."

"Hey, it's okay." She patted him on the shoulder, slowly releasing herself from his embrace. "I'm happy you're both out okay and in good hands here." She patted him on the hand and moved over to Bella who was watching in the next bed.

"Hiya, Bella. Looks like you've got the full five-star treatment, huh?" Bella smiled and nodded. Mac looked at the doctors and the nurse, then back at Bella. She moved closer. "When this is all over, one day, when baby bubble here is old enough, you call me and I'll take them for their first ride in a fire truck. How's that sound?"

Bella smiled. "We'd love that very much." Tears ran freely down her face. She reached out and grabbed Mac's hand and hoarsely whispered, "Thank you."

Mac reached out and gently touched Bella's cheek. "You are most welcome. Rest up now. I'll try and drop in a bit later and see how you're all doing. Okay?"

"I'd like that." Bella's eyes were shining with fatigue and the effects of the medication they had given her.

Mac stayed a few more minutes until Bella had lightly dozed off. She gently extricated her hand and tucked Bella's back under the bedcovers. She turned to see Dr. Macarthur watching her intently. She shyly lowered her head. "Thank you for letting me see them."

Dr. Macarthur smiled and nodded as Mac turned quietly and left through the swing doors back to reception, where Bettsy had arrived and discovered the bag with the jam doughnut in it and was halfway through devouring it, sugar dusting his ginger beard.

He had the good grace to look sheepish as he looked up with a mouthful. "I hope that was mine. I figured you didn't want it, having left it behind here with your gear."

Mac shook her head and laughed. "Lucky for you then, hey, big fella?"

Smiling, they picked up the gear and headed outside to the waiting truck.

CHAPTER THREE

Four a.m. had been and gone some time back. Mac knew she should have been tired, and in truth, she was exhausted, but the after wash of adrenaline from the call-out kept her going. She would hit the wall, it was inevitable, and when it came, it would crash over her like a wave, all but knocking her off her feet. But she wasn't quite there yet.

She'd dropped Bettsy off, restocked, reequipped, and done the paperwork and was going over the night's events, mentally looking for cracks or things that could have been done differently should there be a next time.

She rang the report in, got washed and changed and made ready for bed, even though most nights after a call-out, she rarely slept. Just the routine was comfort enough sometimes. Then she waited. The wave slid closer. Her mind passed from active, productive thoughts, to restlessness, finally slowing to a state of numbness. A place of disassociation. Sometimes snapshots of the evening's events flashed across her mind's eye. Other times the blankness was large enough to bleed the mind of its remaining energies. There was nothing left. Totally spent, she embraced surrender, closed her eyes, and slipped into the arms of sleep.

Sunlight pierced through partially cracked lids and stabbed with cruel brightness, daring her squinting eyes to open and do battle with the day.

Rolling over, Mac looked at the clock on the bedside table. "Crap!" She had overslept. "Damn it." She threw off the bedcovers, and her feet hit the floor. Berating herself, she knew she should have checked her alarm before falling into bed only a handful of hours ago. Somewhere along the line she must have dozed off, which was a bit unusual of late. Between bouts of insomnia and late call-outs, sleep had been a very distant friend these past few weeks.

Start the coffee machine, shower, change, grab hot coffee and fruit, head out the door, and get on with the day. Late was late and there was nothing to be done about it now but to get going and try and pick up some time along the way.

It was a beautiful morning, as the sun rose and christened the sparkling dew-covered landscape. Although living on the outskirts meant a fair drive into town most days, it was mornings like these where the drive in transported her soul to a peaceful, refreshed place. It was a nice gentle way to start the day as she drove past bush blocks and small farms, the urban interface increasing with each click closer to town.

All too soon, the traffic and business that come with urban living became more and more concentrated. Mac forced her mind to pick up in sharpness and attentiveness as she weaved her way through the solid morning traffic. Stopping at the lights, she began to run down mentally the checklist of things to do, people, places, appointments to keep. Hopefully, if the day went well, she might be able to swing by the hospital and check on Bella. Who knows, maybe she might even run into Dr. Hot Chocolate Eyes. What did she say her name was again? Funny how she just magically appeared and disappeared without making a sound.

Blaring horns startled her. She had missed the change in lights and now had frustrated people behind her, honking their horns for her to move on. She waved an apology, put the truck into gear, and moved off. She must have been more tired than she thought. What an airhead. With a more concentrated effort she continued the journey into the office. Pulling up in the car park a few minutes later, she grabbed her briefcase, only to be slapped in the face with a cold breeze that took her breath away as she disembarked from the car. Any colder and it might as well snow.

By contrast, the office was hot and stuffy as she pushed through the doors. As she slid past the service desk, she smiled and waved. "Morning, Martha."

She was greeted with an echoed, "Morning, yourself, young lady. Heard you and John had another late night last night."

Martha not only commanded the service desk, but was station mother to all who worked under the firehouse roof. Martha could have retired several years back but opted to stay on and supervise her family. The station house was Martha's house. With her milk-coffee complexion and deep brown eyes from her Maori parentage, she boasted a subtle state of stocky that comes with middling to later years, but was always smartly dressed, with hair immaculately styled short, swept up in a classic style. And she seemed ageless. She looked over the rims of her glasses at Mac.

Mac stopped by the mail pigeonholes and was sorting through what needed attending to and what could wait. "Mm, just one of those busy weeks I guess." Mac's official status was a combination of part-time and voluntary, and whenever she was in the office, there was always plenty to play catch up on. "That's one lazy wind outside. Did you catch the weather report? Do they think it might rain?"

"Perhaps, tonight they think we might see a storm."

Mac waved the mail, smiling at Martha. "Well, I'd better get on with it. Catch up with you later on."

Martha stood up and handed over a container, along with a mug of hot chocolate. "Take these with you as you go. A little sugar sustainer to keep you going through the morning."

Mac closed her eyes and sniffed the air. "Those biscuits smell like another wonderful low-fat recipe of yumminess. You spoil me." Her stomach rumbled in anticipation.

As Martha started to walk out the door she chuckled and threw over her shoulder, "Low fat indeed! I don't know any of those recipes, which is just as well because you don't eat enough, young lady." Martha waved her away. "Okay, petal, go gently."

"You too, Martha." Mac walked down the corridor to her office. She sank into the chair and turned her computer on, quickly checking the weather update for the next twenty-four hours before diving into reports and putting the finishing touches on the training program for the intake of new recruits later in the month.

Taking a break, Mac chuckled and sat back at her desk, munching appreciatively on one of the biscuits when the chief stuck his head around the corner. "Hey, Mac. You got five minutes?"

"Sure, Chief. What's up?"

Captain "Chief" Thomas O'Reilly was firefighting blue blood. His father had been captain, and his father's father before him. He was as tough and courageous as any human being could be, but still proudly embraced his fire family with a gentle family man's disposition. But the Irish blood ran through him, sure and solid. Chief O'Reilly could tell a fine yarn in a good mood, or he could lay you on the carpet and rip you a new exit hole as soon as look at you if you screwed up. There weren't too many people in the station that hadn't been on the receiving end of both the chief's good and bad side, but all to a letter were proud to serve under the man and wouldn't want it any other way.

He lowered himself to the visitor's chair in her tiny office. "I was doing the half-yearly personnel reports and noticed you haven't taken any leave for close to two years now. Want to explain what that's all about?"

Wow. Of all the things she thought the chief would want to talk to her about, she would never have picked the subject of going on leave. She shrugged and put her pen down. "I never really gave it much thought, to be honest. Not much of an explanation, I know, but I love doing what I do. Why would I want to take a break from that?"

Chief offered her a smile. "Because this is a *part* of life Mac, not life itself. Everybody needs a break sometimes, or to do something different. You need to rest and recharge your batteries. You have the highest number of call-out stats of both paid and voluntary ranks. I'm concerned that you're going to burn out if you keep going the way you are. I would much rather you be away for a couple of weeks on R & R, as opposed to losing you to something more serious somewhere down the track."

Mac looked down at the paperwork on her desk. She had made firefighting her life. It challenged her and pushed her to her limits some days, but it also provided her with a sense of stability and safety that came with knowing your place in the scheme of things. It filled her days and nights with purpose. It left her too tired to do other things, to think, to socialize, and to put herself out there. She liked her life just fine like it was. She was content.

"Mac, there's no easy way to say this, but you are starting to look like I feel some days. It's time for you to get out of here, meet new people, have a change. *Live* a little."

She sighed and looked up. "I feel fine, honest. I don't need a break."

"Uh-huh, well, I thought you would say as much. So I am taking you off the roster for the next month and reassigning you to some community-education projects."

"What?"

"You'll be going to a couple of schools and healthcare facilities, conducting inspections and running fire safety courses."

"You're not serious, Chief. *Really*?"

The chief nodded.

"But Eddie normally does that stuff. He loves it! C'mon, Chief, giving classes is not my thing."

"Eddie and Barbara are heading off for a month to help their daughter, who is due to provide them with their first grandchild any day now. I need someone to step in, and I have nominated you."

"I don't suppose—"

The chief shook his head. "Nope. You're it. You can finish the day here, then tomorrow you can swing by my office and pick up the portfolio of places and classes needed, and you can have the rest of the week off roster to plan how you want to do it." The chief stood with a hint of a smug smile on his face. Mac was frozen in place in shock. She was stuffed. The chief had obviously had this all planned out for some time before presenting it to her. She was the next senior in line to Eddie and had the necessary instructor and inspector qualifications. Shit. There was no getting out of it.

"You'll be fine, Mac. It'll be a good change. And you know what they say, a change is as good as a holiday." With that, the chief winked at her and walked out.

"Shit, shit, *shit*!" She put her head in her hands. It wasn't the cleaning up of her desk, or loose ends to tie up—she'd always managed to be fairly organized and on top of things, so there were no major concerns there, but going out and playing nice to people? In groups? Really? Damn the chief.

Chapter Four

It was just gone seven p.m. when Mac headed out the station door to her truck. She had a parcel tucked under one arm. Martha had left her a sample of a new spicy Cajun creation to try. She planned to quickly duck into the hospital to get an update on Rob and Bella, go home, have a nice hot bath, heat up dinner, and enjoy it with a nice chilled glass of wine, vowing to deal with the chief's curveball tomorrow.

At the hospital, she discovered they had moved Bella up to the maternity ward. The report was that Bella and the baby were doing okay. The bleeding had stopped about an hour after Bella was brought in, and she had been closely monitored for most of the day while her labour progressed. She and Rob were now upstairs in one of the delivery rooms. She left a note with the ward clerk, wishing them well and that she would call in and see them tomorrow.

It was strange—she hadn't gone with the intent of searching out a certain pair of strangely fascinating brown eyes, but as she walked out of the hospital to her vehicle, she had a brief moment of disappointment, realizing she hadn't seen that face again. There was something about the good doctor that made her curious, but she didn't really know exactly what it was.

❖

Mac slept like a baby for the first time in many weeks. Martha's wonderful dish of chicken and deep, earthy spices had enough bite to it that the wine she had chosen had been the perfect accompaniment to settle the edge of the spicy buzz. This new dish would definitely be a favourite. A hot bath, food, and wine had done their job, and she didn't remember much after turning out the light until the alarm woke her at five a.m.

Curveball day. Sighing, she tried rationalizing the change to herself. The time period wasn't too horrendous—it was only for four weeks. She'd get it organized, get it done, and get back to normal. Sounded easy enough, right? Crap. Who was she kidding? Okay, she needed to break it down. Hand over truck and swap for official department car. This was not a bad trade—the heater worked better in the car than it did in the fire truck: one positive tick. Next, swap turnout and work clobber for the office uniform. Bugger. She hated wearing the dress blues. The shirts made her itchy and she would have to iron her uniform every day: a definite big cross.

When she wasn't out doing inspections or giving a class, she would probably be in the office doing paperwork and designing classes. She was not a fan of paperwork or sitting still. Another cross. On the positive side, the hours would be regular, with set start and finish times, if planned well enough. It had been a while since she had last done anything other than fire stuff. She hadn't done any sculpting in months now, and if she wasn't on call-out duty, getting overtime, she could do with some more money coming in. She'd never had any problem selling her work, and she had several dealers and reps who would get in contact a couple of times each year and ask if she had anything to sell. Possible tick.

Mac donned a tracksuit and runners and headed out the door. Part of her morning routine, when she could, was to run to the local cat and dog refuge five kilometres down the road to help out. Some days she helped with the feeding or cleaned out the runs or took dogs for walks, and sometimes she just enjoyed cuddle therapy with a kitten, puppy, or another animal that just needed some unconditional love. When she was done, she would jog on home, have a shower, get changed, and head off to work. Some mornings, because of call-outs, she didn't get there, but whenever she could she was always welcomed as an extra pair of hands. She had been so busy lately that she hadn't been in a while, and she was really looking forward to putting it back into her morning routine.

The run to the refuge felt comfortable, and as she made her way around to the back of the shelter, she saw Maree come bounding up to her with a huge grin on her face. Maree and her long-time partner Terri had once owned a very successful string of restaurants in Sydney, Adelaide, and Melbourne. Five years ago they sold up and moved to the country to set up the refuge. They were busier than ever and happy as pigs in mud. They had an excellent rescue and rehoming record, provided education sessions for schools, and helped out with behaviour education programs for troubled animals.

She'd first met Maree and Terri not long after they moved in. There was a fire in the old farmhouse shed on the property, and Mac and her fire crew were amongst the first on scene to help put it out. Ever since then, the girls had all been firm friends, spending many a dinner party together with wonderful food, wine, and company.

Maree threw her arms around her. "Mac, how are you? We haven't seen you for forever. What's your news? Walk and talk with me, huh?" Maree was already on the move with Mac following in her wake. She loved coming here, and seeing Maree again made her realize how much she had missed these last couple of weeks.

"Hey, Maree, it's great to be back. Sorry I haven't been around much. Been a bit busy of late. You know how it goes."

"Yep, sure do, girlfriend. But boy, I'm glad you're here. As you can probably tell, we have close to a full house."

Funny, she hadn't really noticed the racket before, but now Maree mentioned it, there were cries, excited yelps, and loads of barking. "Well, put me to work, boss. Where do you want me?"

"We haven't fed the dogs in run six yet. Can I get you to start with cleaning out the kitten pens inside? We should be finished feeding the dogs by then, and then if you could clean out run six, that would be great."

"Too easy. I'll see you in a bit."

Once inside Mac headed to the kitten wing of the cat section. Lots of little mewling noises greeted her as she walked past the pens. "Hello, everyone. Ooh, aren't you all delicious."

She continued through to the utilities room, got all the necessary cleaning gear and fresh paraphernalia needed for the task, then moved cheerfully from pen to pen cleaning, talking, and cuddling all the tiny bodies. They had obviously not long had breakfast, as most were sporting fat, full little tummies.

After packing and washing up the gear, next she made her way back outside to the dog wing. Run six was on the end and was reserved to house dogs that were young, shy, abused, or not socialized and showing signs of nervousness. Normally Maree preferred to handle run six herself, so that she could provide them with a consistent person for the first few weeks, so it was a bit of a buzz to be asked to clean the run solo. She collected a broom, dustpan, pooper scooper, and a mop and bucket. She left them outside the pens and walked the path outside of the run to establish and observe who was in residence.

There was an old female cattle dog with one eye who watched her warily. "Good morning, my lady," she softly crooned. She walked over to the pen, squatted down, and placed her hand on the wire door. "You look like you've seen some adventures, old girl." At the sound of her voice, the old dog stiffly made her way over to cautiously smell her hand. Mac had grabbed some cat biscuits earlier and offered them up as pungent, yummy treats. The old dog, although licking its lips in anticipation, didn't make a move to take them from her hand. Mac left them on the floor inside the door. "You have those, princess, and I'll be back soon to clean your parlour. How does that sound, hmm?" The old dog just looked at her, not sure what to make of her.

She did the same in the next two pens for a badly scarred hunting dog and a young mixed-breed terrier. When she went to the last pen on the end, she initially thought it was empty. She couldn't see any animal inside. She started to turn to walk away when she noticed the soft doughnut-shaped bedding moving slightly. She looked again, not sure if the bedding really moved, or if she only imagined it had. No, there it was again, just the smallest of movements at the edge of the bedding. There, in the back recess of the pen, barely visible from underneath the bedding, was a pair of eyes blinking at her.

She squatted and made soft nonsense talk. "Hey there, little one. Looks like you're today's scaredy-cat winner. You want to come out and say hello? Come on, pumpkin, I won't bite." The only movement from the bed was more blinking. "Tell you what, little one. I'm going to clean up your neighbours' penthouses, and then I'm going to come on back and make your house feel nice and clean and cosy. How about that for a plan?" More blinking. "Okay. You sit tight and I'll be back in a little while." She left a few nibbles as a peace offering before heading back to start cleaning the pens.

Mac quickly ascertained that the old female cattle dog was fine, provided Mac didn't move too quickly. Any sudden movements, and the dog growled and backed into a corner nervously. Mac slowed, trying to move rhythmically, chatting away the whole time until she was done. She left a few more treats as a thank you to the old girl for letting her into her space.

Second pen along belonged to the hunting dog. Most of his kennel had to be cleaned up using the dustpan and brush. It became pretty obvious the broom freaked him out, so she didn't even bother with the mop, opting instead to wash and wipe the floor with some rags. Mac guessed that he had more than likely been beaten with sticks of some sort. It ended up being a bit slower to clean his pen, but worth the effort when, as she went to leave, he approached her, wagging his tail tentatively. She didn't want to push him though, so she didn't make any move to touch him, opting to leave him some treats on the ground not far from her feet. As he timidly made his way up to pick at them, she told him what a lovely and brave boy he was.

Then there was the mixed-breed terrier. Mac was able to go into his cage and clean and tidy it up without too much hassle. The dog made no move towards her. Instead he was a constant blur of motion as he paced incessantly backwards and forwards. Sometimes he watched her while he paced; other times it was like he was in a trance. Mac vowed to ask Maree about the history of this one when she had finished up.

Finally, it was time to clean whoever was hiding in the last pen. Quietly, Mac walked into the pen, leaving the equipment on the ground near the door. She never looked directly at the bedding but kept talking away, saying nonsense things like, "Well, today is a bit of new start for me too. I know a bit about what you're feeling. Been shoved into a place you don't want to be, and you don't really know what's going on. It's a bit scary, isn't it?" Slowly, while she was talking, still not looking at the bedding, she started to clean the pen. As she picked up the mess, she maintained the dialogue. "But the way I look at it is that we're both here, in these situations. They don't look like they're going to go away, so we just have to figure out, you and I, how we're going to get our heads around this, huh?" As she walked past the bedding, she didn't stop, moving smoothly past, dropping a few tasty morsels as teasers about an inch from the edge of the bedding.

She continued over to the doorway for the mop and sneaked a glance over her shoulder. She caught sight of the blinking eyes and what appeared to be a twitching nose starting to poke out from under the bedding. She kept mopping the floor. "Well, little one, I'm as good as done here. I tell you what, though, this wasn't too bad now, was it? How about I come back again tomorrow, hey? Would you like that? Hopefully tomorrow I might get to see a bit more of you, hmm?" Now when she looked up at the bedding, the eyes were still watching her. "I'll be off now. I'll see you tomorrow."

Quietly she picked up her gear and headed off to put them away. Then she would try and find Maree and get a quick rundown on what the dogs' stories were before heading off back home for a shower. But by the time she packed her gear, time was getting away, and she ended up leaving a note for Maree and Terri on the counter, promising to call later that night.

Just as she was heading out the gate, Terri wolf-whistled and gave her the call-me sign. Mac nodded and gave her two thumbs up in acknowledgement and headed off for the run home. Once home, she quickly showered, grabbed a bite to eat, changed into her office dress blues, and jumped into the truck. She gripped the wheel tightly for a brief moment and squared her shoulders. Curveball: day one. "Let's get this started." Putting the truck into gear, she pointed it towards town and let the engine eat up the distance before her.

Chapter Five

Sarah was finally sitting down finishing off notes from the night shift, ready for handover. She glimpsed an official memo in her mail tray alerting her that her attendance, along with every other employee at the hospital, was required for the annual series of workplace health-and-safety training sessions. As the doctor in charge of Emergency, she was also required to be involved in the WH&S fire safety inspections.

Sarah was tired. It had been a long night. One case after another had been brought in, ranging from run-of-the-mill injuries, such as a broken nose from a bar fight and a broken collarbone from boisterous football tackling practice, all the way through to the more demanding cases like an overdose, electrocution, a baby scalded with hot water, and an infant with fever-related seizures. It meant that Sarah had been on her feet fairly constantly now for nearly sixteen hours. The last thing she wanted to do, let alone think about, was the annual time-consuming, mind-numbing compulsory classes.

She saw that the inspections were first up on the Monday morning. Terrific. At least she could do them after shift. The classes looked to be scheduled during the day over the next two weeks. She would need to do a swap with Don, her second in charge. Sarah left a note in Don's mail tray suggesting he take the first class at the end of the first week and she would do the later class midway through the following week.

Sarah was watching the time closely. She had the monthly case review meeting in an hour, which should take her up close to lunchtime, and then she had four luxurious rostered days off. She couldn't remember the last time she'd had a couple of days off. Her first day would no doubt be spent catching up on sleep, shopping, and doing chores around the house. After that, apart from catching up with family, she didn't have any firm plans. The thought made her giddy. She felt positively schoolgirlish, waiting for the holiday bell to ring.

Sarah liked living in the country, and an added attraction to the move was being closer to her only family—her sister Jean and her little boy Thomas. Jean was a single parent, having divorced and moved away from a domestically violent relationship. Sarah loved having her sister close by, and she liked nothing better than to have Thomas come and stay over when she had time off. It had been nearly eighteen months now since they had moved into town. Sarah had talked to Jean about getting Thomas a kitten for his sixth birthday, the following week. Over several dinners they had talked about it, and Jean felt that they were settled enough now that it would be good for Thomas. They both agreed it might help bring him out of his shell a little bit and give him someone to love and look after. The plan was to pick both Jean and Thomas up tomorrow night, and they would have dinner somewhere, come back to Sarah's for a sleepover, and head out to the animal shelter early the next day to look for kittens. Sarah looked again at her watch and realized it was time to head off to the meeting. Smiling to herself, she couldn't wait for the day to be over already.

❖

As Mac walked into the station office, Martha stood and took her glasses off, looking Mac up and down, smiling and nodding in approval.

"Look at you—you should wear the dress shirt more often. You are looking mighty fine in your pressed officialdom."

Mac rolled her eyes, pulled at her tight collar, and grimaced. "It makes me itchy," she grumbled.

Martha came out from behind her desk and walked around her making clucking noises. She stopped in front of Mac, straightened her tie, and tilted her chin up to look straight into her eyes. "Itchy be damned. You should wear that get-up more often. Much better than that other shapeless stuff you live in."

Mac felt herself blush a little and laughed, then kissed Martha on the cheek. "Thank you. Is the chief in?"

"He said to tell you to go straight in."

"Thanks."

Mac walked down the hall, pausing to tap on the chief's door. Looking up from his paperwork he smiled and waved her into his office to sit in the chair. There were several folders on the desk.

The chief tapped the files. "Eddie has files on the hospital and two schools for inspections, maps, people to contact, et cetera, and the other folders are the education programs, one each for the two schools and the aged-care residence, and another separate series for the hospital. The hospital is the biggest challenge, as you will need to run several classes across two weeks to give everyone a chance to attend and organize their shifts. Eddie's roughed out a series of timetables that all the places have agreed to. It's just a matter of making contact and confirming that you'll be there on the agreed date. I've included the latest state recommendations for you to look over. Feel free to add your own touches where you want to on the programs. Any questions, you know where to find me."

Mac spent the next couple of hours working on the files in her office. She looked at the inspections and tweaked a few things to hopefully make it a bit easier, based on the maps of the various buildings. With her eyes and brain weary from the concentrated paperwork, she closed the files, pleased with what had been accomplished. She'd planned on heading over to see Bella and Rob on her way home. Tapping thoughtful fingers on the topmost file containing plans of the hospital, she decided she could kill two birds with one stone. She took the hospital inspection maps with the aim of giving herself a quick head start by doing a walk-through and locating some of the outer facility buildings that she was not familiar with.

After a short drive across town, Mac had the hospital plans in her hand and was standing outside the Emergency staff entrance bay, looking at the signs pointing out the directions of the various buildings. Wanting to find and identify the facilities maintenance buildings, she headed off around the corner, only to walk smack bang into Dr. Hot Chocolate Eyes. They bounced off each other lightly and stood momentarily still in shock.

"I'm so sorry—"

"I didn't mean—"

Mac held up the map. "I was so absorbed in the map and didn't notice you. I really am sorry."

Having recovered, Sarah laughed lightly. "I'm sorry too. I was busy trying to get out of here after a long day and wasn't watching."

Sarah looked at Mac and tilted her head, trying to remember why she looked so familiar. The woman in front of her was very striking, with long, wavy chestnut hair, cutting a very classy figure in the uniform. She wouldn't be someone who was easy to forget and yet…wait, the eyes, clear blue crystalline with a hint of storm-dark edges. And the uniform. Fire uniform. "Fireman Mouse!" she cried out triumphantly, having finally remembered.

Mac looked down at the ground, her face as red as a beetroot, which only made her eyes look bluer.

Sarah shook her head slightly. She must have been more tired than she thought—what an idiot she must look. "Sorry, long day. You look quite different to the other night. That was you who brought the couple in from the MVA, wasn't it?"

Mac looked up. "Yes, that was me." She extended her hand. "I'm sorry, it was late the other night and I don't think I introduced myself properly. My name is Mackenzie James, from the local fire station. Please, call me Mac."

Sarah took the hand offered in hers and warmly exchanged the handshake. "Hi, Mac, I'm Sarah, Sarah Macarthur." A person could get lost in those eyes. "You were looking at a map?"

"Ah yes, sorry." As if realizing she was staring, Mac broke eye contact and looked at her map. "I've been given the job of doing the inspections and fire training sessions this year. I was coming to see Bella and Rob, to see how they were doing after the other night, and I thought I would get a head start while I was here and just try and get a bit of an idea of where a couple of things were, rather than stumbling around like a lost sheep on Monday."

Sarah laughed. "Don't you mean a lost Mouse?"

Mac joined in. "Touché."

Sarah moved in and leaned over to have a look at the map. It was very detailed. She was pleased she didn't have to read it. Maps were not her forte—it was much easier to navigate around a human body. Fatigue was suddenly forgotten. "Was there any place in particular you wanted to have a look at? I'm off shift now and could help, if you wanted."

"Seriously? That would be great. I won't keep you long. But if you could just point me in the direction of the maintenance facilities, like the workshop and the laundry, that would be great. I just wanted to walk past and make a note of where they are for next week, if that's okay."

"I'll do better than that, I can take you there if you like. It's behind this building and around the corner, sort of set back. Come on, I'll show you."

"Thanks, Sarah, that'd be great. I didn't mean to trouble you."

"It's no trouble, follow me." Sarah felt a little buzz. *It's no trouble at all. I think I could actually find myself looking forward to Monday's inspections, go figure!*

The map quite forgotten, Mac had to really concentrate on where Sarah was taking her. Mac couldn't remember the last time she went on a date, let alone the last time someone caught her eye. But she wasn't blind and she still had a pulse and was most certainly enjoying the unexpected company. Maybe the chief was right. Who knew, maybe this gig wouldn't be too bad after all. The safety classes were compulsory for all hospital staff, so she was definitely going to run into Sarah at least one more time. Besides, it would be good to have a familiar face in the crowd. Or at least that was what she was telling herself.

Sarah walked Mac around to the workshops, the laundry, the incinerator, and the back of the kitchen areas, pointing out various features of each as they went past. On a few occasions Mac asked a couple of quick questions, pausing to add some notes on the maps. All up, the tour took about forty minutes.

Back at the corner where they first started, Mac held her hand out again to Sarah, who readily gripped it. "Thanks again, Sarah. You've given me a great head start for next week. I really am grateful for you taking the time to show me around."

Sarah smiled quite openly and returned the handshake. "It's been a pleasure. I look forward to seeing you next week."

"Cheers. See you next week, then."

Mac realized they were still holding hands and sheepishly let go of Sarah's. Sarah waved and headed off to the car park while Mac folded her map and turned to go inside to see Bella and Rob.

"Hey, Mac?" Mac turned to see Sarah waving at her. "Bella had a baby girl!"

Mac waved back. "Thanks! See you." Mac detoured slightly and headed towards the gift shop.

Chapter Six

Mac enjoyed visiting Bella and Rob and meeting their new baby daughter, who were all doing well. Mac didn't normally follow-up on people she helped out on the job, but sometimes it did happen. There were days when they got to see things that no human being should have to see, but in the end, someone had to. A feel-good outcome—like Rob and Bella being okay and a baby safely arriving in the world—was the thing they all fought so hard for. That was what motivated hurried steps, tumbling out of bed in the middle of the night when the pager sounded off. The happy endings helped make their job all the more worthwhile.

She had spent a pleasant evening at home, adding a few more things to her school programs and catching up with Maree and Terri on the phone, getting some more details about the dogs on run six. Their stories were all sad tales: abandoned rather than being looked after in old age, thrown off a truck and never collected, found in an abandoned building. The pup with blinking eyes had been left in a box at the gates of the refuge in the middle of the night. He had obviously been neglected, but other than that, not much was known about the dog's history.

Mac loved a challenge; she couldn't wait to see the animals again. Next morning she was up at five, into her runners, footsteps pounding down the road to the refuge. Last night she had cooked some chicken and saved some extra bits for her new friends. As timing would have it, she met up with Maree again as she came through the gate. The noise was almost deafening. It seemed everybody was up and excited, ready for breakfast. She ran over and gave Maree a hug. "Morning."

"Hey, gorgeous. Two mornings running." Maree froze on the spot and her eyes went huge in horror. "You haven't quit your job have you?"

Mac burst out laughing and put her arm around Maree's shoulders as they walked, arms around each other, to the office. "No, nothing like that. The boss has given me a change of scene for a month, doing inspections and education classes, which means I get to work regular-people hours for a while. So unless we have one of those movie-scale epic disasters, my plan is to be here most mornings, if that's okay with you two."

Terri walked around the corner and dove straight in for a group hug. "If what's okay with us two?"

"Mac here is pretending to be a normal person for a month, with regular job hours. So she wants to come and play with us and all the fur babies in the mornings."

Terri whooped in delight, then stood back. "Hang on, Mare, did you say she's pretending to be a normal person? Yeah, good luck with that!"

Mac mock-punched her on the arm, put her arms around both women's waists, and they all walked into the main office together. Mac turned around to face them. "I'm sorry. I've been a crap friend lately. I've missed this—I've missed laughing with you guys, and I miss your cooking. Hey, are you guys doing anything weekend after next?"

Maree and Terri looked at each other and shook their heads.

"Because I have been such a crap friend of late, how do you feel about coming over to my house for some dinner, music, wine, and general catch-up? And yes, I will cook for you."

Maree and Terri looked at each other, failing to keep straight faces. Terri turned to Maree and in a semi-mock-whisper said, "Oooh a night out would be good. And it would be good to catch up with Miss Missing in Action over there, but she said she was gonna do the cooking. Is that wise?"

"Hmm, yeah," Maree answered in kind. "Remember the last time she cooked? We had to order in pizza and sit outside eating while the smoke cleared from the house."

"Oh yeah, and then there was the time when—"

Mac was chuckling and held up her hands in surrender "Okay, okay, so cooking's not my thing. But I've got this covered. Really."

Terri and Maree both looked at each other and then back at Mac, not looking at all convinced.

They were all laughing now. "Seriously guys, I *will* do dinner."

Terri was giggling. Maree slapped her playfully on the arm. "Okay, then we'll bring the wine, how's that?"

"Super! Okay, lock it in."

Maree looked at her watch, then to Mac. "You happy to do the same routine again this morning? Kittens, then run six?"

"Too easy."

As before, Mac did the kittens first. She had a bit more time this morning, so each and every kitten got loads of attention and extra cuddles before she was done. She talked to each kennel occupant and left them treats before going back to start the cleaning with the old cattle dog. "Morning, princess," she crooned and was pleasantly surprised to see the old dog wag her tail in recognition this morning. Mac cleaned out her kennel and sat on the floor next to the old dog, feeding her some of the leftover chicken. She pulled a brush out of her pocket, showed it to the dog and allowed her to sniff it, then gently started brushing her.

Mac finished by gently scratching behind the old dog's ear. "How was that, princess? You like that? I think you do. How about we have a beauty session each morning, hey? How does that sound, hmm?" The dog leaned into her and wagged its tail and Mac scratched her behind her ear. "It's a date, then. Same time tomorrow then, my lady. I had best be off and see to the youngsters."

She did the same with the hunting dog, although he was slightly more stiff in his reception. Poor bugger had probably never been brushed in his life. Still, he didn't object and barked cheerfully once at her as she left as if to say thanks.

The terrier was still pacing and wasn't interested in the chicken. She noticed he hadn't really eaten much of his breakfast either. She would talk to the girls about him. He was too highly stressed. Mac left, a hefty ball of concern weighing heavily on her mind for the little dog.

Lastly there was the kennel on the end. As before, there were blinking eyes. Today however, she didn't put out the nibbles near the bed. Mac went about her business and cleaned the kennel. Then she sat down on the floor about two feet from the bedding. "Hey, little eyes. Last night I made some chicken dinner and I cooked a bit extra and brought it in to share. I was kind of hoping that you and me could get together over a piece of shared bird."

While she was talking, Mac brought the chicken out of her pocket and was shredding it into little pieces. She gently tossed one piece right on the edge of the bedding. The eyes blinked double time, and a small black nose appeared and quivered as it scented the chicken in the air. A pink tongue quickly darted out and snared the morsel. Mac kept up the dialogue.

"Now normally, I am a crap cook, and my friends Maree and Terri agree completely on this, but"—she tossed some more chicken just a little farther away from the bedding and closer to her by a couple of inches—"I was especially careful last night and chose the best piece of chicken." A golden muzzle appeared from under the bedding and snagged the second piece before retreating, so Mac tossed another piece, a little farther out and closer to her.

"I thawed it out and cooked it in a pan." Mac held her breath as a whole beautiful golden head slowly appeared to take the chicken, and this time it did not retreat but stood statue still and waited.

"I confess, I used a smidgeon of butter when I seared it." Another piece of chicken was released barely two inches from her. The dog would have to come all the way out to get it. "I thought perhaps the butter might just give it the little winning edge of approval that I was looking for."

Mac placed the rest of the chicken directly alongside her outstretched thigh. The dog emerged ever so slowly, as if magnetically drawn, mesmerized, by the hypnotizing power of the chicken, to cautiously eat the remaining titbits beside her. Mac made her movements slow, so as to not alarm the dog. "And I was kind of hoping for some feedback from you guys here this morning on what you thought." Mac ever so gently put her hand on the shoulders of the tiny golden body, who initially froze at the contact, then continued eating the chicken as Mac stroked the furred back.

It was a tiny body, still a puppy really, hard to tell how old. It was skinny. Too skinny. It broke her heart just a little. Mac gazed over the pup from head to toe. She could count each of its ribs quite easily. It was a little girl, the colour of sun-ripened wheat from head to tail, with the tip of the tail white as if someone had dipped it in paint. She had a dark nose and walnut-coloured eyes. What was it with the brown-eyed beauties this week? Probably a mixed breed. Looking at her paws, she guessed at maybe a middle-sized dog when she grew up. Given her poor start in life, Mac suspected she would probably remain a small-framed lass.

Mac held the last piece of chicken in the palm of her hand in the middle of her lap. "You know, I watched a movie once, about a child in the woods, raised by her gran, I think." Mac stopped patting the puppy and let her eat the last of the chicken on the ground. "Anyway the gran had a stroke and eventually died, and this girl was living a bit wild, on her own. She was a blond young wild wisp of a lass, a bit like you really." The puppy had finished the food and realized that the only piece left was in Mac's lap. If the puppy wanted to take it, it would require an enormous leap of faith.

Mac kept her voice steady and calm. "She had her own language and when she met this man they had to learn to talk to each other. Eventually they became friends." The puppy, in the slowest of motions, put one paw on Mac's thigh. Mac didn't move. Two paws. Three. Then slowly, ever so slowly, the fourth leg was raised and the pup crawled onto Mac's lap to nuzzle her hand, where the last of the chicken lay.

"I remember Jodie Foster played the role in the movie. It was breathtaking. I can't remember if it was a true story or not." Mac started to stroke the puppy's back. "Anyway, the movie and the young girl were called *Nell*. Y'know, you kind of remind me of her in a way." The puppy looked up at her and seemed to figure Mac was okay. The newly christened Nell had a full belly, was sitting in a warm lap, and had a gentle hand running down her back in a warm, rhythmic motion. Nell yawned, then turned around three times before curling into a ball, falling fast asleep up in Mac's lap. This was the ultimate gift of trust offered to Mac. She knew the enormity of it and tears coursed down her cheeks as she continued to stroke the puppy's back. "So I guess you liked my chicken, huh?"

❖

As predicted, Sarah had spent her first day off cleaning the house, grocery shopping, washing, and throwing open the windows, encouraging fresh air to sweep the house clean. That was one thing about working nights—the house rarely felt fresh. She left in the dark and came home as the sun was up, only to shut everything closed to keep out the light and noise so she could get some sleep. But here it was, daylight, and she was home. Sarah had a smile on her face all day. Luxuriating over a nice cuppa on the balcony felt positively decadent. Funny, she had forgotten how the simple things like sunlight and free time felt so damn good.

The spare rooms for Jean and Thomas were all ready to go. Right on five, Sarah headed across town to pick them up. First they went into the mall and picked up a new video game for Thomas for the weekend. They happened to go past the pet store. Thomas tugged on Sarah's coat and pointed to go inside. Both Jean and Sarah looked at each other and smothered a smile. Sarah nodded and they all went inside.

Thomas walked around the store, carefully looking at all the accessories for any and every pet imaginable with a very thoughtful expression on his face. Sometimes he would stop in front of a particular item, look at the price and the varieties on offer, and then move on. It appeared he deliberately left looking at the animals on display until last, almost like he was savouring it. He worked his way past the fish, the mice, guinea pigs, and rabbits. There were only two puppies in the store and they were both curled up, fast asleep. Finally he walked to the kitten enclosure and there he stood, fascinated. He watched them all with great intensity. He laughed at their tumbling antics and their bumbling pouncing manoeuvres. They were all colours and a mix of sizes, but he kept coming back to a clutch of tiny kits who were obviously still working out how their bodies worked.

It was getting on time for dinner. Jean signalled to Thomas that it was time to go. Thomas put his hand to the glass and sighed, dutifully turning to join Sarah and his mum as they walked out the door. As it was an early birthday outing for the family, dinner was Thomas's choice. He picked a Japanese restaurant where they had been once before. Thomas didn't like the food so much as the chef who gave a fantastic floor show as he chopped and tossed food around like a well-seasoned showman, getting Thomas to hold up a dish at one end of the servery while he diced carrots in the air to have them land into Thomas's bowl. Sarah and Jean laughed at the chef and Thomas's antics.

All too soon it was time to head back to Sarah's. Thomas fell asleep in the car on the drive home. Jean carried him into the house and put him straight to bed while Sarah poured them each a glass of wine. Sarah put on a new CD one of her work colleagues had recommended.

Jean walked in, grabbed her wine, and crashed down on the couch next to Sarah. "Mm, this is nice. Hey, who's the CD? Sounds great."

"It's The Waifs. Alice at work put me on to them—they're great, aren't they?"

"So, tell me, how's work? And when was the last time *you* had a couple of days off? How nice."

"Yeah, I know. I was just thinking this morning how nice it was to be home. I even enjoyed cleaning the house—how sad is that, huh? God, I must be getting old."

They both smiled.

"Work isn't too bad—busy as always, but I can't complain. Every day is different. Some days aren't so good, but then, some days you get to be a part of something special and that keeps you going through the tough days."

"Has this been a tough week?"

Sarah sipped her wine and thought through the week and smiled. "No, it hasn't been too bad. The usual. Kids with burns, drunks, broken bones—oh, and I met a firefighter called Mouse."

Jean sipped her wine. "Okay, you've got my attention. Please explain."

Sarah told her the story of the MVA. She even told her about Mac doing the fire inspections on the Monday.

"She must be cute, this Mouse."

Sarah's glass stopped midway to her mouth. "Why do you say that?"

Jean laughed gently and patted Sarah's thigh. "Well, apart from the fact that you're smiling like a cat that found the fridge door open, you sound like you're even looking forward to doing the fire inspections! I mean, come on, Sare, fire inspections are definitely not that interesting, so she must be cute."

Sarah laughed and swatted Jean's hand playfully. Sarah's face felt warm and she couldn't blame the flush all on the wine. "Mm, let's just say that the inspections might not be too much of a hardship to bear this year."

They sat in companionable silence for a while. Jean leaned over and topped up both their glasses. As she handed Sarah's over she tilted her head to the side and looked at Sarah.

Sarah couldn't help but notice Jean's intense scrutiny. "What? Have I got food on my face?"

"No, I was just trying to think how long it had been."

Sarah looked at her puzzled, not quite sure where Jean was going with her question. "Since…?"

"Since you went out on a date."

Sarah choked on the wine.

"Seriously, Sare. How long has it been?"

Sarah looked away. God, how long had it been? Thinking back through the few times she even went out, let alone on a date, the last couple of…years? Shit. "Two years? Three years? It's been a while."

"Well, what about this Mouse?"

"Oh, now hang on, I don't think—"

"Well, maybe you *should* think about it. I don't remember the last time you lit up like that over anyone, let alone someone you just met. What's the harm in finding out?"

Sarah opened and shut her mouth a couple of times. *Lit up?* Jean was right. She had only met Mac briefly twice and she couldn't get those blue eyes out of her head. Hell, she was even looking forward to Monday. It wouldn't hurt to find out a bit more…would it?

"Seriously, Sare, there's more to life than just work. I want to see you happy."

"I *am* happy."

"I'd say more like staying busy and trying to be content, wouldn't you?"

"Content is good."

Jean shook her head. "Nuh-uh. Not good enough. Not when you can do better."

Sarah swirled the wine in her glass thoughtfully. Colleen had had a go at her the other evening about hardly ever seeing her and that she was always working nights. Maybe she *was* turning into a nocturnal old maid.

"All I'm suggesting is that you keep your options open, honey. Don't close yourself off and hide in your work. Hey, maybe on Monday you can talk this Mouse into having a cup of coffee—after the inspections, you know?"

Sarah shrugged.

Jean bumped her on the shoulder playfully. "It would just be coffee, no commitments, no sex—that should all come *after* she takes you out for dinner."

Sarah did snort her wine at that and just shook her head and laughed. "Okay, okay, just coffee, no sex. I get it!"

They both laughed.

Sarah reached for and held Jean's hand. "What about you? What about *your* happiness Jean?"

Jean smiled sadly. "My happiness will be knowing that Thomas and I can just settle down in one place and live normally. Not looking over my shoulder all the time, or jumping at shadows. You know, this is the longest we've stayed in any one place for the past two years. It feels nice. *This* makes me happy." Jean's eyes filled with tears as she looked up. "But I'm always waiting, watching, knowing he can turn up anytime, and that we might have to move again. Just this week, I've had a few phone calls. I don't know how he got my number, but I know it's him."

"What does he say?"

"It's never very much. Sometimes it's just heavy breathing. Yesterday he just said *I haven't forgotten about you.*" Jean shook her head. "It breaks my heart. Every time we settle, Thomas makes some new friends, and then Richard finds us, and we have to move." Tears flowed freely down Jean's face. Her throat closed up and she hoarsely whispered, "It's just so hard. So damn hard. I keep wondering how long I can keep doing this."

Sarah leaned over and pulled Jean into her arms. "Have you heard from your solicitors or the police lately?"

Jean shook her head. "No. He's been in counselling, and it's been so good for a while. But last week, I had a call from the police to say he didn't check in with his probation officer and he'd missed his last couple of treatment appointments. They don't know where he is." Jean fingered the stem of her wine glass. "I feel like I'm in limbo land, and I don't quite know what to do next."

Sarah hugged her tight. "We'll figure something out."

CHAPTER SEVEN

Mac had finished all the preparation work for next week's inspections and classes, leaving the rest of the day to be hers. She took herself off to the pet store in the mall to look for some treats for the dogs on run six. Wandering up and down the aisles, she picked out some nice collars and leads, a box of toy mice for the kittens, and a couple of toys for the puppy, Nell. On the way back to her truck, she spied a reasonably priced pocket-sized digital camera in another store, a sprinkle of spontaneity sparking inside of her as she decided that she could afford to treat herself to it. Smiling smugly, she justified that her impulsive purchase could also be used to take some photos of the upcoming inspections and education classes, which she could add to the reports she would submit at the end of the month.

As the day was hers, she thought she would spend the rest of it at the refuge rather than just an hour or two in the morning. As she drove, she got to thinking about Maree and Terri's upcoming five-year anniversary of opening up the refuge. She wanted to do something special for them. She looked at the camera, still in its box, as an idea began to dawn. She would take the camera in with her for the next week or two and get some shots of the refuge, which would help with the inspiration for the plan that was taking shape in Mac's mind. Mac was smiling and humming to herself as she pulled into the car park, thinking that her first practice shots could be her new buddies in run six.

Maree and Terri both spied her as she walked in with her box of goodies. Terri turned to her partner. "Well, well, what have we here? You know, I was only thinking this morning, when Mac didn't turn up, that a couple of mornings in a row helping us and playing at being normal, might have been too much."

Maree was chuckling. "Actually, my love, I think it's worse than that. It looks like she's trying to move in."

Everybody was laughing. Mac raised an eyebrow at them both. "Ha-ha, you two clowns. I thought I might spend a whole day here helping out, if you're interested, as opposed to just cleaning up after you two."

Terri looked at Maree with a huge grin on her face before turning to look back at Mac. "Serious? A whole day of free labour?"

"Yep, a whole day…and I like to think of myself as cheap and easy, not free."

Terri whooped with delight. "You're an idiot, y'know that?"

Maree laughed. "Yes, but she's *our* idiot, and for a whole day! Don't suppose you brought your tools with you?"

Mac smiled. "You bet. How about I go over to run six first. I brought the guys some treats, and you two make out a list of the things you want done and we'll go from there."

The girls gave Mac a huge group hug.

"Well, if you're going to help out today, then lunch and dinner are on us," Maree said.

"Hey, if you're cooking, then I'm eating. What say I meet up with you in the office in say"—Mac looked at her watch—"about forty-five minutes?"

"Too easy."

"Okay, see you in a bit." Mac turned and headed to the run, while Maree and Terri had their heads together working on the list for Mac.

Mac had brought the old lady cattle dog a stretcher bed with a woollen liner on it, to get her stiff old bones off the cold cement, and a lovely fire-engine red collar and lead. For the young hunting dog she brought a couple of rawhide chews and rope tug toys. His collar and lead were an embossed leather set in dark earthy tones. The terrier got a stuffed rabbit toy for him to cuddle up to and some calming herbal drops that she planned to put in his water bowl if it was all right with the girls. His collar and lead set was of a rich emerald green.

Last was little Nell. Mac sat on the ground of her pen and held her hand out, with some small liver treats in her palm. Nell timidly came over and took the treats from her hand. "Hello, Nell. How are you this morning, little one?" Nell crawled into her lap. "I brought you some things I thought you might like." She reached into the box and brought out a lavender-coloured collar and lead and let Nell sniff them. "All the big girls wear collars, you know. And later on, we can put a name tag on for you." She slowly and gently put the collar around Nell's neck and did it up. The puppy just looked at her with big trusting eyes. "You are such a good girl. We might try the lead out a bit later on, hey? What else is in here?" She reached into the box and pulled out a ball, a squeaky turtle toy, and a big soft teddy.

She put the teddy between her and the puppy so both of their scents would be on the toy. "This big guy can go in your bed for you to cuddle up to so you don't get lonely at night." She was scratching behind the puppy's ears as it watched her. She grabbed the squeaking turtle. "You can chew on this funny guy." She squeaked the turtle not far from Nell's face. But something wasn't right. The puppy didn't look at the turtle. She squeaked the turtle again. Nell didn't even blink. Mac put the turtle down and put one hand behind the puppy's head, out of its line of sight, and clicked her fingers, first behind the puppy's right ear, and then the puppy's left ear. There was no reaction. Mac repeated it again with her fingers and then again with the turtle. The pup just kept looking up at her. Nell made no reaction at all to the noises. Mac drew the puppy in to her chest and hugged her. She would have to tell Maree and Terri. Nell would need a vet to check her out to be sure, but it looked to Mac like Nell was deaf.

Tears welled in Mac's eyes. She knew this would make it even more difficult for Nell to find a good forever home. Not many people wanted a deaf dog. She gave Nell a last hug, left her some treats, and headed off to find the girls.

Over a coffee they talked about Nell. The girls had drawn up a great list of jobs for Mac, more than enough to do in one day. Inside, she changed washers on taps, put new hoses in the washrooms, installed brackets on the wall for a dryer, and fixed some cupboards and drawers that had seen better days. Outside, she hung up new signs and installed some hand railings that the girls had bought last month. Mac was starting to measure up where the girls wanted a cement path laid between sheds when Terri came over and grabbed her for lunch.

"Hey, girl Friday, you ready for something to eat?"

Mac stood up and dusted off her hands on her pants. "You bet."

As they walked back together, Terri put her arm through Mac's. "I can't believe how much you've done already. It looks great. Thanks heaps, chick."

"You're most welcome. I'm really enjoying it, and if it helps, well, that's a bonus."

"It really does, it helps a lot. But more than that, it's super to just have you here."

"Well, it's super to be here. And if you promise to feed me, then I just might keep coming back."

Terri punched her arm. "You crazy fool."

Grinning, Mac punched her back. "Yep."

Having washed up outside, they walked into the tea room behind the office. Maree waved them in. "Sit, sit…how's it all going?"

"Pretty good, I think," Mac said. "I've finished most of the little jobs, and I'm just about to start measuring up to mark out where I need to set the formwork up for your path. Were you able to get the concrete to come out tomorrow?"

Terri nodded. "Yeah, the concrete guy said they could be here about half past nine."

"Okay, that'll work out well. We can set the formwork up today and be ready for the pour tomorrow."

Maree put a steaming dish of vegetable soup in the middle of the table, followed by fresh warm bread rolls. "Help yourselves."

Mac's mouth was watering so much at the delicious smells that she thought it might just be possible to drown with the anticipation of it all. They each dished themselves out a portion and tucked in. Mac closed her eyes in sheer pleasure at the first mouthful. "Maree, you are a magician. This is *amazing*."

Terri raised a piece of bread in salute. "What she said. This is beautiful, babe, thank you."

"You're both welcome."

The rest of the meal was consumed in silence until all was gone. Terri was pouring fresh juices all round. "So, apart from blessing us with your presence, how's your week been, Mac? Do you have to do much preparation stuff for the classes and inspection thingies?"

Mac told them briefly about the call-outs at the beginning of the week, including Bella and the baby, and the preparations she'd been working on for next week. "Most of the paperwork was done by Eddie, the guy that usually does this stuff. I've just tweaked it a bit here and there and thrown in some extra fun stuff that I hope will be okay for the different groups. My first inspection is on Monday, and it's at the hospital. That'll take me a couple of days, as it's a pretty big area to cover, with a few education classes around town thrown in."

"What's so good about the hospital inspections?" Maree asked.

Mac looked at Maree and wondered if she'd finally steamed her brains when making lunch.

"Don't give me that look. When you mentioned doing the hospital inspections on Monday, you were smiling. Is there a story there that we should know about?"

Damn Maree, she never missed anything.

Terri bounced in the seat excitedly. "Oooh, there is. Come on, spill it. What can possibly make you smile about a fire inspection?"

"Well Bella—you know, the pregnant lady in the MVA I was telling you about?"

Maree and Terri nodded.

"Well, when I dropped her off to the hospital, the doctor on duty, was…"

"Was she hot?" Terri couldn't help herself.

Mac felt her face go red as a beetroot.

Terri was rubbing her hands with glee. "She was!"

Maree slapped her on the arm. "And does this doctor have a name?"

"Sarah. Sarah Macarthur. I remember standing there that night—she asked me a question, and I couldn't speak. All I saw where her dark chocolate eyes. She must have thought me a right daft twit. And then I literally ran into her a couple of days later. We both walked around a corner at the same time and smacked into each other. I didn't see her. I was looking at a map of the hospital buildings, trying to work out where the maintenance stuff was. Anyway, she ended up personally taking me around and pointing out where the buildings were out the back of the hospital. She's part of the staff that I need to work with for the inspections next week."

"Who'd have thought inspections could be so interesting, huh? Is she…y'know?"

Mac shrugged. "You know me. I wouldn't have a clue unless she wrote it on the back of a beer coaster."

They all laughed at that and both Terri and Maree agreed. "That's true, girlfriend. When they gave out gaydar you must've been out of the country."

Terri waggled her eyebrows. "Maybe one of us could go ahead and act as a spy for you."

Mac was smiling but shaking her head as she picked up her dishes and walked them over to the sink. "Maybe…maybe."

Maree got up too. "Leave that, I'll fix this up. You two go back out and play."

Mac kissed Maree on the cheek. "Thanks for the great lunch."

"It's the least I could do for my workers."

❖

Terri explained how they wanted the path to join the buildings together and eventually connect another building, not yet constructed. So with that in mind, Mac made some adjustments to her measurements, and using a tin of spray paint, marked out the path. Terri stayed and watched the process of marking before waving off to exercise some of the dogs and put others through some basic training while Mac prepared the stakes and borders for the formwork.

Mac set to work digging out the grass and levelling out the dirt. She was just putting the first of the formwork pegs in when Maree came over to see how she was doing. Digging out the pathway had been hot work and Mac had stripped down to a singlet.

"Thought you might like some water after all the labour you've been doing." Maree handed over a bottle.

"Thanks, Maree, that's gold." She took the chilled water gratefully.

"The vet just rang to say he's about ten minutes away. I thought you and Terri might want to see what they have to say about the terrier and the puppy. He's going to look over a couple of the cats and another dog that came in earlier in the week, but I'll get him to start with those two first. I'll just get Terri and we'll meet you in six."

"Thanks. I'd like to see what he says about the two of them."

"Okay, meet up in a bit."

Mac nodded and tidied up some of the stuff she was working with. She was just washing up before heading over when the vet pulled in. As she was there, she greeted him and took him over to run six, where the girls were already waiting.

The vet looked over all the dogs on the run, leaving some anti-inflammatories for the old cattle dog with the stiff joints, giving the hunting dog a clean bill of health, prescribing some light relaxants for the terrier, and confirmed Mac's worst fears by pronouncing Nell a bit undernourished and deaf. He felt a small healed dent to the side of her skull and thought perhaps her deafness might not be congenital, but rather as a result of either an accident or a blow to the head. The girls mentioned how they came about the puppy and that they had suspected it had been abused. The vet, having thoroughly assessed the puppy, agreed with the girls' conclusions.

They were talking over the puppy's prospects when the sound of a car pulling into the car park could be heard. Mac had heard all that she needed to. "I'll get that if you like."

Maree patted her shoulder. "Thanks, I'll be there in a bit."

Mac waved and headed off to see who had pulled up. Just as she was approaching the office, she froze. It was the doctor from the hospital with another woman and a young boy. *Shit.* She looked down at herself. She had dirt on her clothes and no doubt her hair looked wild and all over the place. *Oh well, can't be helped.* She took a deep breath, straightened her shoulders, and walked to greet the small group.

"Hello, Sarah. Nice to see you again."

For a moment, Sarah looked like a rabbit caught in the headlights, as if Mac was the last person she thought she would meet. The woman with her jabbed her in the ribs. "Are you going to introduce me?"

Blinking, Sarah quickly recovered. "Sorry. Mac, this is my sister Jean and her son Thomas."

Mac held out her hand to Jean. "Hello, it's nice to meet you."

"Jean, Mac is the firefighter I was telling you about."

Jean's eyes went wide briefly, quickly replaced with a huge smile. "Hello, Mac, it's a pleasure to meet you too."

Jean lightly touched Thomas on the shoulder and the boy glanced up. Jean used sign language to talk to Thomas. "Thomas, this is your Aunt Sarah's friend, Mac. Mac is a firefighter. Say hello to Mac."

Thomas was deaf.

For a brief moment, Mac was lost in a time warp, back to when she was little. Her younger brother was deaf from birth. All the family had learned sign language. She hadn't signed in a long time. Watching Jean brought back some dusty memories.

Mac knelt down next to Thomas and hesitantly signed back. "Hello, Thomas. Nice to meet you." She held out her hand to Thomas, who took it and shook back with a smile on his face.

Mac stood to see Sarah and Jean staring at her. Jean was the first to come to her senses. "You know how to sign?"

Mac shrugged. "I learned a long time ago, but I haven't used it in a very long while. I'm afraid I've probably forgotten more than I remember. My friends, the owners, are just with the vet who's doing some check-ups on some of the new animals. They'll be along in a few minutes. Is there something I can help you with in the meantime?"

Sarah was still rattled. Here was fireman Mouse looking far too good in a singlet, *and* she knew sign language? Really? Was this too good to be true or was it just plain spooky and weird?

Jean dug Sarah subtly in the ribs again. Sarah swallowed and regained her composure. "I promised Thomas that we could come out and see the animals. Is that okay?"

"Sure. Is there anything in particular that you're interested in?"

Sarah stood behind Thomas so he couldn't lip read what she was saying. "We thought Thomas might like a kitten for his birthday next week, but it's a surprise. He thinks we're just out here to look at the animals in general. Would that be okay?"

Mac nodded. "I think we can manage that. What say we look at some dogs and then we can finish up with the cat and kitten house?"

Jean gave Mac the okay sign.

Mac knelt down again next to Thomas. "Your mum and aunt said you would like to see some of the animals today."

Thomas nodded.

"Okay, follow me."

Mac took them over to the old dogs' run, then to the small dogs' run. He diligently stopped and looked at all of them, signing a few questions as he went. "Why don't these dogs have homes? Why is that dog's eyes different colours?"

The group crossed the grassy verge on their way back over to where the cats were kept and Maree met them on the walkway. Mac introduced them, using sign language so Thomas could understand.

"Maree, I'd like to introduce you to Thomas who has come to see the animals. Thomas has brought his mum Jean and his Aunt Sarah along with him."

Maree shook Thomas's hand first, then Jean's and Sarah's. "It's lovely to meet you all. Thank you for coming out today to have a look at all of our furry friends." Jean was signing to Thomas what Maree was saying. "If you'd like to follow me, I'll show you through the cat house." Maree pointed to the path which led to the building.

Mac whispered something to Maree, and Maree nodded in understanding and gave her the thumbs up. "Gotcha!" she mouthed before ushering them inside.

Mac walked slowly back to the formwork she'd been working on earlier. She stood there looking, but not really seeing. She didn't notice Terri saying goodbye to the vet and heading over her way. Terri came up beside her quietly and laid a hand on her arm. "Hey, Mac, you okay?"

Mac jumped a little and came back to reality, shaking her head lightly. "Um, sorry? Did you say something?"

"Yeah, I asked if you were okay. You looked a bit lost and out of it there for a minute. Did the news of the puppy upset you?"

"No, I mean, yes, it did, it made me sad, but I had sort of guessed that would be the case."

"Okay. Is something else worrying you? The people you were just with…is everything okay?"

Mac closed her eyes and gathered herself. *Stop being so stupid, get it together woman.* "No, yes, they're fine. Maree's taken them over to the cat house."

Terri looked at Mac with a frown, as if not quite getting what was going on.

"It's Sarah."

Terri, apparently, still didn't get it.

"The doctor."

The penny dropped. "Oh, you mean Dr. Hot with chocolate eyes?"

Mac nodded.

"And this is a *bad* thing?"

"No, not bad. The little boy, Thomas, he's deaf. Seeing him and using sign language again, after all these years, and seeing Sarah out of the blue with them, it's just got my head in a spin, you know? Not bad, but it's just thrown me a bit."

"Ah, I see now." Terri gave her a hug and kissed her on the cheek.

"Thanks Ter. I'm okay. I better get back to this formwork so we'll be ready for tomorrow's pour."

"Okay, I'll just go and put these tablets away and check on Maree, then I'll come back out and give you a hand."

"No worries."

Mac picked up the stakes and the hammer. The physical work would clear her head and give her something else to concentrate on for the minute. Later on she would take out her thoughts and feelings and work through them, but not right now. Right now she needed a bit of distance, and the physical work and concentration needed to get the formwork just right would do the job nicely.

❖

Sarah walked through the pens behind Jean, Thomas, and Maree. She was only half listening to the conversation going on around her. Her mind was racing. Mac knew sign language. *Go figure.* She was obviously rusty, as she was a bit hesitant between signs, but she knew how to do it. What was the chance of that? And what was Mac doing here? She'd said the owners were her friends, so maybe she works here on her days off. She certainly looked like she'd been working. She had a cute smudge of mud on her left cheekbone where she'd obviously wiped her face.

Jean tapped Sarah on the head. "Earth to Sarah, come in Sarah."

"Wha? Sorry." Sarah recovered and looked over at Thomas and couldn't help but smile. Thomas was in front of the tiny kitten cage with Maree, pointing out a small grey tabby kitten. Maree opened the cage, pulled out the kitten, and handed it to Thomas to hold. Thomas looked up with an enormous smile on his face at Jean and Sarah. Jean nodded and smiled back at Thomas. He looked down at the kitten and snuggled it into his jumper. "Looks like Thomas has fallen in love. I think we just found his birthday present."

CHAPTER EIGHT

S o the little grey kitten is the winner?"

Jean was washing while Sarah was drying the dishes from dinner. Thomas had long since gone to bed after his big day.

Jean was beaming. "It was funny—it was like as soon as he saw that little guy, he had this connection thing. Did you see how he and the kitten just looked at each other? Oh, that's right, you were off in la-la land mooning over fireman Mouse."

Sarah flicked her with the towel. "I was not!"

Jean retaliated with a flick of washing-up water. "You so were."

Sarah went to protest more but Jean turned, looking her right in the eye with her hands on her hips. "Okay, well, maybe a little. I wasn't expecting her to be there."

Jean played along. "Uh-huh."

"And she knew how to sign! I mean, really, what are the chances of that?" Sarah was shaking her head.

"Uh-huh."

"And she works with animals."

"And you forgot, cute." Jean was smirking.

"Yeah, cute, and…What? Hey! That's not fair."

Jean had stopped doing the dishes and was watching Sarah prattle on. Sarah chuckled as she realized Jean had played her perfectly.

"I can see why she grabbed your attention. Apart from her eyes of course, and great body. What's not to like? Hard-working, loves animals, good with kids—and deaf kids, at that—and oh, *so* hard to look at. Sarah Jane Macarthur, if you don't invite her out for coffee on Monday, then I sure as hell will."

Sarah held her hands up in mock surrender. "Okay, okay enough already. If the opportunity arises on Monday, I will ask her for coffee."

"Promise?"

"I'll do my best."

"Come on, Sare, what have you got to lose, huh?"

"Oh, I don't know, my dignity maybe?"

"Oh, don't be so precious. Promise me you'll ask her out."

Sarah had butterflies in her stomach. *What's that all about?* She felt like a schoolgirl looking for a first date. Then again, it had been such a long time, it might as well have been the first date. What was she thinking? She hardly knew Mac. She'd met her now, what? Three times? And each for only a handful of minutes. She could be a serial killer for all she knew. A damn cute serial killer, with killer eyes.

"C'mon, Sare, I've got a good feeling about this fireman Mouse."

"Mac, her name's *Mac*."

"Okay, I stand corrected. Mac Mouse."

Sarah rolled her eyes.

Jean persisted. "Be brave, Sare. Reach out and take a chance."

Sarah sighed.

"Please? For me?"

Sarah closed her eyes tight and shook her head. "Yes, yes, all right already. I'll do it on Monday for you because I know you'll drive me crazy until I give in."

Jean hugged her. "Thatta girl. And when it all works out, you know where I am for you to come and thank me." Jean bumped her with her hip. "Oh, one more thing, when you ask her out—can you ask her if she has a brother?"

Sarah put her head in the tea towel and just groaned.

They finished the washing with light banter, retiring to the couch with a glass of wine each. "So, how do we go about doing the kitten thing?" Jean asked.

Sarah scratched her head. "Good question. We'll need to get a few supplies in, but we don't want to give the game away doing it."

They both mused in silence for a few minutes. Sarah had a thought. "Why don't you take Thomas back to the refuge again, to see the animals, and I'll slip into town and get a bed, kitty-litter tray, and a little bit of food, so that we have the first night covered. I can hide them in the garage until we bring the kitten home. The next day, we can take him into town and he can have fun choosing toys and food and all the other stuff."

Jean sipped her wine thoughtfully. "How about *you* take Thomas to the refuge, and *I* go into town for the bits and pieces?" Sarah opened her mouth to protest, but Jean cut her off. "It would be a nice treat for me too. Just to have some time to relax and look in the shops on my own for a while."

Jean was playing dirty. Sarah couldn't say no to her. She wondered if Mac would be at the refuge again. Maybe it was just a one-off day thing, so it would probably be safe for her to take Thomas. They could spend a couple of hours looking around, stop on the way home and have a milkshake somewhere, and text ahead to let Jean know they were heading home. "Okay, how about we head off, say about nine tomorrow, and be back a bit before lunch. Will that give you enough time?"

They clinked their glasses together in agreement. Jean nodded. "That sounds perfect."

❖

It was a bit later than Mac had planned to finish off the formwork. In fact, the last hour had seen her adding the final finishing touches to the last little bit in the dark, with only the illumination of the shed lights, but at last she stood, stretched her back, and looked over her handywork. She was tired, but feeling pretty satisfied that everything that could be done today had been achieved, and all was ready for when the concrete truck arrived in the morning.

Terri had helped her, in between feeding the animals and putting them to bed for the night. She looked at the path framework. "You all done then?"

"Yep, just finished up now. I just need to pop the gear away and then I'm all done."

"I'll give you a hand."

"Thanks." They worked in companionable silence for a few minutes before heading into the house to wash up for dinner.

As they walked into the kitchen Maree greeted them. "Beer or wine, ladies?"

"A beer for me please," said Terri

"Same for me too, please, Mare."

"Two beers coming up. Go and sit down and relax for a bit. Dinner's about half an hour away yet."

The girls had not long sat down when Maree came in with the two promised beers and a G and T for herself. "Did you manage to get the path frame finished?"

Mac sipped her beer. "Yep. All done. All we need now is the concrete and some good weather and it'll be done and dusted in no time."

"Thanks for all you've done, Mac. Terri and I are gobsmacked at how much you got through today. I can't tell you how much it means to us to have you here, helping."

"Well, you are both very, very welcome. If truth be told, I've had a great day. The weather was beautiful, great company, lots of fixing stuff, which I love, and now I have a gorgeous woman cooking for me. What more could a girl want?"

Terri shook her finger at Mac. "Hey, that's my wife you're buttering up, missy."

Mac chuckled. "Ah, my apologies. No offence intended for the hostesses with the mostesses."

Terri raised her beer. "Here's to a good day's work all round, I say."

Maree and Mac raised their drinks and all called cheers in unison.

Maree looked at Mac over the top of her glass. "So, Terri tells me this afternoon's Aunt Sarah is the fabulous doctor that you'll be doing inspections with next week."

Mac played it cool. "Mm."

"I see what you mean about her eyes. They really are quite captivating."

Terri snickered. "The whole damn package was pretty captivating, if you ask me."

Maree playfully slapped her on her thigh. "No one is asking you."

"Oh, come on, you both have to admit, that's a *hot* package. She can take my temperature anytime, I don't mind telling you."

Mac and Maree looked at each other, grinned, grabbed a cushion each and threw them at Terri. "Hey! Watch the beer, you guys!"

Maree kept going. "Her sister Jean seemed nice. Did you know about the boy being deaf?"

Mac shook her head. "No. I've never met them before today. It blew me away for a bit, to be honest."

Maree sipped her drink. "How so?"

Mac's fingers worried the label on the bottle. Her voice grew husky. "I was trying to think the last time I signed. The last time was in the accident. I was signing to David, telling him it would be all right, and to stay awake, help was coming…" Mac closed her eyes at the memory.

Maree leaned over, put her hand on Mac's forearm, and spoke quietly. "No wonder it was a bit of a shock for you. I must say, I was impressed."

Mac looked up at Maree.

"Well, actually, now I'm doubly impressed. I thought when I saw you signing that was pretty cool, but now that I know you haven't done it in such a long time, I am *really* impressed. I mean, I barely remember what I did last week and you looked like you'd been doing it for forever."

Mac shook her head and chuckled. "Actually, I was really nervous and *very* rusty. It was kind of nice though when I realized I still remembered some stuff, but I sort of stuttered my way through for most of it."

"Well, if it's any consolation, I think you blew the good doctor away."

Mac looked at Maree, confused.

"When I took them into the cat house, she looked positively distracted, and I don't think it had anything to do with the kittens they were looking at."

CHAPTER NINE

Mac was up early, having turned the alarm off before it had a chance to sound, and eagerly consumed breakfast, before packing a few more tools into her truck and heading off to the refuge. She wanted to spend a bit of extra time with Nell this morning before the concrete truck arrived.

When Mac got home from dinner at the girls' house, she'd sat up Googling training tips for deaf dogs. She had a pocket full of treats all ready and wanted to try to put into practice some basic steps she found online. If Nell was to find a forever home, she would need all the appeal she could get. A well-trained dog might be one of those selling points to help people look past her disability long enough to see the special little dog that she was.

As she approached Nell's pen, the puppy recognized her, leaping out of bed to run over and greet her at the gate. "Well! Good morning to you too, sunshine. What a lovely, cheerful surprise. Did you miss me, huh?" Mac knelt down and ruffled the puppy's ears. "Hey, wanna try out your new lead this morning?" The puppy's tail was wagging.

"Okay, what say we go over to the play pen and have some fun, huh?" The puppy didn't care where she was going, she was just happy to be going with Mac. Mac picked her up and carried her over to the play pen. It was quiet and furnished with lovely soft grass. This was the area that the girls used for special one-on-one training with the dogs. It also acted as a quiet place where they could take potential owners to meet the animals they were interested in adopting as their own. It was away from the pens and close to the office.

Mac walked in and shut the gate behind her. She put Nell on the ground and sat on the grass, letting Nell sniff and explore the new place. All she wanted to do today was to make a start with the concept of *sit* and get Nell used to the lead. She'd read on the Internet that you could get a collar that vibrated to get a deaf dog's attention. One day next week she thought she might make some inquiries at the local pet store to see if they had one. Today, though, she opted to keep it simple and start slowly.

Nell had finally finished exploring, returning cheerfully for a pat. Mac slowly raised her hand with a finger pointed and put it at Nell's eyebrow level so the puppy had to tilt her head back a little. With her other hand she gently pushed down on Nell's hips. "Sit." Mac pointed again and lightly pushed on Nell's rump. "Sit." The puppy sank down onto her haunches, still looking up at Mac. Mac reached into her pocket and gave her a treat, ruffling her ears. "Good girl!" They repeated this manoeuvre a few more times, with all successes rewarded with treats and praise.

They had a quick break and played with a ball, and then had a few more goes at sitting, before Mac tried a game using the lead. Her aim was to get Nell to think of the lead as a fun thing. They played tug of war and chase the snake, the puppy pouncing joyfully upon the lead and chasing it tirelessly. Then Mac clipped the lead onto Nell's collar and just let her walk around and play, with it dragging behind her. At first the puppy reacted to the weirdness of it, but with a few more treats offered to her she soon took no notice of it. Mac stood and was about to try holding on to the lead when she heard a quiet throat being cleared.

Mac turned to the sound behind her.

There, at the gate, were three sets of smiling eyes, watching her and Nell.

Maree had the biggest smile on her face. "Hey, sorry to bother you, but I just thought you might like to know…"

Mac knew Maree was saying something to her but she wasn't really taking it in. She couldn't get past the vision of Sarah, holding Thomas's hand while they were both looking at her. Terri was right. Sarah *was* the whole damn package. She was fit looking, but soft in all the right ways. Her hair was gently blowing with the breeze and shining in the morning sun. Her eyes were covered in smoked sunglasses, which was probably just as well, as it saved Mac from potentially drowning in them.

"Is that okay?" she heard Maree say.

Focus Mac. Focus! "Umm, sorry?"

Maree chuckled quietly. "The concrete will be here a bit after ten. Is that okay?"

"Ten? Yeah, that's fine. Thanks."

"Mac, can you do me a favour please? Some people have just pulled up and want to have a look at some puppies. Can I leave Sarah and Thomas with you for a little bit while I sort these other people out?"

Mac looked at Maree. She was smiling ever so sweetly at her. She glanced over at Sarah and Thomas, looking expectantly at her. How could she say no? "Yeah, sure, I can do that."

Maree openly grinned and turned with a wave. "Thanks. I'll come back when I've finished." As she turned to leave, she winked at Mac.

Mac was still in a bit of shock at Sarah's unexpected reappearance, but she was conscious enough to sign for Thomas. "Hello, Sarah. Hello, Thomas."

Sarah gave a little wave to Mac. "Hello, again. This *is* a lovely surprise."

It was a lovely surprise for Mac too.

"Jean's gone into town for the morning, so Thomas and I thought we would come out for another look around, if that's okay?"

"No, that's fine. It's lovely to see you both again. Did you both enjoy yesterday?"

Thomas eagerly signed back, "Yes. I met a lot of dogs. Then we went and saw the cats and the kittens. And Maree told me they each had stories."

"And who was your favourite animal yesterday?"

Thomas didn't hesitate. "Henry."

Mac looked at Sarah and Sarah's hands went up in a search-me gesture.

"Who is Henry?" asked Mac.

Thomas's face lit up. "The tiniest kitten of them all. He was grey, with green eyes, white toes, and a white chest."

Just then, Nell, who had been sitting patiently by Mac's side, decided she couldn't wait any longer and raised a paw and tapped Mac on the leg as if to say *Hey, remember me?* Mac laughed and leaned down to pat Nell on the head and tell her she was a good girl, then gave her a treat. Mac looked over at Thomas who was captivated. She signed to him, "Thomas, this is my friend Nell. Would you like to come and say hello to her?"

Thomas looked up at his Aunt Sarah and she nodded.

Mac pointed her chin over to her left to Sarah. "Come on in, the gate is over there next to the wall."

Sarah and Thomas came in and stood next to Mac and Nell. Mac knelt down next to Nell and Thomas. "I was teaching Nell how to sit, so that when she grows up, she has good manners." Thomas nodded sagely. "When I want Nell to do something, like sit, then I use my voice." Mac saw Thomas's face fall slightly as he knew he could never do that. Mac gently touched Thomas on the leg to get his attention. "But I also have to use sign language as well."

Thomas looked first at Mac and then at Sarah in confusion. Sarah shrugged her shoulders as well. They both looked expectantly at Mac to explain.

"Nell is a very special puppy. I use sign language with Nell, because she's deaf."

Both Thomas's and Sarah's eyes opened wide at the revelation.

Thomas signed, "So she's like me?"

Mac smiled and signed back. "That's right. I use my voice so she can feel the vibrations, but I use sign language to ask her to do things. Today, I'm teaching Nell to sit. Would you like to have a go?" Thomas vigorously nodded. Mac looked to Sarah. "We'll need your help too, to be Thomas's voice. You okay with that?"

Sarah had no voice. She felt like she was a puppet as she nodded at Mac that she would join in. It was a morning of surprises for Sarah. She had talked herself into coming, thinking yesterday was a one-off and that she would not run into Mac again. And here she was, Mac, looking cleaner than yesterday, and twice as gorgeous. Mac had her hair tied back, with a cap on and sunglasses on top of the cap. She was wearing old faded jeans that hugged her perfectly and an oversized T-shirt. Her face had a slight blush to it, probably from too much sun yesterday. Her eyes were the blue of the Aegean Sea. Mac was the picture of fitness and health. Sarah was never one to swoon, but even she had to admit, Mac made her head spin.

Mac showed Thomas how to hold his hand with the finger pointed. "You need to hold it just over the top of her head, so she has to tilt her head back, then you push down gently on her bottom and your Aunt Sarah says *sit*. And if Nell sits, you have to tell her she is a clever girl and then give her a treat." Both Sarah and Thomas were a captive audience. "How about I show you once, and then you both have a go?" Both Thomas and Sarah nodded. Mac showed them, then handed Thomas a treat to put in his pocket. She stepped back. "Okay, now your turn."

Sarah and Thomas stepped forward together. Thomas looked up at Sarah, who smiled and nodded. He stood in front of Nell and got his hand signal ready. He looked to Sarah as if to cue her. Sarah said *sit* and Thomas pointed at Nell and pushed gently down on her rump. Nell sat obediently. Sarah smiled both at Thomas and Nell and at Mac, who stood there beaming like a proud parent.

Mac signed to Thomas, "Tell Nell how clever she is and offer her a treat." Both Sarah and Thomas made a fuss over Nell, who lapped it up with equal enthusiasm.

Mac smiled and applauded and signed to them both. "Well done, everyone. That was super." Thomas looked up at Mac. "Because Nell is only a baby, we have to make the lessons short. So in between lessons, she can have some play. Do you want to play with her for a few minutes?" Thomas nodded, and he and Nell took off with a couple of the balls and tug toys in the yard and were having a whale of a time.

Mac and Sarah sat down on the grass together and watched them play. Sarah turned to Mac. "That was really lovely of you, showing Thomas how to teach Nell. Thank you."

Mac blushed and found a loose thread on her jeans. "That's okay. It's nice to see them hit it off together."

There was a brief silence before Mac heard Sarah take a deep breath. "You know, this might sound really weird, and I can't believe I'm saying it out loud, but I've only met you a couple of times, and each time you surprise the hell out of me. It's in places I don't expect and in contexts that are all completely different."

Mac smiled shyly.

Sarah had started. She decided if she was going to have egg on her face, it wouldn't matter if it was one egg or the whole damn carton, so she decided to keep going. "This is probably going to sound weird, and maybe there won't be time, I mean you'll probably be busy and everything, and it's okay if you don't want to, I mean, I completely understand, but I wondered if you'd like to go out for coffee or something on Monday, after the inspections at the hospital." There. She'd said it. Okay, it was rushed and probably garbled, but she'd said it. She'd asked her out. Just like she promised Jean.

There was silence.

Great. So much for dignity. *I should have just kept my mouth shut. What was I thinking?*

"I'd like that very much."

Sarah looked up startled. Did she just say yes?

"Coffee with you, on Monday. That sounds lovely. Thank you."

She said yes! Sarah smiled so hard she thought her face would split.

Thomas and Nell both came bounding up together, saving Sarah from melting down completely. She and Mac stood up and Mac signed, "Nell has had a big morning, but she's still only a baby. So we should take her back to her kennel so she can have a rest. Would you like to pick her up and carry her to the kennel for me?" Thomas nodded and picked up Nell, cradling her as if she were the most precious thing in the world and he her personal protector. He stood near the gate and waited for Sarah to open it for him. They walked through and followed Mac over to run six, where they deposited Nell back into her pen. They left her with the remaining treats in her bed. As they left, Nell was contently chewing on the last of the nibbles with heavy eyelids.

As they walked back, Maree intercepted them and offered to take Sarah and Thomas off to the kitten wing of the cat house. As they were leaving, Sarah turned to Mac, who was standing by the pathway formwork. "Are you here for a while?"

Mac nodded. "Yeah, I'm just waiting on the cement truck. I'll probably be here up to my eyeballs in concrete when you come back."

Sarah smiled. "Okay, we might see you on the way out, then."

Mac smiled back. "I'll be here."

And with that, Sarah turned and went with Maree and Thomas to see Henry and friends in the kitten wing.

An hour later, Maree, Sarah, and Thomas came outside to watch the last of the concrete pour. Thomas was no different to most boys and was fascinated by the truck. Mac waved Thomas over. "Would you like to have a go raking the cement?"

Thomas signed, "Can I?"

Sarah gave the okay sign, and Mac handed Thomas the rake, showing him how to drag from the centre and pull to the sides so that the concrete spread evenly. With his tongue sticking out in concentration, Thomas dutifully fulfilled his brief, huffing and puffing with the effort.

Maree paid the cement man and waved as the truck headed back to town.

Terri leaned on her rake and gestured to Maree and Sarah. "How about you two pristine beauties grab rakes and keep going on the sides here, while Mac and I do the dirty stuff and start to smooth it out a bit with the floats?"

Maree and Sarah looked at each other with raised eyebrows, smothering grins. Sarah chimed in, "I think we can manage that."

The small group worked away at the cement for a good hour and a half until, finally, Mac stood up, stretched her back, and declared the job finished. "All we need now is time to allow it to dry."

Maree brushed her hands together. "How about I make us some lunch, while you guys wash up?"

Terri's stomach grumbled. "That's sounds great. I'm starving."

Maree turned to Sarah and Thomas. "Would you like to stay for lunch? There's plenty to go around and it would be our way of saying thanks for all your hard work this morning."

Thomas tugged on Sarah's sleeve to translate, which she did. And he signed, "Can we? Please?"

Sarah looked over at Mac, who was watching with interest. "I don't see why not, although we don't need payment. Thomas and I have had a wonderful morning. It should be us thanking you. I'll just text Jean and let her know."

Mac cleared her throat. "Before you all go, all the workers need to sign off on the job." Everyone looked at her. Mac picked up a stick and walked over to the corner of the path, writing her initials in the cement. She held the stick out to Thomas, who came over and added his initials. He in turn gave the stick to Sarah, and then it was passed to Terri and then Maree.

They stood and admired their handiwork. Terri piped up, "Okay, clean-up time, gang."

Twenty minutes later they all converged in the sunny dining room. Thomas was setting the table with Maree, Terri was cutting up bread, while Sarah was stirring something delicious smelling in a pot on the stove.

Mac went over to see what Sarah was stirring. She leaned closer to the pot. "Wow, that smells great."

Sarah chuckled. "I confess, I cannot take any credit for this, other than stirring it."

"Maree and Terri are whizzes in the kitchen. One of the many reasons I love helping out here. I can't stay away from their cooking."

Sarah chuckled.

Mac frowned. "What's so funny?"

Sarah leaned over and touched Mac's chin gently. "You have a dob of cement on your chin."

"Oh, bugger."

Mac raised her hand to rub it off, but Sarah intercepted her hand, pulling a clean hanky from her pocket. "Here, let me." Sarah cupped Mac's face with her left hand and gently wiped off the smudge on Mac's chin with her right. When she was done, they both stood there looking at each other, barely breathing. Sarah's hands were shaking.

Mac recovered first and whispered, "Thank you."

Just then the hiss and spit of the pot's contents boiling over could be heard. "Shit!" Sarah turned to quickly stir the contents and turn the heat down a little.

Mac turned and silently left the room.

Sarah's heart was pounding and her legs were shaking. What the hell just happened? She followed Mac through a door that led to a verandah. "Mac, are you all right? I turned around and you were gone."

"I'm sorry. I don't know why I did that."

"Are you okay?"

Mac nodded.

Sarah raised a hand to Mac's cheek. "You're very flushed." She left it there.

Mac raised her hand and placed it over Sarah's. "Am I?"

"Mm, you are." Sarah's thumb gently caressed Mac's cheekbone.

"Must have been too much sun." Mac's voice was hoarse.

Sarah smiled and whispered back, "You think?"

They heard the door open and turned to see Terri's head sticking out. "When you two are ready, we need a translator in here for Thomas."

Sarah stepped back, grinned sheepishly, and felt her face flush. "Ah yes, sorry. Coming." Terri held the door open for Sarah as she walked through.

❖

Lunch was a cheerful affair. Maree and Terri told Thomas some of the animals' stories, while Sarah translated. This worked well for Mac as she could just sit back and get her act together. She watched as Sarah signed for Thomas. Sarah had strong hands with long fingers and was very expressive as she conveyed the conversations to her nephew.

Mac was beginning to understand the saying *like a moth to a flame*. There was something happening here with Sarah. Mac could feel it pulling at her, drawing her in. Every now and then, she would catch Sarah looking at her. Did she feel it too? She was beginning to feel a bit out of control. And she hated feeling out of control. If she was to be honest, it unnerved her. But like the moth, it was like she couldn't resist.

Mac's thoughts were interrupted as her pager went off. There was a grass fire just out of town, heading towards a small stretch of bushland. Even though the paid part of her work had changed for the next month, as a volunteer, she could still attend call-outs on weekends and after hours.

"Sorry, guys, gotta go."

Maree gave her a hug. "No worries, we'll finish up here. You be careful out there, okay?"

Mac kissed her on the cheek. "Always." She turned to the group and signed. "Thanks for a great morning. I had lots of fun."

Sarah waved. "See you Monday?"

Mac smiled and waved back. "See you Monday." She jogged outside to her truck, grabbed her kit bag from the storage space from the back, put it on the front seat, and headed off to the fire.

❖

Sarah turned to Maree and Terri. "That was a beautiful lunch. Thank you both for letting us stay."

Maree started to pack up the dishes. "You are both truly welcome. Thank you for coming out today and agreeing to be roped in to do some work."

"That was no trouble. We had fun, didn't we Thomas?"

Thomas nodded.

"But we should be getting back, otherwise Jean will wonder where we got to." Sarah turned to Thomas. "Can you help carry the plates into the kitchen, please?"

Thomas nodded and helped Maree clear the table.

Terri turned to Sarah. "You guys okay earlier, out on the verandah?"

Sarah folded her napkin on the table. "I think so, mostly."

"You sure?"

Sarah sighed and shook her head. "No, not really. One minute we're in the kitchen, and the next thing I know, Mac disappeared outside. I thought maybe I read things wrong." She looked to Terri for help.

Just then Maree came in and stood behind Terri with her hands on her shoulders. "You two look serious."

Terri leaned into Maree's arms and smiled. "Sarah and I were just talking about Mac. I think Sarah witnessed one of the reasons Mac got her nickname of Mouse."

"Ah, I see." Maree looked at Sarah. "As you've probably already guessed, Mac is fairly quiet and shy. She's a bit like a puppy, really.

She has an enormous heart and will repay you with love and loyalty in spades, and she will defend you to the hilt. But it takes a lot to break her protective shell. She built it for a reason. If you want to get to know Mac"—Maree looked very intently at Sarah, who nodded that she did—"then tread gently."

Terri was smiling at Sarah, but the smile had an edge to it. "Nothing would make us happier than to see Mac happy. But if you hurt her, you'll answer to us. Mac is family."

Sarah nodded sagely. It was plain to see that these two friends loved Mac dearly, and she could imagine that no amount of health insurance would ever help anyone who hurt Mac. She didn't want to hurt Mac. She wanted to get to know Mac. She found herself being more and more drawn to her. She wanted to run headlong in, but she took seriously Maree's words and she would go gently. She would be patient. Something told her it could be worth it.

CHAPTER TEN

Mac didn't get home until later that night. It took the best part of the afternoon to knock the worst of the fire down. The fire ended up making it into the front part of the bushland reserve, but the crews attending were able to put it out quickly before it could get too strong a hold. The last couple of hours were spent going back over and blacking out any hotspots and embers, making sure there was nothing left to reignite. Mac was tired and dirty and longing for a shower. She had stripped down to her shirt, socks, and shorts, and had just finished texting Maree and Terri to let them know she was home and that she would see them tomorrow, when her phone rang.

"Hello?" Mac's voice was a bit croaky from an afternoon of smoke.

"Hey, it's Sarah. You're home."

"Hi, yeah, I just got in and was about to have a shower."

"I won't keep you. You sound tired. You've had a big day."

"Mm, it has been a big day. But a fun day. It was really lovely that you and Thomas could stay."

"We both had a lot of fun. Thomas hasn't stopped talking about Henry and Nell and how he helped with the concrete. Thank you for making it a special day for him…for both of us."

"You're most welcome. I had a lot of fun today too."

"Well, I promised I wouldn't keep you long. I just wanted to see if you got home safe, and to say thank you for today."

"That's really lovely of you. Thank you."

"Okay, I'll see you on Monday then?"

"Yeah, see you Monday, Sarah."

"Sleep well."

"Will do. Bye."

"Bye, Mac."

Mac put the phone down. That was lovely of Sarah to check that she got home all right. It wasn't something that happened very often, and Mac had to admit, it felt kind of nice. In fact, the whole day felt kind of nice. Starting with Nell, watching Nell and Thomas playing, sitting talking to Sarah, then everyone helping out and laughing and talking while they did the path all together—it was a really good day.

Flashes of Sarah's hands on Mac's face when she cleaned her chin, or was stroking her cheek, kept replaying in Mac's tired mind. Even now, Mac's face felt flushed as she put her hand to her cheek. Her heart rate had picked up just thinking about how close Sarah had been. Sarah's dark, smouldering eyes, wandering over her face. Her lips had been only a breath away when Terri had found them. She'd wanted the kiss. Even now, Mac could feel the tiny sparks and ripples of energy short circuiting in her chest. She'd never felt it before and it unnerved her. She had wanted Sarah to kiss her—in fact, she had felt powerless to stop it.

She wasn't sure if this was a good thing or not. On one hand, the thought of spending more time with Sarah excited her and she was looking forward to it, but on the other hand, she was nervous. If truth be told, even a bit frightened. Surely this couldn't be a good thing if it made her feel so jumpy.

Mac shook her head and stood up. Her nose wrinkled. She desperately needed a shower. She smelt like the bottom end of a fire pit. Her eyes were gritty, her mouth was dry, her throat was scratchy, and she had a headache creeping over her. She was too tired to analyse this tonight. *Shower and bed, that's what I need.* And true to her word, she had a long hot shower and fell straight into bed, falling asleep minutes after her head hit the pillow.

❖

Sarah wasn't getting much sleep at all. When she and Thomas had gotten home that afternoon, it was obvious from their flushed faces that a good morning had been had by all. Thomas talked nonstop about all that he had done. He was in love with Henry the kitten but was fascinated that Nell was deaf like him and needed sign language. His joy at being able to play with the concrete had capped off everything. He wanted to take Jean out to show her where all the workers, himself included, had signed their names in the wet concrete as testimony to their craftsmanship.

Jean's morning had been largely successful too. She had acquired the necessary things in readiness for when the kitten arrived, squeezed in some decadent time looking in shops, buying Thomas some extra birthday bits and pieces, before returning back to Sarah's to spend the rest of the time on the phone to her solicitor and the police, trying to seek advice on what her options might be, given Richard's recent menacing phone calls and his failure to meet any of his recent appointments. Sadly, in the end, there wasn't much that they could offer her, other than to suggest she change phone numbers, with the police promising to file and send a report to Jean's new local town police precinct updating them on the current situation.

After putting Thomas to bed, Jean and Sarah sat up having a hot chocolate. Jean gave Sarah the brief update on Richard. Both women were sombre with the news, or rather the lack thereof. Lost in their own thoughts, the hot drinks were consumed in silence, neither one wanting to voice their concerns.

Jean said, "I heard all about how Thomas enjoyed the day, but you haven't said much."

Sarah smiled. "It was a good day. Thomas had an absolute ball."

"Mm, I know. He hasn't stopped raving about it all afternoon. Thomas said you both spent a lot of time with Mac, what with the puppy and then doing the concrete. How did that go?"

Sarah ran her finger along the top of the mug. "How did it go?"

"Mm."

Sarah blew out a breath she didn't realize she was holding. "Where do I begin? When we first rocked up and she was there, I was surprised. I honestly wasn't expecting her to be there. We were with Maree at first, but then she had to go off and look after another customer. So Mac introduced us to the little deaf puppy." Sarah closed her eyes and relived the memories of the morning. "The way

Mac talked to Thomas, about how special the puppy was and how to use both your voice and sign language to train the puppy…She was amazing and beautiful. I couldn't stop watching her."

Sarah opened her eyes. "Then doing the concrete and getting Thomas to sign his name in it—he was so proud. I swear he grew six feet tall when he stood back and saw his name on the path."

Jean just listened, as if waiting for Sarah to put the thoughts and feelings into words.

Sarah's head dipped down. "We had a moment in the kitchen, when I wiped some dirt off her face. I think I scared her."

"Why do you say that?"

"I turned around for a second and when I turned back again, she was gone. I thought I'd done something to upset her. I followed her outside, to see if she was all right."

"And was she?"

"Yes, yes, I think so."

"You think so?"

Sarah nodded and sipped her chocolate, thinking about why Mac took off like that. "I think it was like the fright, flight, fight thing, y'know?"

"Oh?"

"I know it sounds weird, but Maree and Terri said something a bit later that made sense. They said the reason she's called Mouse is because she's shy."

"And you think maybe it was a bit much for her?"

"It kind of makes sense, now I think about it. I have to admit, *I* felt overwhelmed and a bit nervous." Sarah stared into the bottom of her cup. "I almost kissed her."

"That sounds pretty intense."

"Mm, it was."

"What else did Maree and Terri say? I take it they've put two and two together."

Sarah barked out a laugh. "Oh yeah. In fact, now I think about it, I'm not sure Maree didn't throw us together this morning on purpose when she went off to help another customer. I don't remember seeing another car in the car park." Sarah took another sip of chocolate. "They were good and said just to take things slowly, and that if I hurt her they were probably going to kill me, or something to that effect."

"Oh, well that's all right, then."

"Hey! What do you mean *that's all right then*?"

Jean was giggling and just shrugged her shoulders. "Hey, I'd do the same if someone hurt you, but there *are* two of them and only one of me, so common sense says I should just let them kill you."

Sarah was laughing now too. "Oh, that is nice, real nice."

"You did ask."

"I did, didn't I?"

Now, lying in bed, Sarah was replaying the morning over in her head. Especially the kitchen and the verandah scenes. She had been so close to Mac that she'd seen the dark stormy blue outlines of Mac's irises and how her pupils dilated when her hand came up to touch her cheek. Mac's skin was so soft, and being that close, Sarah could just make out a hint of pine and something else. Sandalwood, maybe? Sarah closed her eyes. She remembered perfectly how Mac's lips opened slightly as she moved closer, her bottom lip full and round, trembling just a little…

Sarah groaned and sat up. Her mouth was dry. All moisture had headed south and her heart was racing. *What the hell is happening?* She got out of bed and padded into the kitchen. Maybe having a glass of water might help. Then again, maybe a cold shower was a better idea.

❖

Mac was in working with Nell when Maree came past. "Hey, cutie, how'd it go yesterday?"

"Pretty good, thanks. We managed to head it off before it took hold on the reserve, which was a relief."

"That's great news. We're nearly finished up here, how're you going?"

Mac looked at Nell. They had been doing some more sitting, and Mac had started to walk around with Nell using the lead, but it was coming up time when the pup could do with a break. "I'm nearly done here."

"Feel like a coffee? Terri baked a fresh batch of lamingtons this morning, and she would appreciate an impartial guinea pig."

Mac's throat was still a bit scratchy from eating too much smoke yesterday. A warm coffee and some of Terri's cooking sounded perfect. "Sounds great."

"Okay, come on over to the house when you're ready."

Fifteen minutes later, Mac knocked on the door and walked in. Terri was in the kitchen with a tea towel over one shoulder, testing a tray in the oven. The smell was heaven on a stick. "Hey, Ter, if that tastes half as good as it smells, it'll knock my socks off."

"Hey, sweet, how'd you pull up this morning after last night?"

"Not too bad. Bit stiff and sore in places and a bit of a dusty throat, but other than that, pretty good, I think."

"I hope you don't mind, but Sarah rang and asked for your number last night. She wanted to ring and say thanks for a lovely day. Did she get you?"

"Ah, I wondered how she got my number. Yes, thanks. She caught me just after I texted you guys that I was home. That was nice she rang. She said Thomas hasn't stopped talking about the day. Thanks for everything yesterday."

"No worries. It was lovely to have the extra company, and the extra hands all helped get the path done. It looks good doesn't it?"

"Yeah. It does. It was a great team effort."

Maree came breezing in and waltzed up behind Terri who was cleaning up the stovetop and wrapped her arms around her from behind and nuzzled her neck. "God, that smells unreal, babe. The cake isn't bad either."

Terri laughed, turned in her embrace, and kissed her on the lips. "You are incorrigible, woman."

Maree laughed. "I know, that's why you keep me." Maree kissed her again and pulled away. "Who'd like coffee?" Both Terri and Mac said they did.

Maree made three cups of her famous coffee mix and brought them over to the dining table where Mac was sitting. They sat in companionable silence appreciating the coffee and the chocolate treat.

Mac had three pieces and sat back, patting her stomach. "That was terrible as always, Terri." Mac was grinning at her.

"Oh yeah, I can tell you hated it, you big fraud. How many pieces did you have again?"

They all had a chuckle. Mac slouched down in her chair. "Good thing we got the concreting done yesterday. I don't think I could do it today—I am so wonderfully full. You guys rock, you know that?"

Maree brought refills for the coffee and kissed Mac on the top of the head as she went past. "We think you're all right too, chick."

Maree was sipping her coffee and watching Mac over the rim of her mug. "So, Sarah seems nice."

Mac picked up crumbs of coconut with her fingertip from off the tabletop. "She does."

"It was nice to get to know her a bit better yesterday."

Mac nodded.

"Next weekend, when we come over to your house to be poisoned, why not ask Sarah if she'd like to come? It might be a nice chance to get to know each other a bit better."

Mac's fingers stopped as she thought about what Maree had said.

Terri chipped in. "It might be nice. And there'd be safety in numbers and all that. From a purely selfish point of view, it would be good to have another person on hand if we have to ring for help when you set fire to the kitchen again."

Mac barked out a laugh and shook her head. "You kill me. You really do."

Both Maree and Terri were looking at her with eyebrows raised.

Terri grinned. "Well? Is it a foursome then? Come on, Mac, we need the safety ratio."

Mac rolled her eyes. "How about I see how coffee goes first, tomorrow?"

Maree nodded. "Fair enough. One step at a time, huh?"

Mac nodded.

"Well, just let us know when you're ready."

Mac looked up. "Thanks. Well, I had better choof off. I've got some things I need to do at home. I'll leave the frame on the path while it cures and have a look at it tomorrow."

"Too easy. So we'll see you in the morning?"

"Yep. I need the run to work off Terri's baking. Speaking of which…" Mac grabbed the last lamington off the plate, then blew them each a kiss. "See ya!" Then she cheekily absconded out the door.

During the course of the morning, Mac had taken some shots around the refuge with the new camera and printed off a couple that looked like they might fit the bill. She took the pictures into her workshop where she spent the next couple of hours working on an idea she had had earlier, for Maree and Terri's refuge anniversary. She emerged briefly to grab a sandwich for dinner and a glass of milk, then headed back out for another couple of hours. She fell into bed feeling pretty pleased with her afternoon and evening's efforts. There was a fair way to go, but she was pleased with the start she had made.

She thought briefly ahead to tomorrow's big hospital meeting. The plans were all in order, ready to pick up from the station. She had a meeting at half past nine with the heads of the various sections to go over inspection time slots, and then she hoped to start the first inspections a bit after eleven. As she lay in bed, a bubble of nervousness bounced around in her chest about how it would all go, but the preparations were solid, which eased her mind marginally, so fingers crossed, it would all go okay. In truth she was more nervous about the coffee afterwards. But she shut that out of her mind. What she needed was a good night's sleep. With that, Mac rolled over and turned out the light.

Chapter Eleven

Mac finished up early at the shelter and was in her office at the station going over some last-minute details. If the heads of departments were all happy with the schedule, then Mac hoped to start at the top with the ICUs and work her way down to Emergency. She would do the back-room technical sections like the morgue, pathology lab, kitchen, and facilities maintenance buildings the following day. She organized her paperwork so that her tasks were all grouped and sorted. It would then just be a matter of picking up the files when she needed them and she would be right to go.

Having commandeered Martha's help for the upcoming dinner party with the girls, Mac bid a hasty farewell. She wanted to ensure that she arrived in plenty of time for the big meeting at the hospital.

Mac pulled into the hospital car park and walked in the main entrance. She got directions to the main conference room and headed on up to begin the meetings. One by one the heads of the various sections rolled into the meeting room, including Sarah. Mac and Sarah only had time to smile and nod at each other across the room before everyone was present and the meeting got under way. Mac started off with a brief presentation and slide show of what she hoped to achieve with their help and how she proposed going about it. She had handouts for each section, outlining the things that she particularly wanted to check in their areas, and then she invited comments, questions, and suggestions for things that they would like to see covered in the inspections.

The meeting went smoothly, with positive exchanges of banter and ideas, finishing up a bit before eleven, so she was running a bit ahead of her schedule. She looked at her watch. She had time for a quick bathroom break before the inspections started.

Mac was standing in front of the mirror straightening her collar and tie when the door opened and Sarah walked in. Was Sarah following her?

Sarah casually leaned on the wall. "That was a nice presentation."

Mac washed her hands and dried them on a piece of paper towel. She blew out a nervous big breath. "Thanks. I was chewing on butterflies for the first little while. I wasn't sure how it would go. But I think it went okay." Mac was worrying the towel.

Sarah smiled. "You might have been nervous, but you looked like a natural."

Mac smiled shyly at the compliment. "Thank you."

"I was impressed how you showed them what you hoped to achieve with *their* help and then asked them for ideas. You made them feel involved. Usually it's a dry process and just something we all have to stomach for the sake of a workplace health and safety accreditation check."

Mac nodded and filed that information away.

Sarah came over and washed her hands next to Mac and leaned sideways to offer a stage whisper. "Besides, you're much nicer than the other fella we usually have. He's okay, but a bit old fashioned and dry, and not nearly so good looking."

Mac didn't need to look up and see her face in the mirror to know that she was blushing. She could feel the heat rising up her throat, to pool and settle in her cheeks.

Sarah laughed. "You still okay for coffee afterwards?"

"Sure." Mac looked at her watch. "Oops, I'd better get a wriggle on. I'll see you about four?"

Sarah winked at her. "Four it is. Good luck."

"Thanks. You have a great morning."

"Okay, bye then."

The mornings inspections went well. Mac found a couple of things that could be done a little differently and used the opportunity to talk over the options with the various heads. She had one or two things she needed to follow up and promised to bring back some more information when she came back the following week for the first of the staff fire and safety education sessions.

She managed to grab a quick bite to eat from the cafeteria and kept going on through the sections until at last she reached Emergency at two minutes before four. Sarah was busy with a patient, so Mac told the nurse on duty that she would start outside with the ambulance bays and progress through to the waiting room. Outside, Mac noticed one of the exit night lights had been smashed, so she made a note to put it in her report. She might even be able to mention it to the maintenance staff tomorrow, if they didn't already know about it, and it could be easily fixed and sorted. It would look good on paper if they could get it fixed; it would show that the hospital was alert and responsive to safety changes and measures. Mac figured it never hurt to rack up brownie points when it came to red tape.

The waiting room checked out as fine and the nurses' station similarly had no issues. Sarah was still busy, so Mac completed her other inspections and returned to the waiting room…to wait. It was now nearly five and Sarah was still with her patient. Mac passed the time by grabbing a water from the drinks machine, writing up some notes, and marking maps where points of interest had been identified. Mac heard the heavy plastic doors swing open. Lifting her head from her notes, she watched as a bed with a number of staff and frightened-looking parents came through. On the bed was a small girl, aged around four or five, flushed in the face and twitching uncontrollably. She was on a ventilator and had IV tubes and monitors galore surrounding her tiny body. Sarah pointed the team to the lift. "I'll be up in a minute."

Sarah broke away and came over to sit next to Mac. "Hey, sorry I'm late."

Mac smiled gently. "That's okay. Looks like a tough day at the office."

Sarah closed her eyes briefly and nodded. "Little girl with febrile convulsions. There's an infection of some sort, but we're struggling to pin point it at the minute. We're just taking her up now to the paeds ICU. I'll probably be about another hour. Is that too late? I can do it tomorrow if that's easier."

Mac looked at Sarah. She looked tired and strained around the eyes. "I can wait. Tell you what—how about I get one of the staff to show me in there. I'll take some notes and I can run it past you when you're finished, so then you can knock off and go home. You look beat."

"You sure that's okay?"

"That's fine. You go on up and I'll see you when you're done."

Sarah stood up, leaned over, and kissed Mac on the cheek. "Thanks, Mac." Sarah turned and quickly headed over to the stairwell, taking them two at a time and swiftly disappearing.

Mac realized she was sitting there with her mouth open and quickly shut her mouth, suddenly self-conscious, turning her head to see if anyone was looking. She was alone and was able to take a few minutes to settle herself. *Holy smokes. She sure knows how to rattle my chain.*

Mac walked over to the nurses' station to see if someone was free to help her finish the last bit of her inspections. She was introduced to Don, who was second in charge behind Sarah, and he took Mac through the last couple of rooms. Half an hour later, she was done. Mac knew of a great mobile café van service that she sometimes used when she and the crew were on a late call-out. She phoned in an order of a dozen coffees and a mixed platter of chocolates, doughnuts, and sandwiches to be delivered to the ambulance bay. She asked them to put it on her tab.

Mac had seen the faces of the hospital staff as the little girl was wheeled through. Even though they were professionals and saw this stuff all the time, Mac figured that they were probably like fireys—two things they hated the most were burns and sick or injured kids. Mac knew the coffee and food weren't much, but it might act as a bit of a pleasant distraction.

One by one, the staff who went upstairs came down and resumed their normal duties. Forty minutes later Mac's phone went off. It was the mobile food van at the ambulance bay door. Mac went over to the nurses' station.

The nurse on duty looked up. "Can I help you?"

"Can I ask a quick favour?"

The nurse looked at Mac and must have figured she was okay. "Sure, shoot."

"Can I leave my notes here at the desk for a minute and borrow that trolley over near the door? I'll be two minutes—I just need to collect something from the ambulance bay and bring it in."

The nurse shrugged her shoulders and held out her hands for the reports. "Sure, go right ahead."

Mac threw her a smile. "Thanks." She grabbed the trolley and headed to the bay.

Mario, the van's owner, greeted her. He hugged her and kissed her on both cheeks. "Miss Mac—look at you, sharp uniform. You're so lucky I'm a happily married man."

Mac laughed and gave him a return hug. "Hey, you're lucky you *are* a happily married man, because Theresa might kill you if she heard you talking like that. How have you been? And how is Theresa after her hip operation?"

"All good, all good. I am too fit and too stupid to fall over, which is just as well, huh? Theresa is good and almost back to her old self again. Soon, she'll be as good as new."

"That's great news."

Together they loaded the trolley up.

"I've put in some of those pastries you like."

"You spoil me, Mario, thank you so much."

"You are very welcome. Have a good night, my dear."

She kissed Mario on the cheek. "You too, and give my love to Theresa."

"I will do that. Ciao, Mac."

"Ciao, Mario."

Mac wheeled the trolley into the bay and through to the staff area. The nurses saw her first and their eyes lit up.

"Who's that for?" the nurse watching Mac's notes asked.

Mac pushed the trolley into the staff area and started to unload the goodies. "It looks like you guys have had a tough day of it and I thought you might like a pick-me-up."

One of the male nurses came over. "Are you serious?"

Mac nodded and smiled. With a big grin, he strode over to Mac and planted a big wet kiss right on the side of her face before grabbing a handful of the pastries, grinning like a Cheshire cat. Mac laughed.

Mario had in fact outdone himself and had provided far more coffees and edibles than Mac had ordered. Mac also knew he wouldn't charge her any extra for them, as Mac was one of his favourite customers. She quickly rescued two coffees, a couple of chocolates, and some of Mario's fabulous pastries and put them aside in a bag.

Word got around about the food pretty quickly, and staff came and went at a brisk pace. Mac turned to see Sarah, arms folded, leaning on the doorjamb of the staff room. "I wondered where my staff had disappeared to."

A couple of stragglers grabbed their coffees and what was left of the goodies, muttered, "Sorry, boss," and scuttled sheepishly out of the staff room and back to work.

"I heard what you did. That was really nice of you. Thank you."

Mac shrugged her shoulders. "You all looked like it had been a tough day. Food and coffee doesn't change that, but sometimes it makes for a nice reprieve."

"It does indeed."

Mac held up the coffees and a bag. "I saved you some. Coffee should still be hot if you're interested."

Sarah pushed herself off the door frame and came to sit next to Mac on the couch. "I'd love some, thanks."

Both sat and just enjoyed the coffee and pastries.

"How's the little girl doing?"

Sarah rubbed at tired eyes. "She's holding her own at the minute. We might know a bit more tomorrow when some more test results come back."

Mac nodded.

"How did you go with the inspections? I'm really sorry that I got tied up."

"That's no drama. I've finished them. Don showed me round the last part while you were upstairs. I've written some notes up. Basically it all went well. There's a couple of things we can either fix or replace, but essentially it's all good."

Sarah nodded. "That's good to hear."

Mac could see Sarah fading. "What time do you get off tonight?"

Sarah looked at her watch. "I was officially off three hours ago."

Mac stood up and took Sarah's empty coffee cup and napkin. "Why don't we meet up tomorrow for a coffee, and we can go through the report then?"

Sarah looked up. "Would you mind? I'm really sorry, but I don't think I would take much of it in if we did it tonight, to be honest."

"That's fine. We'll rain check for tomorrow."

"Thanks, Mac. Thanks for waiting and for the treats. That was really lovely."

"You're welcome. I'll push off and see you tomorrow, then."

"See you tomorrow."

❖

Sarah went to her office, checked her mail, and wrote up some notes on the cases from the day. She also caught up with Don on the day's happenings and the inspections. There was nothing more Sarah could do other than to go home.

As she drove, she reflected on the day. She ran over the cases in her head, but mostly she just thought about Mac. She thought how gorgeous she looked in her tailored outfit in front of everyone. Mac had said that she was nervous, but Sarah had been honest when she'd told Mac she was a natural. Sarah also hadn't been lying when she'd hinted that part of the reason the mostly male room was mesmerized was because Mac was gorgeous to look at. The morning's session was particularly good—Sarah had a chance to really look at Mac, without being caught staring. Sarah was the first to admit, she liked what she saw.

Mac wasn't overly tall, but she was beautifully proportioned. She had great shoulders and graceful arms that hinted at their tone, even through her dress coat. When Mac took her coat off halfway through the presentation, Sarah could have sworn the temperature in the room rose a couple of degrees. Mac's navy slacks were beautifully cut and sat perfectly snug, accentuating Mac's curves and toned bottom and legs. Mac moved with the fluid confidence of someone who was confident in their own skin. She made a point of working the room with her eyes as she addressed each and every person. There was no escaping her intense blue gaze. At one point, when Mac looked directly at her, Sarah broke out in goosebumps. Sarah smiled to herself. Mac could have given her talk in Swahili and she still would have held the attention of the room.

When Sarah caught up with Colleen after the presentation, Colleen had noticed Sarah staring at Mac and teased her without mercy. Colleen pointed at Mac with her chin. "Isn't that the firefighter from last week who brought the pregnant woman in from the MVA?"

Sarah was watching Mac as people came up to ask her questions. She nodded. "Uh-huh."

She'd realized she had been staring at Mac and turned back to Colleen, only to see her smiling at her. Sarah frowned "What?"

Colleen chuckled quietly. "You do realize you're staring at her, don't you?"

"Don't be absurd. I'm just interested in what she was saying."

"Uh-huh, sure you are."

"Really." Sarah looked at Colleen and knew she was not convincing.

Colleen was shaking her head at her. "Are you just going to window-shop, or are you going to ask her out?"

"What? No! Colleen, I hardly know her."

"Well then, ask her out and *get* to know her, Sare. When was the last time you lived a little, huh? You know what they say, all work and no play makes for a dull doctor."

Colleen was right. Mac fascinated her. A lot. She really did want to know more about Mac. "We're getting together for coffee later this afternoon, after the inspections."

"Well, that's a good start."

Sarah had just nodded.

Pulling into her driveway, Sarah turned off the engine, then took a moment to just sit in the darkness of the car. She and Mac had managed a brief coffee, but it didn't work out the way Sarah had planned. Still, there was always tomorrow, and on that note, Sarah pushed herself out of the car and headed inside.

Chapter Twelve

Mac had the plans and notes ready for the second day's set of inspections at the hospital.

She started with the kitchen, followed by the morgue, then onto pathology, ending with the laundry. Despite her initial misgivings when the chief gave her the job of undertaking inspections, Mac found each section fascinating, with the staff who were showing Mac around only too happy to explain how things worked and how the various facility services fit into the overall scheme of things, helping to keep the hospital running smoothly.

It was getting on lunchtime and Mac's next meeting was in an hour's time with the facilities maintenance section. This meeting would take a couple of hours, so Mac reasoned it would be best to grab a bite to eat while she could.

Mac had no sooner sat down at a table in the cafeteria when she heard a throat being cleared.

"Mind if I join you?"

Mac looked up into Sarah's smiling face. Mac mirrored the smile and extended her arm to the seat opposite her. "Please."

Sarah opened her salad container. "How's your morning been?"

Mac toyed with her yoghurt. "Really good. Most things went pretty smoothly. Everybody's been really helpful and receptive. I've learned heaps and really enjoyed it. How about yours?"

"Well, touch wood, it's been fairly uneventful so far, which has been good. Means I can catch up on some much-neglected paperwork."

"Have you heard how that little girl is, from yesterday?"

Sarah shook her head. "They're still doing tests. They've managed to get her temperature down and the seizures have eased off, but they're still struggling to identify the cause."

They both ate in silence for a while. Sarah finished her salad and pushed the container to the side. "I want to thank you again for the weekend and for yesterday's feeding of the staff. It seems you have a fan club developing."

Mac, who was sipping a juice, sputtered when she miscued the swallow.

Sarah laughed and handed her a napkin. "My staff want to know if we can offer you a job, and Thomas hasn't stopped talking about the animals and the concrete path from the weekend. He wants to know if you're building more paths next weekend."

Mac grinned. "I'm pleased that Thomas had a good time. He seems like a nice kid."

"He is. It's funny, Thomas is normally quite shy, but on the weekend, it was like he had known you all forever. It was wonderful."

"I'm glad." Mac stirred her juice with her straw.

"How long have you been signing?"

Mac stopped stirring. She knew Sarah was watching her face and could probably read the mix of emotions roiling just below the surface.

Sarah waited.

Mac looked down at her juice and took a deep breath. "My brother David was born deaf. Once we had it confirmed, we all learned how to sign. I think I was four when I started." She started stirring again.

"Since you were four? Wow. That's impressive. How many in your family?"

"Just the four of us, Mum, Dad, David, and me."

"So what does David do now?"

Mac let go of the straw and pulled her hands from the table and clenched them in her lap. Mac shook her head and said, softly, "Nothing."

Sarah waited, a question in her expression.

"David died when he was twelve. There was a car accident. Mum and Dad and I were all okay, but David…" Mac blew out a soft breath and smiled weakly. She resumed stirring her juice. "So that's why I was a bit rusty on the weekend. It's been a while since I've signed."

Sarah gently placed her hand on top of Mac's. "I'm really sorry to hear about your brother."

Mac met Sarah's eyes. Mac's eyes glistened with the fullness of unshed tears at the sudden onset of the memory. Sarah's heart ached on behalf of the teenage Mac, who had lost her only sibling.

Mac pulled her hand away to nervously tuck a stray lock of hair behind her ear. "Sorry. I don't usually tell people that story."

Sarah recognized that Mac needed a bit of space to recover. "It must have been a bit confronting then, meeting Thomas and signing again, after all those years."

Mac took a sip of her juice. "It was, a bit. But I was surprised at how much I remembered. And Thomas is such a nice boy. That made it easier in the end."

Sarah noticed Mac was still stirring her drink, but in a gentler, calmer way.

"Thomas reminded me a bit of David, when he was younger. So keen to take everything in." Mac stopped stirring and her hand rested on the table. She looked up at Sarah. "I had a moment, when I first realized that Thomas was deaf, when the memories of David came flooding back. I thought for a minute I couldn't do it, that it was too much."

Sarah once again placed her hand over Mac's on the table. This time Mac didn't pull away. Sarah used her thumb to gently caress the back of Mac's hand. "What changed your mind?"

Mac smiled at Sarah. "I saw the love for Thomas in your eyes, and Jean's. It helped me to see Thomas, and not David. I saw the questions in his eyes, and I knew in my heart how to talk to him, with my hands."

Mac was crying, but she was smiling too at the memories of her brother, and Sarah hoped they were healing tears. Sarah recognized the significance and the weight of the emotional moment.

Mac continued, "I'm pleased you told me that the weekend was a positive thing for Thomas. Looking back, it was for me too. I took Thomas's lead and stopped thinking and just laid myself open to the experience." Mac laughed softly as she brushed away the errant tears.

"I know it doesn't look like it, but he helped me to visit a part of my past in a way that didn't leave me feeling sad." She took a deep breath and squared her shoulders as a happy peaceful look settled on her face. "So I'm the one who should be thanking you for bringing Thomas to the refuge. You tell Thomas, he can come and build paths with me any time he likes."

Sarah laughed at that.

They both looked down at their joined hands. Mac frowned slightly. "You're welcome to say no, but I was wondering if you were doing anything on Saturday night."

Sarah's mind went blank. Was she on duty? Was she on nights or days?

Mac stiffened and pulled her hand away, then looked back down at the juice, anywhere except Sarah's eyes.

Sarah realized that she had taken too long to reply, and she could see Mac getting nervous. *Say something you idiot!* "What did you have in mind?"

Mac shrugged. "Oh, well it's not much. I was having Maree and Terri over for dinner and wondered if you wanted to come. For dinner. On Saturday. But if you're busy, that's okay. You're probably working and—"

Sarah gently cut her off. "I would love to come. What time?"

Mac opened and shut her mouth. "Six be okay?"

Sarah smiled. "Six would be fine. What can I bring?"

"Just yourself. It's nothing fancy, just a relaxed dinner."

"It sounds wonderful."

Mac wrote her address on a piece of paper. Sarah didn't know if she was rostered on that weekend or not, but either way she would have a look and see. If she was rostered on, there was plenty of time to organize a swap with someone. She was the one who usually accommodated other people's shift swaps, so she felt confident that she could pull in the favour without too much trouble at all.

❖

The rest of the inspections went equally as well for Mac. She'd had a good last session at the hospital with the facilities maintenance staff. They had identified the local in-house things to fix, and together they had worked out a replacement and upgrade plan for the sprinkler systems for some of the older parts of the hospital, like the laundry and the pathology labs. They also looked at some of the suggestions that came from talking with other sections of the hospital, and between Mac and the maintenance crew, they felt that they could be accommodated fairly easily and still ensure that they were compliant with the safety standards. Mac finished the day feeling positive with what had been achieved by all involved.

The next two days saw Mac give a fire safety session to a college cooking class in town and the annual fire inspections at one of the town's retirement villages. Mac popped in early to the station on the Friday to put some finishing touches on the inspection reports she had done during the week and left them with the chief to look over. She decided the rest of the day could be hers.

Mac drove home, changed into her comfy workshop uniform, and headed to the shed. She wore an old wool jumper, a pair of stained work pants with pockets everywhere conceivable, and an old soft T-shirt whose cotton was so fine and smooth from use that it felt like she wasn't wearing anything at all. The stunning workshop ensemble was finished with an old pair of oil- and paint-stained work boots.

Whenever Mac was in her shed, time ceased to exist. The shed was her cocoon. Once Mac walked inside and shut the door, the outside world was left behind. Here, in the inner sanctum of the workshop, lived her true raw essence. The shed was the private part that no one saw. Not even Maree or Terri had seen inside the workshop. It was a place to which only she and what she created bore witness.

Life, money, work, circumstance—all were irrelevant. When the wood spoke to Mac, her mind and her hands moved as one in a language all their own. Some days there was no conversation of creativity, only silence. Other days, it was like the wood and Mac were raging a battle against each other as each element was determined to go in an opposite way to the other. Mostly though, it just was.

The workshop was a sacred place and just being in it was like a living meditation. It soothed Mac's soul, cleansing and restoring her balance. Sometimes Mac didn't work in the shed. She just came in, sat on the stool, looked out the window, and enjoyed a cup of tea in the silence. The smells of wood, the shavings, and the order of things in the shed soothed her ruffled feathers, enveloped her with its very essence, making Mac purr on the inside with restored contentment.

During the course of the week, when Mac had been at the refuge, she had taken some more photos. These additional images had been printed and were now added to the original set along the wall. Mac sat on her stool with a cup of tea lightly clasped in both hands. She was studying the pictures, noting the angles and the perspectives of the curves on several of the shots. By the time she had finished her tea, she had a plan of approach in her mind. She put the mug and stool to one side and set a block of blond wood in the clamp on the bench top. Crossing the room, she opened cupboards and racks, collecting chisels, hammers, a rotary tool, carving knives, and a small bow saw, laying the equipment out on the side arm of the bench in readiness. She looked again at the wood, glanced at the pictures, and back to the wood, which she readjusted slightly in the clamp. A smile stole over her face as the excitement of her plan cracked open a tiny valve to her internal creative adrenaline pump. Her hands and fingers tingled in anticipation as she reached behind her ear for her carpenter's pencil and began to sketch an outline of a figure onto the wood.

When Mac was in the shed, only her fire pager and the call of nature could shatter her process. Several hours later, it was the latter that grabbed Mac's attention. She stood up straight and stretched her back, glancing over to the clock on the wall. It had just gone on two in the afternoon, and she decided she might as well have a break and grab a bite to eat. She had reached a stage in the work where she was happy to stop. Sometimes, when things were flowing freely, it paid to keep going rather than lose the creative groove, but other times, like today, Mac had a confident picture of what she wanted and where it was going. She knew she could pick up right where she left off after a break. She walked in the back door of the house, humming to herself. She was reaching into the fridge just as the phone rang. Closing the door with an outstretched leg, Mac picked up the phone. "Hello?"

"Hi, Mac, it's Sarah."

Mac's eyebrows rose in surprise. "Hello." She smiled at the unexpected surprise of hearing Sarah's voice.

"I tried the station but they said you'd gone home. I tried earlier but you must have been out. I hope you don't mind that I called you at home."

Mac didn't mind in the least. "No, I don't mind. Sorry I didn't hear you, I was out the back. What's up?"

"Oh, nothing bad, I just wanted to know if I could bring something tomorrow night. I know you said not to, but I was wondering if maybe I could bring some wine. But then I thought, I didn't know if you liked red or white, or if in fact you even liked wine. Maybe you'd like something else?"

Mac chuckled at Sarah's nervous verbal dribble. Adorable. "Yes, I like wine, and if you would like to bring some, then that would be lovely."

"Red or white?"

"Either would be fine. The dish will be spicy, so maybe a white? Oh, shit, sorry, I didn't think to ask, do you like spicy food?"

"Love it." Mac could hear the smile in Sarah's voice over the phone. "White it is, then."

"That sounds great. How's your day going?"

"Steady. Nothing too weird or wonderful, which is always nice. How about yours? What have you been up to? You said you were out the back."

"Yeah, just pottering around and playing in the shed, doing bits and pieces. I've just come inside to grab a bite to eat before heading back out again."

"Oh, right then, I won't keep you. It was just a quick call to say hi and to ask about the wine."

"That's okay. I'm glad you called."

"Me too. I'll see you tomorrow night."

"Okay, see you tomorrow. Bye."

"Bye, Mac."

Mac put the phone back in its cradle. Up until now, she'd tried not to think too much about having Sarah over for dinner, but now, having stopped and thought about it, the first hint of butterflies were restlessly making themselves known in the pit of her stomach. Just a gentle flutter, nothing too overwhelming. At least Terri and Maree would be at the dinner, which would help. Shaking her head, Mac decided to put the thoughts aside as she quickly made a salad wrap and headed back out to the shed. Here her thoughts narrowed, focusing down to the piece of wood in front of her. She sat on the stool looking at what she had done that morning while she ate the wrap. As soon as she had finished, she wiped her hands on her pants, picked up her tools, and resumed work on the piece. The shape was coming together nicely, and as she continued to refine the curves and the features, time disappeared.

CHAPTER THIRTEEN

Sarah hadn't managed to get the whole weekend off, but she wrangled a shift deal: she doubled Friday and into Saturday morning, and Don and Claudia picked up the remainder of Saturday and all of Sunday. She wouldn't have to be back until Monday morning at seven.

As Saturday was Thomas's birthday, she made arrangements with Jean to collect Henry the kitten after shift and meet up at Jean's for a birthday lunch with her and Thomas. That would still leave her plenty of time to go home for a nap before getting ready to go to Mac's for dinner.

Saturday morning dragged slower than a billy cart with two flat tyres, but finally Don came in to tag team her, allowing her to clock off and head to the refuge. As she pulled into the car park, her pulse quickened. She wondered if Mac would be there this morning. Even though Sarah would see her tonight, she was hoping to perhaps run into her and say hello.

Sarah got out of the car holding a carry basket to collect the kitten and its things. The previous weekend, Maree had suggested they drop off a blanket and a soft toy so that the kitten could sleep on both during the week, placing its scent on them, so when the kitten was picked up to go to his new home, the blanket and toy would go with it. That way, on his first night in a new, strange environment, the kitten would have something warm and familiar.

She walked into the office, tripping the door buzzer. She didn't have long to wait before Maree came out to greet her.

She kissed Sarah lightly on the cheek. "Hey there, lovely to see you again."

"Hi, Maree, good to see you too."

"So, today's the big day for Thomas and Henry?"

"Absolutely. I can't wait to see his face when he sees the kitten. I'm not sure who's going to get the biggest kick out of all of this, Thomas, Jean, or me. Even though it's a surprise for Thomas, I think Jean and I are excited enough for him."

Maree laughed and pointed to the door. "Well, let's not delay it any longer. Let's make it happen for both little men. What say we get the official paperwork out of the road first and then we pick up Henry?"

"Lead on."

After finishing the office part, together they walked outside towards the cat and kitten house along the new path. Sarah and Maree both glanced down when they crossed the piece where everyone's initials were etched in the concrete. "That was a good team effort wasn't it?" Sarah said.

"It certainly was," agreed Maree.

As they approached the door Sarah turned to ask, "Is Mac here today?"

Maree held the door open for Sarah to walk through. "No, she rang last night and said she wouldn't be in today or tomorrow as she had some things she needed to do."

Sarah felt a twinge of disappointment, even though it would only be a matter of hours until she'd see Mac.

They pulled up outside Henry's cage. Maree opened the door. "Here we are. You ready, little man? Your Aunt Sarah is here to take you to your new home." Maree reached in and grabbed the blanket, lining the carry basket Sarah had brought. Next she placed the soft teddy into the basket, and lastly some toy mice that he'd been playing with. Finally, the little man himself was picked up, given a last cuddle and a kiss on the top of his head, and put in to the basket. "You are one lucky man, Henry. There's a little boy waiting for you, and I suspect you two are going to be the best of friends."

Sarah and Maree exchanged waves as Sarah backed out of the car park to head towards Jean and Thomas's house. She had texted

Jean to let her know she was on her way. They had prearranged that Jean would take Thomas outside while Sarah snuck the kitten inside into Thomas's bedroom. She would then go back out to the car and pretend she had just arrived.

The plan worked like clockwork. Sarah had put the kitten on Thomas's bed and was back out at the front door when Thomas opened the door to greet her. Sarah signed, "Happy birthday," picked him up, and gave him a big hug and kiss.

Thomas held her hand and dragged her inside to the kitchen where Jean was making lunch. Thomas was so excited, he kept signing, "She's here! She's here! Now can we open my presents?"

Both women laughed.

"Yes," signed Jean with a big smile on her face. "Now we can open the presents."

Thomas raced to the lounge room, sat on the floor, and waited to be presented with his gifts. In no time at all he'd unwrapped a new action figure, a video game, some socks, fancy new runners, and some Star Wars Lego. All too soon all the wrapped presents had been opened. All that was left was a plain white envelope with his name on it. Thomas opened the envelope. In it was a note. Thomas read it a couple of times and looked up puzzled, showing the note to his mother and aunt.

What has five letters, and needs a best friend? Go to the napkin drawer for your next clue.

Thomas held his hands up, signing, "What's this?"

Jean signed back, "You better do what the note says and find the next clue."

Thomas went to the drawer in question, opened it, and found another envelope with a note in it:

I'm now the youngest in the family. Will you look after me please? For your next clue, go to the linen cupboard.

Thomas read the note twice after showing it to his mum and Sarah, and then ran to the cupboard. Here, on the bottom shelf, was another envelope. Thomas tore it open. Sarah struggled to hold a deadpan expression as she read the note Thomas shared:

Sneak quietly into your bedroom to receive the reward of your birthday puzzle.

Thomas looked again at Jean and Sarah. They shrugged their shoulders and Jean signed, "Go on, start sneaking."

And so sneak he did, down the last of the hallway and into his bedroom. Jean and Sarah followed him and saw his face light up, first in disbelief and then in pure joy, as he saw Henry curled up in his carry basket, looking up at him. He ran to the carry basket, then froze, ran back first to Jean and then to Sarah to give them each an enormous hug, before returning to the bed and slowly, gently lifting Henry out to cradle him in his arms.

Sarah had her arm around Jean, whose smile was tempered with happy tears gliding down her cheeks. Sarah pulled Jean in for a hug. "I think you nailed it, Mum. I would say that is the picture of the best-ever birthday present."

Jean sniffed and hugged her back. "I think you're right."

Both adults went out to finish lunch preparations, leaving Thomas and the kitten to themselves for a while. They sat at the breakfast bar and exchanged pleasantries about their week. Jean took a deep breath and turned to Sarah. "I have a meeting with the solicitors and a detective on Tuesday after I drop Thomas off to school. They want to go over a few details from the last time we saw Richard. They think they might have an idea where he is, but they want to make sure they have all the details right."

"Okay, that sounds positive…Doesn't it?"

"Oh, Sare, I don't know any more. I just know that I'm not going to be able to relax until I know where he's at and what his game is."

Sarah nodded. "That's completely understandable. Tuesday, huh? Do you want me to come with you?"

Jean shook her head. "I should be all right. It's just a meeting on where things are at. If it's anything like some of the others, it won't take long. Thanks, though. I'll call you after and let you know what they say."

"Okay. Well, let me know if you change your mind."

"Will do. Thanks. So, what about you?"

"What about me?"

"Have you seen fireman Mac Mouse again? Oh, hang on, there was a coffee date wasn't there? How did that go?"

Sarah suddenly found the bench top fascinating and was tracing an imaginary pattern on it. "A bit of a balls-up really. We agreed to meet after inspections, only things got busy at work and it didn't go quite to plan."

"Oh?"

"We had a little girl in, with convulsions that we struggled to get under control. It was a tough case for everyone. The convulsions lasted so long, we were all worried about brain damage. Anyway, Mac hung around. While I went upstairs to the paeds unit, Mac ordered in coffee and snacks for the team. She could see they were all a bit on edge."

"Wow."

"I know. We did manage a brief coffee afterwards, but I was too tired." Sarah finished the sentence with a shrug.

Jean pursed her lips and nodded. "I see. Not quite like you planned then?"

Sarah half smirked. "Not quite. But it wasn't so bad. We caught up and had lunch the next day."

"Oh, well that sounds better."

Sarah nodded. "Yeah, it was nice. I asked her how long she had been signing. It turns out her brother was born deaf, which is how she and her family learned to sign."

Jean's eyebrows rose in surprise.

As Sarah explained about the accident, Jean's hand went to her mouth in fearful anticipation of what Sarah was going to say next. Sarah nodded. "Her brother was killed."

"Oh my God, that's terrible."

"I know. I can't imagine it myself. I don't know what I would do if I lost you or Thomas. The thought just makes me sick."

Jean just kept shaking her head in disbelief.

"But Mac said meeting Thomas and signing again was a good thing. It was sort of healing for her, in a way."

"That's amazing."

"Isn't it just. We talked about other general stuff, and then she invited me over to dinner tonight, with Maree and Terri, at her house."

"Dinner? Then you had best go and get Thomas so we can have some lunch because you are going to need to go home and have a beauty sleep before you go out tonight."

❖

After a busy morning, Mac carried in the last of the bags of shopping and safely unpacked the basket of goodies from Martha's. Mac smiled. Martha had known Mac hadn't had people over for dinner in quite some time and was determined to find out just what had triggered the change.

"Are you going to share, Mackenzie James, or am I going to have to drag it out of you?"

"I don't know Sarah very well, but when I'm with her, the world tips upside down. I can't speak half the time. My heart feels like it's either going to explode, or it wants to stop. It's hard to breathe. I feel drawn to her, but when I'm with her, I feel..."

"Frightened?"

Mac nodded silently as her eyes filled with tears.

Martha handed her a tissue from her apron pocket, then reached over and took Mac's hands in hers. "For a long time, after my Leonard died, I shut up shop inside. Oh, I still went about with the day-to-day things and looking after the children, but my heart was broken. It took me a time to learn to love life again and to get back into the art of living. Your heart does heal in time. You carry the scars of those wounds, but life goes on, Mac." Martha's thumbs caressed the backs of Mac's hands. "You've been curled up tight like a flower bud for long enough, child. The time has come for you to open up again, to feel, to flower, to blossom."

Unable to be held in check any longer, the tears spilled over and coursed down her cheeks. "I feel like a train speeding out of control. My emotions are all over the place." Mac's throat was closed up. She shook her head and whispered, "I don't know what I'm doing."

"You're starting to live again. To feel again. You need the tears to wash away the glue that's been holding you together so tightly. It will settle down in time. Dinner is a good place to start. Talk to her. Let her know how you're feeling, and why you're feeling it."

Mac was an intensely private person. She wasn't sure that she could open herself up just like that.

"If Maree and Terri think she's all right enough to ask for dinner, then she must be okay. But she needs to know why you feel the way that you do and that you need to go one step at a time." Martha leaned over and lifted Mac's chin with her hand and made sure their eyes met. "If you don't tell her, Mac, then she might think she's done something wrong. Just talk to her, and see where it goes from there. Okay?"

Carefully placing the instructions Martha had given her, she set about organizing plates and cutlery and putting fresh flowers on the table. Flipping through her music collection, she chose some albums and loaded them into the player, before setting the fireplace in readiness to light later on, if needed.

Blowing out a nervous breath, there was nothing else left to do but wait. Mac walked distractedly around the house, mulling over what Martha had said earlier. It was good advice. All she needed was to be brave enough to try. The more she thought about it, the more nervous she got, wondering what in the hell she was doing. Mac needed focus. The shed. She quickly changed and went out to the workshop.

The block on the bench now had some shape to it, but the next phase required more detailed attention to achieve the finer definitions. Mac sat on the stool and looked at the block, turning it around. She went to the back cupboard, opened the doors to reveal a sound system, and looked for an album. She needed something she could lose herself in, but not melancholic. It needed to be bright, but not distracting, to have light and shade. She flicked through the album choices and found a P!nk album. Perfect. She put it on just loud enough to fill the silence in the room, which helped her to stop thinking too much about anything other than the job at hand. Mac walked back over to the bench, sat down on the stool, grabbed her carving tools, and set to work.

Chapter Fourteen

Sarah had managed a brief nap not long after she had gotten home. After grabbing a coffee and shower to brighten herself up, she now found herself standing in her room, wondering what on earth to wear to dinner. Mac had said the night would be relaxed and nothing fancy. Sarah felt far from relaxed. In fact, she felt positively giddy, like a teenager going out on a first date. She tried on several different combinations, finally deciding on a pair of black jeans with a white singlet top under a silky burgundy blouse. To top it off she wore her favourite black suede boots.

She turned and looked at the small mountain of discarded clothes on the bed before shifting her gaze to look at the clock. It was only five o'clock. She drummed her fingers against her thighs—she was too early. To pass the time, she picked up the clothes that she'd thrown on the bed and hung them back up, but that only killed ten minutes.

Sarah remembered she hadn't picked up any wine, so grabbing her keys, she headed out the door, happy to have something positive to do. Making herself go slowly, row by row, looking intently at all the bottles of white, time still dragged. She selected two Semillon Sauvignons that would hopefully complement the dinner and sighed, realizing it was only half-past five. She decided she couldn't wait any longer and planned to justify her early arrival with the guise of offering to help get dinner ready.

She found Mac's place easily enough on the outskirts of town down a side road. As she pulled in, she was impressed at the simple elegance of the tree-lined driveway which effectively tucked the house away in a nestle of trees.

Sarah parked the car, then traversed the gravel drive to knock on Mac's front door. There was no answer. Looking around she saw that Mac's truck was in the driveway next to her car. Sarah wondered where Mac was, so close to dinner. She was about knock on the door again when she heard the soft beat of music coming from behind the house. Following the music, she made her way around the side of the house and out to the backyard. Behind the house there was a second wooden building with shuttered windows and a set of sizeable barn doors. That's where the music was coming from.

Tentatively Sarah approached. She could make out a figure behind the window sitting at a table or bench of some kind, leaning over something. Sarah went to the barn door to knock. The door wasn't shut, so as she knocked, it pushed open. Inside Sarah could see a workshop. Tools were beautifully arranged and organized on walls or on purpose-built shelves along benches. The place was light, open, and airy, with rich deep-red beams and rafters adorning the ceiling, adding to the workshop's warmth and charm. Sarah could see the open cupboard at the back of the room where the music was coming from. She smiled at Mac's choice of P!nk. She had the same album in her car.

Her eyes swung back to Mac bent over the bench top, so intent on what she was doing, she hadn't yet noticed her. It gave Sarah a chance to study her. She had a slight frown on her face and was nibbling on the corner of her bottom lip, deep in concentration as her hands moved in slight up and down motions over the piece she was working on. Sarah now understood where Mac's unique scent came from—there were elements of it in the workshop. A hint of cedar, a smattering of pine and cypress, and something else Sarah couldn't quite put her finger on. Mac had a sweetness, in addition to the spice of the wood, and it set Sarah's blood to race. Sarah found it positively intoxicating and heady. There was a break in songs and Sarah cleared her throat to get Mac's attention.

Mac heard the noise and froze. She turned slowly and saw Sarah standing there.

Sarah waved. "Hi. Sorry, I'm a bit early." Mac looked completely spun out. *Shit! I've completely freaked her out.* "I tried knocking on the front door and there was no answer. I heard music coming from out the back and I followed it to here. I hope that's okay." *What was I thinking, coming early? This is all wrong. I should go.*

Mac closed her mouth. Sarah was here. She had obviously gotten carried away and forgotten the time and how late it was getting. Now Sarah was in her shed. No one had ever seen her shed. And here was Sarah, standing in the middle of it. For a brief second Mac was too shocked to move. Looking at Sarah's face, it looked for all the world to Mac like Sarah was beginning to spin out too. Mac realized her silence was starting to freak Sarah out. She needed to get herself together before Sarah hightailed it out of there. Martha's words echoed in Mac's brain *If you don't tell her, Mac, then she might think she has done something wrong.* Mac took a deep breath. "Hi, Sarah. Sorry, I didn't hear you come in."

Sarah still didn't look very confident. "You looked like you were pretty focused on something."

"Yeah, I get like that when I'm in here sometimes."

Sarah smiled tentatively.

Mac took a deep breath. "I was a bit thrown because no one has ever been in here before, so I was a bit shocked when I heard you. Sorry if I freaked you out."

Sarah's eyebrows rose. She looked around the workshop, then looked back at Mac and pointed a finger at her own chest. "You mean, no one has seen this place? I'm the first one?"

"Uh-huh, the very first."

"Wow, and I barged right in. No wonder you looked startled. I'm so sorry."

"Don't be. It's okay." And strangely, Mac realized, it was okay. "This is my inner sanctum, of sorts. Although I'm working full-time this month, I usually only work part-time at the station. I sometimes supplement my income with other things, like sculpting."

Sarah was shaking her head. "Sculpting?"

"Uh-huh. From time to time I get commissions and do some work about the place."

Sarah looked at the figure on the bench top. "Is that a commission?"

Mac smiled. "No, that's a gift. Maree and Terri's five-year anniversary of owning the refuge is coming up. They've been great friends over the years, family really, and I wanted to give them something special."

Sarah stepped forward and had a good look. "It's a dog!"

Mac nodded.

Sarah looked at the clamp holding the figure. "Can I turn this?"

"Uh-huh."

Sarah reached out to the clamp and slowly spun it around, having a good look from all sides. "It's Nell, isn't it?"

Mac nodded.

Sarah noticed pictures on the wall and walked over to have a look at them. There were pictures of Nell and of kittens. She looked back at the dog again and looked at its posture, then tilted her head on its side.

Mac smiled. She could see the cogs ticking over in Sarah's mind. "I wondered if you could help me for the next bit."

Sarah looked at Mac, clearly puzzled. "I'm not sure I would know how."

Mac brought out a sketch from behind some of the photos on the wall and handed it to Sarah.

Sarah drew in a breath of surprise as she looked from the sketch up to Mac. "This is beautiful. Oh my God, it is *really* beautiful, Mac."

The sketch was of a small boy, holding a puppy in his arms, with a kitten winding around his legs. The puppy was Nell and the boy in the sketch was Thomas.

"Thank you."

Sarah looked at the sketch and then back to the carving of Nell. "How on earth can I possibly help?"

"I was wondering if you had some photos of Thomas that I might be able to borrow. So I can get a better understanding of his face and his expressions."

Sarah was nodding. "I can do that. Yes, in fact, I would love to do that."

"That'd be lovely. It would help me a lot. I closed my eyes and tried to remember, but if I can have a couple of photos, that will make it so much easier. So thank you."

Sarah was still looking at the sketch when Mac happened to glance up at the clock on the wall. It was five to six. "Shit!"

Sarah looked up suddenly alarmed. "What?"

"The time! Oh, crap, I've got to put dinner on. Oh, shit-bugger-poo-bum!"

Sarah was laughing. "It's okay, I'll give you a hand. Come on, lead me to the kitchen."

"Hang on."

Mac spun around, put her tools to one side, turned the stereo off, and grabbed Sarah's hand. After turning out the lights and locking the door behind them, they ran hand-in-hand in the back door of the house. By the time the pair of them had reached the kitchen they were both laughing and puffing.

Mac went to the fridge and pulled out the pots and put them on the stove. "I need to cook the rice, warm this up on the stove, and then warm the bread." Mac closed her eyes trying to remember what Martha had told her. The rice would take about twenty minutes. The spicy mix needed to be brought to the boil, being stirred the whole time, and then it could sit on simmer for ten minutes. So the rice would have to go on first. The bread would only take a few minutes in the oven, but she couldn't remember now what temperature Martha said to do it at.

Sarah reached for Mac as she spun by and held her with still hands on Mac's waist. "How about I get the rice on and warm the mix, while you go and get changed? By the time you're out, you can warm the bread up, how's that sound?"

"Really? You could do that?"

Sarah was laughing again. "Yes, I can cook rice and warm up a pot of dinner."

"You are an angel. I'll be quick, I promise." Mac reached up and kissed Sarah on the lips, turned, and ran down the hall to her room.

Mac raced around her bedroom. "You're an idiot, you're an idiot, you're an idiot. What the *bloody* hell am I going to wear?" What had started off calm and organized was very quickly falling apart. Thank God, Sarah was helping out in the kitchen.

She looked through her wardrobe and tried to figure out what to wear. She thought about how Sarah looked: absolutely fan-*bloody*-tastic. The burgundy really showed off the warm, rich depths of her eyes and the light-coloured contrasts in her hair. "God, I'm a dick-brain. I didn't even tell her how lovely she looked." She looked through her cupboard, pulled out a pair of black tailored pants and a white cotton blouse with three-quarter sleeves. She threw herself in the shower and was out in minutes, dressed, and pulled on some comfy black boots. She smoothed her shirt down a final time and hurried back out to the kitchen.

Walking down the hallway, she could hear Sarah humming. When she turned into the kitchen, Mac saw that Sarah had the rice on the boil and was stirring Martha's pot of spicy magic, with a glass of wine in the other hand. Mac stopped in the doorway and thought how beautiful Sarah looked. It seemed so natural with Sarah by the stove, humming. It made Mac's heart ache with unrealized possibilities. Mac slowed her breathing, gathered herself, and walked up to stand behind Sarah. She placed one hand on Sarah's hip. "How's it going?"

Sarah turned to face Mac, smiling. "It's all under control."

Sincerity rolled off Mac in waves. "Thank you."

"It's no problem. I poured you a wine, it's over there on the bench."

Mac couldn't move. She was spellbound by Sarah's eyes. "I apologize for not saying it earlier, but you look lovely, and thank you for the wine."

Sarah's hand came up to tweak Mac's collar. "You look very sharp yourself, except"—Sarah reached up and pulled something out of Mac's fringe—"you forgot this." She held up a wood shaving.

Mac felt herself blush. Before she had time to think, Sarah leaned in and gently claimed her lips in a kiss. When they finally separated, they were both breathless.

Mac smiled shyly. "I think I need to go back out to the shed."

Sarah frowned. "Did you forget something?"

Mac shook her head. "Uh-uh, but if one shaving in my hair gets me a kiss like that, then I think I might go and roll around on the floor and pick up some more."

Sarah's head tipped back as she laughed. Mac thought her laugh was golden. Before anything more could happen, the doorbell rang.

Sarah gently pushed Mac away. "You hold that thought. Go and answer the door and I'll put the bread on."

Mac flashed her a smile as she went to greet Maree and Terri. A brief burst of happiness shot straight to her chest when she opened the door to see her two best friends standing there, Maree in a white linen top and milk-chocolate pants with a rich brown jacket, Terri in a black coat over a deep purple shirt and black pants.

Mac took their coats and hung them near the door before turning and offering a hug and kiss to both. "Wow, you two look divine."

Terri stepped back and gave her the up-and-down eyeball treatment. "You're looking mighty fine yourself, chick. I take it that's Sarah's car out the front."

Mac tried to look cool. "Yes, she arrived earlier." She could have gotten away with it, except for the silly grin she knew she had plastered on her face, but to Maree's and Terri's credit, they didn't call her on it. "She's in the kitchen, giving me a hand."

Maree held up a cooler bag containing the wine. "How about I put these in the fridge?" They made their way into the kitchen where Maree and Terri said hello to Sarah. Terri walked to the stove, closed her eyes, and smelled the air appreciatively. "Smells unreal—except something's missing."

Everyone looked at Terri a bit confused. Terri waved Maree over for a smell. Maree leaned in and sniffed and looked at Terri with a serious face. Terri looked at Maree. "You noticed it too, didn't you? Something's definitely missing."

"You could be right, babe."

The suspense was too much for Mac. "What?"

Terri looked to Maree. "Should we tell her, love?"

Maree agreed with equal seriousness. "I think it's only fair, we should."

Mac looked from one to the other. "C'mon guys. There's nothing missing. Is there?"

"Yup," said Terri. "What's missing is that burning smell. There's no smoke." Maree and Terri couldn't hold it together any longer and burst out laughing.

"Oh, very funny, you two. Very funny. Ha-ha. Remind me why I invited you again. I've a good mind to just feed you bread and water and none of this delicious delicacy."

Maree and Terri filled Sarah in on the joke, and pretty soon they were all laughing.

Mac grabbed the glasses from the bench top and filled them. She handed them out to the girls and topped up Sarah's. Mac raised her glass to the group. "To good friends, a good meal, and a night off."

To which Terri chimed in, "And no smoke!"

They all raised their glasses, clinked sides, and cried, "To no smoke."

Mac sipped her wine. "Mm, that's nice. How about you all move into the dining room and get yourselves comfy while I finish in the kitchen. Dinner's about"—Mac looked to Sarah who held up a waggling hand, then ten fingers—"ten to fifteen minutes away."

Maree led the way and each took a seat at the table. Maree and Terri sat opposite each other with Sarah sitting next to Terri. There was a platter of cheese and biscuits on the table. Maree lifted the lid and offered it to the other two. She looked at Sarah. "Have you been here long?"

Sarah shook her head. "Not long. I had a bit of time up my sleeve, so I took a chance and came a bit early to see if I could help. Mac was running a bit close to time, so I offered to put the rice on, and then you both turned up." Sarah hoped that sounded convincing enough.

Terri was just spreading some cheese on a cracker. "Did Mac say what the dish was? It smells gorgeous."

"No, I'm sorry. I didn't think to ask."

Maree looked at Sarah. "How was Mac when you got here?"

Sarah looked at Maree for a minute. That was a strange question to ask. "All right, I guess. May I ask why?"

Maree looked at Terri as if to ask *How much do I say?'* Terri nodded. "This is the first time in a while that Mac has had anyone over for dinner."

Sarah looked to them both. "Oh?"

Maree continued. "Not long after we moved here, we met Mac when she came out to help put a fire out in one of the sheds at the refuge. Right away we all clicked and over the years we've spent a lot of time at each other's homes. We would take turns cooking on weekends."

Sarah smiled. "Mac can cook as well as all the other things she does?"

Terri shook her head. "Mac's partner Tina did the cooking."

Sarah could sense something else was coming. "Okay."

"About twelve months after we got here, Tina died. She had an aneurysm, in the brain."

"Oh."

"Yeah. It blew us all away for a good while, especially Mac."

"I see."

Maree reached out and held Sarah's hand. Sarah looked into Maree's face and was surprised to see a gentle warm smile. "So this is the first time she has had anyone around for a meal since then, and we were wondering how you thought she was doing?"

It all made sense now. That's why they wanted to know how Mac was doing, and why they were so protective. As Sarah processed Mac's loss, she also realized how much trust Maree and Terri were placing in her. She suddenly realized what a special honour the girls were affording her by taking her into their confidence. Sarah sipped her wine and digested this new information. She thought again about how Mac was when she arrived. "Well, she was a bit rattled about the cooking, but in good spirits within herself. The timing of things threw her a bit, but as I was a bit early, I offered to help with a few things. Basically, it was all pretty much all organized by the time I got here. And then you arrived not long after." It was like both ladies were holding their breath as to how Mac was coping. But her answer seemed to have been the right one, as it looked like a weight had been lifted off their shoulders.

"Thanks for that, that's super," Terri said, grinning.

Maree held her glass aloft. "I'll drink to that." And the others joined in.

Sarah was aware of silence in the kitchen. "Will you excuse me a minute?" She got up and made her way into the kitchen where Mac was setting up a couple of trays. One had plates on it, and the other was bare except for a cloth. Mac had oven mittens on her hands.

"Hey, there. Need a hand?"

Mac looked up at the sound of Sarah's voice. "Yes, please. Can you take those plates in for me? I'm just about to bring in the bowls."

Sarah wandered around to the other side of the bench to collect the tray of warmed plates. Just before she picked the tray up, she leaned into Mac and gave her a quick kiss on the lips. "I just want to say that this is the first night in ages that I've been out for dinner, anywhere. Thank you for inviting me. It's made it a very special night for me." Before Mac could say anything, Sarah picked up the tray and headed back out to the dining room.

CHAPTER FIFTEEN

Food, wine, and laughter flowed freely. When dinner itself finished, they took their wine glasses and retired to the lounge room where a cheerful fire was blazing in the fireplace. The girls quizzed Sarah why she'd wanted to be a doctor, and how she'd ended up in their regional neck of the woods, with Maree and Terri reciprocating by sharing how they met, their restaurant successes, and their change of lifestyle.

Sarah turned to Mac. "What about you? Why did you want to become a firefighter?"

Mac shrugged her shoulders. "When my family had the accident, the firemen were great. Two of them sat with me and David throughout it all. What they did stayed with me for a very long time."

Sarah nodded. "That makes sense."

"One day, I saw a recruitment ad in the paper and I thought I'd try my hand at it. So I gave it a whirl and I found that I liked it."

Maree leaned over and emptied the last of one of the bottles into Mac's glass. Terri stood up. "I'll get another bottle."

Maree asked, "I've always wondered—are their many women in the fire brigade? You know, as a profession?"

"There's not a lot, but the numbers are steadily increasing. It's still predominantly a male-dominated industry, but we're getting there."

Sarah looked at Mac. "Have you ever had any problems, being female?"

Mac nodded. "Sometimes some of the equipment is a challenge to use, simply because it's built for a man's bigger body frame to operate, but it's usually just a matter of thinking your way around the issue in order to make it work for you. And we work as a team, so what one person has trouble doing, someone else might be good at, and in return, you swap the favour when the roles are reversed."

"Have the guys ever given you a hard time?"

Mac laughed. "There was one guy, when I first started out, who used to be a bit of a pig. He would leave condoms in my locker and constantly belittle me in front of the other men. He didn't like having a woman in the unit and he didn't bother to hide his disgust. He was never one for teamwork with any of us, not just me."

Maree said, "You never told us this before. That sounds horrible. How'd you manage it?"

Mac shrugged. "It wasn't so bad. It made me work twice as hard to learn things and to use equipment. I wanted to lessen his reasons for ragging me all the time. But the best thing was, one day, we had a situation where he and I had to work lead together, getting a kid out of a drainpipe. I was the smallest, so it made sense to send me in, but he wouldn't let me. He said because I was a girl I would get scared in the dark, and if there was a grate in the way I would be too weak to lift it out."

Maree was getting visibly steamed. "What an arsehole! What happened?"

Mac chuckled. "I let him go in. He was too big, but he couldn't see past his pigheadedness and insisted. He got stuck so tight trying to prove that he was right, and it cost the council a lot of extra money they didn't need to spend on digging both him and the kid out. The chief never let him live it down and tore strips off him for being a pigheaded, irresponsible jerk. Not long after that, he transferred out and I've never had any issues since."

They were all having a bit of a chuckle when Terri came back in, brandishing another bottle of wine. As she walked around topping everyone's glasses up, she turned to Mac. "I have to say, Mac, you outdid yourself with dinner tonight. That was quite simply amazing."

Mac smiled. "I'm glad you liked it."

Everyone agreed it was superb.

Maree nodded. "The blend of spices was mind-blowing. What was in it?"

Mac smiled. "Oh, a bit of this, a bit of that. You know how it is." Mac threw her a wink. "I can't tell you all my secrets."

Terri pulled a piece of paper from her pocket and waved it between her fingers in midair with an evil grin on her face. "That's okay. I'll just ring and ask Martha tomorrow how she made it."

Mac had just taken a sip of wine and choked on it, coughing and spluttering, while Sarah reached over and patted her on the back. Terri was laughing at Mac's expense, enjoying the moment of victory immensely.

Maree looked at the two of them. "What's going on?"

Terri piped up, still waving the note, "I found this in the kitchen when I was looking for the corkscrew. It's a note in Martha's handwriting, telling Mac how to heat up dinner."

Everyone looked at Mac, who had recovered from being found out as a fraud. She shrugged her shoulders with a cheeky grin on her face, raised her glass, and made a toast. "Here's to outsourcing."

With much laughter they all raised their glasses. "To Martha."

They talked, shared stories, and laughed for another hour before Terri caught Maree yawning for the third time. "I think, my love, I had best take you home before you fall asleep on the couch."

Maree nodded. "Hmm, probably a good idea. Between the fire and the wine, I'm starting to fade. We should help clean up first before we go."

Mac shook her head. "Don't worry about the dishes—they'll take all of five minutes to clean up. You two head on home."

Everyone stood up. Terri came over to Mac and wrapped her in the biggest hug. "Thank you so much for a fantastic night. I've missed this."

Mac nodded. "Me too."

Terri kissed her on the cheek. "Let's do it again soon, huh?"

"I'd like that."

Maree gave Sarah a hug, then kissed her on the cheek and said, "Thank you for helping make this night so special."

Sarah hugged her back. "Thank you for letting me be a part of it."

Maree kissed Mac. "Give our love to Martha, and tell her I want that recipe!"

Terri kissed and hugged Sarah, and then Mac walked them to the door while Sarah transported the dishes out to the kitchen.

Mac stood in the front doorway. "Thanks again for coming over. It was a really great night."

"Thanks for having us. We had a great night too." Maree's hand went to Mac's cheek. "I'm glad to see you so happy, babe. Sarah seems like a really lovely person."

Mac nodded and smiled shyly. "She is, isn't she?"

After another hug and kiss and a promise to drive home safely, Mac waved them off as they drove down the driveway. Having seen the taillights turn onto the main road, Mac closed the door behind her and made her way into the kitchen where Sarah was washing up.

"You don't have to do that. I can do that later."

"It's the least I can do after such a lovely meal."

Mac picked up the tea towel and started drying the dishes.

"So, who's Martha?"

Mac smiled. "Martha works at the fire station. She's in charge of running the office. The chief is the boss, but Martha…let's just say, she's unofficially in charge of most everything else."

"Sort of like a mother hen?"

Mac chuckled. "Yeah, sort of. Being the only girl on staff, Martha took me under her wing a bit when I first started. She never had a daughter, and since my parents had moved states to go and live in Adelaide and work on a vineyard, I didn't have any nearby family, so we each helped fill a space for one another."

Sarah finished washing and turned to watch Mac wipe the last of the plates. "She sounds lovely."

"She is. You'd like her. Everyone likes Martha. She's a wonderful lady." Mac finished wiping the dishes and was folding the towel. The silence in the room grew heavy.

Sarah took a step towards Mac, placing her hand over Mac's restless ones to still the nervous folding. "Thank you for tonight. I don't remember when I last had such a wonderful meal and such wonderful company. It's been amazing."

Mac looked down at their hands. She could feel her heart starting to hammer in her chest. "Thank you for coming. Tonight was pretty special for me too."

Sarah's thumb caressed the back of Mac's hand. "Maree told me this was the first time you've had people over since Tina died."

Mac nodded.

"Then that makes this evening doubly special, for you *and* for me. It's an honour to be asked to be a part of that. Thank you for trusting me with that honour."

Mac looked up into Sarah's eyes. She could hear Martha's voice in her head. *Just talk to her, and see where it goes from there.* "I don't know why, but I feel comfortable with you, like I can trust you with anything. Even though when I'm with you, I feel like the world is turning upside down. I've never felt that way before." Mac shook her head. "I can't explain it."

Sarah smiled. "I know what you mean. I feel drawn to you. I look at you, and it's like there's something pulling me in. I want to know more." Sarah shook her head. "No, it's more than that, it's like…a need." Sarah's hands slid up to Mac's shoulders. As she stepped closer, Mac's hands automatically found Sarah's waist.

Mac's voice thickened with the emotional tension. "It's been a long time."

Sarah's hands framed Mac's face. "For me too. We'll take it slow. If you want me to stop, then just tell me. Okay?"

Mac nodded.

Sarah's head dipped as she leaned in to kiss Mac's lips. It started off as gentle, tentative probing. Sarah's tongue darted out to lightly brush the top of Mac's top lip, and she was rewarded with a groan from deep inside Mac.

Mac deepened the kiss as their bodies drew closer, locking tighter together. Sarah left Mac's lips to travel down Mac's throat, kissing and licking as she went. A whimper tore from Mac's lips as she arched her neck to receive Sarah's caresses. As if unable to resist or deny, Sarah returned to Mac's mouth. Her voice was thick with desire. "Do you want me stop?"

Mac shook her head. She had lost the power of speech.

Sarah kissed her again. Mac's hands, which had been circling Sarah's waist, came up to caress Sarah's sides. One hand dropped, finding the small of Sarah's back, and continued to dip lower, pulling Sarah's centre in tight against hers. Sarah broke the kiss. They were both panting. Sarah leaned up to nip Mac's ear and she whispered, "Show me your bedroom, love."

Soundlessly, Mac gripped Sarah's hand, leading her to the bedroom, pulling up next to the bed to turn and face Sarah, whose eyes had darkened with the rising promise of more passion. They kissed again, hungrily exploring each other's mouth.

Sarah again broke the kiss to run her fingers through the lengths of Mac's dark hair. "We don't have to do this, Mac, if you don't want to."

Mac closed her eyes. This was it. This was the moment, here, in Sarah's arms, to let go of the last bastion of her past and to move forward. The intensity frightened her, but she also knew she wanted it more than anything else. Mac opened her eyes to meet Sarah's. Her hands came up to hold Sarah's face gently, reverently. She looked deep into Sarah's eyes and whispered, "I want this. I need you, please."

Sarah dove into Mac's mouth. Any noble restraint she might have had before disappeared as Mac's fingers started to undo her blouse. It was Mac's turn to kiss and nuzzle Sarah's neck as she slid the shirt from Sarah's shoulders. Somehow the singlet top and bra followed, and Mac was once again claiming Sarah's lips as her hands roamed the newly bared warm flesh of Sarah's ribs and back.

Sarah felt her nipples tighten with the cool air. As they brushed against Mac's shirt, jolts of electricity went straight to her groin. She needed to feel Mac, she needed to taste her. The hunger was driving her crazy. Quickly disrobing Mac, she pushed her gently to the bed. Without breaking the kiss, Sarah followed and lay on top. She could feel Mac's nipples against her chest. Her hand found one breast and cupped it lovingly, her thumb caressing the erect nipple. Mac pressed her body firmly upward to meet the increasing attention and resulting sensations, groaning into Sarah's mouth with the mounting pleasure.

Unable to resist any longer, Sarah left Mac's lips, taking first one, then the other nipple into her mouth, rolling the engorged tips around with her tongue and lightly grazing them with her teeth. Mac's hands gripped the back of Sarah's head as she arched with each tug and pull of Sarah's mouth.

Mac could feel the roughness of Sarah's jeans against her centre. She needed to feel Sarah's body on hers. She needed flesh on flesh. Mac gently rolled Sarah onto her back, leaned in, and kissed her. Her hands found the restraints on the jeans and quickly undid them. Sarah raised her hips, allowing Mac to slide the rest of Sarah's barriers off, tossing them to the floor. Kneeling, Mac took a moment to look at Sarah lying before her.

Mac whispered, "You are so beautiful, Sarah."

Sarah raised herself to a sitting position, stroked Mac's arms, and moved to caress her chest. "So are you. I look at you and my heart races." Sarah pulled Mac down, and together they lost and found themselves in each other.

Chapter Sixteen

The sun peeking into the bedroom window teased Sarah's eyelids until they could no longer resist opening. Somehow, when she and Mac had finally fallen asleep, exhausted from hours of lovemaking, Sarah had ended up on her side with Mac spooned behind her, her arm wrapped around Sarah's waist. Sarah gently raised Mac's arm to turn over and face her. Mac's beautiful dark hair was splayed out on the pillow behind her. Sarah remembered how soft it was when her fingers trailed through it last night, or when Mac was teasing and kissing her breasts, or when Sarah bent her head to kiss the top of Mac's head. She stretched carefully, knowing they would both probably be stiff and sore, but she didn't mind. Mac was the most attentive lover she had ever met, taking her to places she never even knew existed.

In sleep, Mac's face was relaxed with the little frown crease between her eyebrows having smoothed out. She had gorgeous dark arching eyebrows with a soft aquiline nose, and her mouth…Sarah could feel her temperature rising again at the remembered magic that Mac's mouth could make.

Mac's eyes fluttered open. It took a moment for her to focus. As her vision sharpened, she saw Sarah, lying on the pillow facing her. Her eyes were bright, her face was flushed, and Mac thought she was the best thing she had ever seen. The hand that was caressing Mac's arm slid over to cup her breast. Mac's voice was husky. "Good morning."

Sarah rolled Mac over until she was on top of her. "Mm, it is." Sarah's thigh slipped between Mac's legs, and Mac knew Sarah could feel how wet she was. As Sarah claimed Mac's mouth hungrily she brought her thigh in tight to Mac's centre. Mac moaned and her hands began to explore Sarah's body as her hips rocked against Sarah's thigh. Breakfast could wait.

❖

Wandering around the kitchen opening cupboards, Sarah shook her head. The few items in the fridge could have run around like crazy and still not bumped into each other. Finally, standing in the doorway of the pantry in an oversized navy-blue fire-brigade T-shirt, she put her hands on her hips and looked at Mac, who was leaning on the kitchen bench watching her. Sarah saw the goofy grin on Mac's face and knew Mac's eyes were watching her bottom. She cleared her throat in mock indignation and put her hands on her hips. "You know, I do believe that a pantry in your house is a wasted resource."

Mac looked at her, smiling with her head on its side, clearly not quite getting Sarah's drift.

"A pantry is a place you store food items in. Yours is empty. And so are your fridge and cupboards. What do you eat?"

Mac smiled sheepishly. "Fruit, yoghurt, and I make a mean toasted cheese sandwich."

Sarah put her head in her hands. "Oh my God, I can't believe I'm falling for a food heathen."

Mac froze at the same time Sarah did.

Sarah couldn't believe what she'd just said. It just fell right out. Looking at Mac's face, it didn't look like she could believe it either. Sarah thought about her statement. *Where did that come from? I've only known Mac for what, two, three weeks? Bloody hell. And yet, I don't think I have ever felt more comfortable or more alive with anyone else I have ever known.*

Mac felt like someone had thrown a rock straight between her eyes. She stopped breathing and felt a bit dizzy. Sarah rushed over and put her arms around her, guiding Mac into the dining room to sit down.

"Hey, Mac, take a deep breath for me. Mac? Come on, breathe, babe."

Mac took a breath, and then another, and slowly the darkness receded from her vision. As the dark swarming spots dissipated, she saw Sarah's concerned face in front of hers. Mac blinked several times. "Sorry about that."

Sarah brushed the fringe out of Mac's eyes. "You okay now?"

Mac nodded.

Mac saw how stressed Sarah was becoming. She reached out and took Sarah's hands in hers and slowly brought them up to her lips to tenderly kiss them.

Sarah's mouth fell open.

Mac smiled shyly. "I'm sorry. You know how I told you last night that you turn my world upside down?"

Sarah nodded.

"Well, you can add to the list, that you take my breath away."

Sarah smiled and said, "Let's eat."

They jumped into Mac's truck and headed into town to get some groceries. Sarah's hand rested on Mac's lap as they drove in. Yesterday she'd been so nervous, that she didn't really take in the surroundings on the drive. Today, the world was a beautiful place and Sarah was blissfully taking it all in.

Mac was in soft faded jeans, an old softball shirt, and a hooded jumper. Sarah was in her black jeans but had kept Mac's shirt and had acquired a fire department jumper to match the shirt. As Sarah had put it on, she'd closed her eyes, taking in the essence that was Mac's. She could identify the wood scent now, but there was still a hint of background sweetness and spice mix that she hadn't yet worked out. Sarah loved a challenge; she was fully prepared to hang on to Mac's clothes until she figured it out.

As they approached the outskirts of town, Sarah's stomach let out an enormous growl of protest at not having been fed. Both girls looked at Sarah's stomach and giggled. Mac leaned over and tenderly patted Sarah's grumble. "Perhaps we should grab something to eat before we get the groceries?" Before Sarah could answer, her stomach growled again. Mac laughed. "It would appear that your gastrointestinal tract agrees."

They stopped at a cafe, placed their orders, and were soon rewarded with steaming mugs of coffee and their meals. Mac had two thick pieces of fruit loaf, while Sarah had eggs and bacon. Sarah tucked in like she hadn't been fed in a week, while Mac sat back, smiling.

Sarah polished off her breakfast and spied an uneaten piece of Mac's bread. "You going to eat that?"

Mac shook her head as Sarah rescued it from the plate and inhaled it. Sarah sat back and patted her stomach. "That's better. Fully fuelled and ready to go again." She saw the contented smile on Mac's face. "You look happy."

Mac said, "I was just thinking the same thing. I am happy."

Their legs were intertwined under the table. Sarah put her elbows on the table, rested her chin in her hands, and let her gaze feast on Mac. She felt like the cat that had found and licked the cream bowl clean. "Mm, me too." *Cream, now there's a thought.* Sarah stood up and grabbed Mac's hand with a cheeky grin. "Come on, let's go grocery shopping."

They rushed through the shopping and, in no time at all, had it stacked away. Somehow the unpacking turned into a game, which naturally ended up with them naked and in bed. Mac was lying on her back, while Sarah was half on her stomach and half on Mac's chest, running Mac's hair between her fingers, while Mac's fingers, far from idle, were lazily grazing Sarah's spine.

Sarah raised her head and planted the softest of kisses on Mac's lips. "What are you plans for work this week?"

"Tomorrow is a safety class at one of the retirement villages, followed by an inspection at the Kingsley School."

Sarah raised herself up onto her elbows. "That's Thomas's school."

Mac smiled. "Really? Oh, of course it is, it's the school with the special-needs unit."

Sarah was tracing an imaginary pattern on Mac's chest. "Maybe you'll see him tomorrow."

"Maybe. I'll be sure and keep an eye out for him. I think I'm doing some classes with the kids the following week. Maybe he can be my special helper."

"I'm sure he'd love that. What else will you be doing?"

Mac frowned, trying to remember, and Sarah playfully reached up and smoothed her brow. "Then, from Tuesday through to the end of the week, I'll be back at the hospital doing fire-safety classes. I was talking to George, in maintenance, and he said the contractors were coming in this week to start replacing the older sprinkler systems. So I can also be on hand to help look over those, if needed."

Sarah's face lit up. "We can meet for coffee and lunch maybe. Oh, hang on, I'll have to see what shifts I'm on. I know I'm on a couple of days, and the courses are compulsory for everyone, so I'll have to go to one of them too."

"That would be nice."

Sarah's eyes lit up mischievously. "Hey!"

Mac looked at her. "Mm?"

Sarah was beaming. "Maybe I could be your special helper."

Mac nuzzled Sarah's neck. "Maybe you could." Mac rolled Sarah over until she was lying on top, planting kisses down her torso, Sarah's body arching for greater contact as Mac continued a path of torture with her lips and tongue. "Then again, maybe you would be too much of a distraction." She could hear Sarah's breathing quicken as she continued to kiss lower. "I might have to take you aside and give you lessons in private, my good doctor."

Mac stopped talking as her lips reached her goal. Sarah gasped, "Yes, please!"

❖

Mac bid Sarah a reluctant farewell when she left for home later that night. They had shared a wonderful meal in front of the fire, taking turns feeding each other.

Mac fell into bed just after ten, tired, sated, but very happy. She lay in the bed thinking how strange it felt to be on her own. Less than forty-eight hours ago, being alone had been a completely normal occurrence. Tonight, the bed felt too big and cold without Sarah.

Eventually the weekend caught up with Mac and she slept soundly. It was strange getting up the next morning, opening the fridge and seeing food in it. Instead of grabbing a piece of fruit and yoghurt to eat on the run, as was her usual fare, this morning she had choices. She saw some fruit loaf with a sticky note and a love heart drawn on it. Mac smiled. *How can I possibly have yoghurt now?* She grabbed the loaf, cut two slices, put the merest smidgeon of butter on it, and ate it, humming away, as she mentally ran through her safety class for later in the morning. She had to drop by the station to pick up the inspection plans for the afternoon, return Martha's pots, and give her a parcel of chocolate brownies from Sarah.

Mac headed into the station. She walked inside to find her partner going through the mail pigeonholes. She went over and gave him a hug. "Hey, Bettsy. You're out early—or are you coming in late?"

"Hey, Mouse. Coming in late. We had a derailment last night. Nothing special. Just messy to clean up."

"Uh-huh."

"When you coming back?"

"Aw, does this mean you miss me?"

"Yeah. The other guy they've got me with, he doesn't smell nearly as nice as you. He's stinking up our truck, and he talks too much."

Mac laughed. Bettsy looked about six years old, all pouty mouthed. She leaned over and gave him another hug and whispered, "I miss you too, big fella."

Bettsy grinned. "I knew it."

"Hey, what are you doing next week? Have you got a half day you can spare me?"

Bettys shrugged. "Depends what day. What's up?"

"You know the Kingsley School, with the special-needs unit for kids?"

"Uh-huh."

"Well, I'm giving them a safety class next week and I wondered if you wouldn't mind helping me. I thought maybe we could take the pumper over and let them have some fun in it, but I could do with an extra pair of hands, if that's okay. I was thinking we could do a couple of games too."

"Yeah, I could do that, sounds fun. Just let me know what day, and I'll pencil it in for you."

Mac was hoping that John would say yes. She'd seen him with kids before, and they just loved the big man-mountain. He had a knack with them. Special needs or not, when it came to kids, two firefighters were always better than one. Winking, she mock-punched him on the shoulder. "Thanks, partner. Owe ya."

Next Mac headed to Martha's service desk to deliver the pots and the brownies.

Martha pointed to the chair next to her. "Sit and spill, child. How did it go?"

"It was a lovely evening. We all had a great time. Your dinner was the hit of the night." Mac pulled Sarah's parcel from the bag that held the returning pots. She handed it to Martha.

Martha accepted it and looked to Mac. "What's this?"

"It's a little something to say thank you for the lovely dinner."

"So it went well then?"

Mac nodded. "Uh-huh."

"And…?"

"And I listened to what you said, and I talked to her, and we had a lovely time."

"You had a lovely time?"

"Yes, a lovely time."

Martha tidied the papers on her desk with a straight face. "In my day we would have said it was a hot night in. But if you say you had a lovely time, then that's terrific."

"Martha!"

Martha looked at Mac indignantly. "What? I might be old, honey child, but I still remember what good food, good company, and great sex feel like!"

Mac couldn't help herself any longer and burst into a fit of the giggles, which Martha joined in.

❖

A knock at Sarah's office door made her stop writing up a supplies report. A happy Colleen Baker from Obstetrics walked in.

"Hey, Sare, I heard a report of a strange noise coming from Emergency, so I thought I would come down and check it out."

Sarah looked up at her, frowning. "What noise?"

Colleen sat on the edge of Sarah's desk, grinning from ear to ear. "It was you, humming."

Sarah laughed. "What are you talking about?"

Colleen looked at Sarah and tilted her head at her friend. "Look at you. You look happy. No, it's more than that. You look positively glowing."

"I don't know what on earth you're talking about."

Colleen leaned over and put her finger under Sarah's chin and leaned in close, whispering in a conspiratorial voice, "If I didn't know any better, I would say you looked well loved, girlfriend." Sarah expected she'd gone as red as beetroot. Colleen started chuckling. "Yup, well loved."

Sarah smiled smugly and winked.

"It's that firefighter, isn't it? The one with the gorgeous eyes?"

Sarah nodded.

"Oh, nice, Sarah Macarthur. Nice."

The nurse, Alice, knocked on the door. Both doctors looked up. "Sorry to interrupt—these were just dropped off at reception." Alice held a beautiful bunch of flowers, bright colourful gerberas mixed with pink roses. "They're for you." She handed them to Sarah before turning and leaving the room.

There was a card attached. Sarah opened it and smiled. It simply said, *You take my breath away.*

Colleen looked at Sarah and her face sobered up. "Is it serious?"

Sarah puffed out a big breath *You can't get much more serious than blabbing out loud you're falling for someone.* "It's early days yet, but yeah, Colly. I think it could be."

"Well I'll be damned! Someone finally caught you?"

Sarah smiled contentedly. "Maybe yes, maybe no."

"Details, girl, spill. I want details."

"Well, we had a lovely dinner, which in and of itself is a story. Two of Mac's friends were there, the girls from the animal refuge I was telling you about?"

Colleen nodded.

"Anyway, it was a great night. We all laughed and talked heaps. I learned that Saturday was the first time Mac had had anybody over for dinner since her partner died three or four years ago."

"Oh, wow."

"Yeah, I know. Maree and Terri were telling me about it. Anyway, the dinner—it turns out Mac doesn't cook, it was made by a surrogate mother figure, a lady from Mac's work called Martha, and Mac was being all secretive about the dinner, until Terri found a note in Martha's handwriting with instructions on how to heat it up and called her on it. So we all had fun teasing her about it all night."

"And?"

"And it was the most fun I've had in a long time."

"And?"

"Mac's friends are really nice."

Colleen was laughing and waving her hands "*And?*"

Sarah laughed again before leaning into Colleen's ear and whispering, "And it was the best sex I've ever had."

"Ha! You go, girl!"

Laughing, Sarah was fanning her face with the card from the flowers. "Now get out of here, Colleen Baker, and let me get some work done."

Colleen gave Sarah a hug. "I'm so happy for you, Sare, and I want all the details at lunch."

Sarah laughed and swatted Colleen's retreating bottom with the card.

Chapter Seventeen

After Mac finished up for the day, she had enough time to go home, change, organize some dinner, and be back at the hospital in time to pick Sarah up by seven, when she got off shift. Sitting in the car, she watched as Sarah approached. Mac's mouth went dry just watching her. By the time Sarah got into the car, Mac's blood was fairly racing. She took a deep breath.

"Hey, how's your day?" Sarah asked, fastening her seat belt.

"Yeah, good. Yours?"

"Not too bad as days go. Are you okay?"

"Perfect."

"You sure? You sound like you're wound up tight."

"Yeah, I am. I just need to get out of here. Can you give me a minute?"

Sarah was clearly wondering what was going on. "Okay, sure."

Mac turned the truck on, driving in silence for a good ten minutes before pulling over. She cut the engine and undid her seat belt, turning in her seat to face Sarah. "Has anyone ever told you, Dr. Macarthur, that you have a damn sexy way of walking?"

Sarah barked out laughing. "What?"

"I'm sorry, but watching you walk across the car park, and seeing you smile that gorgeous smile, all I wanted to do was ravish you the moment you got in the car. But I didn't want to embarrass you at work with all the people about."

Sarah was laughing in a disbelieving way. "Are you serious?"

Mac nodded self-consciously. "I told you, you make me feel like I've never felt before. You turn my world upside down."

Sarah undid her seat belt, slid across the seat, and claimed Mac's mouth in a hungry, desperate kiss. They finally separated, panting, foreheads leaning against each other. Sarah started giggling. Mac pulled back a little to look at her. "What's so funny?"

Sarah shook her head. "It's really corny, but it's a good thing you're a firefighter because I am seriously on fire. I kept looking at the clock all day, wondering when it would end so I could get back to you." Sarah kissed her again, her tongue darting in and out of Mac's mouth, tasting and teasing, her hands starting to roam under Mac's dress jacket and up her sides. Sarah pulled back and licked her lips. "Your place or mine. I don't care, just step on it."

Tyres kicked up the gravel as Mac pulled up into her driveway. Grabbing Sarah's hand, she ran to the front door and into the house, just managing to shut the front door before the first items of clothing started to be shed. They only got as far as the lounge room before falling onto the couch in a mass of writhing, hungry, and impatient limbs.

❖

Sarah's head rested on Mac's chest as they lay on the couch, and she listened to the sounds of Mac's heartbeat and the timbre of Mac's voice buzzing in her ear when she talked. Sarah raised her head and put her arm and chin on Mac's chest. "Did you see Thomas today when you went to the school?"

Mac's fingers were trailing through Sarah's hair. "Only briefly. Enough only really to wave at him and tell him I'd see him next week. I think I spun the principal out a bit when she saw me signing to him."

Sarah chuckled. "I bet. I know it did me, when I first saw you. I guess it's just not something you expect people to be able to do, so when you meet someone who can, it's a bit of a buzz."

"Yeah, I suppose. I hadn't really given it much thought."

They lay in each others arms just enjoying the peace. Sarah could see the cogs ticking over in Mac's head. "Penny for them."

Mac's attention came back to Sarah. "Sorry?"

"You look like you disappeared in thought. So I said, penny for them."

"Oh, I see." Mac smiled. "I was just thinking about Thomas. What's his and Jean's story?"

Sarah rested her head on Mac's chest again and sighed. "Not a happy one, I'm afraid. Jean met a charming man a few years her senior at university. They fell in love, moved in together, and eventually got married. For a few years they moved around a lot with Richard's various jobs, and eventually Jean fell pregnant with Thomas. We hardly ever saw each other, and when we did, it was never for very long. I never really got to see much of Thomas until he was close to two years old."

Mac's fingers moved down from Sarah's hair to gently stroke her back and shoulders.

"That must have been tough."

"Mm, it was a bit strained there for a while. Then one day she turned up on the doorstep, black and blue, with a broken wrist. Apparently Richard came home drunk one day, having lost his latest job, lost the plot, and took it out on Jean. He accused her of all sorts of things, including alienating him from his son by teaching him nasty things with her evil voodoo finger language."

"Shit."

"Yeah. Jean said that the first year or two they were married were okay, although he did suffer from the occasional wild mood swing, but as the years went on and he couldn't hold down a job, he started to drink more, sometimes disappearing for days on end, only to return home in a state. Sometimes he would be depressed, other times he would be violent."

"Poor Jean."

"He never learned sign language, so the fact that he couldn't communicate with his son, and Jean could, only made his frustrations and paranoia worse. She tried to leave him a couple of times, but he would always somehow find them, bring them back, only for it to start all over again. The last year, she was constantly on the move. I didn't know about any of this for ages. The last time he found them, he locked them in a house and was threatening to kill them. Fortunately, the neighbours heard the noise and called the police who broke in and managed to subdue him, but not before he had beat the crap out of Jean. He was charged with assault and battery, with part of his sentence including getting some treatment. After that, Jean went to court, got a divorce, and was awarded sole custody of Thomas. She later moved states to come and live afresh here."

"Poor Jean and poor Thomas. That's just crap."

Sarah sighed sadly. "Yeah, it is. I guess, in a way, it's been a small blessing that Thomas is deaf and he wasn't subjected to the verbal part of the abuse. But even though Jean tried to shield him as best she could, he saw enough. He's never really had much of a chance to go to school, have friends, be a kid. This is the longest they've had in one place, and they're both finally starting to relax and live normally."

Mac's hand stopped. "I hear a but coming."

"Yeah. Richard was released a couple of weeks ago, and he's supposed to check in with a probation officer and a counsellor once a week. Jean got a call to say that he's missed his last few appointments and no one seems to know where he is."

"Shit."

"Yeah. Shit."

"Is there anything we can do?"

"Not really. Jean has a meeting with her solicitor and the police this week to discuss what options she might have, and maybe, by then, they'll have news."

"Well, if there's anything I can do, just let me know. You're welcome to give Jean my number and let her know that she can call me anytime. I'm never very far away, and having a truck with lights and sirens means I can usually get somewhere a bit faster than most."

"Thanks, babe. That's lovely of you."

"Well, she's your family, and that makes her and Thomas important to me too."

Sarah's eyes filled with tears. "Why is it you always say the most amazing things?"

Mac leaned in and kissed Sarah's tears away tenderly. "Because you make me feel amazing."

❖

Sarah stayed over at Mac's but had to get up to make the two a.m. shift. Mac drove her in, as she'd left her car at the hospital. As Mac pulled into the car park, Sarah sighed, reluctant to make a move. "Thank you for driving me to work. We didn't think it through very well yesterday, did we? I could have driven to your place yesterday and you could have had a few more hours' sleep this morning."

Mac shook her head. "I wouldn't have slept anyway. I discovered the bed's too big when you're not in it."

Sarah leaned over and kissed her. "I know what you mean."

Sarah wasn't keen to get out of the car and Mac wasn't keen to let her go. "What time do you get off?"

"I should be finished by lunch."

"I'm here giving classes today. Do you want to meet for lunch?"

"If I can, I'd love to. I'll text you to let you know how I'm going."

"Okay. Um, I was thinking about Jean and Thomas and Martha."

"Mm?"

"Do you think they'd be interested in having a dinner together? Sort of a getting-to-know-each-other thing, in one fell swoop?"

Sarah stopped and thought about what Mac was really asking. *Do I think that this relationship is at the point of meeting family?* Mac had already met Jean and Thomas—was she ready to meet the closest person to family that Mac had? "I'll ask Jean and Thomas, but I think it would be a lovely thing to do." Sarah could see Mac's shoulders relax marginally.

"Okay, how about I ask Martha and you ask Jean and Thomas and we'll work on a night after that, depending on what they say?"

"That's sounds wonderful."

"Okay. I guess I'll see you for lunch then, maybe."

"I hope so."

"Have a great shift."

"You have a great rest of your night."

They kissed and Sarah slid out of the truck and watched as Mac pulled away.

As Mac's headlights sliced through the silent darkness, she knew she wouldn't be able to get back to sleep. She decided that she could use the extra few hours to work on the sculptures in the shed, figuring she might as well make the waking hours useful hours. She pulled into the driveway, quickly changed while the kettle boiled for the makings of an inspirational mug of tea, and headed out the back.

Sitting on the stool, sipping her tea, she stared sightlessly at the carving on the table. Mac realized she didn't know where Sarah lived. She'd never seen her house, let alone been inside. It struck Mac as a little odd. Not wrong, just odd. *I'll talk to her about it over lunch. I don't want to stuff this up by being thoughtless or selfish.* Then Mac picked up her carving tools and set to work.

Three hours later, Mac stood up and dusted off the shavings. She was happy with her progress. Except for some finer sanding, the wooden figurine was done for the moment. She hunted around the workshop and found the pieces of wood she had already picked out for the figure of the boy. Setting these on top of the bench, she took the dog off the clamp and put it to one side, so that the bench would be clear and ready for her to start when she was next in. She glanced at her watch—time to head off to the refuge for the morning clean and feed. She was looking forward to seeing Nell again and to see how much of her training she remembered.

Chapter Eighteen

From the moment Sarah walked into work, she was run off her feet. It was one case after another: the hypothermic drunk with gangrenous toes, an angina attack, a badly inflamed appendix, and an overdose. It was getting on midmorning and Sarah was hiding out for a brief minute in the utilities room, looking into a mirror, cleaning up a series of angry scratches running down her neck from the overdose patient. Wincing briefly at the last of the antiseptic sting, she straightened as her phone went off. It was a text from Mac, who was between safety classes.

Can you do coffee or would you like me to do a drive-by drop off?

Sarah smiled. There weren't any new cases in at present, so she could afford to take a break. She told the nurses' station that she would be on a break, with instructions to page her if they needed her. She met Mac outside on a bench in the sun where she was waiting with two coffees and something to eat. There were dark circles under Mac's eyes.

Mac arched her neck to meet Sarah's lips. "Hey, babe, how's your morning been?"

Sarah grunted. "Ugh. Busy. Thanks for the coffee, you're a darling."

"No problems." Mac gently tilted Sarah's chin and neck to the light to get a better look at the scratches. "Did you get some hellcats lobbed on you last night?"

Sarah shook her head. "Nah, just a junkie pissed at the world because I wasted a good trip with a shot of Narcan."

Mac chuckled. "Damn you do-gooders."

"Yeah, it's always a dilemma—what to choose, death or sobriety? According to them, sobriety is not always the ideal choice." Sarah was chuckling. "I wonder if someone can invent a *happy* Narcan, so when they come out of it, they thank you all very much and wish you a pleasant evening."

Mac laughed and shook her head. "Good luck with that one."

"How about you, how are your classes going?"

"Pretty good so far. I think most people have walked away with something positive or new. If you hear any feedback in the staff room, I'd love to know what they thought of it—if I need to make any changes or if things made sense or not."

"Okay, I'll keep my ear to the ground and let you know. And of course, I can always give you first-hand feedback tomorrow, when it's my turn to do the class." Sarah wriggled her eyebrows up and down mischievously. Mac playfully bumped her with her shoulder.

"I spoke to George in maintenance. He said the contractors are in and are starting to remove the old sprinklers and are making preparations to fit new lines and pipes in the laundry. They've downscaled the laundry work for a couple of days, so the contractors can get in. So some of the laundry staff are helping out in the classes."

"How's that going?"

"Not too bad. One guy's a bit of a pain, but I don't have to deal with him again until tomorrow morning's session."

"Have you told George?"

"No, not yet. I thought I'd give him another go tomorrow and see if we can work something out. Some fellas don't appreciate being told what to do by a woman. I just have to find a way that makes him feel more positive about it."

"And if he doesn't?"

Mac had an evil cheeky grin on her face. "Then I know of a few good places to bury the body."

Sarah spat her coffee out onto the grass in surprise.

Mac calmly handed her a napkin to wipe her face. Sarah shook her head and laughed, bumping Mac's shoulder in fun. Sarah's pager went off. There was an MVA coming in with an estimated arrival time of five minutes. She sighed. "Gotta go, babe, duty calls. Thanks for the coffee. Let me know when you break for lunch."

Mac relieved Sarah of her empty coffee cup and placed it on the bench. Then she faced Sarah and caressed her cheek with her thumb. "Go get 'em, love." Leaning in, she tenderly kissed her on the lips. Sarah rose to head back to work, leaving Mac to collect the bits and pieces and put them in the bin.

❖

Sarah never made it to lunch but had arranged for Mac to meet her at her place after work, sometime after five. She gave Mac her address. Sarah had managed to pick up some groceries on the way home and grab a quick nap. She put her feet up on the coffee table and cradled a coffee, then snagged the phone and called Jean to catch up on the latest news from her meeting with the solicitor. "Any news?"

Sarah could hear the tension in Jean's voice. "No. Nothing." Jean sighed. "I had another phone call this morning...more of the same."

"How are you holding up? Honestly."

"Honestly?"

"Uh-huh."

"Well, the longer this goes on, the more nervous I get. I'm starting to jump at shadows, wondering if it's him."

"How's Thomas holding up?"

"I haven't told him anything, but he's not stupid. He knows there's something going on."

"Are you going to tell him?"

"Yes, I was just hoping to spare him for a little bit longer, but you're right. Putting it off won't make it any easier."

"I was thinking this afternoon, on the way home...How would you feel about moving in to my place?"

"Oh no. That's a lovely offer, but—"

"Hang on, hear me out first. This place has security cameras. It's in a secure complex of units and there's a guard on duty in reception. It's not going to make the Richard thing go away, but it might make things a bit more comfortable for you until this blows over. What do you say?"

"Having the two of us there, Sare, it might cramp your style. We might drive you crazy."

"You guys wouldn't drive me crazy. To be honest, I've hardly been at home much these last few weeks, so it's been largely empty. You two would have the run of the place most of the time."

"Have you been pulling double shifts again?"

Sarah cleared her throat. "Not exactly."

"What do you mean, *not exactly*?"

"I've been staying at Mac's place."

"So it's all going well then, I take it?"

Sarah smiled. "Yeah. It's good. No, it's better than good—it's great."

"Oh, honey, that's the best news I've heard in ages. I'm so happy for you."

"Me too. In fact, we were wondering if maybe you and Thomas would be interested in having dinner with us and a close friend of Mac's."

"I'll talk to Thomas, but I'm pretty sure we'd love to. He thinks the world of Mac. Let us know when."

"Okay, and Jean? Will you think about the offer of moving into the unit? I'd feel a lot happier knowing that you had that extra bit of backup."

"I'll think about it."

"Thanks. Well, I'd better get a move on. I'll get back to you about dinner."

"For sure. Say hi to Mac for me."

"Will do. Talk to you soon. Bye."

"Bye, Sare."

❖

Mac arrived a bit later than she had hoped and was still in her uniform. Sarah had left her name with reception, so she was buzzed through, and Sarah met her at the door.

"Hey gorgeous, come on in." Mac entered, then stood in the hallway, looking into the elegant lounge room as Sarah came up behind her and wrapped her arms around Mac's waist. Sarah nuzzled the back of Mac's neck. "How did the rest of your day end up?"

Mac turned around in Sarah's arms and gently kissed her lips. "The last class went smoothly and everything is right to go again, ready for tomorrow. I suspect, by the end of the week, I won't want to see another fire extinguisher for a while."

Sarah returned the kiss. "Mm, that's understandable."

Mac half turned around. "Nice digs, Doc. Very elegant." The lounge room was decorated in a cream leather couch suite, plush rugs, and some colourful large pieces of art on the walls.

Sarah took Mac's hand. "Would you like a tour?"

Mac smiled. "I'd love one."

The rest of the house was equally as nice. They ended up in the kitchen, with Mac sitting at the breakfast bar, while Sarah stirred a pot on the stove. "If you look in the fridge there should be a bottle of white on the door. Can you do the honours? Glasses are in the top cupboard on the right."

"Love to." Mac poured two glasses and put the bottle back in the fridge. She walked Sarah's over to her. She gently ran her fingers to the side of the score marks on Sarah's neck. "Anyone else get tagged today, or was it just you?"

Sarah took a sip and gently shook her head. "No, just me. I wasn't quick enough to avoid his hands." Sarah turned, reaching up to put her arms around Mac's neck, looking straight into her eyes. "In Emergency, we see people at their worst. They come in frightened, sick, in pain, or in another state of mind. Sometimes they're not happy to be there. On occasion, when they're distressed, they need to hit out at someone or something. Sometimes, that's us. It doesn't happen very often, but I'm not going to lie to you, sometimes we get pegged. I imagine that you see that too sometimes."

Mac nodded. "Sometimes." Mac knew Sarah was right. It was a part of the job. It didn't mean she had to like it though, but she did have to accept it. After all, who was she to talk? Her job had risky elements to it too. She was a trained professional and took all steps possible to minimize the risks and to stay safe, but even she knew sometimes that things happened on the job. "You're right. I know you're right. You're good at what you do. I just need to pull my head in a bit."

Sarah's hand went to the back of Mac's head and undid the tie holding up her hair, and she smiled as waves, finally freed, cascaded down her shoulders. "Anyone ever tell you you're cute when you get all protective?" Sarah kissed her cheek tenderly. "Thank you for caring, and thank you for trusting me. I've never had anyone worry like that before." Sarah put her head on Mac's shoulder and just stayed there in the safety and love of her embrace for a few minutes. Sarah pulled back slightly. "Dinner's a little way off yet. Did you bring a change of clothes?"

Mac shook her head.

"How about you go and have a shower and I'll grab you some comfy gear to change into, and we can put your uniform on to wash, ready for tomorrow?"

"Okay. Sounds good."

Mac padded down the hallway and through Sarah's room, to the en suite tucked into the back. It wasn't until the blast of water on her shoulders had started to relax her that Mac realized how tired she was. The near-sleepless night was beginning to catch up with her now that she had stopped. She rested her forehead against the cool tiles as the water worked its soothing magic on her tired shoulders and back.

Mac heard the door open and turned to see Sarah walk into the shower. Wordlessly, Sarah turned Mac back to face the tiles, took a sponge from the shelf, applied some shower gel, and began to wash and massage Mac's shoulders and back. Mac's head again went to the tiles, but this time in pleasure, all thoughts of weariness forgotten.

❖

Sarah topped up her wine glass, then raised the bottle to Mac, in question. They had retired to the lounge room after dinner, with Sarah sitting on one end of the couch and Mac lying with her head in Sarah's lap.

Mac put her hand over the top of her glass, which rested on her chest. "No, thanks. If I have any more, I'm going to fall asleep right here on the couch." Sarah reached over and put Mac's empty glass on the coffee table.

They had spent the time swapping stories, talking about their growing-up years, Sarah's years studying medicine, and how Mac discovered sculpting. They talked about music and movies and learned they had some very similar tastes in both. Mac only briefly discussed her family and didn't once talk about Tina. Sarah had come to understand and respect Mac's need for privacy, but she hoped that she would feel comfortable enough to talk about it one day with her. Sarah thought the next time she saw Maree or Terri she might ask them a little bit more about Tina. Not to pry, but for a better understanding of who Mac was.

Sarah looked down to see Mac's eyes close. She smiled. Even dozing, Mac still held a tension around her eyes that caused a little frown crease to gather just above her nose. Sarah smoothed the line with her forefinger. Mac's eyes fluttered open.

Mac yawned. "Sorry. I think I nodded off for a minute."

Sarah chuckled. "Yeah, you did, and you were snoring your head off."

Mac's eyes opened in alarm. "I was not! Was I?"

Laughing, Sarah shook her head. "No, you weren't. I was only teasing. How about we go to bed—we're both beat and we have another big day tomorrow."

"You won't have to ask me twice."

Hand in hand they went to the bedroom. Sarah held the sheet back for Mac. Mac slipped between the sheets and had no sooner lain down before Sarah moved closer, snuggling up beside her, resting her head on Mac's shoulder. Mac kissed the top of Sarah's head as Sarah kissed her neck. Within minutes they were both sound asleep.

❖

Mac woke first, and the first thought that crossed her mind was that she felt like she had come home. Mac took the time to just watch Sarah as she slept. *This is the most peaceful and happiest*

I have felt for a very long time. I loved Tina dearly, with all my heart. I never thought in a million years that I would ever fall in love again. Is it possible to love like that twice in a lifetime? Silent tears ran freely down Mac's face as she realized the enormity of the gift she had been given in Sarah. There was no comparing Sarah and Tina. Tina taught Mac so much, but Sarah made it all feel so complete. She was falling in love with Sarah, big time. Mac's heart felt so full it almost hurt.

Sarah woke to Mac's tears. "Hey, honey, what's wrong?"

Mac shook her head and whispered, "Nothing."

Sarah gently wiped her tears away. "Why are you crying, love?"

Mac caught Sarah's hand, brought her fingers to her lips, and kissed them. "I woke up and couldn't believe how lucky I was to have met such a beautiful person."

"Oh, sweetheart. I think we both got lucky." Sarah reached up and kissed Mac tenderly. She then lay back down on Mac.

Mac's stomach grumbled and Sarah giggled into her chest. Sarah patted Mac's tummy. "I think we had better feed the beast."

Breakfast was a leisurely affair, but eventually duty called. The drive into town was shorter than Mac was used to, and all too soon they were both pulling into the car park. Sarah got out of her car just as Mac stepped out of her ute. Sarah walked over and stood in front of Mac, reaching up to smooth her collar and straighten her tie. Mac grimaced. "I can't wait to get out of the monkey suit and back into ordinary gear."

Sarah laughed, tweaking her tie playfully. "Don't be in such a hurry. I like you in your uniform. I love the way it shows off your gorgeous curves, in all the right places." Sarah pulled on Mac's tie until her head dipped and Sarah claimed her lips.

Sarah's pager went off and they parted. Mac closed her eyes, breathless, and leaned back heavily on the ute's door. When she opened her eyes, she was pleased to see Sarah was just as flustered. "Boy, am I glad I've got a bit of time before I give the first class this morning. You sure know how to wind me up, Doc."

Sarah chuckled and held her hands to her flushed cheeks. "I sure know how to wind *me* up too. God, you're intoxicating." Sarah's pager went off again. She grabbed it and silenced the alarm. "All right, all right, I'm coming." She gave Mac a quick kiss on the cheek. "See you later for coffee, maybe?"

"I'll be looking for you. Have a good morning."

"You too, babe."

As Sarah's pager went off for a third time she broke into a jog across the car park and disappeared through the entrance doors.

CHAPTER NINETEEN

Mac lined up the last of the extinguishers in readiness for the next class when her phone chimed. It was a text from Sarah.

Hey, babe, can't make coffee. Sorry. Need to finish up here first. See you in class in half an hour. S xxx

Despite feeling like she had made some small progress, Mac had had a trying morning. The difficult man from the day before had picked up where he left off the previous afternoon, making quiet smart-arse comments on and off during the last class's practical session. Breathing deeply in an attempt to find some patience, Mac had one more trick up her sleeve she wanted to try in the next class, before she'd seriously consider looking for an isolated spot in a forest somewhere to leave him.

The formal part of the class in the conference room began on time, with a few stragglers sneaking in the back. As she turned to lower the lights for the first streaming video clip, Mac noticed that one of those stragglers was Sarah. She grinned, thinking about how she was going to have to give Sarah some homework to make up for her late entrance.

Once that part of the class concluded, the massed group made their way outside to complete the practical component. Sarah filed in beside her. "Sorry I was a bit late, I got tied up."

Mac pulled a straight—almost stern—face. "Do you have a late note? The classes are compulsory, you know, Dr. Macarthur."

Sarah laughed. "I was only a few minutes late."

"You'd best see me after class then, to catch up on what you missed." Mac couldn't hold a straight face any longer; she flashed Sarah a smile and a wink. Sarah laughed. Mac walked to the front of the group. There were several different types of extinguishers, a metal tray, and a drip torch. Off to one side lay Mac's turnout gear and spare fuel. Mac began by introducing each of the different types of extinguishers and how, and on what, they could be best applied. The practical part would involve each of them stepping up and using one of the extinguishers so that they could see how they worked.

"It's much easier to have a practice run first, rather than the first time you've ever used an extinguisher be in an emergency situation. Having a go and learning how to use one now will help give you that extra bit of confidence if a situation should ever arise when you need to use one of these."

"It's a fire extinguisher for Christ sakes not a NASA rocket. Any girl can use one." Mac sighed. The smart-arse, Tony Felucio, had started up again, true to form.

A few heads turned to Tony, subtly indicating their annoyance. Pursing her lips, Mac decided now was the time to try her idea. "Hey, Tony. I've noticed you don't seem thrilled to be doing the class. Mind telling me why?"

Tony spoke up, "Yeah. It's simple—any moron can use one. I don't see why we have to be out here, wasting time, learning how to use something that doesn't need any learning to use it."

Mac held her arm out to point at Tony. "You know what, folks, a lot of people would agree with what Tony has said. Seriously. How hard can it be to use of one these? Right, Tony?"

Tony looked a bit taken aback, as if this wasn't the response he was expecting. But confident, he forged ahead "That's right. It's got a handle, it's got a nozzle, you point it and shoot. Voila. It ain't rocket science."

Mac was nodding as Tony spoke. "You're right, Tony. It shouldn't be that hard. Can you come out the front and show the group how it's done, please?"

The look on Tony's face was priceless. He wasn't expecting Mac to call him on it, but he had gone too far to back out, so he accepted the challenge and walked forward to the front of the group. Mac's plan had hinged on Tony accepting the challenge, with a small sense of relief she directed him to stand to her left where she had put a number of extinguishers out ready to use. She pointed Tony to a spot nearest the dry chemical powder extinguisher, which was the first in the line. She was banking on him blindly picking the nearest one to him for the plan to work.

Next Mac put on her turnout coat, poured some fuel into the metal tray, pausing briefly to light up the contents of the tray with a drip torch. She then turned to the group. "This morning, we have heard about the different types of fires from when we were in the room earlier, for the sake of this particular exercise, we are going to pretend that this is an oil or fat fire. Tony is going to select an extinguisher and demonstrate how to put it out for us." Mac turned to Tony, extending her arm towards the line of extinguishers. "Tony, if you would be so kind?"

The pan was starting to heat up, and popping noises could be heard from the fuel and water mix. The group was silent as they watched Tony choose an extinguisher. To Mac's relief, Tony picked up the dry powder extinguisher which was closest to him, turned to the crowd, and shrugged his shoulders as if to say *How hard can it be?* He pulled the safety pin, stepped towards the burning pan, aimed the nozzle at the fire, and squeezed. Powder went everywhere. He had a bit of trouble controlling the flow and the direction at first, but he soon managed to work it out, enough to put a light coating over the surface of the pan, and the flames disappeared.

Mac stood to the side of the tray smiling.

Tony turned back to the group, put the extinguisher down, and faced his amassed audience with a triumphant smile on his face. "See? Easy."

The audience were snickering at him. His victory smile very quickly waned, then turned puzzled.

One of the kitchen orderlies leaned forward and pointed past Tony's shoulder. "Hey, Einstein, look behind you."

Tony spun around and discovered that the pan had reignited. What the group hadn't noticed was that Mac had tapped the pan with her boot, breaking up the thin powder cover, allowing the oxygen to meet with the hot fuel, and reigniting the contents of the pan.

Mac calmly stepped forward and, using one of the extinguishers, successfully suppressed the contents of the pan, snuffing the flames completely. Tony stood in front of the group, completely red faced. It had not been Mac's intention to embarrass him, so much as to bring him around and get him on her side.

She quickly moved in with part B of the plan. Mac put her hand on Tony's shoulder. "I want to thank Tony for helping me out this morning. We put on a little show between us to demonstrate what most people think—How hard can it be to use an extinguisher?—and in truth, once you know a little bit about fires, fuel types, and the types of extinguishers to use, then it's not hard at all. Can you all put your hands together for Tony, for helping me out here this morning?"

Everyone applauded and a few of Tony's mates cheered. "Nice work, buddy! On ya, Tony."

No one suspected Mac's plan. Tony didn't lose face and Mac felt confident that his comments would stop. Mac turned to Tony and quietly spoke to him. "Hey, Tony. Thanks for that. Sorry to spring it on you, but you were great. Can you do me one last favour? It's hard to talk, and help people, and light the tray. While I talk to the group about the different types of extinguishers here, can you put on the fire gear and help me, by lighting up the pan when I nod?"

Mac had learned a long time ago that most young boys were fascinated by uniforms and action, whether it was playing at being a cowboy, a policeman, a special forces agent, or pretending to be a firefighter. Mac also knew that inside every grown man still lived that little boy. She saw Tony's eyes light up when he looked at the fire gear and was happy that her plan was working out.

Tony nodded to her. "No worries, Mac, I can do that."

Mac slapped him on the shoulder. "Thanks, Tony. I owe you one."

While Mac talked to the group, Tony put Mac's coat, trousers, helmet, and gloves on and stood with his chest puffed out, looking right at Mac and waiting for her signal to light the pan.

One by one, everyone got to have a turn, even Sarah, who stepped up to the pan and successfully put the flames out. She stood up and gave Mac a triumphant gorgeous smile. Mac smiled and winked at her as Sarah handed the extinguisher off to the next person.

Being highly aware of the staff's responsibilities, Mac was pleased the class had finished on time. The group had started to disperse, cheerfully talking about the morning amongst themselves. Tony was off the side, still in the turnout gear, surrounded by his mates who were good naturedly slapping him on the shoulder and looking at him in the gear with what appeared to be a little bit of envy.

Sarah wandered over to Mac. "Was Tony the class pain you were talking about?"

Mac had a very satisfied smile on her face. "Uh-huh."

Sarah looked at Tony and then back at Mac's face. "You set that up, didn't you?"

Mac's grin got bigger. "Uh-huh."

"You're feeling quite pleased with yourself, aren't you?"

Mac bounced up and down on her toes. "I am, at that."

Sarah was laughing and shaking her head. "How did you know to do that?"

Mac shrugged, holding her hands up. "Well, after all these years of working with men, you learn a few tricks here and there. I just got lucky today, was all."

A shrill bell sounded just as George came running around the corner of the building to where the group was. "Laundry's on fire! Two contractors are still inside. Hurry!"

Mac ran over to Tony. "Give me the coat and hat. You and your mates grab the fresh extinguishers from over there and follow me."

Mac tossed her navy jacket to one side and donned the turnout coat and helmet. She had several of the men with hoses pointing the water spray in through the laundry entrance door. She knelt down next to them. "Stay low to avoid the heat. Aim the hose in through the door and out to the window to help vent the fire."

Next she turned to George, who was standing next to her with an extinguisher. "Have you called the fire in?" George nodded. "How many inside?"

"Two of the contractors. They were welding in the new lines. There was an explosion and then it went up in flames."

Mac looked around at the building. Thick black smoke was starting to billow out. She was trying to remember the layout of the laundry rooms from the plans. The fire hadn't yet taken hold. Looking at the smoke, Mac knew there was only a small window of time left to do anything. She turned to George, grabbed the extinguisher he was holding, and yelled, "Get another hose line in here and try and keep the doorway free of flames, in case someone comes out. When the fire truck arrives, tell 'em what you told me." Mac quickly did up the collar of her coat, pulled her helmet on snug, and ran through the door into the laundry. As Mac went through the door, she vaguely heard someone scream out her name.

The first room Mac ran into was filled with smoke, but flames hadn't yet reached this part of the structure. She ducked down low and called out, "Can you hear me? Call out." She started coughing. She knew it was risky running into the building without her full protective outfit, particularly her breathing gear, but that was on the fire truck and she didn't think she could wait for it to get here, if these guys were to have a chance. She coughed, took another breath. "Can you hear me? Call out."

She reached a doorway, dropping down on her hands and knees as the smoke got thicker. She could feel the radiating heat starting to build up. The smoke was thick and her eyes were stinging and watering so badly she could only take small blinking glances before it got to the point where she couldn't see any more. "Can anyone hear me? Call out." In front of Mac, off to the right, she could hear moaning. "Call out. Where are you?" With every breath, she coughed. The smoke was getting thicker.

"Here! I'm here."

Mac crawled over and felt out with her hands. She found a man lying on the floor. "Are you hurt? Can you walk?"

"I'm okay. Have you seen Jimmy Lee? Where's Jimmy?"

"I haven't found him yet. Where was he?"

They were both coughing. "In the next room."

Mac took a breath and coughed. "Jimmy? Jimmy, can you your hear me?" She looked at the man in front of her and made a decision. "Come on, buddy. Let's get you out of here and then we'll find Jimmy." Mac put her arm around the man and together they half stood in a crouch and stumbled to the front doorway. She pushed him out into the waiting arms of the men on the hose line, turned around, and headed back in.

Mac couldn't see much at all. Crawling back to the doorway where she found the first man, she could feel the heat and see the flames starting to crawl along the ceiling, spilling out of the back room where the fire had obviously started. "Jimmy!" She coughed, and sucked in hot air. "Jimmy! Can you hear me? Jimmy!" She could hear parts of the back room starting to collapse as it became fully involved in fire. *I don't have much time.*

Mac crawled on her stomach with her hands outstretched, blindly feeling in the dark. It was getting harder to breathe. She could feel her thoughts starting to slow. Every breath hurt, and her eyes stung so badly they were closed shut. *Have to get out. Too hot. Can't last much longer.*

Mac spun around and started to head back, crawling and coughing the way she came, when her arm felt a foot. She stopped. She ran her hand up a leg and up a thigh, pelvis, chest, and head. She'd found him. He was partly wedged under a dryer which had fallen on him, probably in the explosion. Mac rose up to kneel, flinching as she felt the intense heat coming off the ceiling, searing her face and neck. The dryer was metal and red-hot. She leaned in to the dryer, but it wouldn't budge. She shoved harder. The effort was using up precious energy and strength. She was running out of oxygen. She couldn't afford too much more time. She was about to give it one more shove when there was an explosion, lifting her and throwing her into the dryer with such force that it was dislodged from the prone Jimmy.

Mac rolled over, then slowly got up and grimaced. She felt like she'd been kicked, but there was no time to worry about it. She had to get them out. She grabbed Jimmy by the collar and dragged him out to the doorway. *Get to the door...the door.* Her arms and legs felt like lead weights. She could barely move them. *Find the door...*Her thoughts were barely registering. *Can't breathe.* She was coughing so hard, she stumbled. She vaguely registered the sirens outside. *Can't. Tried. Sorry.*

Without air, her body couldn't go any farther. Mac finally felt the door frame just as a spray of water hit her on her face. She collapsed on the threshold.

❖

Sarah stood behind George, from Maintenance. She'd gotten there just in time to see Mac run into the burning building. She stepped forward and screamed her name as George's arms wrapped around her and held her back. They all stood helpless outside while they watched the smoke thicken and grow like a greedy billowing monster as it began to pour from the windows and out from under the eaves.

More men came with hoses, and a bucket line started with staff from every part of the hospital helping out. Sarah got herself in the queue and was passing the buckets when she saw two dark silhouettes appear in the doorway of the laundry. One figure was pushed from behind and stumbled out. Several of the front people ran forward to pull him out to safety. The second silhouetted figure turned and disappeared back into the smoke.

Sarah felt like she had been partially separated from her body, as she stood there frozen, knowing that was Mac who'd gone back in. George grabbed her by the shoulder and shook her. "Doc! Doc, we need your help."

Sarah's working brain snapped on. She looked over to where her team were standing with a gurney. She waved them over. "Put him on the gurney. What's your name, sir?"

He was coughing badly but managed to rasp out, "Peter, Peter Chesterfield."

"Okay, Peter. I'm going to put this oxygen mask on. I want you to take some nice deep breaths for me, okay?" She turned to her crew. "Get an IV going and wash his eyes out. Take him straight through. I'll call and tell Don you're on your way." The nurse nodded and whisked Peter away after the IV line was in place. Sarah picked up her phone and dialled the triage desk. "Hi, Alice, it's Sarah, put Don on, please."

Within seconds Don was on the line. "Hey, Sarah."

"Don, first one is headed your way. His name is Peter Chesterfield. There's still two inside."

"Do you need me out there? Claudia's come in early, she can handle the first one."

Sarah closed her eyes. She was terrified for Mac. If anything happened to her…"Yes, please come." Sarah hung up. She couldn't give voice to her fears, or they would consume her alive. She heard the sirens, then saw the flashing lights. It had felt like an eternity ago that the fire had started before the fire truck arrived, but surprisingly it had only been a matter of minutes.

She saw a man who fit the description of Mac's partner, John, jump off the truck and run over to George for a briefing. He turned and yelled at the crew who were already out of the truck and pulling out and hooking up hose lines to hydrant outlets. "Two inside. One of them is Mac. Let's move!" As he put his mask on and turned to face the laundry entrance, an explosion ripped from inside the laundry and blew out the doorway. Those in front stumbled from the percussive wave of force.

Sarah heard someone scream out Mac's name and realized the sound was torn from her own throat as tears coursed down her face.

Everybody froze in shock before John's voice rose above the noise. "Move it!" Just as they charged the line and started to spray into the structure, a helmeted figure, crawling on the ground, emerged out of the smoke-filled doorway. As the figure was sprayed with water, it collapsed.

Mac.

"There, in the doorway."

"Quick, wet the door!"

Three men ran over and pulled Mac from the doorway. She had a grip on an unconscious figure. John loosened her grip and put his hands under her arms. "I've got you, Mouse. Hang in there, babe. I've got you." He dragged her out, clear of the building, and gently laid her down.

The other two men dragged the unconscious man—the man Mac had risked her own life for—out, laying him off to one side of Mac. Sarah and her team rushed forward.

John gently took off Mac's helmet. "Hey, Mouse, you're out now. Good job, little buddy. I got you."

Mac rolled to her side and coughed, struggling to breathe. Sarah waved for the oxygen as she knelt down next to Mac, opposite John. "Hey, sweetheart. I'm going to put this oxygen mask on to help your breathing."

A gurney appeared beside John. Mac was instantly surrounded by firefighters who gently picked Mac up and laid her on the gurney. As the medical team stepped in, John and the men took a silent step backward. Sarah quickly looked to her team. "Let's get her inside."

CHAPTER TWENTY

The two gurneys rolled into Emergency, one after the other, and were parked next to the gurney that Claudia was working on. Sarah looked up at Claudia. "How're you going there?"

Claudia nodded. "All good. Some smoke inhalation and minor contusions, but other than that, pretty stable. I want to monitor his breathing for a while, to keep an eye on his airway. We're just waiting on a bed upstairs so he can stay overnight for observation."

Sarah nodded. "Good. How about you, Don?"

Don didn't look up. "Low sats, looks like we've got a mix of partial- and full-thickness burns to about forty-five per cent, and I'll need head and chest X-rays."

Alice was busy wrestling with Mac's heavy turnout coat. Alice cursed under her breath, and Sarah looked down at the noise. There was blood covering the left side of Mac's light blue shirt. The team quickly rolled Mac and removed the jacket. Alice and another nurse set to cutting Mac's shirt and trousers off, which revealed a large piece of shrapnel embedded between her ribs.

Sarah winced. She watched as Mac's trouser legs were removed. There were burns along her beautiful legs, blisters were starting to form on Mac's hands, as well.

At the head of the bed, a nurse was washing out Mac's eyes and dabbing her face. Sarah watched as pools of soot and saline soaked the pristine white sheet below. Sarah made out the redness of Mac's face and noticed that Mac's hair was shorter and singed on the edges. *Oh, honey, your beautiful hair.*

Mac opened her eyes briefly and saw Sarah looking down at her. Sarah brushed a stray lock of hair behind Mac's ear. "Hey, sweetheart. Do you know where you are?" Mac nodded. Sarah noticed she was taking shallow, short breaths. "You got both men out, honey. They're in here with you too." Sarah had her hand on the top of Mac's head. "It's hard to breathe because of the smoke you inhaled, and it looks like you have a bit of shrapnel in your side. We're going to need to take some X-rays to see what's going on."

Mac nodded and whispered something into her oxygen mask. Sarah lifted the mask and leaned in. Mac gave a little cough and tried again in a raw whisper. "Feels like I've been kicked by a horse."

Sarah put the mask back down and glanced over at the monitor to see what Mac's vitals were doing. She was stable enough that they could give her some morphine to take the edge off the pain, but not too much, because they still needed to monitor her breathing. Only time would tell if Mac had sucked in enough hot air to burn her airways. They would know soon enough. So far, Mac appeared to be okay, but it still was too early to call.

Sarah turned to Alice. "Push five of morphine, please, Alice."

Alice nodded, turned and loaded the syringe, then pushed it into Mac's IV. Sarah stroked Mac's fringe back off her forehead.

"Sarah," Don called, "I need your help over here with this man's airway. Claudia, can you look after Mac for a minute?"

Sarah didn't want to leave Mac's side for even a second.

Mac pulled down the oxygen mask and signalled for Sarah to come closer. Sarah leaned in to catch Mac's hoarse whisper. "Go. I'm fine. He needs you."

Tears started to fill Sarah's eyes. Mac signed, "Go."

Sarah nodded, leaned in, and kissed Mac's cheek. "I won't be long."

Mac nodded and closed her eyes as Sarah reluctantly went to help Don.

It was a good three hours before Sarah got back to Mac's side. Jimmy had been taken upstairs and was being admitted to the burns unit. The dryer that fell on him cracked his sternum and he had a concussion. His legs and one arm were burned, but the dryer had shielded his torso and face from the worst of the heat. He had started to develop some pulmonary oedema from breathing in hot air, but the burns unit were cautiously optimistic for him. The main concern was over one of his legs. From the knee down, the burns were extensive and looked to be full thickness.

Mac had been settled into a semiprivate room upstairs. The second bed in the room was unoccupied, which was just as well, as there were several beefy firefighters sitting on it. Sarah couldn't help but think how tiny Mac was next to all these men. A woman in her mid to late sixties was sitting in the chair next to Mac with her hand on her arm. It warmed Sarah's heart to know that so many people had Mac's back.

A half-hour later, having changed into fresh scrubs, Sarah stood in the doorway and looked around, pleased to see that Mac was resting. She still had the oxygen mask on and her face was shiny, the cream they had applied glistening in the room's reflected lights. Her hands were bandaged and resting on the sheets either side of a protective cage hiding under the bedcovers, protecting her legs. An IV pump ticked away rhythmically next to her bed. Sarah knew the pump contained antibiotics, saline, and morphine, all working to keep Mac comfortable and hydrated and to help fight off any potential infection. On the other side of the bed a monitor measured Mac's pulse, blood pressure, and oxygen levels.

Sarah stepped into the room. A man near the spare bed, wearing a similar uniform to Mac's, approached her. "Hello, I'm Captain Thomas O'Reilly. This wayward lot call me chief." He shook her hand.

"Hello, Chief O'Reilly."

"How's our girl doing, Doc?"

Sarah grabbed Mac's notes and looked them over. She closed the folder and smiled at the fire crew in the room. "She's doing well. She'll need to stay in for a little while, just so we can monitor her breathing and get some antibiotics into her, but all things considered, it looks like she got lucky. She has a number of stitches in her side and she's going to be a bit sore for a while. It looks like she tried to take home a part of one of the dryers. It embedded itself in her side, but other than muscle and tissue damage, it appears to have missed the major organs. She has some burns to her legs and hands, but they will heal with a bit of time. What she needs most of all now is some rest."

The relief in the room was palpable. The woman in the chair looked to the captain and they exchanged nods. The chief handed Sarah his card with his contact details on it. "Don't hesitate to call if she needs anything."

Sarah put the card in her pocket and patted it. "Thanks, Chief."

He turned to his men. "You heard the doctor. Mac needs rest." He thanked Sarah again and kissed the woman sitting next to Mac's bed. "You know where I am."

The woman nodded. "I do."

The room was strangely empty after the men filed out, echoing with the noises of the pump and the vitals monitor. Sarah pulled a chair over from the other patient's bed area and sat on Mac's opposite side. The visiting woman looked at Sarah and leaned one extended hand out across the bed. "I don't believe we have met. I'm Martha."

So this was Mac's Martha. Sarah got up out of her chair and came around to Martha, then leaned down to briefly hug her. When she finished the embrace, she knelt next to her chair. "Hello, Martha, I'm Sarah. It's a pleasure to finally meet you, although I wish it were under different circumstances."

Martha touched Sarah on the cheek. "It's nice to finally meet you too, Sarah. Now tell me, how's she really doing?"

Sarah closed her eyes and gathered herself. This was the first time she had stopped all day, and the enormity of what had occurred began to wash over her. Before she could stop them, the tears came.

Martha gently pulled her into her lap and rubbed her back soothingly until the worst had passed. She handed Sarah a clean hanky to wipe her face.

Sarah straightened up. "I'm sorry, Martha. She's fine, really. She'll be fine. It's just…"

Martha patted Sarah's shoulder. "I know, dear. My husband, Leonard, was a firefighter. I know what you're feeling. But you said it yourself, she will be fine."

Sarah smiled weakly. "Yes, yes, she will." Martha patted Sarah's hand and stood up stiffly, grimacing. "Don't get old, Sarah. There isn't anything graceful about it. Give her my love, and tell her I'll be in to see her tomorrow."

Sarah nodded. "I will." Mac was right, Martha was lovely. "Thank you, Martha."

Martha tutted at her and waved a dismissive hand. "You try and get some rest too, young lady. I will see you both tomorrow."

Taking a seat, Sarah rubbed weary eyes, stilling her movements as she heard Mac's heart rate pick up. She raised her head to see that Mac was growing restless. Sarah gently caressed Mac's forehead, smoothing out her frown. Mac's eyes fluttered weakly open.

"Hey, sweetheart, how're you doing?"

Mac grimaced and tried to pull off her oxygen mask.

Sarah gently took her hand, placing it back onto the bed. "Hey, hey, it's okay. You've got some stitches in your side, which is why it hurts to breathe. Hang on and I'll get something for the pain." Sarah leaned over and adjusted the rate in the morphine pump. "You just missed Martha. You're right, she's a lovely lady. You need to hurry up and get out of here so we can get together for that dinner."

Mac tried to smile and nodded.

"John, the chief, and the boys were all here from your unit. They send their love and said they'll see you tomorrow too. And I had a phone message from Maree and Terri. They'll be in in the morning after they've finished up."

Sarah could see the morphine starting to work as Mac's eyelids started to grow heavy. Mac said something into the mask that Sarah didn't understand. She leaned in closer and gently lifted the mask and gave Mac a kiss. Mac licked her lips and tried again, managing to rasp out, "Bed's too big."

Sarah got her meaning and shook her head. "Bed's too tiny, babe, and I would only hurt you."

Mac shook her head and tapped the bedcover with her bandaged hand. Sarah could read her lips moving in the mask. "Need you."

Sarah shook her head. "Mac, it's not a good idea, honey."

Mac pegged her with pained blue eyes and mouthed, "Please."

Sarah couldn't deny those eyes, even if she'd wanted to. Carefully, she climbed up and lay next to Mac, with her head on Mac's shoulder, being careful not to touch the stitches in her side.

Sarah listened as Mac's heart rate slowed and settled to a steady rhythm. Her own nervous tension, that had been building up inside of her since the fire had started, was beginning to ease now that she had Mac in her arms. Sarah closed her eyes and started to doze, lulled by the rhythmic music of Mac's heart.

❖

Mac woke in the early hours of the morning. Sarah was still asleep next to her. Her throat was dry and raw. At arm's length on the bedside table was a cup of water. Mac looked at Sarah and back at the cup, trying to work out distance and reach in a drug-befuddled brain. Her throat and head hurt. She slowly reached out, grimacing at the pain in her side, but she desperately wanted the water, so she determinedly kept reaching. Her fingers brushed the edges of the cup. She reached again. Fine beads of sweat formed on her brow. So tantalizing close, fingers tickling the edges of the rim, she hooked it and dragged it over with a bandaged finger, closer to the edge. With her hands bandaged she couldn't wrap her hand around the cup to pick it up, so she tried again to hook it with her finger, and lift, gently, a bit more—

Crash.

The cup slid off the edge and fell, clattering to the floor, spilling its contents everywhere. Mac's head fell to the pillow in frustration. The cup woke Sarah up. She opened sleepy eyes. She saw Mac's face and the cup on the floor. "Hey, honey, you want some water?"

Mac nodded.

Sarah got off the bed and filled another cup of water and put a straw in it. She lifted the oxygen mask off Mac's face and brought the cup over. "Just small sips, love." Mac lifted her head and took a few sips before falling back to the pillow again. Sarah put the mask back down. "Better?"

Mac nodded.

Sarah looked at Mac's monitor and walked over and glanced at her notes. "How 'bout we get rid of that mask?"

Mac nodded.

Sarah buzzed for a nurse, who appeared very promptly, and requested some nasal prongs and ice chips for the water. Within minutes the nurse returned and the mask was gone, replaced by the more comfortable nasal tube. Sarah sat on the bed and stroked Mac's forehead. Mac's eyes closed.

"Want some more water?"

Mac nodded.

The icy cold water was heaven on her sore throat. Mac knew it was best not to talk, not that she was tempted, as she was sure someone had put razor blades in her throat while she slept.

"More?"

Another nod, followed by sipping.

Sarah buzzed the nurse again and asked for an antiemetic and another bag of IV fluids. The nurse returned, handing Sarah a loaded syringe while she hung the fresh bag of saline up. Sarah pushed the drug through the line. Mac watched her, raising her eyebrows at Sarah in question.

"It's to help settle your tummy, love."

Mac mouthed, "Thank you."

The nurse left as quietly as she came. Sarah sat on the edge of the bed, gently cradling Mac's bandaged hand in hers. The outlines of Mac's hands blurred as the tears rose to well in her eyes. She looked up and saw Mac watching her. She wanted to say so much but was struggling to get past the lump in her throat. "I am so proud of you. You were amazing. You saved both of their lives—I couldn't believe the way you ran in there. The smoke and the flames, and when it exploded..." Sarah was shaking her head and had her eyes tightly closed as the images flashed before her. Her throat closed and all she could do was whisper, "I have never been more terrified in my life. I thought I had lost you"—Sarah started to sob—"just when I'd found you. I thought I had lost you. And then you came out..."

Mac pulled Sarah into her arms, holding her close as she sobbed into her chest. As Sarah's tears began to subside, Mac tilted Sarah's chin until their eyes locked. Mac licked her lips and rasped out, "I will always come out. You're my lifeline. I love you."

Fresh tears came to Sarah's eyes. "Oh, Mac. I love you too." Sarah gently leaned in and kissed her.

❖

Mac dozed on and off for the next few hours. She woke briefly to find that Sarah had gone to find something to eat and Martha was sitting in the chair, reading. Mac turned her head as Martha put her book down.

"Hey, sleeping beauty, you decided to join the party?"

"Hey, Martha," she croaked.

"Would you like some water?"

"Please."

Mac took a few sips before laying her head back down.

Martha explained where Sarah was. Mac nodded. She turned to Martha. "You've met her then?"

Martha smiled. "I have indeed. She seems like a very nice person. We've had a couple of good chats, she and I."

"Should I be worried?"

"Not yet. I haven't told her how truly terrible you are. I was saving that for later. I don't get out much, so I like to spin the fun out."

Mac giggled, grabbed at her ribs, and hissed in pain.

Martha waited until she had settled, fixing her with a serious gaze. "You need to keep an eye on her, Mac. You and I both know what you do for a living and how things sometimes unfold. Yesterday, Sarah had that thrown at her in a very big and personal way. It's going to take her a while to process what happened. And it's going to take a while for those images to get out of her head. She's going to see those images the next few times your pager goes off."

Mac half fidgeted with the bed sheets. "I know."

Martha patted her arm. "What about you?"

"What about me?"

"What do you see when you close your eyes?"

Mac was quiet a long time. Martha waited. "I keep seeing Sarah's worried face."

Martha nodded her head. "Good."

Mac looked puzzled. "Why is that good?"

Maratha smiled. "Because that's your rope, your anchor. That's the thing, when things get tough, that's what guides you home, child. Before, it was all about you and the decisions were easier. When you love someone, there's suddenly a whole lot more to consider, to risk, to fight for."

Martha stood up and kissed Mac on the cheek. "On that note, some of us have to get to work. I will see you later."

Mac kissed Martha and thanked her for coming. She lay back on the pillows and thought about what Martha had said. She was right. Before Sarah, Mac had sized up a situation, thought about the options, picked one, and got on with it. Mac knew she would still need to do that, but now she also needed to consider Sarah and their relationship. Mac was still thinking about it when Sarah walked through the doorway. She had obviously had a shower and put clean scrubs on.

Sarah walked straight up to Mac and kissed her warmly. "Nice to see you awake."

Mac smiled. "Nice to be awake."

"How's your throat? You still sound a bit husky."

"Mm, a bit scratchy, but better than before."

"That's good. It'll need a couple of days, if you don't strain it too much. Mind you"—Sarah wriggled her eyebrows suggestively—"it sounds very sexy, but you might have to cancel those concerts you had planned for the weekend."

Mac chuckled and grabbed at her ribs.

Sarah grimaced. "Sorry."

Mac was still smiling at the thought of her giving a concert. She couldn't carry a tune if she wrapped it up and stuck it in a backpack.

"I met Martha last night."

Mac put her head on the side. "Hmm?"

"You're right. She's lovely."

CHAPTER TWENTY-ONE

By lunchtime, Mac was well enough to come off the oxygen. Maree and Terri had called in to see her and to tell her not to even think about coming into the refuge for at least a week. Maree promised to continue training Nell until she could get back to it. Terri had been busy making soups that would be kind to a sore throat, offering to drop them off when Mac got out. Before heading off, Terri collected Mac's ute keys, to drive her truck home.

Sarah popped in and out during the day as best she could during her shift. Mac still hurt, but it was manageable. She had a nap after lunch, but never one to sit still or idle for long, by midafternoon Mac was restless and bored.

Sarah finished up for the day just after five, and walked into Mac's room with a huge grin on her face. "Hey, cutie, wanna blow this joint and go home?"

Mac had been aimlessly staring out the window before Sarah came in. "Serious?"

"Uh-huh. All the reports say you're doing fine, so there's no reason for you to stay if you don't want to."

"Um, slight problem."

Sarah frowned. "What?"

"I have no clothes to wear. Your team cut them up. I don't think it would be too good for your reputation if I walked out of here naked."

Sarah threw her head back and laughed. "Actually, my love, I think it would be *great* for my reputation. However, it is a bit chilly outside, so I took the liberty of getting you some warm clothes to wear from home. Is that okay?"

Mac smiled. "Very okay."

As per hospital protocol Mac was wheelchaired right to the door. Sarah had brought the car around and Mac was safely tucked inside and on her way home in no time at all. Sarah drove straight to Mac's house. "I thought you might be more comfortable in your own bed for your first night home."

Mac turned her head to Sarah. "Will you be staying?"

"If you want me to."

"I'd like that, very much."

Sarah smiled. "Well then, good thing I packed a bag then, hey?"

Smiling, Mac rested her head back on the seat and closed her eyes. "Good thing indeed."

As soon as they got home Sarah settled Mac onto the couch with a blanket over her legs. They shared a pot of soup and cuddled on the couch afterwards. Sarah wriggled in behind her so Mac could rest back against her chest, and Sarah stroked Mac's hair. "Do you want to have a shower before going to bed?"

"Can we do that? I'd love to wash my hair. I'm a bit over the singed Mouse smell."

"Jean did hairdressing a thousand years ago. Would you like me to call her and see if she can come out and give your hair a trim? I'm afraid the fire-frizzled look is a bit lopsided here on one side at the back."

"That sounds lovely. If you think she wouldn't mind."

"I'm sure she'd be happy to. I'll give her a ring in the morning."

Sarah taped bags around Mac's hands and legs to keep the dressings dry while she was in the shower. She ended up going in with her as Mac's legs were still a bit shaky. It was a quick shower as Mac was starting to tire. She sat on the toilet catching her breath while Sarah dried herself off. Turning her head back and forth, Mac caught sight of her hair in the bathroom mirror. Sarah was right, it needed a trim. She had probably lost a few inches off the ends from the fire, and although she didn't remember it happening, there was no denying the ragged evidence.

Mac couldn't help but notice the dark circles under Sarah's eyes and hoped that she could be coaxed into getting into bed with her. They could both do with the rest. After a few moments of careful body adjustments to make sure Mac was comfortable, Sarah turned out the light and snuggled into Mac's side. As the welcome of being home enveloped them and held them safe, Mac listened as Sarah's deep, even breathing harmonized smoothly with her own, carrying them into the small hours.

❖

Mac had a restless night. She couldn't access the pain medication by the bed because it was in a blister pack, and her hands were still wrapped up like mittens. Lying there, she resolved to tough it out for the night for as long as she could, rather than wake Sarah. She had looked so wiped the previous night that Mac didn't have the heart to disturb her. Mac managed to last until five a.m. before her fidgeting roused Sarah into wakefulness.

Sarah rose up to her elbows. She leaned over and gently felt Mac's cheeks and forehead to see if she was running a temperature. "Hey, honey. You okay?"

Mac shook her head. "Can you get me some of those tablets, please?"

"Sure." Leaning across her, Sarah quickly popped some free of the blister pack, then helped Mac to sit up and take them with some water. Mac lay back down and closed her eyes, trying to will the pain away. Sarah stroked her forehead in comfort. "Why didn't you take some earlier, love?"

Mac shook her head.

"There's no point being tough—they're there to make your life easier."

Mac held up one of her bandaged hands. "Couldn't open it."

"Why didn't you wake me? I would have gotten them for you."

Mac shook her head again. "You needed sleep too…thought I could wait until breakfast."

"That's very noble of you, sweetheart, but I would rather you'd woken me than spend half the night awake yourself. Tell you what, I'll take a look at your hands later and see if we can rewrap them to make things a bit easier, if you promise to wake me if you need help in the night. Deal?"

Mac nodded. "Deal."

Sarah kept stroking Mac's forehead until the medication kicked in and she finally dozed off. Sarah got up a couple of hours later as quietly as she could, so as not to disturb her.

As Sarah made herself some breakfast, she thought over how much had happened in the last few days. She would never, in her wildest dreams, have thought anything like this would happen to her. She rang Jean and updated her.

"You're kidding me? She did what?"

"I know. I couldn't believe it myself when she ran into the burning building. It was incredible. I think we all held our breath in fear, for what seemed like ages. And then it exploded, and she still managed to crawl out, dragging this man behind her."

"Is she okay? She must be okay because she's home, right?"

"Yes, she's okay. She got a bit burned in places and she picked up some shrapnel in her side from the explosion, but she's going to be fine."

"Oh my God! I don't believe it."

Sarah ran her fingers through her hair. "I know. I don't quite believe it myself. And then last night, she stayed awake in pain rather than wake me to help her get some pain meds."

"Why'd she do that?"

"She didn't want to wake me because *I* had been so tired the night before. She wanted me to sleep."

"Sare, are you for real?"

"Uh-huh."

"Bloody hell. You don't know where I can find me one of them, do you?"

Sarah chuckled. "I don't know how I got to be so lucky. I just know that I did and I'm going to hang on tight."

"Well, good for you. Okay, how about I drop Thomas off to school and come on over. Is that too early?"

"That would be great, thanks, Jean. See you soon."

"Okay, see you then."

Mac appeared in the doorway rumpled and sleepy eyed. Sarah noted she had dark circles and bags under her eyes still, which was not surprising. Perhaps she could coax Mac into a nap later in the day. "Hey, there."

"Hey."

"Feel like some breakfast?"

"Yes, please."

"Okay, you sit down and I'll just be a minute."

Sarah made scrambled eggs served on toast, accompanied by a steaming mug of coffee. She thought the eggs would be easiest for Mac to eat with a spoon, and she cut up Mac's toast into pieces that she could scoop up. The coffee was a bit more of a challenge, as Mac couldn't hold the mug in her hands, but Sarah had found some straws in one of the drawers earlier, which ended up solving the dilemma nicely. "I spoke with Jean—she said she'll be around this morning to cut your hair."

"As long as it's no trouble."

"She said she'd be very happy to do it."

"What time do you have to be at work?"

Sarah shook her head. "I'm not going in for a few days. Thought I'd hang around and keep you company, if that's okay?"

"That's very nice of you. Thank you. But you don't have to stay. You can go back to work."

Sarah was a bit puzzled. "I'm happy to stay."

Focusing on pushing her eggs around, Mac shrugged. "I'm just saying, you don't have to feel obliged. It's okay."

Sarah was a bit taken aback at Mac's response. "I don't feel obliged. I'm here because I want to be here. Is that all right?"

Mac shrugged again. "Yeah."

"You don't sound convinced. Do you not want me to be here?"

Mac closed her eyes.

"Mac? What's going on? Talk to me."

Mac blew out a sigh. "I just don't want you to feel like you have to be here. I don't like being needy, and I don't like the idea of you feeling like you have to stay out of some sort of…"

Sarah knelt in front of Mac. "Hey, hey, let me stop you right there. I don't feel like I *have* to be here. I'm here because I want to be. When I told you I loved you, I meant it. I am not here because of some feeling of obligation, okay?"

Mac nodded sullenly.

"Mac, look at me."

Mac did.

"Where has all this come from?"

"I just thought…I didn't want you feeling obliged, or trapped into staying."

"I'm not. Would you like me to go?"

"No."

"Okay, so I'm happy to stay and you're happy for me to stay. Is that right?"

"Yes."

"All right then, that's settled. How about we get you dressed for the day, then take a look at the bandages. Okay?"

"Thank you…I'm sorry."

"For what, love?"

"For being miserable. I think the lack of sleep and drugs are messing with my head."

Sarah kissed her on the top of the head. "Mm, you're probably right. How about we just take one step at a time, and if something worries you, then just let me know and we'll see what we can do. Okay?"

"Okay."

Sarah pulled the chair out for Mac. "Besides, why would I want to pass up the opportunity to help you get undressed and to see you naked?"

"You are crazy, Sarah Macarthur."

Sarah laughed softly. "Only for you."

❖

It took nearly an hour for Sarah to clean and dress Mac's burns and stitches. The stitches were all nice and clean, and she managed to rewrap Mac's hands so that the fingers were a bit more independent, rather than all wrapped up like a mummy.

The fresh white bandages adorning her newly wrapped legs stood out starkly against the shorts Mac opted to wear around the house, to avoid trouser legs brushing against the bandages. Sarah completed the ensemble with a fleecy hooded top and some soft, thick white socks.

Mac sat quietly on the edge of the bed, watching, while Sarah cleaned and wrapped her extremities. Sarah tried to be as gentle as she could, knowing it must hurt like crazy where the burns had exposed the nerve endings. Mac never made a sound the whole time Sarah attended the wounds. Having done all that she could, Sarah was packing up the wipes when she stole a look up to see how Mac was faring. Mac looked pale and wiped.

"Jean probably won't be here for another hour or so. Why don't you lie down and take a nap before she gets here?"

Mac nodded tiredly. "'Kay."

Sarah quietly finished cleaning up. She had no sooner finished the dishes when a knock sounded at the front door. She opened the door to Jean and Thomas. "Well, hello, you two. What a lovely surprise. I wasn't expecting you for a little bit."

Jean stepped in, enveloping her in a hug. "Sorry. I told Thomas what had happened and that I was coming over to cut Mac's hair. He said he couldn't possibly go to school and wanted to come over to make sure his friend Mac was okay."

Sarah knelt down in front of Thomas and gave him a hug. "Mac is having a nap at the minute, because she's very tired. How about you come inside and do a drawing for her? I just know it would make her feel better if she had one of your beautiful pictures."

Thomas nodded and patted his backpack, signing that he'd brought his pencils.

"That's super, how about you come on through and I can set you up in the lounge room?"

Once Thomas was set up, Sarah and Jean retired to the dining table.

"How's she doing?"

"Not too bad. We just finished replacing the dressings not that long ago. Between that and not sleeping much last night, she's a bit wiped, so the nap will hopefully do her the world of good."

Jean reached over and put her hand over Sarah's. "And how are you doing?"

"I'm doing okay. Yesterday was pretty tough. It'll probably take a while for some of the images to get out of my head, but I'm okay." Sarah shook her head, frowning slightly. "I still can't quite believe it, really."

"This might help." Jean pulled a newspaper from her bag.

The fire had made the front-page news. The headline read HOSPITAL HEROES. There were pictures of the laundry on fire, the bucket line and the fire crew, and one of Mac being dragged out by John. There were also photos of the hospital staff attending the injured. The most eye-catching picture was at the bottom. It was a stunning close-up of Sarah, with her hand on Mac's forehead, leaning down talking to her after she had put the oxygen mask on.

"Oh, my."

"Oh, my indeed. Looks to me like the paper got it right with the headline. You *all* were heroes. It looks like an incredible team effort."

Sarah stared at the paper and the images. Jean was right. What Mac did was amazing. But looking at the pictures, they all played a part. Jean rose from her chair and patted Sarah on the shoulder. "How about I make us a coffee?"

"That'd be great. Thanks."

The doorbell sounded. Jean turned to Sarah. "Do you want me to get that?"

Sarah got up. "No, I've got it."

It was John, Mac's partner, with several big flower arrangements in his arms. "Hi. I feel like I've known you for ages after yesterday, but we've never been formally introduced. I'm John, Mac's partner from the station."

Sarah rescued one of the arrangements from the big man's arms. "Sarah. Lovely to meet you. Come on in. You're just in time for a cuppa." They walked through to the kitchen.

John put the arrangements on the side counter. "These arrived at the station. They're some of the flowers from the families of the two fellas Mac pulled out. There's more at the station, but I figured she won't want them all, so I just brought the nicest ones out."

"They're beautiful. Thank you for that. Mac will love them."

John looked around.

Sarah guessed what he was thinking. "She's just having a nap. She had a bit of a rough night."

"She okay?"

"Yes, she's doing well. We changed the dressings this morning and everything looks good. First nights home are usually a bit tricky."

He nodded in understanding.

"John, I'd like you to meet my sister, Jean. Jean this is Mac's partner at the fire station."

Jean extended her hand. "Hello, John, it's lovely to meet you."

John blushed slightly as his big hand encircled Jean's smaller one. "Hello, Jean, the pleasure is mine."

Much to Sarah's delight, she thought she detected a reciprocal faint colouring of Jean's cheeks. They took their coffees into the dining room. Jean had made a hot chocolate for Thomas, who was introduced to John. Thomas looked at the newspaper on the table and back over at John. Thomas signed to Jean to translate.

"Thomas wants to say thank you for being Mac's friend and for looking out for her."

John turned to Jean. "Please show me how to say *Thank you— that's what friends do, we look after each other.*"

Jean showed John how to sign. When he had finished, John held his hand out. Thomas took his hand, and they shook, nodding to each other each.

There was a gentle throat clearing from the doorway. Mac stood there, looking at the group gathered around the table. "Is this a private party, or can anyone join in?"

Thomas was the first to react. He rushed right over, stopping two feet dead in front of Mac, then carefully stepped forward to gently wrap his arms around Mac's waist and set his head on her chest. Mac wrapped her arms around him in return. She looked over the top of his head to Jean. "Can you tell him that's one of the nicest hellos I've ever had. Thank you."

While Jean set up her hairdressing equipment, Sarah took Mac aside to ask if John had a wife or girlfriend.

"No, there's no one that I'm aware of at the moment. Mind you, he would make an excellent catch for someone one day."

Mac looked on as Sarah watched Jean. "Are you matchmaking, Dr. Macarthur?"

Displaying an almost believable innocent face, Sarah put her hand to her chest. "I'm sure I don't know what you're talking about."

Mac bumped her with her hip. "I'm sure you don't."

Meanwhile, John was inside drawing fire trucks with Thomas. From time to time John's laughter could be heard filtering through the doorway.

Jean took great care, evening up Mac's ragged ends and the lopsidedness at the back. By the time she had finished, Mac's hair had lost several inches and now sat two inches below her collar, falling in gentle waves. Jean was brushing Mac off. "How long have you worked with John?"

"Um, about eight or nine years now."

"He seems like a nice man."

"He is. I still can't figure out how he's still on the market."

"Oh?"

Mac chuckled. "You know, as firefighters, we're pretty good at putting out fires, but when it comes to relationships, I think we might be a bit clueless. I reckon that's why John and I make good partners. We think similarly and we're both a bit shy, so being in each other's company is easy." Jean continued to brush away the loose hair from Mac's shoulders in silence. Mac was secretly smiling. She could almost hear the cogs ticking over in Jean's brain. "Speaking of relationships. I hope you don't mind, but Sarah and I were talking about you and Thomas the other day. Sarah told me about Richard."

Jean's hands stilled.

Mac carefully reached into the pocket on her jumper and pulled out a piece of paper. She handed it to Jean.

Jean looked at the note. "What's this?"

"That's my home and mobile phone numbers. If ever you get stuck, or need a hand, please don't be afraid to call."

"That's lovely of you. Thank you. We'll be all right, though."

Mac turned around to look at Jean. "You and Thomas mean the world to Sarah, which makes you both very special and important people. I have access to lights and sirens and can summon extra help pretty quickly if needed. If you never need to call those numbers, then that's okay, but if you do, then you have them."

Jean looked at the numbers, folded the note and put it safely into her pocket. She looked to Mac. "Thank you…for this." She patted her pocket. "And for making Sarah so happy. I like you. I hope we get to spend more time together, getting to know each other."

Mac got up and hugged Jean. "Sarah makes me happy too, and I would love to get to know you and Thomas better. And thank you for fixing my hair. Now I won't have to walk around with my head on its side, trying to make the ends look even."

They were both smiling when they headed back into the dining room. Sarah came over and turned Mac around, while looking at her hair. "Mm. Lovely."

John, Jean, and Thomas ended up staying for lunch, with John leaving to go back to work shortly after. He didn't leave empty handed though. Tucked under his arm was a drawing Thomas gave him from their combined artistic efforts of the morning. Jean and Thomas left not long after John, leaving Mac and Sarah alone in the house.

Sarah managed to convince Mac that it was okay to lie down on the bed in the afternoon. Mac agreed, on the condition that Sarah join her. Mac lay on her back, with Sarah lying alongside, her head propped up on one hand. "That was nice of John to drop the flowers off and check on you."

"He's a nice man. Jean could do worse—if she were looking, of course."

Sarah smiled sadly with a slight shake of her head. "I don't know if she's even thought of another man since Richard. I think she's a bit scarred, truth to tell. Can't say I blame her. He was an arsehole. But you know"—Sarah leaned over and caressed Mac's stomach—"nice firefighters have a way of sneaking up on you when you least expect it and steal your heart."

Mac's eyes darkened as Sarah's caresses made their way up to encircle a breast. "Oh, do they now?"

"Uh-huh, they sure do." Sarah leaned over Mac, greedily capturing her lips.

Mac broke off with a moan. She held up her bandaged hands. "That's not fair."

Sarah chuckled. "Well then, you'll just have to get creative, won't you?"

Mac's moan was lost as Sarah proceeded to use her own imagination.

CHAPTER TWENTY-TWO

Although still tender, Mac was managing well enough that she had been cleared to start back on light duties the following week. Sarah was running out of clothes to wear—not that she minded pinching Mac's clothes, but she thought a change might be good and suggested that they spend Sunday night at her place in town. Sarah could drop Mac off at the station the next morning and one of the boys could drop Mac back to Sarah's when she'd had enough.

On their way to Sarah's place, they decided to call in at the refuge to see Maree and Terri.

Terri met them at the gate. "Hey there, you two. Mac, nice to see you've graduated to trousers. Not that looking at your pins is a chore, mind you. How's everything feeling?"

"Hi, Ter. Not too bad. I just have to be a bit careful and, as Sarah keeps reminding me, slow down half a step."

Terri put her arm around Sarah's shoulders. "Good luck with that one, my friend."

Sarah wrapped her arm around Terri's waist as they walked ahead, laughing. "Oh yeah, tell me about it. Has she always been this bad?"

"Uh-huh, doesn't do the whole sit-still-for-ten-minutes routine at all well. And if it's an enforced layabout, look out—even worse."

Maree came towards them with Nell trotting in tow on a lead. Nell pulled up excitedly beside Mac, who noticed Nell was wearing a new collar. "Hey, baby girl."

Maree gave Nell the commands to sit and stay so she didn't jump up on Mac's burned legs. Mac knelt down gingerly next to the puppy, patting her and rubbing behind her ears. Nell licked Mac's neck but stopped abruptly and curled against Mac's hip.

Mac laughed. "She must have caught a taste of the burn cream."

Maree gave Mac a kiss as she stood up. "How you doin', babe?"

"Not too bad. Both of my bosses have said I can try going back to work tomorrow for a few hours each day, and build up from there."

"*Both* of your bosses?"

"Yep the chief at work and the chief at home."

"Two chiefs, huh? Well, my sympathies to both of them."

Sarah and Terri burst out laughing. Mac stopped still and indignantly put her bandaged hands on her hips. "Hey, guys, I'm not that bad."

They all burst out laughing again.

"Am I?"

They looked at each other, crowded in, and gave her a group hug.

Maree broke away from the group. "I'll catch up with you in a minute. I'm just going to put Nell back. Mac, do you want to tag along so you can see how she's doing?"

"Sure, love to."

Terri said, "Okay, well, Sarah and I'll rustle up something nice for when you two dog whisperers get back." She and Sarah walked back to the house.

Back in the kitchen, Terri made a hot-chocolate base, while Sarah found a pie in the fridge. Sarah put the pie in the oven to warm and set the table. She leaned on the counter, watching while Terri stirred the pot on the stove.

"Wow, that smells nice."

"Thanks. I must confess, I love hot chocolate when it's made from scratch. It takes a bit more time, but it's a favourite old recipe, and I reckon it's well worth it. So, how's everything going with you guys? You both seem pretty happy."

"You know, I was just thinking, as we came in, even though we haven't known each other for a very long time, and we're still getting to know each other, it just feels so right. It feels normal and comfortable and, well, it feels good."

"Well, I'm glad. I have to thank you for being the person to bring the light back into Mac's eyes. It's nice to see her living again, instead of just existing."

"Thank you. That means a lot. But I'll be honest with you, Mac makes me feel the same way. I mean, I can't say I was miserable *before* I knew Mac, but looking back, I'm not sure that I was really living either." They were silent for a moment before Sarah took a deep breath. "Can I ask you something, about Mac? If you don't want to answer, I'll understand, but I was hoping to ask you two about Tina."

"Hmm?"

"Mac doesn't ever talk about her. I hope that one day she might be comfortable telling me about her, but I was kind of hoping that you might be able to fill me in on a few things."

"Like what?"

"Well, are there things I should avoid—things that might upset Mac—to do with Tina?"

Terri stirred the pot for a while, thinking. "One of the big things with Mac is that she holds a lot inside. Too much, if you ask me. I think she's been holding stuff tight inside right from when she lost her brother in the car accident. And then when Tina died, she just kind of stepped back from everybody, closing herself off from all emotions and expressions, keeping everyone at arm's length. I suppose it's her coping mechanism."

"I think I know what you're saying. The first morning home from hospital, after the fire, she more or less told me that I didn't have to be there, and that I could go. When I pushed her for what was really going on, she had trouble finding the words. I just put it down to lack of sleep and the painkillers, and while I think, in all honesty, that contributed to it, there was more. What you said kind of makes sense."

"Go on."

"Well, normally she's great. She's funny, kind, thoughtful, and a very considerate and generous partner, but when it comes to really emotional things, she's really knocked for six. Was it me, or was there other stuff going on? So I'm curious as to how she's been since Tina."

Terri closed her eyes briefly and shook her head sadly. "After Tina died, Mac shut down for a while. She went through all the motions—the funeral, dealing with Tina's family, sorting out Tina's things, and then going back to work, but Maree and I were really worried about her. Martha was worried too. We don't know if she cried or not, when she was alone at home, but none of us ever really remember seeing her cry. There were the odd tears, but…it was like she locked that part of herself away."

"I see."

"So, in answer to your question—is there something to look out for, or to avoid? I think maybe all I can hope is that whatever the magic is between you two, you hold on tight to it. Mac's just starting to poke her nose out from a really big black hole. So if you can stop her from going back in again, then you'll be rewarded with a woman who will take your breath away."

Sarah smiled. "She does that now. It's hard to imagine that there's more."

Terri wiggled her eyebrows at Sarah. "Just think of the fun you'll have finding out."

Both of them burst into giggling, just as Maree and Mac walked in the door. Maree said, "Uh-oh, that sounds like these two are up to no good at all."

Terri batted innocent eyes at Maree. "Oh, baby, how can you say that?"

Maree came up and swatted her behind. "Because I know you, and I know that laugh."

❖

Sarah and Mac ended up getting Chinese take away for dinner, a nice chicken and cashew stir-fry, which had lots of flavour but wasn't too hot or spicy, in deference to Mac's throat. Sarah gave up on the chopsticks and opted for the fork. "How's Nell going?"

"She's coming along in leaps and bounds. Maree got one of those vibrating collars for her, and it seems to be really helping. Whenever Maree wants her attention, she presses a control button and the collar vibrates. This lets Nell know that she has to look at Maree. Once she does that, Maree can get her to come, or sit, or whatever. She's a really bright puppy and she's learning really fast."

"That sounds brilliant. That must have been great to see."

"Oh yeah. She's a special puppy, that one."

"Well, she was lucky it was you who saw that potential. You helped her shine."

Mac shook her head. "Maree's the one getting her to shine."

Sarah leaned in and kissed Mac. "How about we agree that you both did?"

Mac shrugged her shoulders and grinned. "You know I'll agree to anything you say when you kiss me."

Sarah laughed and ducked in for another kiss. "Oh, I'll have to remember that."

Mac toyed with a loose thread on her jeans.

Sarah could see Mac wanted to say something. "What are you thinking, babe?"

"Thank you for looking after me these last couple of days, and thank you for being patient with me. I know I'm not the easiest person to deal with and I'm not very good at being sick and sitting around. And I'm not very good at saying what I feel, and sometimes when I do, the wrong stuff comes out my mouth. I just wanted to say that you make me feel safe, and loved, and that I appreciate it very much." Mac blew out a big breath with a rush.

Sarah held Mac's hand in hers and turned to face her until their eyes locked. "Thank you for telling me that. I don't know how or why we met and connected like we have. I just know that being with you makes me feel whole in a way I can't explain. I'm sorry that you got hurt, but I'm pleased that I could be here for you, and that you let me look after you, because I'm discovering that there's nowhere else I want to be, unless it's with you."

Sarah slid her hands up past the bandages on Mac's hands to her forearms, so she could stroke Mac's skin with her thumb. "Honey, I know that we're still learning about each other, but I'm hoping that we can keep talking, to help each other out. If there's something that I do that you don't like, or if there's something that you want me to do, then I need you to tell me, love. I don't have a great track record in relationships, and sometimes, I'm really clueless. I want this, *us*, more than I've ever wanted anything in the world. But I need you to help me."

Mac nodded.

Small steps, Terri and Maree had said before, so Sarah thought to lighten up the mood a little. "My shift doesn't start until nine in the morning. I was wondering if you had time to show me around the station, when I drop you off."

Mac's eyebrows shot up in surprise. "You want to see where I work?"

Sarah grinned. "I'd love to see where you work. I want to be the best partner I can be for you, and to do that, I think it's important to see and understand a little bit more about what you do. You've seen what I do. I figure it's my turn to learn about what you do. Is that okay?"

"Sure, I can do that. There's not that much to see. But we can do that. I suppose you'll want a ride in a fire truck, and to use the sirens too, don't you?"

Sarah laughed. "Doesn't everybody?"

The next morning Sarah helped Mac with her new work shirt. They'd washed it on the weekend to try and get the stiffness out, but not nearly enough to make it soft. Mac was pulling faces as Sarah did up the buttons. "This is worse than the other one."

Sarah brushed her hands away. "Don't be such a baby. It'll get better as the day goes on."

Sarah was trying to knot the tie and failing hopelessly. "How do you drive this damn thing? It always looks so easy."

"I got it." In no time at all, Mac had wrapped it around, pulled it through, and tugged it smooth and even. Sarah did the last bit tight and smoothed the collar down.

Sarah stepped back and held Mac at arm's length. "Mm, nice."

Mac pulled at her collar. "Mm, itchy."

Sarah laughed and slapped her on the butt. "Come on, gorgeous, take me to your fire truck."

❖

Sarah pulled up to the station. She turned to Mac, who had gone quiet. "You ready?"

Mac took a deep breath. "Yep." But she didn't move from her seat.

"You nervous?"

"A bit."

"What are you nervous about? Is it putting the uniform back on?"

"No."

"Is it the thought of facing a fire again?"

"No."

"Then what's giving you butterflies?"

"I don't like fuss. I just want to go in and be normal."

"People fuss because they love and care about you." Sarah looked at Mac and could tell that she needed to take a different tack. "Did you know, when you were sleeping in the hospital, there were firefighters in the corridor shushing anyone being noisy so that you could sleep?"

Mac smiled, crinkling up her nose. "They get pretty protective."

"Honey, they do that because they care. You'd do the same for them too, wouldn't you?"

Mac nodded.

"You know, if you were a bitch, then they wouldn't give a toss. But you're not, so you just need to suck it up and accept that people love and care about you."

Mac sighed in resignation. "I'm being an idiot, aren't I?" Mac knew that Sarah was right. She had good friends at the station. They were her family. So of course they cared about her.

Sarah chuckled. "Yes, but you're a damn cute one, so how about we do this?"

Mac blew out a nervous breath. "Okay." Mac held Sarah's hand and together they walked in. Mac only got as far as the service desk foyer before John spotted her and a whistle went out. This signal brought firefighters out of every door and hallway to surround her.

Martha approached her first and wrapped her in a hug. Second in line was the chief, who clapped her on the shoulder and kissed her cheek. "It's good to have you back on the floor Lieutenant James." The chief shook Sarah's hand. "Dr. Macarthur—thank you for looking after our girl." His eyes were getting suspiciously moist. He cleared his throat. "I'll be in my office if anyone needs me."

As soon as he walked around the corner, pandemonium erupted, with each firefighter trying to get to Mac. As Mac's partner, and as the biggest man there, John muscled his way to the front and got the first hug. "Welcome home, Mouse." He then gave Sarah a kiss on the cheek.

Mac cleared her throat. "Thank you guys. It's nice to be back. Most of you have met my girlfriend, Sarah, at the hospital. She would like to have a look at where we all work. So if you could all keep your clothes on for the next half an hour, that would be great."

There was laughing and good natured wolf whistles from the group. Martha stepped in and rescued them from the jovial crowd. "All right, you lot. Go back to doing something useful and let the girls catch their breath. You take Sarah and show her around while I go and make us a hot drink."

Mac hugged Martha. They stood there for a good few seconds just holding each other, before Martha broke away and shooed them down the hallway.

Mac walked Sarah through the back room areas, like the lockers, laundry, storeroom, and kitchen. As promised, Sarah got to sit in one of the pumpers as well as the smaller rescue-equipped vehicle that she and John often went out in. Sarah looked over all of them, asking lots of questions about the radios and the vast array of equipment.

Mac let Sarah try on a turnout jacket and breathing tank. "Wow, this is really heavy. How do you guys run around in all this gear? I'm only wearing half of what you do and I can barely move."

"Just practice. You get used to it after a while. It's why I feel a bit weird wearing the fancy shirt. I sort of feel naked without all the gear on."

Sarah froze, and Mac realized where Sarah's mind was headed as she leaned into Sarah's ear to whisper, "Don't make me turn the hose on you, Dr. Macarthur."

They were both laughing as Mac helped Sarah out of the gear. Then back in the main part of the building, Mac showed her the briefing room and her small office space, where a bunch of flowers, two steaming mugs of coffee, and some of her favourite sweet biscuits, Tim Tams, were waiting for them on the desk.

Stuck to the side of the flowers was a card. Carefully, Mac opened and read it.

You're my hero. Love you lots. Sarah xxx

Long silent moments ticked by as Mac stared at the card.

Sarah sat very still.

Breaking the spell, Mac plucked one of the rosebuds from the arrangement. She trimmed the stem, stood and leaned over Sarah, then threaded the bloom through Sarah's lapel buttonhole. She kissed Sarah tenderly on the lips and whispered, "And you're *my* hero, Dr. Macarthur."

"Thank you for showing me around this morning. It's helped give me a better idea of some of the things, like the trucks and the gear. It's really quite fascinating, and I've really enjoyed it. Thank you for sharing that part of your world with me. And it was lovely to be made feel so welcome. They're a nice bunch of people you work with, and it's obvious they think the world of you."

"They're good people. I wouldn't want anyone else to have my back. But don't tell them I said that, because their heads would swell and we wouldn't be able to get them into the truck."

Sarah chuckled. "Fair enough. Not a word. Well, I'd better push off and get my day started. You sure you're right to get home when you're done?"

"I'll get one of the guys to run me home."

"Just remember, it's your first day back. Pace yourself, huh?"

"Yes."

"Promise?"

Mac was smiling. "Yes, mother."

They kissed and hugged briefly before Sarah left.

Sitting back at her desk, Mac stared at her flowers, thinking back to the welcome she received from all the men. She *was* lucky. Even though all the attention felt uncomfortable, she'd survived. Sarah was right. It was because they cared about her. She just needed to learn how to deal with that.

CHAPTER TWENTY-THREE

Sarah's mobile rang just before two. Colleen. "Hey."

"Hey, stranger, you had lunch yet?"

"I'm just having it now."

"You in the caff?"

"Uh-huh."

"Mind if I join you?"

"I'd love it."

"All right. See you in five." When she came through the door a few minutes later, Colleen spied Sarah at one of the tables, waved, and came over. "Hey, thanks for waiting."

"No problems. All quiet on the baby front?"

"Yes, not too bad. How 'bout you? You guys busy?"

"We're not too bad either, which makes for a nice change."

"How's Mac doing?"

"She's good. She's gone back to work today for a few hours."

"Really? How's she managing that with her hands and legs?"

"Actually, she seems to be a pretty good healer. I'm a bit surprised myself. We're still keeping them wrapped, especially her hands, as they're still pretty raw, but she can manage a lot of things. She's on light duties, so she's not required to haul heavy equipment or attend call-outs for a while, and she's got people who'll help her out with inspections and classes, which is good."

Colleen was shaking her head. "I still can't believe that she ran into that building."

Sarah put her sandwich down and rested her elbows on the table and her chin in her hands. "You know, I can't get my head around it either. You and I try to save lives by patching people up. Mac saves lives too, but to do that, she and all the other firefighters have to put themselves into places most sensible people would never go."

"Does that freak you out?"

Sarah sipped her juice and thought about that question. She'd thought about it a lot in the last few days. "Yes and no, if that makes sense?"

Colleen tilted her head in question.

"Does it freak me out that Mac sometimes has to be right in the danger line? Yes, absolutely. If I close my eyes, I can still see her running into the laundry, and the explosion ripping out the door, and I'm still waiting, for what feels like forever, for her to come out, not knowing if she will or not. But she's good at what she does. I trust her. I know they're well trained and she told me that she'll always do her best to come home to me. I can't ask for more than that, can I?"

"Well, when you put it like that, I suppose not."

Sarah laughed. "Oh, don't get me wrong. I would feel happier if she were a sheep herder or a plumber, something a hell of a lot safer. But then I probably would never have met her if she was, and the thought of never having met Mac would be criminal, now that I have."

"Oh Lord, listen to you, you big romantic."

Sarah felt herself blush. "You know what? I think I am. I can't help myself. Isn't it weird? I guess when you're with the right person, you just go with what feels good."

"So you guys are good then?"

"Yeah, we are. We're still learning about each other, and we each have baggage from the past that we need to deal with, but, I think…I *feel* like we have something really special going on. For the first time ever, I want to be with somebody, Col. I want to have a future with Mac. I've never wanted that before, with anybody."

"That's a big first."

Sarah sat back in her chair. "I know. Enjoy the company, then get out fast. That's always been my playbook. But I don't want that any more."

"Does Mac know how you feel?"

"I think so. I mean, I haven't spelled it out in quite so many words. We've sort of mentioned bits and pieces around it."

"I hear a but coming."

"I don't want to rush her or scare her off. I want us to just take our time, sort of a take it as it comes sort of thing."

"Why would she be scared off? You're not planning on marrying her next week, are you?"

Sarah laughed and shook her head. "No. Mac is still recovering from the death of her first partner, Tina, a couple of years ago. She's still pretty vulnerable. And you know me, probably better than anyone else, Col. If truth be told, I've never been in a long-term relationship. I have perfected the art of staying on the move. I have commitment phobias. So I have to learn how to be a partner and not just a short-term hook-up."

"Well, that makes sense. But I still think you should tell her."

"You're probably right. It's just finding the right moment and the courage to do it."

"Well, with a bit of luck, you'll know when the moment arises and you won't have to think too much about it. It'll just happen."

"Hope so, Colly. Because I don't even want to think of a future without her."

"That bad, huh?"

Sarah nodded and blew out a breath. "Oh yeah."

❖

Mac had spent the morning finishing off reports and tweaking a few of the class formats for the weeks to come, so that she could do them in a slightly modified physical format to cater to her healing body.

The shrapnel wound still had a tendency to catch her when she moved suddenly, or twisted the wrong way, but she was learning to compensate, using other muscles when trying to lift and carry things. In some cases she had to ask for help, which was a bit of a new experience for her. Mac had always prided herself on being very independent and proved herself in the field to be both competent and equal to whatever task was before her. Asking for help did not feel comfortable, but she was learning to tolerate it in the short term.

Her legs weren't too bad as long as she didn't bump them. But her hands frustrated her the most. She could do things, especially now that Sarah had wrapped her hands a new way so she had some use of her fingers, but it was still frustrating to only be able to do the rudimentary basics. Mac never thought being able to get yourself dressed in the morning could be so important. She was having to learn patience. She was learning that she sometimes had to ask for help and more importantly she was learning that she had to let other people help and care *for* her. This was probably the most exhausting part of all. It left her feeling more raw and exhausted than having the dressings changed.

Mac yawned. Now that she had a full stomach after one of Martha's lunches, the morning was catching up with her. She had only taken a very light dose of pain medication at breakfast so she wouldn't be too bombed out for work, but the edge of discomfort was starting to creep in and she knew when she had the next lot, it would probably leave her feeling a bit washed out for the rest of the afternoon.

Martha stuck her head around the office door before Mac could stifle her yawn. "You nearly finished up here?"

"Mm, just have to print and file this report, and I think I'm all done."

"All right, you do that and I'll ask one of the boys to drop you home."

"Thanks, Martha. And thanks for the beautiful lunch."

"My pleasure."

Mac signed her finished reports just as John knocked on the door. "Hey, Betts. You my ride?"

John tipped a pretend cap. "Yes, ma'am. I am your humble driver."

Mac slapped him playfully with a report folder. "You clown. You couldn't be humble if you tried."

John laughed. "C'mon, Mouse. You've done enough for one day. Time to get you home before you turn into a pumpkin."

They drove in a comfortable silence. John was smiling. "Missed this."

Mac smiled wistfully too. "Me too. Only a couple of weeks left. God, listen to us, like an old married couple."

"Ha, you're right—'cept there'd be no point asking you what's for dinner, hey?" John knew well Mac's lack of cooking talent.

"Nope, not unless you like pizza or a toasted cheese sandwich." They pulled up outside Sarah's complex. "Want to come inside for a coffee?"

John shrugged. "Sure, why not. Lead on."

They made their way up to Sarah's unit. Mac opened the door and John whistled. "Nice, Mouse, nice."

Mac led the way to the kitchen, where she put the kettle on, scrabbling around for a biscuit to go with it. As soon as it was done, they headed to the lounge room. John sank into the leather couch with a groan of pleasure. "Roll me over if I go to sleep on this."

"Nice, huh?"

"Mm."

"Thanks for this morning. It meant a lot."

"You're welcome. You mean a lot to us. We're family. You know that, right?"

"I know. And I love you guys for it. Thanks for making Sarah feel welcome too—that was nice."

"Well, looks to me like she might be joining the family. Is that right?"

"Could be, Betts. You okay with that?"

John nodded. "Yep, always good to have a doctor in the house. Sure is pretty too. She make you happy?"

"Yeah, she does."

"Then I'm definitely okay with that."

"Thanks, Betts."

"Anything for my best mate. Hey, I've got something I'd like to run past you, if that's okay."

"Sure, shoot."

"Sarah's sister, Jean. Is she married, or seeing anyone?"

"No, not to my knowledge. Why's that?"

"She seemed like a really nice lady, when I met her the other day, at your house. We hit it off pretty well. I wondered if she and the little fella might like to go on a picnic somewhere, maybe, if she wasn't involved with anyone."

"I think that sounds like a nice idea. Why don't you ask her?"

"Yeah, yeah, I might do that. You wouldn't happen to have her number, would you?"

"I would. I don't think she'd mind if I gave it to you, though."

"Is there a problem?"

Mac told him about Richard. John's face set grim with the news. "What an arsehole."

"I know. I'm just telling you, though, so you're aware if she's a bit gun-shy."

"Yep, I hear you. Hey, can you teach me sign language?"

Mac laughed. "Sure. It takes a while to learn, but I can get you started on some basics if you like. You can try it out on Thursday at the school."

❖

Lying in bed, Sarah traced the letters on Mac's T-shirt. "So, your day in the office was okay?"

Mac was lying with her eyes shut, just enjoying the peace. "Uh-huh. Got the paperwork all done, sorted stuff out for the next two weeks, and had lunch with Martha. *And* showed off the station to a really cute piece of—"

"Ahem! Not *too* cute I hope."

"Oh, a stunning piece. You know, the sort that makes your mouth water just standing next to her."

"Oh, really?"

"Mm-hmm. Seriously thought of ditching my girlfriend, 'til I remembered she *was* my girlfriend, and well, after that, you know how it goes."

Sarah was laughing. "No, do tell."

"Ah, well, I take her back to my office"—Mac paused for effect—"and she spoils me with beautiful flowers." Mac wriggled her eyebrows up and down suggestively. "And we share"—Mac dropped her voice for dramatic effect—" a hot cup of coffee."

Sarah rested her head on Mac's chest, chuckling.

Mac stroked Sarah's hair. "Tell me about your day."

Sarah sighed. "Same old, really. A faculty meeting early on, followed up by a steady stream of patients coming in after that. Oh, and I grabbed lunch with Colleen. I think you met her the night of the MVA—she's in charge of obstetrics."

Mac nodded.

"Anyway, we managed to catch up for lunch, which was nice. Colleen and I have been friends since med school, but often our shifts don't match up, so we don't run into each other much or for very long. Speaking of which, she and her husband, Brian, are having a barbecue soon—they want to know if we'd like to come."

"Sure, that sounds nice."

"She also asked me how you were, and how we were going."

"What did you say?"

"I said you were stubborn and pig-headed, but the sex was great, so I'd hang on to you for a bit longer."

Mac nodded. "Sounds sensible."

Sarah leaned up and kissed her. "Actually, I said I thought what we had was pretty special, and that I think you may have cured me."

"Cured you? Of what?"

"Commitment phobia."

Mac raised her eyebrows in question.

"Let's just say that I have a track record of loving and leaving. Loving someone scares the hell out of me. So my way of dealing with it was not to deal with it. I got hurt badly early on in the piece, when I first came out. So I resolved not to let anyone do that to me again. I got pretty good at it too. But then one night, I met you. Everything changed." Sarah rested her chin on Mac's chest. "I'm going to be honest with you here, I don't really know what I'm doing. This is territory I've never been in before. All I know is that you mean the world to me. I can't imagine my life without you in it. I love waking up next to you. I love it when we talk at breakfast or dinner, or drive into town."

Sarah laid her head on Mac's chest. "I can only begin to imagine what it must've been like for you to lose Tina. I know that she has a big place in your life, and in your heart. I just hope that maybe…" Sarah's voice thickened with emotion. "I hope that maybe you and I could build a future together."

Mac was quiet for a while as she absorbed how Sarah had opened herself to her. She lifted Sarah's face until their eyes were even. "You're too late. I think we've already started." She frowned, trying to gather her thoughts, to find the words that, up until now, she had been too afraid to say out loud. "I never thought that I would love again." Mac shrugged a shoulder. "I thought that, when I lost Tina, that was it. I'd had my chance, y'know? But you and I"—Mac shook her head—"we're on another path, *our* path. I'll be honest with you. I'm thrilled to bits, but I'm a little bit terrified too." A nervous laugh escaped from Mac's lips. "It's amazing and freaky all at the same time."

Sarah sobbed in what Mac hoped was relief. Mac drew her in and held her close. "Speaking of relationships, I think John wants to ask Jean and Thomas on a picnic date. I gave John Jean's number. I hope that's all right."

Sarah leaned up and kissed Mac tenderly on the lips. "I think that sounds wonderful. John seems like a nice man. It would be nice to see Jean go out again. It would be ironic, don't you think, if she and John got together?"

"What do you mean?"

"Two sisters, dating a fire crew?"

Mac chuckled. "Guess we should be grateful you don't have eleven more brothers and sisters, huh?"

CHAPTER TWENTY-FOUR

Smoothing the collar down over her tie, Sarah's hands continued lovingly down Mac's chest and ribs, coming to rest at and encircle her waist. "How much time have we got before we have to head in to work?"

Mac looked at her watch. "About ten minutes. Why?"

Sarah shook her head and blew out a frustrated breath. "Not enough time."

"Time for what?"

Sarah's face broke into a lecherous grin. "To ravish you and get you dressed again."

"To *ravish* me?"

"I can't help it. I think it's the uniform. It's positively distracting."

"I'll have to remember that."

"Don't worry, I'll remind you. Come on, let's get going before I change my mind and have my way with you anyway. I'll go get the keys."

Mac checked herself in the mirror one last time. She put her jacket on and adjusted the sleeves; satisfied, she nodded to her reflection in the mirror. She was ready. As she closed the door behind her, the bandage on her left hand snagged and caught on the handle. Her momentum forward was stopped suddenly as the caught bandages snapped tight. Mac hissed in pain. "Shit." She bent over double, clenching her hand between her thighs, her eyes shut tight as she desperately tried to breathe through the waves of pain.

That was how Sarah found her, bent over, leaning on the wall in the hallway. Sarah knelt in front of Mac. "Hey, honey, what happened?"

Through clenched teeth, Mac explained, "Stupid…caught my hand on the handle. I just need a minute."

"Come and sit in the lounge room for a minute, 'til you catch your breath."

"Okay." Sarah put her arms around Mac and walked her through to the couch.

Mac sat with her head back and eyes closed, cradling her hand.

"Let me take a look, love."

Mac held out her hand, her eyes still closed.

Sarah patted her on the lap. "Sit tight, I'll be back in a minute." Mac nodded.

Two minutes later, Sarah returned. "I know you don't like taking these, love, but I think this morning we might make an exception, what do you think?"

Mac opened her eyes and saw some pills in the palm of Sarah's hand. She also saw new dressings and bandages ready. She looked at her hand and saw the red stain seeping through. She'd obviously opened something up and the pain was pretty intense, the nerve endings screaming. Getting it redressed again was only going to make it worse. Painkillers were a sensible option, but if she took them all, she's be too doped to think straight in the classes.

"Can I try half?" Sarah didn't look convinced that half would cut it. "I'll take the rest with me and take it if I need it."

"All right. If you're sure?" Mac nodded. "Okay, swallow this, then I'll take a closer look."

Mac did and then lay back with her head on the back of the couch and closed her eyes again. Sarah set to work cutting off the old bandage and gently peeling off the dressing. Sarah gently cleaned up the wound, redressed it, and bandaged it. "How are you going?"

"Okay. Thanks for that." Mac blew out a breath. "Sorry."

"Sorry for what, love?"

"Rushing and not being careful. Now we're going to be late."

"We'll be okay, it's only a few minutes. Do you want to stay home?"

Mac shook her head. "No. I'm good to go."

"Sure?"

"Yes, thanks."

They stood up together. Mac took a deep breath and nodded. "Okay."

It was a quiet trip in to the hospital. They pulled up in the car park and Sarah turned in her seat. "You're sure you're okay?"

Mac smiled gently and waved her hand slightly. "Yep. I just gave myself a reminder to go steady and let Tony help today."

"And you'll take the other tablet if you need it?"

Mac patted her pocket. "Yes, I will."

"Okay, then. I guess I'll see you for the morning break."

"I'm looking forward to it already."

They leaned over and kissed before heading off out their respective doors and into the day ahead.

Mac had another half an hour before the class started, so she headed over to find Tony and to make sure that everything was all set for the practical part later in the morning.

John had dropped off the extinguishers fully charged for the next round of safety classes. As part of her assistant's role, Tony would help Mac recharge the extinguishers in the afternoon, ready for the following day.

Mac walked around the corner of the building to see Tony lining up the extinguishers. He was in his own personally issued turnout gear, shining with newness, minus the helmet, which he'd laid on the ground nearby. When he'd come to the station to be sized for the gear, he'd signed up to join as a volunteer. He was so excited, and Mac was proud that what she was doing at the hospital had convinced him to join up.

"Well look at you, Mr. Felucio! Don't you look awesome."

Tony spun around and blushed "Hey, Mac. Cool, huh?"

"You bet. You look great. How does it feel?"

"Awesome. I want to thank you—you inspired me. I can't wait for training to start. Will you be doing any of the training?"

Mac laughed. "Probably. We share it around. I can assure you, you'll be sick of me soon enough. Seriously though, I'm really glad you decided to join up. I think you'll make a great firefighter."

"Hey, did you see? They put my name on the coat. How cool is that? Can't wait 'til the other fellas see it."

"You never know, maybe you might inspire some of them to join up too."

"Hey, yeah, wouldn't that be great?"

"It sure would." Mac nodded at the equipment set out. "I see you've got it all set up, ready to go."

"Uh-huh. I've got the pan, fuel, drip torch, and the extinguishers ready. What else do you need?"

"How about a fire blanket?"

"Okay, there's one in the truck. I'll bring it over."

Mac touched him briefly on the shoulder. "Thanks, Tony, and thanks for helping out this week. I really appreciate it."

Tony looked at the dirt and blushed and kicked a few pebbles with his new boots. "You were amazing the other week. When you pulled those guys out? I couldn't believe it. And I was such a prick when I first joined the classes. But then I saw how cool it was, and you picked *me* to help out, even though I gave you a hard time. I figured helping you out was the least I could do, to say thanks for giving me a chance."

"Well, looks like we've helped each other then, so let's call it even, hey?"

"Even it is." He gestured towards Mac's hands. "Are they sore?"

Mac leaned in in a confidential whisper. "Hurts like a bitch, but don't tell anyone I said that."

Tony winked at her and tapped his nose. "Gotcha."

Mac looked at her watch. It was time to head inside and get the formal part of the safety sessions started. "Okay, Tony. See you in a bit."

"I'll be here."

Mac made her way inside to the conference room. Her hand was still sore, but it was settling down into a dull throbbing pain, which was manageable. She set the machine up for the presentation and opened her notes. People started to slowly wander in and take a seat. A few who had come to know Mac gave her a wave when they saw her.

Very quickly, the room was full, with a few latecomers having to stand at the edges. It was Mac's biggest class yet. She noticed a lot of the maintenance and laundry staff had turned up and thought she might even have caught a glimpse of Tony up the back. Mac decided to turn the lights down and make a start before the butterflies kicked into gear at the thought of facing such a large group. She smoothed down her jacket, straightened her shoulders, and took a deep breath. She looked up and favoured the audience with a smile.

"I'd like to thank you all for taking time out of your day to attend the annual fire safety education classes. This morning's session will be in two parts. The first part will be here, and we'll go through some of the principles of fire, fire behaviour, and fire safety, and then we'll make our way outside to the front of the facilities buildings for the practical component, to wrap it all up. I know and appreciate that a lot of you are fitting this in with shifts, so I will do my utmost to keep to time. If you have any questions, or if there's something that doesn't make sense, please let me know and I'll do my best to answer. I will also make myself available at the end if anyone wants to come over and have a chat about what we'll go through here today." Mac scanned the audience. "Are there any questions before we get started?"

A hand went up from the east wing doorway. "Excuse me, Lieutenant James?"

Mac shaded her eyes in an attempt to look past the bright overhead stage lights to see who wanted her attention, only to discover that it was the hospital's chief of staff asking the question.

"Yes, Chief?"

The chief started to walk down the aisle towards the front of the room. "If you could humour me for just a minute, I have a brief announcement I'd like to make, if that's okay?"

Mac nodded and waved for him to take the floor. She moved to stand off to the side.

"Actually, this involves you too, Lieutenant."

Mac's eyebrows went up in surprise. She looked briefly out into the audience and spied Sarah standing in the doorway, along with Chief O'Reilly and John. Her mouth grew dry, instantly knowing that something was afoot.

The chief of staff cleared his throat—not that he needed to, as you could have heard a pin drop in the room with all eyes keenly focused to the front.

"Not that long ago, as most of you know, the laundry caught on fire. We all got to see first-hand how to put fire-safety education into play. Many of you were there helping out, either directly with the fire, or indirectly by dealing with those people involved. I want to express my deep appreciation and gratitude to each and every one of you for how you handled yourselves on that day, and the days succeeding it. You did both yourselves and this hospital proud in your undertakings. I would like to call on the managers from Emergency, ward three, and the burns unit to come down to the front. In addition, I would like to pay tribute to the men and women of the local fire station, who came so swiftly to our aid and contained the danger before it could become a much larger disaster. Chief, if you and your colleague would care to join us out the front too, please?"

To much applause and cheering, Chief O'Reilly and John made their way down to the front to stand next to Mac, along with Sarah and the unit managers from the burns unit and ward three.

The chief of staff waved to the audience for quiet. "As you know, two men were trapped inside that fire. Both of these men are family men. Their families are here today and would like to say thank you to you all, for being there and for helping their men the way that you did." The chief extended his hand to the families, inviting them forward.

The audience clapped and cheered. Once again, the chief raised his hands for quiet. "They especially would like to say thank you to Lieutenant Mackenzie James, who risked all to bring them out. Chief O'Reilly, Mrs. Chesterfield, and Mrs. Lee would like to make a presentation, in recognition of Lieutenant James's actions that day."

Mrs. Chesterfield stepped forward holding a box. The chief stepped in front of Mac, opened the box, and withdrew a meritorious award, pinning it on Mac's navy suit coat. The chief saluted her and stepped back. Mrs. Chesterfield hugged Mac and kissed her on the cheek. Finally, Mrs. Lee stepped up, with her young family, to envelop Mac in a group hug. Mrs. Lee whispered into Mac's ear, "I can never thank you enough for saving our Jimmy. You will be forever honoured and remembered in our family. Thank you."

The smallest of the Lee children, a tiny doll-like girl in a pink stripped dress, stepped forward to present Mac with a posy of flowers.

Mac knelt down and hugged the child, who clung to Mac's neck with great enthusiasm until her mother pulled her off.

The families returned to their seats at the front of the class. There wasn't a dry eye in the house. Mac turned to the chief and John, who both patted her on the shoulder. Looking down the line past them, she found Sarah, who was clapping and grinning at Mac, tears streaming freely down her face. She stepped forward to Mac and handed her a tissue to wipe the tears that she didn't realize were flowing down her own face.

One by one, the representatives left the stage, to leave Mac standing there alone as quiet descended on the room. Mac cleared her throat, took a deep breath, and looked to the now silent crowd. "I'm deeply grateful and humbled by this morning. To Peter's and Jimmy's families, I thank you. Knowing that we all helped make sure both of your men get to come home to their families…I think everyone in this room would agree, these are the things that we all strive for, and that give us the greatest joy and satisfaction."

Mac took a moment to look at the audience. She looked first at John, and then at Sarah. "I thank you for the honour you have given me this morning. However, the day of the laundry fire was a day of great teamwork. Many hands achieved great things that day. The safety class participants, the hose-and-bucket lines, my colleagues in the fire service, through to the wonderful hospital staff who treated us all with great skill and care. This honour belongs to all. Thank you." Mac bowed her head to the audience and mimed clapping with her bandaged hands, joining the audience applause.

The chief of staff came over and kissed Mac on the cheek. He turned to the audience again. "And now, folks, I think we need to hand the floor back to Lieutenant James, so she can finish her class. Lieutenant, I leave them in your hands." The families, the unit managers, Chief O'Reilly, and John followed the hospital's chief of staff out the door.

Mac put her posy down and gathered herself briefly before turning back to the audience. "Wow, that's a pretty hard act to follow." There were a few good-natured chuckles from the group. "Well, we've had a pretty good example of how important having some basic understanding of fire, fire behaviour, and safety is. So let's dive in to finding out a bit more about it." Mac dimmed the lights and went through the program.

❖

Tony was a very able and willing assistant during the practical session. Mac even spied him demonstrating to one of the kitchen staff orderlies how to bend low and make sweeping actions with the extinguisher. Because it was such a large group to get through, it took until lunchtime before Mac had finished.

Sarah had commandeered a bench by the time Mac met her. She leaned over and kissed Sarah before sitting down. Sarah smiled as Mac tried valiantly to open the container of yoghurt.

Sarah took the container and removed the lid before handing it back.

"Thanks."

"I thought your speech was beautiful this morning. *You* were beautiful."

"Thanks."

Mac's hand holding her spoon was shaking. Sarah placed her hand on Mac's thigh. "You okay?"

Mac nodded.

"Sure?"

A brief smile flickered across her lips. "I just feel a bit overwhelmed. It's why I was hoping we could have lunch outside. People are really lovely, and it's been very nice, but I'm on overload."

Sarah gazed lovingly at Mac, then leaned over and kissed her cheek. "How's your hand going?"

"Fine."

Sarah looked at her with a single raised eyebrow. "How is it really?"

"It hurts."

"Have you taken the other tablet?"

Mac shook her head. "I thought I should have something to eat first. I find when I take them on an empty stomach, it really messes with my head."

"Fair enough. You do seem to be pretty sensitive to them. I might try and get you some different tablets that, hopefully, won't knock you around quite so much."

"Thanks, that would be good."

Sarah's phone rang. She looked at the screen. "It's Jean."

Mac watched Sarah as the call progressed. From Sarah's curt replies and the look of concern etched on her face, she suspected the news was nothing good.

Sarah hung up and Mac asked, "Everything okay with Jean and Thomas?"

Sarah shook her head. "I don't know. Stuff's been happening and she thinks it's Richard—odd phone calls, her mail destroyed...I made her the offer a while back, if she ever wanted to stay at my place, she could. You've seen the security around the place, she'd be safer there than where she is on her own. Anyway, she just asked if the offer was still open."

Mac picked up her water bottle, swirling it thoughtfully in her hands. "Can you drive me home after work?"

"Sure. Is there something you want to pick up?"

"I was just thinking, you might want to spend some time with Jean and Thomas, to help them settle in."

"I would love to spend some time with them and, yes, show them where everything is, but I was hoping we could do it together."

"I don't want to crowd things, or be in the way, or make things awkward. I just thought it might be easier, might be more comfortable for everybody, if I went home."

Sarah shook her head. "I feel most comfortable when I'm with you. How about we stay for one night and help them move in, then if it seems to be going okay, I'll pack some things and we can head back to your place?"

"Okay, if you're sure."

"I'm sure. Now, are you going to finish that yoghurt or not?"

Mac picked up her half-touched container. "Yes, ma'am."

CHAPTER TWENTY-FIVE

On the way home from picking up some groceries, Sarah rang and organized security clearance for Jean and Thomas. She and Mac had not long finished the unpacking when the doorbell sounded, heralding their arrival. Jean stood in the doorway with bags, while Thomas stood behind her with a backpack, carrying Henry in his cat cage. Neither Thomas nor Henry looked very happy.

Jean put her bags on the floor and stepped into Sarah's waiting hug. "Thank you so much for this. I'm really sorry."

Sarah held her close. "It's all right. I'm pleased you're both here. Come on, let's get you inside. Are there any more bags to bring up?"

Jean nodded. "Yes, a couple more in the car."

Sarah turned to Mac. "Do you want to show Thomas where his room is, and I'll help Jean get the other bags?"

"No worries."

Sarah watched as Mac got Thomas's attention and signed, "If you follow me, we'll take your bags into your room and get Henry here settled in. How's that sound?" Thomas nodded in a resigned fashion, which broke Sarah's heart. But she felt a glimmer of hope as Mac put her arm around his tiny shoulders, and together they walked down the hallway to his new room.

She followed Jean to her car. Jean lifted the last bags out of the back seat and closed the door. Standing behind her, Sarah put her hand on Jean's shoulder. "You okay?"

Jean shook her head. Sarah turned her around to enfold her in her arms. When they first arrived, she could see that Jean was trying to be solid and positive for Thomas, but now that they were alone, Jean could let go in safety, to cry freely without needing to maintain the facade of a calm and in-control parent. Sarah held her until the tears finally stilled. As Jean pulled away, Sarah pulled a tissue from her pocket and offered it.

"Thanks, I'm sorry."

"Don't be. I'm glad you've come. I've been worried about you on your own. I'll feel a little bit easier, knowing that you're both here."

"Like I said, maybe I'm making this bigger than it is. The phone calls rattle me, but lately…it's escalating, and I'm not sure but I think a car has been following me around town." Jean looked down intently at the tissue, worrying the corners. "I've learned to trust my instincts over the years. I have no proof, but I think Richard is close by."

"Have you told the police?"

Jean nodded. "Yes, and I told them I was coming to stay at your place. They're going to do some precautionary patrols around here and Thomas's school for the next week or so."

"Does Thomas know?"

"No. I haven't told him. But he's been through this before. You saw his face tonight. He knows something's up. I feel bad that we're crashing in on you and Mac like this, though."

"Don't be. Mac and I talked about it, and it's fine. We're going to stay here tonight. Then, if everyone's okay, we'll head over to Mac's tomorrow and sleep over. She needs her car and some more clothes, so we figured by the time we finished work and picked up everything, we might as well stay. That way, you and Thomas can settle in at your own pace. If you feel worried, we can come back and stay, or you and Thomas can have the run of the place and call it your own. We'll just take it one step at a time, huh?"

Jean threw her arms around Sarah. "Thanks, Sare. I really mean it."

Sarah gave her a squeeze. "All right, well, let's get these bags on up and we can get some dinner going while you and Thomas settle in."

They opened the door to see Mac and Thomas lying on the floor with takeaway flyers spread out in front of them. They were signing back and forth about the various choices. Thomas was jabbing his finger at two different pizza menus, indicating first one sort, then another, shaking his head and smiling.

Sarah put the bags down and shut the door. "What's going on here?"

Mac and Thomas were smiling. Mac pointed to Thomas to go ahead and explain. He sat up and signed, "Mac and I were playing a game, trying to guess what sort of pizza people you are."

"And what sort of pizza people do you think we are?"

"I'm barbecued beef boy. Mac's a classic Hawaiian. Mum's seafood delight, and Mac said that you're a spicy super supreme, but I think you're more a chicken delight."

Jean burst out laughing and signed back, "I'm sure you're both right."

Mac added, "Thomas and I thought that as we're all together for dinner, we could make it into a pizza party."

"Why not?" Sarah agreed. "What do you think, Jean, you up for pizza?"

"I think it sounds perfect."

Mac nodded at Thomas. "How about Thomas and I order the pizzas while you two unpack?"

Half an hour later, they were sitting at the table with pizza boxes in front of them. Mac and Thomas had set the table, Mac showing Thomas how to fold the napkins into little hats.

Jean touched Thomas on the shoulder. "You guys did a great job. Look at the fancy napkins, who did those?"

Thomas sat up with a big smile. "We did. Do you like them?"

"They're splendid. What pizzas did you order?"

Thomas demanded, "Guess!"

Sarah could smell barbecued beef and figured the little beef boy got his choice. "Barbecued beef?"

"Yep—your turn, Mum."

"Is there a seafood delight?"

"Yes!"

Sarah looked on the table as she sipped her water. There were three pizza boxes. "What's the third one?"

"It's you, Aunt Sarah. It's chicken delight."

Sarah spat her water all over the table as the others laughed.

The pizza party was a hit, with everyone feeling full and relaxed. Mac had saved the prawns from her seafood pizza. "Hey, Thomas, how about we see if Henry would like a prawn for a treat and we can see if our trick worked?"

Jean and Sarah looked at each other. Sarah turned to Thomas. "What trick?"

"Mac said to put a bit of butter on his paws and one of my jumpers on the floor near his bed. Mac said it might help him settle in and not be frightened. And we made him a day bed too. Come and see."

They all traipsed off to Thomas's room. Henry had dragged Thomas's jumper halfway into his bed and was contentedly curled up on it, purring. "Mac said to let him stay in here tonight. Then we can open the doors up and let him explore tomorrow, when he feels braver after a good night's sleep." Thomas walked over to the window and pulled back the curtain. Sitting on the wide windowsill was a cat hammock bed. "See? We made it when you two were out at the car. That's Henry's new daytime bed in the sun."

Jean smiled. "I have to say, it looks like you two thought of everything. Henry's a lucky boy."

Sarah smiled at Mac and Thomas. "I wouldn't mind a cat hammock for myself. What a terrific idea."

Thomas looked at Mac. She winked at him, and he nodded back, smiling.

Jean ran her hand lovingly across the top of Thomas's head. "All right, young man. I think it might be time for you to clean your teeth and for you and Henry to say goodnight. What do you think?"

"Can I read?"

"One book."

Thomas looked at Mac and threw her a very dramatic wink. Mac touched her nose in reply. They obviously had cooked up something between them.

Leaving Jean and Thomas to get ready for bed, Mac and Sarah went out to clear the table. Jean emerged twenty minutes later, walked straight over to Mac, and gave her a big hug. "Thank you for making Thomas's night so special. And by the way—he loves his Buzz Lightyear light."

Mac blushed. "I'm glad."

Sarah was frowning. "Okay. I'll ask. What's a Buzz Lightyear light?"

Jean laughed. "It's a headlamp light, shaped like the character, Buzz. You twist his arm and the light comes on."

"Ha, sounds like some of the footballers that come into Emergency some nights…"

❖

"How are the new pain tablets?"

Mac was lying on her back with Sarah at her side with her head snuggled into Mac's neck and shoulder.

"Mm, much better thank you. My head feels clearer."

"Good. Thank you, for what you did for Thomas tonight. It broke my heart when I saw how miserable he was at the door, but I think it would be fair to say that he ended up having a fun night."

"We put some chocolates on Jean's pillow too. You can't go too wrong with chocolate."

"How very true, my love. You are an amazing woman, Mackenzie James. Do you know that?"

Mac shook her head. "Not really. I just tried to take his mind off things. I think the amazing person is Jean, having to do this in the first place. It's not right. My heart bleeds for them both."

"I know what you mean. I feel so helpless."

Mac kissed her on the top of the head. "Well, I think letting them stay here is a great idea. What does this Richard creep look like, anyway? Maybe I could drive around town in one of the fire trucks, and if I spotted him, then I could accidentally on purpose run over him?"

"Actually, that's not a bad idea."

"Running over him with the truck?"

"No, silly. I should ask Jean if she has a recent picture of him. We could leave one downstairs at the desk and the school will probably need one too. I'll talk to her in the morning. How's your hand feeling?"

"It's not too bad. Signing with barbecue boy worked it out a bit, but those new tablets make the pain manageable."

"Good. More classes tomorrow?"

"Mm, although we must be getting close to the end of it. The group this morning was huge—even with my helpers, it took us longer than I wanted to get through them all—but they seemed okay with it."

"Well, the feedback seems to be all good. Lots of people have said they've enjoyed it. You know, that's the first time I've ever used an extinguisher. It was kind of fun, really."

"I'm glad. It makes it all worthwhile when I hear things like that. What about your day?"

"Fairly run-of-the-mill stuff, although it's starting to get extra tricky as we're having to juggle the rosters at the minute. We've had some more staff coming down with the flu. I was talking to some other unit managers today, and it's the same all over."

"I'll be sure not to kiss anyone with a sniffle."

"Hey, hot stuff, the only one you should be kissing is *me*. And I'm not sniffling."

Mac lifted her head and kissed Sarah hungrily. Sarah slid over until she was straddling Mac's waist. As Mac broke off for air, she started laughing.

Sarah mock-frowned at her. "What are you laughing at?"

"Mm, chicken delight!"

❖

Breakfast was a fun affair with cheerful banter across the table. Afterwards, while Sarah was in the shower, Mac and Thomas carried the plates out to the kitchen where Jean was washing up. Mac knelt down next to Thomas. "John and I will be coming to your school tomorrow to talk to all the kids about how to be safe around fire. I was wondering, if John or I needed a helper tomorrow, could we count on you to give us a hand?"

Thomas's eyes lit up. "Really?"

"Yes, really. You know the kids better than we do and we'll need some help with some of the equipment too. Would you be okay with that?"

"I can do that." Thomas jumped up and down and threw his arms around Mac, then ran over to Jean. "Mum, Mum, I'm going to be Mac and John's helper tomorrow at school."

"Oh, sweetheart, that sounds very exciting."

Sarah emerged from the bedroom in a dressing gown, a towel wrapped around her hair. "What's going on?"

Thomas, still jumping up and down, told Sarah his exciting news.

"Wow. Well, we better hurry up and get you ready for school so you can tell your friends that tomorrow is going to be a very exciting day for everyone."

Thomas took off running to his room to get ready.

Jean turned to Mac and Sarah. "Who's the chocolate fairy I need to thank?"

Sarah and Mac looked at each other innocently. Folding her arms, Jean looked back at them.

Mac caved, smiling. "It was Thomas. He thought it might be nice if you had a surprise treat for your first night here too. So thank him. If you'll excuse me, I better throw myself in the shower." Mac disappeared down the hallway.

Sarah waved at her. "I'll be there in a minute to help." The sisters finished cleaning the breakfast dishes. "Do you have a recent picture of Richard at all?"

Jean shook her head. "No, but the police do."

"Mac and I were talking last night and wondered what he looked like. I haven't seen him in years. I thought maybe if you had one, we could leave a copy at the office downstairs. Have you thought to give one to the school?"

Jean nodded, frowning slightly. "I thought about it the other day, but forgot to do it. I have a meeting with the principal later in the morning, so I can give her one then. I was thinking I might offer to be a helper at the school for the next couple of weeks. I don't know how much help I'll be, but it will make me feel better being busy and being close by until things settle down again."

"That sounds like a good idea. Whoops—I just heard the shower turn off, that's my cue. Mac can't do her shirt buttons up with her fingers bandaged."

Jean grinned openly at Sarah. "Oh, you poor thing. That sounds like a terrible job."

Sarah threw her sister a cheeky wink. "Very terrible indeed."

Sarah walked into the bedroom to see Mac standing, waiting, clad in only her underwear. She shook her head, smiling appreciatively at Mac's sculptured body. Yep, just plain terrible. "You ready?"

"Uh-huh."

With no time to linger this morning, Sarah and Mac were soon bidding goodbye to Jean and Thomas and heading out the door. It was a beautiful drive in, the sun beginning to burn off the early morning mist. Mac turned in her seat to face Sarah. "You sure you don't want to stay with Jean and Thomas tonight?"

"I'm sure. They'll be fine. Besides, who's going to get you dressed and undressed?"

"I'll manage."

"And how do you plan on doing that?"

"Well, I can get you to unbutton my sleeves and collar when you drop me off and I can slip the shirt off and on."

"You've thought this through?"

"I have."

"And how will I manage?"

"What do you mean?"

"Well, the bed will be cold, sleeping on my own, and I'll miss my evening and morning fix."

"What do you mean your fix?"

"My fix of undressing and dressing the sexiest firefighter in town. You might manage, but I think I'm addicted, and I'm not sure that *I* would manage quite so well. So if it's okay with you, I'd like to hang on to the habit for a bit longer."

"Oh, well, when you put it like that, I see what you mean. It would be very selfish of me to deny you of that."

"Uh-huh, very selfish."

They were giggling as they pulled into the car park. Mac carefully closed the car door. "I'll see you for lunch."

"I'll see you then. I'll text and let you know how I'm going for time."

A quick kiss later and they were heading off into their day.

Chapter Twenty-six

Mac's class that day was small, and she and Tony finished well ahead of schedule. They used the time to look over the laundry site, with Mac pointing out some of the fire's forensics to Tony. She pointed to the area of origin, the patterns of charring, lines of advancing, and secondary fire, and how different levels of heat affected different types of surfaces. Tony was a very willing listener and asked lots of questions as they went through the burned-out shell.

"I never knew that a fire could tell a story like that. It's amazing. I thought burned was burned, y'know? But it really is a story in itself when you point it out like that."

"As part of your training you'll be shown some things to look for at the scene of a fire. As a firefighter, you not only have to put fires out, but you'll also sometimes play a very important role in identifying evidence and ensuring that the scene and the evidence are preserved for further forensic investigations."

"I can't wait 'til the training starts next month. I'm so excited— I've got to tell you, I love learning all this new stuff. I can't thank you enough, Mac."

"Well, we're pleased to have you on board."

Mac's phone sounded. She looked down. It was a message from Sarah. *Can't make lunch. Sorry. Short-staffed. Maybe coffee later? Sxxx*

Mac texted back. *No problems love. Catch up later. Mxxx*

She looked at her watch: it was close to lunch. After thanking Tony for the morning, she went past the cafeteria and picked out two lunches. She dropped Sarah's off at her desk and took hers outside to eat in the warmth of the sun.

As Mac had time, she decided to visit Peter and Jimmy. Peter was on one of the general wards. She walked in to find him dressed and sitting on the edge of the bed, with his wife in a chair next to him.

Peter stood as soon as she entered the room, then stepped forward and wrapped his arms around her. "I was hoping I'd see you before I went home. I can't thank you enough, Lieutenant James." Peter pulled back and his eyes were moist. "Thank you doesn't seem enough." Peter's wife handed him a tissue. "My apologies. Lieutenant James, this is my wife, Bonnie."

Bonnie stood and threw her arms around Mac, just as her husband had. "Thank you for what you did. God bless you." Peter offered Mac a second chair next to the bed.

"It's lovely to see you both again. Please, call me Mac. How're you doing, Peter?"

"I'm good. In fact, we're sitting here waiting for the doctor to sign me out so I can go home. The smoke knocked me about for a bit with a chest infection, but I'm good to go now." Peter sat quietly before shaking his head. "I couldn't breathe. I thought I was a dead man…and then I saw you coming through the smoke towards me."

Bonnie reached over and gently grabbed Mac's arm.

Mac smiled. "How are you sleeping?"

Peter shrugged. "In fits and starts. I close my eyes, and I can still see the flames."

Mac nodded. "It'll probably do that for a little while, but it does get better. Soon enough, I'm sure Bonnie will be poking you in the ribs because you're snoring too loud." Mac reached into the inside pocket of her coat and pulled out a card. She handed the card to Bonnie. "Here are some people who're really good to talk to when you come up against something like the fire. They know what you're both going through. We all use them in the service. They're regular, normal people who are really good at helping you understand why you feel the way you do and how to get through it."

Bonnie looked at Mac's hands. "And what about you? How are you doing?"

Mac nodded and smiled. "I'm doing well. I'm back on modified duties at the minute but hope to be back into full swing soon. What about you?"

Peter looked at Bonnie. "Well, we've been talking about retiring for a while now and we decided that we've just been given a bit of a reminder to stop taking things for granted. So I'm going to go back to work, because I want to finish with confidence, not with fear, and then I'll give my notice. Our daughter lives on the Gold Coast, so we thought we might visit with her and the grandkids for a bit and travel a little after that." Peter leaned forward, put his hand on Mac's shoulder, and looked deep into her eyes. "I don't know how we can ever thank you, Mac."

Mac shook her head and smiled. "You just have. Knowing that you're okay and that you're both happy and getting on with things, that's special. If you want to do anything, send me a postcard when you get to the coast."

"We can do that, can't we love?"

Bonnie nodded.

Mac stood. "Well, on that note, I won't hold you up any longer—other than to say, look after each other and take care."

There was a last hug exchanged before Mac took the lift up to the burns unit to see Jimmy. Mac introduced herself to the unit manager who took her briefly aside and explained how Jimmy was doing and, that to see him, she would need to put on a gown and some gloves to reduce the potential of infection.

One of the nurses helped Mac get the gloves over her bandages. She saw Mrs. Lee sitting next to Jimmy's bed, similarly decked out in gown and gloves. As she stepped farther into the room, Mac could hear the gentle hiss of the oxygen, the ticking of the IV pump, and the beeps of the various monitors. Jimmy waved a bandaged hand in recognition.

Mrs. Lee nodded to Mac as she walked to the side of Jimmy's bed. "Hey there, Jimmy."

"Hey, Lieutenant James. Thanks for coming." Jimmy's voice was raspy and he started to cough.

Mac raised a finger to her lips. "It's okay, try not to talk too much. I know what it's like when you chew a bit too much smoke.

And besides, I'm sure the nurse will only come over and rouse on us both."

The nurse in the room smiled at Mac in agreement. Jimmy smiled briefly, nodding in appreciation of Mac's understanding.

"And please, call me Mac. I talked to your doctor outside and he said that you're doing really well, and that the skin grafts are all looking good."

Jimmy nodded. Mac could see tears welling in his eyes. Putting her hand gently on Jimmy's shoulder, she caught and held Jimmy's gaze. "I know it's tough, but you're one of the strongest men I've ever met. I met your lovely family yesterday, and I know that they can't wait to have you back home with them."

Jimmy nodded.

"You'll get through this. I'm going to give your wife my card, so that when you come out of hospital, you and I are going to sit down, and we're going to share a wine or a beer, or something special. And we can make a toast to celebrate. Deal?"

"Deal. Thank you."

"You're welcome. Hurry up and get out of here, huh?" Mac winked at him and made her farewells. Once outside the room, she took the gown off and tossed the gloves. Her next plan was to pick up two coffees and see if Sarah could squeeze in a five-minute coffee break.

Mac walked down into Emergency's reception. She caught Sarah's eye, and Sarah waved, acknowledging she was there. The nurse working the desk told Mac that she could wait in Sarah's office and pointed it out. Mac made her way down the hall.

Sarah's office was neat and tidy and stylish in a subtle, unpretentious way. She had a soft muted piece of art on the wall and a metal horse sculpture on a corner coffee table, counterbalancing the tools of her trade in the other corner: a light box, a computer, and an anatomical figure, next to a side table hosting a small neat stack of medical journals. Mac sat down in the visitor's chair and sipped her coffee.

A few minutes later Sarah breezed in and kissed the top of Mac's head on the way past as she headed for her chair. She sat down with an audible grunt. "What a day! Thanks for the coffee, you're an angel."

"Another busy one, huh?"

"Mm, I had to loan some staff to the high dependency and surgical units who're really suffering with staff out sick. Tomorrow they're going to have to call in temps. What are you up to this afternoon? Are you finished for the day?"

"Pretty much. What about you? Looks like you might be here awhile yet."

"'Fraid so, love. I've got a good couple more hours here, I would think."

"That's no problem. Could I borrow your car keys? I can duck down to the station and finish my reports and some stuff for the school visit tomorrow, then swing back to see how you're going. How does that sound?"

"Sounds like a plan. And thank you for my lunch—it was yummy."

"My pleasure." Mac took Sarah's now empty coffee cup and tossed it in the bin. Sarah stood up and stretched before coming over and draping her arms around Mac's neck. Mac leaned in to languidly kiss her before easing back to rest forehead to forehead with her.

Sarah closed her eyes, as if to hang on to this little isolated bubble in time for a small moment more. Finally, she lifted her head up and brushed Mac's fringe from her eyes. "Do you like dancing?"

Mac shrugged. "I haven't really done much. But I'm willing to give it a go."

Sarah gently kissed her. "I can see a night with a fire going, nice wine, some music, in each others arms…yep, it has potential."

"I hope you also see yourself wearing shin guards and steel-capped shoes for protection against two left feet."

"Yeah, I was actually thinking more along the lines of no clothes at all."

Mac groaned. "How long 'til you can knock off?"

Sarah laughed. "Not soon enough. Hang on, I'll get you the keys."

With a jingle Sarah located them in the desk drawer and handed them over. "If I finish up early, I'll text you."

Mac kissed her. "Okay. See you soon, twinkletoes."

❖

They ended up having a what-if dinner. As Sarah explained to Mac, you looked at what you had in the fridge and in the cupboard, and you put them on the bench and said to yourself: *What if* I put that and that together? It was a fun thing she'd invented when, as a student, there either wasn't enough food in the house, or she was too tired to be bothered cooking a proper meal. The rules were simple—the idea was to pick items that went together and took the least possible time to cook.

Mac poured them each a glass of wine. She'd lit the fire earlier to take the chill off the room while Sarah was debating what to throw together in the what-if pot. Mac sat, curled up on the couch, while Sarah squatted on the floor looking through Mac's music collection. It turned out they had similar tastes, and Sarah selected a classic, Joni Mitchell's *Blue*.

Sarah loaded the CD into the player, then took a sip of her wine before putting her glass down. She held out her hand, inviting Mac to join her.

Smiling, Mac took a last sip herself before rising from the couch to step into Sarah's arms. Their bodies gently melded along their lengths. As they gazed into each other's eyes, the rest of the world dissipated, unnoticed, into the background. With lips full of gentle adoration, love, and wonder, Mac feasted leisurely on the warm depths of Sarah's mouth, as Sarah's hips started to move to the rhythm.

Mac had no idea what she was doing. Closing her eyes, she let her hips mirror Sarah's movements, relinquishing command of her limbs, letting them liquefy, to follow wherever Sarah took her.

Sarah's hands wrapped around Mac's waist. Seemingly of their own accord, they slid their way up under Mac's cotton top to gently lift it off and away from her body, leaving her half-naked. Sarah's hands slid up her ribs to cup her breasts, then dipped to circle her waist again. Sarah lit a fire inside Mac, and she was burning to touch and taste all in kind. Mac quickly disposed of Sarah's clothing.

Flesh melded with flesh, hips swaying in perfect unison, as the music wove its magic all around them. Time ceased to exist as they lost themselves in each other. The language of taste and touch transcending the need for words. Breaths quickened and eased, only to quicken again moments later as they took their time to discover and to tease each other to the limits of sanity and pleasure.

At some point the album had played through as they lay in each other's arms in front of the fire. The only sound to be heard was the gentling of heightened breaths against the hiss and crackle of the flames. Sarah reached over and snared the wine glasses. They sat up to drink, Sarah resting her back against Mac's chest, her head on Mac's shoulder as they stared lazily into the fire.

Sarah's fingers trailed along the length of Mac's thigh. "You dance pretty good for a two-left-footed lieutenant."

Mac smiled. "You made it easy to melt into you. I just went wherever you took me."

"Are you always so compliant?"

"Only when it suits me."

"Oho, I hear a challenge!"

Mac chuckled. "Some people might say be careful what you wish for."

Sarah sipped her wine and hummed in pleasure.

Mac carefully adjusted her legs so they weren't directly facing the fire. Sarah picked up on it. "Too hot?"

Mac nodded. "Just a bit."

"Well, how about we damp the fire down and head off to bed, love? It's been a long day, for both of us, and something tells me tomorrow will be more of the same."

A few minutes later they were snuggled into the bed. Mac traced the outline of Sarah's eyebrow, softly sliding her feather-light touch along the lines of her cheekbone and jaw. "Did you manage to catch up with Jean today at all?"

"She called this afternoon. She's got some pictures of Richard. She said she'll bring a copy to school to give to you tomorrow. The principal has agreed she can stay and be a helper at the school until things settle back down again."

"Has there been any more news?"

"Nothing much. The police have managed to find out that he hired a navy-blue Ford sedan a couple of weeks ago. They have a notice to keep an eye out for him, but nothing solid to date."

"Do you think it'll blow over?"

"I don't know, love, I truly don't."

"Well, I might be able to offer a brief distraction. Let's plan that family dinner we spoke about. Martha said she didn't mind which weekend. I know it's probably a bit tricky at the minute, with rosters and the like, but do you want to see what weekend suits you? I'll mention it to Maree and Terri tomorrow and get them to look at their diaries too. I thought I might head on over to the refuge in the morning and help out for an hour before work, if that's okay."

"What time do you usually go?"

"Usually I head out early and go for a run, but I think I might take my time and drive tomorrow, so about six. I'll be home by seven."

"If I'm awake in time, would you mind if I came too?"

Mac frowned slightly and tilted her head. "Don't you want to sleep in?"

Sarah shrugged. "I can stay if you want to go on your own, that's okay."

Mac shook her head. "No, that wasn't what I meant. That came out all wrong. I would love it if you wanted to come, but if you want to sleep in, that's fine too. There's no pressure or expectation either way. I would be happy if you came, but I'd be just as happy knowing you were catching up on some much-needed sleep."

Sarah yawned and confessed. "I am tired. How about we see if I'm awake in the morning and take it from there?"

Mac smiled and kissed the top of her head. "I can deal with that. Good night, babe."

"'Night love."

Chapter Twenty-seven

Sarah was dead to the world when Mac got up, so she carefully tucked the covers around her and let her sleep. Mac set the table for breakfast, leaving a note next to Sarah's cup. She slipped on some clothes and headed out the door. As she drove to the refuge, Mac thought how nice it felt to be getting back to a semi-normal routine. It was even nicer to know that there was someone waiting at home for her. *God, I've missed that.*

Martha was right. She was starting to live again, and it felt good. Tina would always be a part of her, but Sarah had her heart now. Before Sarah, she'd never gave much thought to the future. *I am the luckiest woman alive.* Mac pulled up and got out of the car, wandering over to the cat and kitten house to find Maree inside the door.

She was greeted with a hug. "Hey, gorgeous, good to see you."

Mac hugged her back. "Good to be seen! Would you like me to do the babies room?" She nodded towards the kitten room.

"That'd be great, thanks, hon. You happy to do run six too? I know someone who'd love to see you."

"I'd love to. And I can't wait to see her either."

"How are the hands?"

"Not too bad. I brought some gloves to go over the top, so I don't get them wet. I should be okay."

"All right, well, Terri's over with the old dogs, so just give her a yell if you want a hand. Just take it easy, huh?"

"Yup. Will do. Oh, hey, I was wondering if you and Terri might like to come to dinner at Martha's, one weekend soon. For a bit of a family meal. You guys, Sarah, Jean and Thomas, maybe John?"

"That sounds great. I'll check with Ter, but count us in. We could bring dessert."

"Perfect. Okay, just let me know what dates work for you. I better get going. See you afterwards."

Run six was pretty quiet. The hunting dog had been taken up by a young farmer and the old cattle dog had been adopted by a family in town. The little terrier mix was still there, but it pleased Mac immensely to see that he was no longer frenetically pacing. One of the girls had given him a rawhide bone, and he was lying on the floor, happily chewing away.

Mac went in to clean his pen. He never once let go of the chewy bone, allowing Mac to come up and pat him, while parading around the kennel with it like a king. Mac laughed, enjoying his newly discovered sense of ponce. With building excitement, Mac went next door to Nell's run.

Nell came flying over, leaping into midair, straight into Mac's arms, her tail wagging hysterically with joy as she licked Mac's face frantically. Mac laughed as she tried to dodge the energetic tongue. Kneeling on the ground, she put Nell down and asked Nell to sit, which she dutifully tried but was too excited to hold for very long. "What say you let me clean up here, my lovely, then we go for a walk and burn some of this energy off, huh?"

In no time, Mac had the kennel spick and span. She slipped the lead on, and they circumnavigated the grounds before heading to the play pen, where they played for about ten minutes, followed up by a few *sit, stay,* and *come* routines. Nell had taken to the training really well, responding with enthusiasm, happy to please, performing like a champion. Mac looked at her watch. Offering Nell a last treat, she slipped the lead back on and returned the happy pup to the kennel. She had not long settled Nell back in when she met up with Terri on the path headed for the house.

"Hey, chick!

"Hey, Ter. How's it going?"

"It's all good. How about you? How's your grilled bits?"

Mac laughed. "They're good, thanks. I see you've found homes for some of the inmates."

"Uh-huh. You noticed run six lost some of the regulars. The people who took them on were really lovely. It's been a good week. We've found homes for several cats and dogs, and we haven't had too many new ones come in, so all in all, pretty good. What about you, how's work going?"

Mac nodded. "Not too bad. I'm still sort of on light duties for a bit, 'til I get clearance"—Mac held up her hands—"but it's good to be back doing stuff."

Terri shook her head and put her arms around Mac's shoulders. "And to think you've only really been incapacitated for a handful of days."

"I know, I'm hopeless. I don't do sitting around very well."

"Maree reckons you've got ants in your pants. God help us all, if you ever get seriously hurt or sick. I think we might have to put you into a medically induced coma, just so you can cope."

Mac laughed. "You could be right."

"Can you stay for a coffee?"

Mac shook her head. "Not this morning. I want to get home and see if Sleeping Beauty is awake yet."

"Okay, well, give her our love. Will we see you tomorrow?"

"Yep. I'll see you in the morning." Mac jogged back to the ute and headed home, humming all the way down the road.

When she got home, she heard the shower running, and it sounded like Sarah was humming too. Mac smiled. She was tempted to join her but knew that would lead to both of them being late for work. Instead, she heated the water for coffee, then got some bread out and thought about having a go at making scrambled eggs. She figured the protein would offer sustained energy throughout the day, which they were both probably going to need, what with Mac running around after heaps of kids and Sarah more than likely to have another flat-out day in Emergency.

Mac opened up the fridge and pondered. Scrambled eggs didn't look too hard when Sarah made them. Heat the pan, a daub of butter, eggs, some milk, mix it up. *I can do this.* Mac got everything ready. First, the butter. Check. Then the eggs. How many? She'd start with four…no, hang on, five, she liked odd numbers. Okay, now mixing, mixing. Shit! Milk. How much? A small splash. Easier to add than take away.

Mac wiggled her hips, doing a little happy dance by the stove.

"What on earth are you doing?"

"Wha?" Startled, Mac jumped, spinning around to face the voice, the momentum making a piece of egg fly across the room to land wetly at Sarah's feet.

Sarah looked down at the egg and then up at a chagrined Mac at the stove.

"Sorry, didn't hear you come in."

"Obviously. Are you cooking?"

"I'm trying…I'm sort of making this up as I go, kind of."

Sarah walked up behind her, wrapped her arms around her waist, and kissed her neck. "That's very sweet of you. Are you scrambling, or making an omelette?"

"Scrambling. Why?"

"Then you need to stir it some more, babe. Like this." Sarah held Mac's spoon hand and helped mix some more. Mac was incredibly conscious of Sarah's warm breath on the side of her neck, her breasts and pelvis pressing against her back. Sarah nibbled playfully on her ear. "Do you always do little dances when you're cooking?"

Mac chuckled. "No. I don't cook, remember? Which probably explains why I don't dance either."

Sarah kissed her neck again. "Well, we can fix both of those."

Mac closed her eyes and groaned, leaning back into Sarah's caresses.

Sarah poked her in her uninjured side. "Aha, keep your eyes on the eggs, lover."

"Cruel, you're just cruel."

"And loving it. Do you want me to toast some bread?"

"Yes, please. Forgot about that. How long do I cook this for?"

Sarah leaned over her shoulder and looked in the pan. "I reckon by the time the toast is done, you can pull it off the stove."

"Okay."

Half an hour later, as they took their time over coffee, Mac smiled to herself, amused that eating a meal took far less time than what it did to make it.

Sarah wrapped her hands around her mug. "How did this morning go?"

"Really good. The girls both send their love, by the way. I mentioned the dinner. They're going to check to see what weekend is good for them, but they'd love to come. They offered to bring dessert, so whatever you do, make sure you save some space at the end of dinner. Their desserts will blow your mind."

"I can't wait. How was Nell?"

"Well, I won't have to have a bath from the chin up. She jumped into my arms as soon as I got there and licked me like crazy."

"The dog does have good taste. I guess she missed you."

"Yeah, I guess she did. I know I missed her. She's starting to grow too, now that she's got some condition on board. She's not going to be a big dog, probably only a bit over medium sized, but her coat is shiny and her eyes are bright. She looks great. The girls have done a super job."

Sarah reached across the table and held Mac's hand. "That was a lovely breakfast, thank you. And thank you for letting me sleep in, and the note. And I have to say, you've got it all wrong."

Mac frowned. The note she'd left simply said *I love you.*

Sarah smiled at her and leaned over and kissed her on the nose. "I love *you* more."

Mac smiled. "More?"

"Uh-huh. The most, in fact."

"Is that right?"

"Oh, most definitely."

"It seems you have a competitive streak, Dr. Macarthur."

Sarah offered a cheeky smile. "Oh yes. I play to win…when the stakes are right."

"I'll have to remember that."

Sarah laughed. "Come on, into the shower with you. I'll change your dressings when you come out."

Mac got up from the table. "So the eggs were okay?"

"They were lovely."

Mac smiled. "That's the first time I've ever done that."

Sarah's eyebrows went up in surprise. "The first time you've made scrambled eggs?"

"Yep."

"Well then, they were superb and I feel honoured."

Mac chuckled. "You should. For once I didn't set the fire alarm off."

Sarah laughed and swatted her behind. "Go on, get out of here."

After a quick shower, Mac sat on the edge of the bed as Sarah knelt to look at her legs.

"They're coming along nicely. We might try airing them without the bandages on the weekend, if you like."

"That sounds nice."

Sarah ran her hand gently down Mac's side. "Okay, let's look at your stitches. Mm, another day or two, and we can probably take them out. Nice and clean. That's good."

"They're starting to get itchy. That means its healing, doesn't it?"

"Uh-huh."

Next Sarah unwrapped Mac's hands. The right hand was healing well, but the left hand was still marginally weepy from the setback earlier in the week. "How are they feeling?"

"Not too bad. I can do a bit more with them, which is good. But they're still really tender, especially the left one."

"Hmm. How often are you taking the tablets?"

"I take one in the morning, and one when I get home."

Sarah nodded. "Let's finish up here then and get you dressed and on your way. How many kids will you have today?"

"I'm not sure, maybe thirty."

"Are you ready?"

"Can you ever be ready for that many kids?"

Sarah chuckled. "I suppose not. Come on, lover, it's time for you to get your gear on and time for my morning fix."

❖

Sarah was in her office finishing up the weekly meeting with her senior staff. Don stayed behind and was showing Sarah the roster for the following week. He shook his head. "It's the best I can do for the minute. I'm guessing that we'll probably just have to take each shift as it comes until this flu runs its course. The people down the bottom in green have indicated that they can do extra shifts during the week if they're needed. We've got four out at the minute, but two should hopefully be back on board early next week. Fingers crossed no one else goes down with it. Between those out and those we lend around the place, it's getting tricky to find enough to go around without putting too much strain on the ones who are still here."

"I know. We'll just keep going as best we can. You're doing a great job."

Sarah's phone rang just as Don left the room. "Sarah Macarthur speaking."

There was nothing but silence on the other end.

"Hello?"

Sarah could hear breathing.

"Hello?"

A deep-throated chuckle echoed down the line.

"Can I help you?"

"I don't think so. You've done more than enough already."

The voice was clearly male. "What do you mean? Hello? Who is this?"

Whoever rang, hung up.

Sarah shook her head and put the phone back in its cradle.

Her mobile sounded. It was a message from Colleen, wanting to know if she was available for lunch. Sarah texted back that she would meet up in half an hour in the cafeteria. Returning the phone to her pocket, her fingers brushed against the note that Mac had left her this morning. She read it again. *I love you.* Sarah stared at the note. No one had ever left her anything like this before. *But then again, I was never with anyone long enough to get one, I suppose.* She carefully folded the note and placed it back into her pocket, smiling.

Alice stuck her head in the office door. "Sarah, you got a minute? Don wants to know if you can offer a second opinion on a patient that's just come in."

"Sure. Lead on."

Sarah followed Alice to a cubicle where several people were gathered around a bed, looking down at a man's hand. Sarah stepped into the circle, surprised to see a rather large lizard biting down very firmly on three of the man's fingers.

Don looked up at Sarah. "We're not quite sure of the best way to separate these two. Mr. Johnson here doesn't want the lizard harmed, but the lizard is not so caring and refuses to let go. Got any ideas?"

"Ice packs."

Don looked at her like she'd gone mad. "Come again?"

"Put some ice packs in a towel and wrap it around the lizard. It will make his metabolism slow down. When he gets dopey, you can prise him off. Then put him in a laundry bag until he can go home. Mr. Johnson will need some pretty strong antibiotics too—it'll be a dirty bite."

Don nodded to Alice who went off in search of the ice packs. "I take it you've done this before?"

"Sort of. One of the guys down the hall from me, back in our uni days, had snakes and lizards as pets. I was the only one on the floor with a fridge, so he used to borrow some space in it sometimes to anaesthetize his little friends."

"Nice one."

"You guys okay here if I take a lunch break?"

"No problem."

Sarah squared away her paperwork and joined Colleen in the cafeteria. "How's baby world?"

"Baby world is booming. It's like popcorn upstairs at the minute."

"So what are you doing, taking a break?"

"So far all the cases have been straightforward and the team are on top of it. There's one lady I'm keeping an eye on, but I figure I've got another hour or two yet, so I thought I'd grab lunch while I could. How's things with you?"

"Steady. Which is good. How's your team faring with staff this week? We've got four out and some on loan. We're stretched, but we're okay, compared to some of the others."

"Yeah, same here. Looks like the medical ward, ICU, and high dependency have copped it the hardest."

"I think we need to lobby again at the next board meeting to provide annual flu shots for staff. If I raise it, can I count on your support?"

"Absolutely. I know it's not a hundred per cent protection, but if it can give us the edge, then surely that's a win in anyone's court."

"Great."

"How's Mac doing? I saw her yesterday, so I guess she's back at work, right?"

"She's sort of on modified duties. She's giving classes again, but she needs someone to help out with the lifting and physical demonstration parts. Everything's improving steadily, which is good. Her hands are taking the longest."

"How's she dealing with that?"

"She seems to be okay, but I can tell it's starting to bug the hell out of her."

"That's understandable. I know it would drive me crazy. How's Jean doing?"

Sarah filled her in on the latest news.

Colleen shook her head. "You know, I complain about Brian, but I know I'm very lucky. He's a good man. He's loving, kind, passionate, and he's a good father. Sure, he has his faults and he does things that drive me around the twist, but so do I. God knows, you and I see plenty of people who aren't nearly so lucky in who they end up with."

Sarah was folding up her napkin. "Well, I think I'm lucky too. I don't know how, but you know what? I don't care."

Colleen looked at her with her head on the side. "In all the years I've known you, I don't think I have ever seen you look so…content. You look happy and peaceful but, most of all, content."

Sarah rested her chin in her hand. "I am, Colly. I really am. A couple of months ago I would never ever have contemplated living with someone. Now, I can't bear the thought of not being with Mac. I don't care where we are, as long as it's together. It's weird. Everything used to revolve around work. Now, I can't wait to get home. And some mornings…" Sarah felt her face go red. "Let's just say it takes great strength of character to get here on time."

Colleen laughed. "Ah, love. There is nothing else quite like it in the whole world."

"You got that right."

❖

Mac and John parked the truck back at the station a bit after two. It had been a busy—but fun—morning at the school. The fire safety classes went well with the games afterwards being an absolute hit, for children and adults alike. There were relay games and target practice with water balloons, finishing with a small group of Safety Buddies deputised to help Miss Kelly, the teacher, in the event of a fire drill. By day's end, everybody had gotten a ride in the fire truck, even the parents.

The class was divided into groups, and each group was given a fire mascot teddy bear to mind. Children were chosen, one from each group, to be the bears' first minders, taking them home at night and sharing fire-safety tips with the family. After being in charge of the mascots for the week, they would select the next week's teddy minders.

After unpacking the truck, Mac and John went into the station's kitchen and made themselves much-deserved hot drinks—Mac had tea, while John had coffee. Martha soon joined them. "So, how did the morning go?"

John laughed "We got monstered. I don't know about Mouse here, but I'm stuffed. It was a heap of fun, but I am spent."

Mac chuckled "I think I'll stick to being a firey—heaps easier, and drier, I might add."

John was laughing merrily away. "Well, you *were* standing in front of the target at the time. Technically, it was a bullseye. Thomas and I pegged you, fair and square."

"I was standing the target back up. That was a cheap shot and you know it."

John was laughing. "Yeah, it was. But it was so worth it. The look on your face was priceless—the kids will be talking about that for weeks. I hope someone got that on camera."

"We'll soon find out. I gave Jean my camera to take a mix of photographs and videos. They're downloading now. What say I put them on a stick, and we'll play it in the meeting room?"

Within minutes Mac had the morning's events playing on the big screen. Chief O'Reilly came down to see what all the noise was about. Mac replayed the files, and pretty soon everyone was in stitches. Martha was dabbing her eyes as John pointed at the screen. "Wait for it, wait for it...*Bam!* Right on the Mouse tail."

Even Mac was laughing. One of the videos showed her walking towards a target that had been knocked down and, in the background, John and Thomas conspiring. As Mac bent to pick up the target, Thomas threw the perfect pitch, hitting Mac fair and square in the seat of her pants with the water balloon. She turned around with a look of absolute shock on her face. The rest of the crowd were cheering and laughing as Mac started to laugh too, wagging her fingers at both of the boys and signing to them, "Just you wait, you two. I am so going to get you back."

Jean had done a wonderful job taking photos of every child in the class participating in the activities. There was a great still of John and Thomas conspiring just before they tagged Mac. To recognize the safety program, there was a special photo of the safety buddies wearing their hats, next to Mac, John, and the truck. Lastly there was Mac's favourite photo, a group shot with kids all over the truck, and the grownups standing in front, everyone sporting huge smiles on their faces.

The chief stood up. "That was far too much fun to be called work, you two. But going by the look on everyone's faces, I would say that the morning was a success. Well done. Lieutenant James, I would like copies of the photos of the safety buddies and the large group, please, on my desk. Officer Bettford, I would suggest that the balloon incident was highly illegal, as play had obviously been suspended, pending equipment adjustments—however I commend you on the accuracy and the teamwork involved. That young man has a good arm for pitching." With that, the chief went back to his office and everyone had another round of chuckling.

Back in her office, Mac made a couple of copies of the photos and videos. She would bring one set home to show Sarah and Jean, and the others she would drop off to the school tomorrow for Miss Kelly, so that each child could have a memento of the day.

Mac had done all she could for the day. She picked up her keys, the files, and the photos and headed off towards home.

❖

Sarah texted to say she was running a bit behind time but hoped to be home for dinner, which left Mac plenty of time to get what she wanted at the shops, including a nice bottle of wine and some Thai takeaway. She was setting the table when Sarah walked in.

"Hey beautiful. How was your day?" Sarah said, smiling.

Mac kissed her and wrapped her arms around her waist. "Today was a fun day. Exhausting, but fun. I've got some footage to show you after dinner if you'd like."

"Love to. Mm, something smells nice."

"How about you hop in the shower and I'll set about heating dinner up, and then you can come out and tell me all about *your* day."

Sarah kissed her and started to undo Mac's tie and unbutton her shirt. "I've got a better idea. How about you hop in the shower with me, and I can tell you all about it while we're in there?"

Mac grinned. "I think I can manage that."

After dinner they retired to the lounge room. Mac set the television up and replayed the day's events. She handed Sarah the file of photographs that she had printed off that afternoon. While Sarah was looking at them, Mac topped up their wine glasses, then took the bottle back out to the kitchen. She returned, carrying a bag.

"They're super photos. They really capture the fun of the day."

"I know, Jean did a great job."

Sarah noticed the bag. "What's in there?"

"I had some time this afternoon and went shopping. I thought Jean and Thomas might like this." Mac pulled out a frame with the photo of Jean and Thomas, in his safety buddies hat, standing next to the truck.

"Look at that! They are so going to love that. Look at Thomas standing to attention. Isn't he gorgeous?"

Mac went quiet. She reached into the bag again to lift out a small gift-wrapped box. She held it in her hand a moment before taking a steadying breath and placing the box in Sarah's lap. "This is for you."

Sarah looked at the box, then looked at Mac, who was clearly nervous. She carefully unwrapped a soft ash-pink velvet box. Slowly she opened the box, to discover a fine silver necklace hosting a tiny silver- and diamond-encrusted key. Sarah's mouth fell open. It was beautifully crafted, finely made, the delicate touch of diamonds on the key's head catching the light and sparkling. Truly elegant. Sarah looked up at Mac, her voice whisper soft with emotion. "This is beautiful."

Mac's fingers nervously traced a thread line along her trouser leg. "I've been wondering what I could get you. I saw this and it felt right."

"Oh, honey, you don't have to get me anything. You are my gift."

Mac shook her head. "I wanted to give you something, to show you how important you are to me. You are the key that has set me free. You've helped me start living again. You have given me love, when I didn't think there would ever be another chance to love again."

Tears gently flowed down Sarah's face. She closed her eyes.

"Too much, too soon?" Mac asked, and Sarah could hear the nervous tremor in her voice.

She opened her eyes. She could see Mac's face closing down at her prolonged moment of silence. "It's beautiful. I feel a little overwhelmed. I was only thinking today, that the note you left for breakfast—that's the first love note I've ever been given. And now you give me such a beautiful gift and tell me how much you love me. I can't believe how lucky I am that I met you, and even luckier that you love me."

Mac's eyes filled with tears. "So you like it?"

Sarah kissed her. "I love it. Thank you."

Mac held up her hands. "I'm sorry, I can't put it on for you."

Sarah reached into the box, gently lifted the chain, and placed it around her neck. Sarah touched it lovingly. "Does it look okay?"

Mac smiled. "You look perfect."

CHAPTER TWENTY-EIGHT

Mac's final class at the hospital went smoothly, finishing on time, which coincided nicely with Sarah's lunch break. Over lunch Sarah showed Mac a photo of Richard. Even on the phone's small screen, Mac could see where some of Thomas's features had come from, such as his colouring and physical build. As she played with her yoghurt, she wondered about the danger Richard might pose to his family.

"Not hungry love?" Sarah asked.

"Not really."

"Why's that?"

"Don't know. I don't suppose I've done enough to be hungry." One of her legs bounced up and down under the table. "I'm just a bit antsy. Is there a storm predicted for the weekend? Sometimes I get like this before a big storm. Sort of restless inside, if that makes sense. Maybe I should do something physical when I get home—that might fix it."

"All right. If that doesn't fix it, then we'll have to think of something else."

Mac grinned. "Oh yeah? Like what?"

Sarah stirred her coffee. "Oh, I don't know, I thought I'd take you for a drive, down a quiet country road somewhere, let you out, and you could run behind the car all the way home."

"Oh, ha-ha. I thought I might clean the house and get a head start on the laundry if I finish up early. Not exactly groundbreaking, but it is useful."

"Good idea. I think I'm on my last pair of clean knickers."

Mac grinned and wiggled her eyebrows. "You could go commando."

Sarah playfully bumped her with her shoulder. "I won't have to if you do the laundry this afternoon."

Mac rubbed her chin in deep thought. "Hmm, choices, choices… clean underwear and clothes, or near-naked partner. Have you got a coin I could toss?"

Sarah scrunched up a napkin and threw it at her, laughing.

Mac stirred her yoghurt again. "I'm guessing Jean and Thomas will be staying on at your place for a while."

Sarah's eyes narrowed. "I guess. Is that a problem?"

Mac shook her head. "No."

"What's on your mind, then?"

Mac gathered her thoughts for a moment in the hope of making sure what she wanted to say came out right. "Some of my furniture is a bit old. I mean, I know that you have your own place, I was just thinking, for the interim, while Jean and Thomas are there, we could maybe look at getting some new furniture. Make it more into *our* place…if you want."

Sarah's fingers went briefly to her key necklace, and then she reached out and took both of Mac's hands in hers. "I've done some thinking lately, about you and me, and I have come to a few rather startling conclusions. The biggest of those is that I don't care where I live, as long as you're there. I need some more things from home, like underwear, obviously, but really? All I need is you."

Mac smiled. "Well, I would still like to go shopping, if that's okay? I'd like it if, wherever we are, it could reflect a little bit of us. Maybe tonight, we can have a look and a think about what we might like to do."

"Okay. How about if you pick us up something nice to drink with dinner this afternoon and maybe some catalogues from some of the stores, and I'll make us dinner and we can sit down and bounce some ideas off each other."

Mac sipped her iced tea. "Okay, I can do that."

"Good, that's settled, then."

Mac was conscious of the time. "I suppose I should let you go, and I had best drop the photos and posters off to the school."

"Thanks. Oh, and can you pick up some paint colour charts too? I want to see what shades of pink might work in the bathroom."

Mac's eyebrows went up in surprise. Pink?

Sarah slapped her on the upper arm. "Gotcha."

Chuckling, Mac shook her head. "All the world's a comedian, and I get you?"

Sarah kissed her soundly and stood up grinning. "You sure do, honey."

❖

Mac arrived at the school armed with a set of all the photos that Jean had taken the previous day. Her favourite was the blown-up and laminated group photo, that could be pinned up in the classroom. She'd also come equipped with a selection of fire-safety posters that would enable Miss Kelly to rotate them throughout the year. Spying Jean coming towards her, Mac slowed up. "Hello, there."

Jean came over and kissed her on the cheek. "Hi, Mac. I have to thank you for yesterday. Thomas hasn't stopped raving about it. He wore his cap to bed, you know?"

"Did he? That's too cute."

"I know. In fact, all the kids are raving. You and John were an absolute hit yesterday. And to tell you the truth? I had fun too."

Mac beamed. "I'm really glad. I have to say, you took some fantastic pictures yesterday. My chief even asked for some copies for his office." She reached into the box and gave Jean her framed photo. "I thought you both might like this to take home."

Jean looked down and smiled. "It's beautiful. Thank you."

"No, thank *you* for helping to make the day so wonderful. But I have to confess, I don't know how you do it, with the kids all day. I was completely busted by the end of yesterday. I take my hat off to you."

Jean took a piece of paper out from one of the folders she had tucked under her arm. "Speaking of photos, I sent Sarah one earlier, but here's a better one of Richard."

Mac looked at the printout. Thomas had Richard's profile, but the subtle fine symmetry of his mother. You could easily pick them as father and son. Mac folded up the picture and put it into her jacket pocket. "Thank you. I'll take this home and show Sarah. Any more news from the solicitor or the police?"

Jean shook her head. "No. Nothing official."

"But?"

"It's like holding your breath, waiting for the other shoe to fall."

"I hear you."

Jean took in a deep, calming breath. "In the meantime, we just have to keep on keeping on."

"Absolutely. Speaking of which, I had better get these to the classroom." Mac leaned over and placed a quick kiss on her cheek. "You know where I am if you need anything."

"I do, and thank you, Mac."

"You're welcome."

Mac knocked on the classroom door. One of the children she had met the previous day opened the door. "Hello, Shelley." Mac smiled at the girl.

"Hello, Mac."

Miss Kelly could be heard clearing her throat in the background. "Ahem, Shelley, what do you say to Mac?"

"Please come in, Mac."

"What lovely manners. Thank you very much." Mac walked into the classroom and set the box on the table to free her hands up to sign. "Hello, Miss Kelly, hello, everyone."

The group cheerily greeted her back in unison. "Hello, Mac!"

Mac presented each child with their photos, and the framed group photo was given pride of place at the front of the teacher's desk. Finally, Mac reached inside the box for the USB stick that contained the complete set, only to discover that it wasn't there. "It must have slipped out on the trip over. May I borrow a couple of safety buddies to help me, and we'll just nip out to the truck and get it?"

Thomas and Shelley headed out with Mac to her vehicle. "What we're looking for is a red-and-silver plastic computer stick, about the size of your finger." Mac opened the front passenger door and the back seat door behind that. Both kids stuck their heads into the car to see if the stick was on the floor. Shelley found a poster that had rolled out of the box just as Thomas knocked on the panel of the door, triumphantly holding the missing USB stick in his hand.

"Good work, Thomas! Okay, let's get these back inside."

As Mac closed the doors she saw a reflection of someone standing behind her. Turning, she found herself looking straight up into Richard's face. Slowly Mac put her hands behind her, shepherding both children protectively behind her back. Mac estimated him to be about six foot two. He was lean, in an athletic kind of way. Even if Mac hadn't seen the photos, there was no denying the connection between father and son. Mac smiled and tried to portray calm. "Can I help you?"

Richard's face was set sternly. "I want the boy."

"Would you care to come into the classroom and have a look around?"

Richard's eyes were flat and hard. "I *want* the boy."

Think, Mac, think. "It's Richard, isn't it?"

"What's it to you? Give me the boy."

"Have you learned to sign yet, Richard?"

Richard's face jerked slightly at the change in tactic. Mac kept going while she had him off guard. "I didn't think so. See, we have a slight problem. I have two frightened children here. You don't want the police, and I don't want any trouble. So hear me out a minute. Let the little girl go back to the classroom, and you and I can sort out what to do next."

Mac took a chance and turned her back to Richard. She could see him standing, shocked, in the reflection in the window. She had to move fast. Kneeling down, she slid her mobile phone out of her hip holster, muted the sound, and slipped it into her sock. With her other hand she took the stick off Thomas and got the folded-up photo of Richard out of her pocket. Wrapping them up tightly together, she gave them to Shelley. Mac gently lifted Shelley's chin with her hand to make sure she was watching her. "Shelley, sweetheart, here is the USB stick. Give this piece of paper to Miss Kelly straight away and tell her that's the file she needs—and tell her Mac is with Thomas. Can you remember that?" Shelley nodded. "Good girl. Off you go, back to Miss Kelly with that file. I'll see you in a minute." Shelley looked uncertainly at Mac. Mac winked at her. "Off you go, love."

Shelley turned her chair and wheeled quickly back to class.

Mac turned back to Richard. "Thank you. Now, about Thomas…" Richard went to shove Mac out of the road but she just stepped sideways, guiding Thomas with her hands so that she remained between the child and his father at all times. "I'm sorry. I can't let you take Thomas. And even if you did get him, how are you going to communicate with him?"

Richard stood for a moment, as if in thought. Mac watched in horror as a mean treacherous leer spread across his face. The hair on the back of Mac's neck stood up. "You're right. I need a slight change of plan. I saw you sign to the boy as you came outside, so you're the change in plan. You're both coming with me."

Mac shook her head. "No, I don't think so."

Richard's hand whipped around and smacked Mac straight across the face, snapping her head sideways, causing her to briefly stagger under the blow. The corner of her mouth stung and her jaw ached. She could feel a trickle of blood from a split lip dribble down her chin.

Richard pulled a Glock pistol from under his jumper. "I wasn't asking, bitch. You and the boy are coming with me." He roughly grabbed Mac and shoved her into Thomas.

Mac signed, "It's okay, Thomas. We're just going to do what he asks. Okay?" Thomas nodded.

Richard shoved them both towards a dark blue sedan parked across the street. "That way. Move." Richard signalled for Thomas to get in the back, then pointed with the gun for Mac to get into the driver's seat. He came around and opened the passenger door as Miss Kelly came running around the corner screaming out Thomas's name. Richard saw her, got in the car, and threw Mac the keys. "Drive." Mac looked at him. Richard reached over and pointed the gun at Thomas. "*Drive!*" Mac started the car, put it into gear, and pulled away from the curb with a squeal of tyres. Richard turned his attention to Mac and pointed the gun at her ribs. "What's your name?"

"It's Mac."

"All right, Mac, listen to me. Do as you're told, and we'll all get along just fine. Fuck me over, and you're both dead. Have I made myself clear?"

Mac kept her eyes on the road. "Crystal."

❖

Mac could see how frightened Thomas was in the rear-view mirror. She caught his eye and winked at him. It was all she could offer him in reassurance as Richard directed her through the city and into the outskirts, to the old, largely abandoned industrial part of town. Richard directed her to turn into a cul-de-sac and drive through to an abandoned warehouse, right at the end. They drove through the gates, around to the back, and into an open shed bay door. Richard made Mac get out and shut the big doors behind them. The doors were stiff and it took considerable effort to get them to close. Mac could see that she must have torn open one of the cuts on her left hand again, as a small amount of blood started to stain the white bandage. She walked back to the car where Richard had grabbed the keys, opened the back seat, and was pulling Thomas out by the arm. Mac grabbed Thomas and wrapped her arms around him. "He's just a child. You don't have to be so rough with him."

Richard backhanded her again. "He's my child, and I'll do what I bloody well like." Richard popped the boot and pulled out a bag and a sawn-off shotgun.

Mac sniffed as blood began to drip from her nose. She pulled a hanky from her pocket and soaked up the worst of it.

Scowling, Richard turned to look at her. "Back there, at the school, how did you know my name?"

Mac shrugged. "I'd heard about you, and I could see the family resemblance. I just put two and two together."

"Who'd you hear about me from? Jean? Or her fuckin' interfering sister?"

Mac bristled at the reference to Sarah.

Narrowing his eyes, looking Mac over intently, he noticed her jaw clench at Sarah's reference. "Oho! Don't tell me you have a thing for the dyke queer?" Richard laughed leeringly into her face. "Oh, two for the price of one. This just gets better and better."

Richard pushed them both towards a metal staircase. Mac put Thomas in front of her and kept her hands on his shoulders to let him know she was there. Together, they walked up the stairs, across a small metal-grated balcony, into what looked like an old office. Mac mentally mapped the room as they walked in. There was only one entrance. A set of windows opened out to what was probably the street they'd driven up, with a second window next to the door they had just walked through, which overlooked the floor of the warehouse space below. A pillow and some bedding lay on the floor next to a metal desk and chair in one corner. A series of cupboards lined a wall opposite that, and two structural steel beams bisected the room, reaching from floor to ceiling. Richard ordered Mac and Thomas to sit against one of these beams. Thomas curled up next to her right side, and Mac put her arms around his shoulders, drawing him in tight against her.

Richard paced backwards and forwards, tapping his head with the nose of the gun.

Mac watched him. "So now what? You've got your son."

"I'm thinking."

"What do you mean, you're thinking? Don't you have a plan?"

"Of course I have a plan. To get my son."

"Okay. Well, you've got him. Now what? What do we do from here? Order takeaway and pretend happy families? What's your plan, Richard?"

"Shut up! Just shut up. Let me think." He started pacing again. He stopped, looked at Thomas and across to the bedding on the floor. He stormed over to one of the cupboards, slid the doors open, threw the bedding inside, and pointed to Thomas to get in. Thomas shook his head and clung to Mac tighter.

Richard looked at Mac and snarled, "Tell him to get in."

"He's frightened, Richard."

Richard leaned over and screamed in her face, "Tell him to get in."

Mac looked at Thomas and signed, speaking out loud for Richard's benefit. "He wants you to go in to the cupboard, sweetheart. You can still see me if you sit in there, near the door. Straighten out the blankets and try and make it comfy, hey? We'll pretend like it's a cubby house. It'll be okay. I'm right here."

Thomas nodded and crawled over to the cupboard and inside. Richard went over and made to shut the door.

"Please, don't do that. Leave the door open. That way he won't get frightened, and you can keep an eye on him. Please, Richard."

Richard hesitated but left the door open before walking away. He searched in his bag on the desk and pulled out some cable ties. He came and stood over Mac. "Put your hands out."

Mac shook her head. "You don't have to do that. While you have Thomas, I'm not going anywhere."

Before Mac had time to think, Richard kicked her in the ribs on the left side. Mac felt her stitches pop and tear. Mac rolled onto her side, gasping for air and holding her ribs. As she lay in that position, he showed no mercy, kicking her in the back, head, and sides. Mac tried to roll into a tight ball, to minimize the areas he could strike.

Eventually puffed, Richard stopped and bent over double to catch his breath, while Mac just lay there concentrating on trying to breathe through the pain. He bent down and roughly grabbed her hands, looped the cable tie around her wrists, and pulled it tight, dropping her hands back to the floor when he was done. Standing up, he grabbed his bag and headed for the door. Mac could just make out the slamming and locking of the door and footsteps heading down the stairwell before she closed her eyes and gave in to the wave of darkness that stole over her.

Mac became aware of a screaming headache. She sneaked a glimpse through half-slit eyes. The light stabbed deep inside her brain like an electric current. Her eyes slammed shut against the assault. Gradually, she became aware of a tiny hand rubbing her shoulder. She gingerly tried to open her eyes again and saw Thomas squatting next to her, patting her shoulder and looking worriedly at the door Richard had stormed out of earlier. Mac realized she needed to sit up and try and reassure him. She tried sitting up, and hissed at the pain in her ribs. Feeling the crunch and grind of bone, she knew that more than just stitches had broken. Taking a breath, she gritted her teeth and righted herself, closing her eyes briefly, trying to narrow her thoughts in an effort to stop herself from passing out or vomiting.

Thomas patted her on the arm and Mac knew she had to rise above the pain for the boy.

She opened her eyes. She could hear Richard storming around downstairs. She figured they didn't have much time before he came back up. She awkwardly reached into her jacket pocket where her keys were and located her ResQMe keychain tool, then used the seat belt cutting blade to cut the cable ties binding her wrists. The circulation slowly made its way back into her hands and fingers. Digging her hand into her trouser pocket, she pulled out a white hanky which she rested on her thigh before reaching up and taking off her tie. She signed to Thomas, "I need your help to put this around my ribs. I want to tie the hanky over the cut. When I nod, I want you to pull the ends tight. Can you do that?"

Thomas nodded and reached behind Mac's back and brought the ends together as Mac held the hanky padding against the cut. She folded the ends over and gave him the nod to pull tight. Thomas did, and Mac finished it off, tying the ends into a knot. She panted through the pain. Downstairs she could hear Richard throwing things and yelling.

She looked at Thomas, who was staring at her with enormously round horrified eyes. She knew her lip was cut and her nose bloody. She could also feel that one side of her face was swollen, and her eyes were starting to close up. Looking at Thomas's expression, she could tell she must look pretty awful and scary. She put the sleeve of her jacket to her lips, dampened it, and tried to wipe some of the blood off. "It's all right, sweetheart. I probably look pretty awful, but it's okay. Are you okay?"

Thomas nodded. "I'm scared."

"I know, baby. Me too. But I'm going to try and get us some help, okay?"

He nodded again.

Mac pulled the cell phone from her sock and checked that it was still muted. She dialled the emergency number and quickly said, "This is firefighter Lieutenant Mackenzie James. I can't talk. Hostage situation. I need police and ambulance to the old east side industrial estate." Mac's head snapped up as she heard Richard coming back up the stairs. She signed to Thomas, "Quick, back in the cupboard, honey." Mac whispered into the phone. "Please hurry and don't talk. If he hears you, we're both in danger. Just trace the call to find us. I'll try and keep the line open as long as I can." She quickly shoved the phone back into her sock and pulled her trouser leg down to cover it. With her hands back in her lap, she sat and rested against the pole.

Richard unlocked the door and threw it open. He grunted in satisfaction and kicked the door shut with his boot. He had a bottle of Jack Daniel's in his hand, which he'd obviously been drinking from, as a good half of the bottle was already gone. He paced the room talking to himself. "We're just gonna rest up here for a bit. They'll think I've left. They won't think to look in town. You know the best place to hide is right in front of someone. When it's dark, I need to swap cars. That stupid teacher saw us. I'll swap. Or maybe I could paint it. Couple of spray cans'd do it. Give me something to do while I wait. Yeah, that'd work. Ha! I'm a genius. See, kid? Your old man's a genius! Bet your crazy-arsed mother didn't tell you that, did she?"

Richard kept pacing, swigging from the bottle, and gesticulating wildly. "Ha! How easy was it?" He started to pace around Mac. "All those months of planning, and you walked straight out with him. Like a gift. I couldn't believe it." He took another swig and bent down low and laughed in Mac's face. Spittle flew from his mouth. His breath smelled so bad, Mac thought she was going to throw up, and she desperately tried to make her breathing shallow. "Here was I, thinking I'd have to wait until they were out playing after lunch, and I'd have to make a snatch and grab, and then you brought him out. Thank you. Hah!"

Mac kept her eyes down, refusing to look at him. Her hands were curled up in her lap. Looking down, she realized to her horror that her keys were on the floor by her side. She hadn't put them back into her pocket.

Richard paced several steps to the left of Mac, then turned and paced back. "I wasn't banking on taking you too, but it might just work in my favour. Oh, and the sweetness of it all. This way, I get back at both those fucking cows." Richard rubbed his hands together with glee. "You can do the driving, and that way I can just sit back and keep an eye on both of you. When we stop, you can teach me to sign. How do you like that for a plan, huh?"

To emphasize his point he kicked Mac again in the thigh. As she started to tumble, she reflexively put a hand out to stop herself from falling over and struck the keys. Richard howled in rage, then picked her up by the coat lapels until she was standing on tiptoe. He slammed her against the pole, growling, "You bitch! I left you tied up."

Mac's mind was racing. She had to try to calm him down. She tried reasoning with him. "I know you did, and I'm sorry, but my fingers were going numb. I can't sign for you if I can't use my hands. I didn't go anywhere. I stayed. I told you I would stay with Thomas.

We didn't go anywhere. We're still both right here. See? Right where you left us."

Mac could see that Richard was beyond reasoning. His pupils were pinpricks, his eyes glassy. There was a fine sheen of sweat on his face and he was extremely agitated. She could feel him shaking as he held her. He slammed her again against the pole. He snarled into her face, "You tricked me, you filthy cow. What other tricks do you have up your sleeve, huh? Show me. Show me!" He shook Mac so hard she thought her eyeballs would fall out.

She shook her head. "Nothing, nothing. I'm right here, where you left me, Richard."

He backhanded her across the cheek so hard, that her head ricocheted off the steel pole. She fell to the ground, onto her hands and knees. Blood poured from a cut above her eyebrow where she had connected with the pole. She could feel herself swaying. It would be so easy to just close her eyes and give in. She shook her head. *Stay awake for Thomas. Don't give in. You have to stay awake!*

Richard screamed in frustration and he started pacing again, leaving Mac kneeling on the floor. He came over and kicked her again in the ribs. Mac collapsed, groaning.

He strode back over to the table, grabbed some more cable ties, and stormed back over. He picked Mac up again by her jacket until she was sitting upright and slammed her against the pole, grabbing her hands and putting two cable ties around her wrists. He pulled them so tight the bands cut into flesh. "I'll fix you this time, you lesbo bitch. Think you're clever, huh? Well, not clever enough." Retrieving more cable ties, he pulled Mac's trouser legs out straight. He pulled her legs so roughly, that the phone jolted loose from Mac's sock and skittered across the floor.

For a brief moment in time, everything seemed to freeze and then slowly restart, only to work in slow motion. Mac's heart skipped a beat as she realized that this could be the thing that tipped Richard over the edge. Richard's mouth was open in surprise as he looked at the phone and looked at Mac. He slowly stood up, walked over to the phone, and picked it up off the floor. He pushed a button, no doubt disconnecting the call.

He looked at Mac with shocked eyes as he put the facts together. Mac could see the realization dawn on his face as he went from white-faced shock, to a purple-red rage. He stormed over and punched her in the face. "You fucking cow. What have you done?" He stomped two paces away from Mac, swung back on his heel, and looked down at her. His face was contorted with hate and rage. He looked down at Mac's leg, where she'd hidden the phone, and an evil angry leer twisted his face.

Mac shivered in fear.

He looked Mac straight in the eye, raised his leg high, then drove his foot down, hard, powered by his rage, slamming his boot down on Mac's leg. The room echoed at first with the snap of bone, quickly followed by a scream of pain torn from Mac's lips. She rolled to the side, clutching her leg, whimpering.

Richard knelt down next to Mac and leaned into her face until their foreheads were touching. "I told you not to fuck with me, didn't I? Didn't I?" He grabbed Mac by the jaw so that he looked straight into her eyes. "Do it again, and I'll kill you both. Understand?"

Mac swallowed and whispered, "Yes."

Richard dug his fingers into Mac's face as he shook her jaw. "Yes, what?"

"Yes, I understand. I'm sorry."

He shoved her to the ground, stood up, and resumed pacing the room. "You bloody women. Always thinking you're smart. Always causing problems. You're all the bloody same. Can't be trusted. Take everything away. Now you've gone and ruined the plan. I have to think. Need to make…"

The phone buzzed in Richard's hands, and he dropped it. He stood, staring at it, as it vibrated on the floor. The screen's face shone brightly as it flashed in time to the vibrations, grabbing and holding his attention. He slowly bent over and picked it up. He pressed the answer button. Mac watched anxiously as Richard listened, growing more red-faced by the second.

"Well, Mr. Kevin McIntyre, I don't care if you're with the police or you're the prime-bloody-minister, I don't want to talk to you, so piss off."

CHAPTER TWENTY-NINE

There you go. Try to keep your stitches dry for the next couple of days. The dressing will need changing in two days. Keep it covered during the day for the first week, just so that no dirt gets in. If all goes well, you can either come back here or see your local doctor in ten days' time to have the stitches removed. Alice here will get a few more details from you, and you can collect a script for antibiotics on the way out. And have a think about putting that safety guard back on, okay?"

The carpenter, who had sliced open several of his fingers on a scroll saw, nodded. "Thanks, Doc. I will."

Sarah was taking off her gloves and throwing them in the bin when her mobile rang. As she walked through the heavy plastic swinging doors to the nurses' station, she reached into her coat pocket to retrieve it. Looking at the screen she could see it was Jean. "Hey, Jean, what's up?" All Sarah could hear was Jean sobbing into the phone. "Jean, take a deep breath for me. Now tell me, what's the matter?"

"Richard's got Thomas. He came to the school and took him."

"What happened?"

"He was waiting for them and when they went outside, he grabbed them."

"Them?"

"He's got Mac too."

"Mac and Thomas?"

Jean broke into fresh sobbing. "Sarah, he's got a gun."

"Do the police know?"

"Yes, they're here now."

"Where are you?"

"I'm at the school."

"Stay there. I'm on my way."

She walked to the nurses' station and spoke to Claudia and Alice. "My nephew and Mac have been taken at gunpoint. Alice, can you get me a trauma kit ready please? Claudia, I need you to call Don and tell him what's happened and get him to come in. I'm going to the school. I'll have my phone on me and will call if I have any news."

Next Sarah rang Martha at the fire station. "Hi, Martha, it's Sarah."

"Sarah, I've just heard. Where are you?"

"I'm at the hospital, but I'm about to head to the school to be with Jean and the police. What have you heard?"

"Only that they have both been taken at gunpoint. The last report was that they were seen driving away in a navy-blue sedan."

"Okay, well if you hear anything, can you let me know?"

"Will do. Stay in touch."

"I will, thank you. Bye."

Just as Sarah hung up, Alice arrived with the kit and a triage vest that had Doctor written on the back. "I've put the radio in as well, in case you need it."

"Thanks."

Alice gave her a quick hug. "Please, be careful."

"I'll do my best." With that, Sarah grabbed the kit and ran out the door to her car.

She threw the bag in, slammed the car into gear, and took off. She knew she was speeding across town, and she was pretty sure she ran at least one red light, but she didn't care. Soon enough she turned the corner to the school and could see the flashing lights of the police cars parked in the school's driveway. She grabbed the bag and ran towards the nearest police officer.

"I'm sorry, ma'am, this is a restricted access area at the moment. I can't allow you to go in."

Sarah held up her bag. "I'm a doctor with the local hospital, and I'm here with a trauma field kit. The two people taken hostage?

They're my nephew and my partner. I need to get in there and be with my sister."

Chief O'Reilly strode over to her. He looked at the policeman and nodded. "It's all right, she's with us. Let her through."

The officer nodded and let Sarah pass to join the chief. "What's going on?"

"The police have not long arrived. We heard over the shared services radio that they're talking to various witnesses now to piece together what happened. Follow me and I'll take you in. John told me the little boy is your nephew."

"That's right."

"Anything you need, Sarah, you let me know. John is here too. He's in with your sister and the police, helping them with descriptions and the like." Sarah followed the chief into the school and towards the principal's office. The chief signalled to the police officer standing outside the office door to let them in.

Jean leaped out of her chair and straight into Sarah's arms, weeping. "Oh God, Sarah, what am I gonna do? He's got them. We don't know where they are."

"Shh, love. I'm sure everyone is doing all they can."

A detective walked over to them. "Hello. My name is Senior Detective David Morales. Dr. Macarthur, would you like to take a seat next to your sister?" Both Sarah and Jean sat down. "We have descriptions of all three people involved. The chief tells me you're a doctor from the hospital."

"Yes, I'm the doctor in charge of the emergency department. I've also brought along a field trauma kit, in case it's needed."

"That's good to know. Let's hope we don't need it."

"What happened?"

"It would appear the suspect was waiting outside the school grounds in a hire car. When Lieutenant James came out of the classroom with two of the children to retrieve some equipment from a vehicle, he approached them. Lieutenant James managed to send one of the children back with a note and a warning for the teacher. The teacher, a Miss Kelly, ran outside in time to see the suspect wielding a gun at Lieutenant James and the boy, before they drove away."

"What happens now?"

"We've issued a KLO4 to all units, a high priority broadcast to keep a lookout for the suspect, your son, and the lieutenant. We have extra patrols combing the city, and we've alerted the nearby towns to help with extra patrols on the crossroads heading out of town. At this stage, there's been no communication, no ransom demand. Some of my colleagues are busy trying to contact the suspect's most recent therapist. We're hoping to be able to build a profile and get a better picture of where he might be at, psychologically, to try and help us." The detective looked at the drawn faces around the room. "Why don't you all go and grab a hot drink from the staff tea room. We'll come and get you if we hear anything."

Sarah nodded. She put her arm around Jean. "Come on, love. All we can do now is wait."

They headed to the staff room with John in tow, carrying Sarah's kit. He put the bag down inside the door. "Why don't you two sit down and I'll put the kettle on."

Sarah smiled and hugged him. "Thanks, John."

John held her and whispered in her ear, "Mac will do her best to look after him. We have to trust in that."

Sarah gave him a squeeze, "I do."

Sarah's phone rang. She hurriedly pulled it out, hoping it was Mac, only to see Maree's name come up on the screen. She took the call outside the room. "Hello, Sarah speaking."

"Hi, it's Maree. I've got you on speakerphone. We're both here. Martha called and told us the news. Are you okay?"

Sarah leaned against the wall and closed her eyes. She was far from okay, but she knew if she lost it now she'd be no good to anybody. "Yeah, I'm okay. Just worried, like everyone else."

"Has there been any more news?"

"No. All we know is that he has both Thomas and Mac and that he has a gun. The police don't know where they are. They've got patrols out looking. All we can do is wait."

"How's Jean holding up?"

"She's terrified. We all are. But there's nothing we can do. John and the chief are here too. We're all just waiting."

"Would you like us to come down there with you?"

Sarah sighed. "I would, but there's already a cast of a thousand here. What about Martha? Is someone with Martha?"

"We were just talking about that. If you think you're okay there, then we might head over to Martha's. If nothing else, we'll cook up a storm together, the three of us, for when everyone comes home."

Sarah's throat closed as a wave of emotion hit her. She could manage a whispered, "Yeah."

"Sarah, you have to believe that. They will come home. We have to stay positive."

"I know."

"You sure you don't want one of us there?"

Sarah took in a deep breath. "No, it's okay. I'd feel happier knowing that you were with Martha. Thank you both, though. I really appreciate it."

"We're right here if you need us. You have my mobile number. Call if you need or want anything, okay?"

"I will. And thanks again, girls."

"That's all right. You hang in there, okay?"

"Okay. I'll call if I hear anything."

"Okay, give our love to Jean too."

"Will do. Bye." Sarah took a minute to centre herself before heading back. Jean looked up as she came in. Sarah shook her head. "Maree and Terri, seeing if we were okay. They both send you their love." Sarah turned to John. "They offered to come here, but I said that we were okay, so they're going to go over and stay with Martha."

John nodded. "That's good. They'll be able to keep each other busy."

All three sat and waited, watching as the minutes turned into hours.

CHAPTER THIRTY

Richard was pacing again and ranting. "Stupid fucking cow! All we needed were a couple of hours and we could have been gone, but oh no, little Miss Fucking Bright Spark…" He stomped past one of the cupboards that had a phone book, a cup of pens, and a box of computer paper on it. He picked them up and hurled them at Mac in rage. Suddenly he stopped pacing. He ran over to the window that overlooked the street. "They still don't know where we are. There's no one there. We might still have time. Can't wait for nightfall. Need to go. Gotta get ready…need to go now." Richard ran to the table and grabbed his bag. He stood over Mac. "You better be here when I get back."

Mac could only manage a whisper. "Yes."

He strode through the door, slamming it shut and locking it behind him. Mac heard him go down the steps. Pushing up on her elbows, then to her hands, she managed to right herself to a sitting position. She put her chin to her chest in thought. She had to come up with a plan. *We're running out of time. Can't take much more of this. Think, Mac. Think.* The stairwell. Maybe she could use that to buy them some time, 'til somebody came. She looked at Thomas in the shadows of the cupboard. He was sitting with his knees pulled up tight to his chest. *Poor baby's terrified. I don't blame him. So am I.* It was hard to sign. The ties on her wrists were so tight that she was losing the feeling in her hands and was very restricted in her movements. She half turned so Thomas could see her and clumsily signed, "When we go to leave this room, I want you to keep your eyes on me. When I say move, you move. Duck or run, whatever you can. Okay? Just move out of the road. You got that? Just move."

Thomas nodded.

"Okay, I need to rest for a minute. But remember what I said. You watch me and move, as soon as I tell you to."

Thomas nodded.

"Good boy."

Mac put her chin back down on her chest and concentrated on her breathing. She was so tired. She could feel that her shirt and jacket were soaked in blood from the cut on her ribs. She also suspected she had some internal damage from all the kicks she'd caught. In the last half hour, it had gotten harder to breathe.

She looked down at her leg and knew if she was going to get out of here, she had to at least try and straighten it so that it could take some weight, if need be. Her shin was slightly misshapen, with a lump in the middle. She closed her eyes briefly and offered up a prayer for it not to be a complete break, in the vain hope that she could put some weight on it. She knew if both bones were gone, her leg would collapse out from underneath her, but she had to be ready in the small hope that she could hold out. She carefully spun around until she faced the pole and hooked the foot of her broken leg around the metal beam. Next she took a deep breath and pushed out on the pole with her good leg, straightening and pulling the bone shafts apart. With grimaced teeth, and tears streaming from her eyes, she leaned forward and felt with her hands to make sure the bones were aligned as best she could manage, before releasing the pressure and falling backward, panting and whimpering with the effort. She bit her lip to stop herself from passing out. *Stay awake. Got to stay awake.*

Lying there, Mac thought through the possibilities. There weren't many. The door opened inward. The balcony was about a metre and a half wide and two and a half long, connected to the steps, which went down in two stages, about eight metres off the ground.

Again, Mac gritted her teeth and slid back into position, with her back against the pole. She dropped her chin to her chest and rested. Every movement was such an effort. She was reduced to taking short rapid breaths. She turned her head and looked at the window facing the street. It had gotten dark outside. She had no idea of what the time was or how long they had been there. It was also starting to get cold. At least Thomas was warm in the cupboard.

A flashing light out the window caught Mac's eye. She looked again. Nothing happened. *Damn. Must have imagined it.* Mac's head snapped around. She could hear Richard running up the steel stairs. The door burst open. His face was covered in sweat. Mac could see the Glock tucked into his belt and he had the sawn-off in his hands. His eyes were wide and panicky as he looked around the room.

He strode over to Mac and kicked her hip. "Fucking cops have found us, thanks to you."

Mac smiled lopsidedly in relief. "God bless the cavalry."

The sound of a loud hailer broke the silence. "Richard Adams. This is the police. Richard, we know that you have two people in there with you, including your son Thomas. We're currently outside the building. I'm going to call you on the phone and I'd like you to pick up."

As promised, the phone rang. Richard pulled it out of his pocket. "What?…No, *here's* the deal. You piss off, and I take my son, and we all get the hell out of here…All I want is my son."

Whatever the cop was saying to Richard, it was making him increasingly agitated.

"I know what you're doing. You're trying to get inside my head. Well I won't let you! And I won't let you take my son away from me again. I am leaving here *with* my son, one way or another. Either way, he's coming with me." Richard disconnected the phone and threw it against the wall, shattering it into pieces.

Mac looked around the room to see if there was anything she could use as a weapon. There was nothing.

Richard strode over to the cupboard, reached in, and roughly grabbed Thomas by the shirt. Thomas kicked and struggled. Richard slapped him upside the head. "Stop it, you little shit." He dragged him to the door. Thomas turned and looked at Mac. His eyes were wide with terror and his mouth open, desperately crying to her with a silent scream for help.

Richard turned to Mac and offered her a last sneer. "See you in hell, bitch." Holding a kicking Thomas in one hand and the shotgun in his other, he turned and was struggling to open the door.

Mac saw her opportunity. She struggled to one knee and pushed off, hoping to God her leg would hold out for just a few steps. The pain was almost blinding. She focused on Richard. She signed to Thomas, "Move!"

Thomas gave Richard one last big kick in the shins, which made his knees buckle. Richard turned to Thomas. "You little—"

Thomas ducked as Mac leaped for Richard. She caught him straight on the chest, the momentum sending them both crashing through the glass window next to the door and out onto the steel balcony. As Mac landed heavily on top of Richard, the gun discharged, both of their bodies jolted by the force of the blast. Panicking, Richard pushed Mac off and tumbled out from under her, only to slip off the side of the balcony. He reached out and clung onto the edge, his body swinging underneath him in mid-air.

Mac lay there, stunned, on her back. Her feet dangled over the edge. She was struggling to catch her breath.

She could hear Richard just below her. "Help me!"

She raised her head to see his fingertips on the edge.

"Help me!"

His hands were grabbing and reaching blindly for a hold. Groping wildly, he found the ankle of Mac's broken leg. She yelled in pain. She could see Richard's twisted smile as he laughed. "If I go, you're coming with me, bitch."

Mac raised the knee of her good leg as she saw Richard beginning to raise himself up over the edge. "In your dreams, you arsehole." With her last remaining strength, Mac kicked out at Richard's head as hard as she could manage and caught him flush between the eyes with the heel of her boot, the force of the blow causing him to lose his grip on both Mac and the balcony edge.

The look of horror on his face, as he lost his grip and realized his fate, was almost comical. As if in slow motion, his arms spread out, flailing. He had a few moments of free fall, before it ended abruptly moments later, with a sickening, wet thud.

Chapter Thirty-one

Jean paced the room. Sarah didn't have the heart to tell her to sit down. Pacing or sitting, it wouldn't lessen her worry. The silence was shattered as the chief came bursting through the door. "They've found them. They're holed up in an abandoned factory over on the old east side industrial estate."

Jean stopped pacing and held her hands to her chest. "Oh God. Are they okay?"

"The police aren't sure, but they think so."

"Can we go to where they are?"

"Yes, you can all come with me. We need to stay back and let the police handle this, but they've agreed we can be there as long as we stay out of the way. Let's go."

They all filed in behind the chief, Sarah collecting her bag as they rushed out the door. They quickly joined the flashing-lighted convoy speeding through town. Soon enough they were turning into the cul-de-sac. A message came across the radio: "Turn all lights off. Nonessential vehicles, please hold the rear flank." The chief parked the car just behind the paramedics. They watched as the police units rolled quietly into position. Officers spread out in strategic patterns. Two heavily armed squads took the lead and made their way to the factory building.

They all got out of the car and went and stood beside Detective Morales, listening as Kevin McIntyre made the phone call to Richard.

Sarah stood there rigidly with a death grip on the kit bag, John had his arm around Jean, the chief's face was set like stone. They all held their breath as Richard's last words, heard over the speakerphone, echoed in their minds. *Either way, he's coming with me.* The phone line went dead. A sob broke from Jean's lips.

The squads were given the directive to go ahead and enter the building. As the lead man approached the door and signalled for the others to follow, a shot could be heard coming from inside. Jean gasped and her knees buckled as John's strong arms held her tight.

Orders could be heard over the radio. "Go, go, go!" The armed squads burst through three of the doors simultaneously and swarmed the building. A second wave of officers stepped up to the outside entrances and waited for the next directive.

Sarah bent down and retrieved the vest. As if in remote control, she put it on and stood there, holding her breath, waiting for a report. Seconds stretched into eons as the silence grew.

"Suspect contained. I repeat, suspect contained. I need a medic in here."

Morales turned and waved to two of the paramedics to move forward. He put his hand on Sarah's shoulder and nodded for her to follow. The three of them followed him into the building. The squad leader met Morales halfway across the warehouse floor. "Suspect is over there. Looks like a fractured skull and broken neck from the fall. Need the medics up on the landing."

One of the paramedics peeled off to check on Richard and confirm the status. The other paramedic took off up the stairs. Sarah looked up and could see a silhouette lying on the landing, through the balcony's grated floor. She could also see blood dripping and splashing onto the floor. She took off at a run and joined the paramedic.

When they got to the top of the stairs, the paramedic went straight over to Mac and knelt beside her. "Hi, Mac. It's me, Trevor, the paramedic. Remember me? It's all right, love, we've got you. You're gonna be all right."

Sarah barely had time to register it was Mac before being physically hit around the waist, as Thomas ran and grabbed her, holding on tight. Sarah hugged him back and kissed his head. Tears were falling down both of their faces. She pulled him off and signed to him. "Are you okay? Are you hurt anywhere?" Thomas just shook his head and threw himself back into her arms.

Sarah felt a touch on her shoulder: Detective Morales. "Let me take the boy to his mother so you can help out here." Sarah pulled Thomas off again and signed to him to go with the policeman. She would see him in a minute, but she had to help Mac first. He nodded and took the detective's hand as they walked down the stairs.

"Doc, I need you."

Sarah quickly came to Trevor's side. She took one look at Mac and sank to her knees. She could barely recognize her. Her face was so swollen, cut, and bruised. There was blood everywhere. "Oh, baby, what has he done to you?"

Trevor put an oxygen mask over Mac's head. He pulled out some scissors and cut Mac's shirt open. Trevor carefully pulled the shirt ends apart to reveal Mac's torso, covered in horrible bruising and blood. "Holy crap! We've got a bleeder here." With one hand he grabbed a wad of padding and applied pressure.

Sarah's brain snapped into action. *Fall apart later. Mac needs you.*

The second paramedic joined them and went to Mac's head and was busy establishing an airway. Sarah ripped open the trauma kit and pulled out a saline and an O-negative bag from a cooler pack, then pulled gloves on. "What've we got, Trevor?"

"Head trauma, LOC, GSW upper-left quadrant. Looks like a through and through. Open pneumothorax, decreased breath sounds on the left. Multiple rib fractures. Probable internal bleeding."

She could hear Mac's chest making sucking noises with each breath. Sarah pulled out her stethoscope and listened. Trevor was right, decreased breath sounds on the left. Mac was deathly pale and covered in a fine sheen of sweat. Her lips had a slight bluish tinge to them.

The second paramedic took Mac's blood pressure. "BP's 55/35. I can't get a line in. Veins are flat."

Sarah turned to him and nodded. "Hang the saline and the O-neg. We need to get her pressure up. I'll put in a central line. While I do that, get a chest tube ready. And she'll need a chest seal. When you've done that, we'll turn her and put a pad on her back.

"On it."

Sarah opened up a central-line kit. She poured Betadine over Mac's shoulder, found the clavicle, used her fingers to find the vein, made a small incision, and inserted the needle. She got the flash of blood she wanted. Quickly she worked through the process, until finally the line went in. She would need to check it with an X-ray when they got to hospital, but for the moment, it would have to do. She taped down the clear seal and the line to Mac's shoulder, to keep it stable. She flushed the lines then attached the saline and the O-neg, opening the lines up wide.

Next, she opened the chest-tube packet on Mac's stomach. She poured some Betadine over the area, located the intercostal space she wanted, made a small incision, and put her finger in and explored the area; once satisfied, she put the tube in, quickly suturing it into place.

Trevor attached a monitor.

"If she starts going tachy, let me know."

"Right, Doc."

"We don't know where the bullet fragments are, so let's collar and spine board."

Trevor gently attached the collar and immobilized Mac's head. The second paramedic returned with the spine board, several police officers, and John, to help carry Mac down the stairs.

John met Sarah's eyes. "How is she?"

Sarah shook her head. "Not good. We need to get to hospital as soon as we can."

John had tears in his eyes.

Sarah had to turn away. If she looked at the pain in John's eyes, she knew she would lose the tenuous hold she had on her own emotions. She needed to concentrate on what she was doing. Sarah hung the last bags of O-neg and saline. Trevor gave her the nod. Mac was secured on the board, her neck in a collar, and her head taped between two rubber blocks for extra stability.

Trevor got everyone's attention. "All right folks, on my count, we're gonna lift and carry down as gently as we can. Lifting on three.

Everybody ready. On my count…one, two, three." Smoothly, Mac was lifted by the six men, with Sarah trailing slightly to the side with the IV bags.

They reached the bottom of the stairs and transferred Mac to the gurney. As the paramedics loaded the gurney into the waiting ambulance, Sarah spared a look behind her. She could see that they had covered Richard's body with a blanket. She hoped that Thomas hadn't seen Richard on his way down the stairs.

Jean saw Sarah and rushed over. "Is Mac okay?"

Sarah shook her head. "How's Thomas?"

"He's scared, but he's okay. We're going to take him to the hospital for a checkup though, just to be sure."

Sarah caught Trevor's eye as he signalled that that they were ready to go. "I have to go. I'll catch up with you there." Sarah scrambled into the back of the ambulance, the doors slamming shut behind her. "How's her blood pressure doing?"

"Not a lot of change, 60/40."

"Tell the driver to put their foot down."

Sarah picked up the radio from the kit. She called in to the hospital base. Don answered. "I need at least eight units of O-neg on standby, tell theatre to get ready. We have a GSW, open pneumothorax. Head and facial injuries, LOC, God knows how many broken ribs. I've put in a chest tube. Have a thoracotamy tray on standby. ETA, ten minutes."

The heart monitor went off. Trevor's voice sounded over the shrill beeping. "She's tachy."

Sarah looked at Trevor. "Tell them to pull over." She pulled her stethoscope out again and listened. "Shit." she could hear muffled heart sounds. She quickly opened the neck brace and saw that Mac's neck veins were hypertensive. She turned to Trevor. "What's the biggest gauge needle you've got?"

Trevor dug around one of the needle trays. "Sixteen gauge?"

"That'll do. I need some gauze too. She's developing a hemothorax. There's too much pressure, I need to drain some blood." Trevor swabbed the area clean. Sarah found the junction of the xiphoid process and the left costal margin, just below Mac's breastline, and inserted the needle. She angled the needle and felt it pop as it entered the space. As Sarah aspirated she saw the flashback of blood. She drained off 100 ml and was rewarded to see the heart monitor respond positively. She carefully withdrew the needle and placed the gauze over the top, applying pressure. "Righto. Let's go, as fast as you can, please."

Within minutes they were pulling up outside the hospital emergency entrance. Don and Alice were both waiting, along with Claudia and Professor Jefferies, the chief thoracic surgeon. Sarah quickly ran down the list of injuries. Left tib fracture. Possible eye-socket fracture, potential cheek and jaw fractures. Mac would pretty much need head-to-toe X-rays before she was done, but the major immediate problems were the gunshot wound and the fractured ribs puncturing her lungs. She'd lost most of her blood volume. The saline and blood already given had barely touched the sides. Blood was filling her pericardial space. She would also probably need an exploratory thoracotomy.

The team worked efficiently, cutting away the rest of Mac's clothes. They had enough blood pressure established to run several more IV lines into her arms to help increase her fluids. The X-rays taken with the portable machine showed a lot of damage. She would need more thorough pictures later, but they were good enough to get her up and into theatre and to get started.

Professor Jeffries patted Sarah on the shoulder. "You've done a great job getting her here. The team are ready and waiting upstairs. I'm going to go with her into theatre now. You stay here and I'll come and get you when I'm finished. Okay?" Jefferies nodded to the team, who swiftly took Mac out and up to theatre.

Sarah stood there, alone in the now-empty room. There was blood on the floor and bits of discarded gauze. There were even some remnants of Mac's trousers. She slowly turned, stripped her gloves off, and walked out towards her office. She passed Martha at the nurses' station, filling in forms, but lacked the energy even to wave.

Sarah made it inside her office door before her knees started to shake and tremble. She staggered sideways to the wall. Then Martha was there, rushing to her side, as the shock finally hit Sarah and her knees went out from under her. Martha helped guide her to the floor. She gasped and gulped in deep breaths. Martha sat on the floor beside her and put her arms around her.

Now that Sarah had finally stopped, the mountain of fear and grief hit her hard. A cry was ripped from her throat as she fell into Martha's embrace. Martha held and rocked her as she cried her heart out.

Chapter Thirty-two

Six hours after Mac was taken to theatre, Professor Jeffries came down to Sarah's office where she and Martha were waiting. Sarah introduced Martha. "Professor Jeffries, this is Martha, she's family. Martha, this is Professor Jeffries, the head of thoracic surgery. Mac is in the very best of hands."

Professor Jeffries held out his hand to Martha. "Hello, Martha, Sarah, please, take a seat."

Martha and Sarah sat side by side on the couch, while Professor Jefferies took the armchair. He ran his fingers tiredly through his hair and sighed. "The surgery went well. We had to do a lot of repair work from the bullet wound. The wound itself is fairly extensive and there are still some shot fragments retained that we decided to leave, rather than risk a longer surgery. The difficult part is that she has both blunt and penetrating chest wounds. She's got myocardial contusion, laceration of the left lung, bruising on the right. She has at least ten broken ribs. We've trimmed up the edges on the nasty ones to try to reduce further damage. We didn't see the need to fixate any of the broken sections. Positive ventilation should do the trick for the minute. In addition to that, we're keeping an eye on her left kidney, which is contused and bleeding. We had to give her seven more litres of blood in theatre, on top of the two you gave her earlier."

Professor Jefferies shook his head. "Those are just the big-ticket items. I don't have to tell you, Sarah, your girl's a mess, but the fact that she has gotten this far means she's a fighter. She's just being moved into ICU now. She will probably need more follow-up surgery, but I think she's had enough for one day. All we can do now is let her rest and keep an eye on her. She's not out of the woods by any means, but the fact that she has gotten this far is a positive thing."

Professor Jeffries turned to Martha and took her hand in his. "I have to warn you, she doesn't look great. She's hooked up, plugged in, and attached to an awful lot of equipment and medication. She's on a ventilator, and probably will be for quite a few days, and she has a number of drains in to help collect the blood and drain off various fluids. We're going to keep her heavily sedated for a while, to give her body a chance to rest and start to heal."

Martha took a deep breath and nodded. "Can we see her?"

Professor Jefferies patted her hand and rose stiffly from the chair. "Yes, you can both go on up. The staff are expecting you. Sarah knows the way. I'll join you in a little while. If you'll please excuse me?"

Sarah held out her hand to Martha, who wordlessly enfolded her own in it, and together they went upstairs. As they came out of the lift, one of the nurses came over to them. "Hi, Dr. Macarthur, my name's Carrie. I'm one of the nurses looking after Mac."

"Hi, Carrie, please, call me Sarah and this is Martha."

"Hello, Martha. If you would both like to follow me, I'll take you through. One of the doctors is with her now." They walked through some glass doors, then straight into Mac's cubicle. The doctor was standing between Mac and the doorway, so all that could be seen of her was the shape of her legs under the sheet on the bed. The room was full of noise—the rhythmic hiss and puff of the ventilator, the ticking of the IV pump, the beeping of the vitals monitor—with lights and numbers constantly flashing across the screens of the machines. Sarah could just make out a couple of bags hanging off the sides of the beds with blood and fluid in them.

The doctor stepped to one side. Professor Jefferies hadn't been lying when he said Mac was a mess. All down the left side of her face were bright red and purple stains from the bruising. Her face was grotesquely swollen, crosshatched with stitches in several places, dried blood matting her hair. There was a large white pad covering her chest and left shoulder, surrounded by bruising on her chest and arms exposed above the bed sheet. No doubt there would be a whole lot more of the same beneath the sheet. Sarah quickly wiped away the tears that ran down her face and stood alongside Martha.

Sarah leaned over and gently kissed Mac's forehead. "Hey, sweetheart. You've just had surgery and you did really well. You're on a ventilator to help you breathe easier. Try and let the machine do the work for a little while, so you can get some rest. Martha is here too, honey. We're both very proud of you."

For several moments, both women stood quietly, trying to absorb the enormity of Mac's injuries with the image of the person they loved lying in the bed before them.

Martha gently squeezed Sarah's hand, then placed a velvet box in it, closing Sarah's fingers over the top of the box and patting them.

Sarah looked at Martha for an explanation.

"This was Leonard's, my late husband's. I have held on to this for a very long time. I believe the time has come for it to pass on to the next generation."

Sarah waited silently as Martha gathered herself.

"Today has been inconceivable, but even with today aside, I know you know what Mac does for a living, and I also know the burden that comes with being the partner of someone who rushes into danger."

Sarah shook her head. "I've never been so frightened for anyone before. I'm not sure I'm going to be able to cope after this when she goes out on a call. I close my eyes and I keep seeing the images…" Sarah fell into Martha's arms weeping again.

When the worst of the tears had stopped, Sarah straightened and blew her nose.

"You learn to be a good actor." Martha had Sarah's attention. "You stand it because you love them. You need to be brave for them and wish them well as they head out the door. After they leave, you can worry your head off, but to their face, you need to be strong. If you worry, then they worry about you worrying, and when they're on the job, they can't afford to be distracted." Martha squeezed her hand, shaking it slightly for emphasis. "And when they come home, you hold them tight and tell them you love them. They are professionals, Sarah. We need to trust them. But they need us to be there for them. We help to hold them steady, so they can be who they need to be."

Sarah thought about Martha's words and remembered back to an earlier conversation she'd had with Mac, about the scratches on her neck after her patient had struck her. It was the same thing, really.

Martha hugged her and held her close and whispered in Sarah's ear, "I don't need to tell you how special she is—I think you know that already."

Sarah nodded.

"Love her with all your heart, Sarah. It'll be the best investment you'll ever make." They hugged again before Martha stepped back.

Sarah opened up the box. Inside was a fine silver chain with a Maltese Cross on it and some sort of figure in the middle, surrounded by some other ornamentation that Sarah couldn't quite work out in the dim room light.

Sarah looked to Martha. "It's beautiful. What is it?"

Martha put her hands over Sarah's, offering her a final squeeze. "Give it to Mac. She'll know."

Sarah nodded, placing the velvet box carefully into her coat pocket. She caressed Mac's forehead with gentle fingers. "I'm going to go and check on Thomas, and then I'll be right back. I love you sweetheart." Sarah gave her another kiss and took a step back. She pulled up a chair for Martha.

Martha sat in the chair and took one of Mac's hands in hers. "Hey, baby, Martha's here. I'm just gonna sit here with you for a while. You just rest up."

Sarah kissed the top of Martha's head. "I won't be long."

Martha nodded and smiled. "You see that the boy is all right. I'll take first watch until you come back."

Chapter Thirty-three

Six months later

As she drove home, Sarah mentally recapped the last few months and shook her head. It had been a hell of a journey, starting with one small moment in time that impacted so heavily on all of their lives. She herself no longer took as many things for granted and had set about making some changes in her life. Work was no longer the be all and end all that dominated her existence. Whereas once she worked predominantly the night shifts, now she evenly shared with her colleagues, not only the night shifts, but also took turns in the weekend shifts. Coming home had taken on a whole new meaning.

Getting stiffly out of the car after a particularly long day, Sarah walked in the front door and through to the dining room to discover the table set, fresh flowers in a vase, and candles softly lighting the dining table. She could hear Mac in the kitchen, and curious, she followed the sounds to see her partner with a tea towel draped casually over her shoulder, standing at the stove, stirring the contents of a steaming pan.

"That smells nice."

Mac turned and rewarded her with a brilliant smile and drew Sarah to her for a welcome-home kiss. Mac's arms looped around Sarah's neck, whilst Sarah's hands wrapped themselves around Mac's waist, linking their hips in tight. After the kiss, Sarah leaned her forehead on Mac's and hummed with pleasure. She pulled back and looked deep into Mac's eyes. "Coming home has never been so wonderful. Thank you."

Mac gently kissed her. "It is truly my pleasure. Dinner's a little way off yet. Why don't you throw yourself in the shower and then when you come out, you can tell me all about your day?"

"You sure? Do you need me to do anything here?"

"Everything's under control. You go and get wet."

Sarah appeared half an hour later, clean and wrapped up in one of Mac's fleecy hooded tops and a soft pair of faded jeans, her favourite clothes. She walked up behind Mac, wrapped her arms around her waist, and nuzzled her neck.

Mac smiled. "You smell nice. Feel better?"

"Mm, I do. Thanks. You know, I don't think I've ever come home to someone cooking me dinner before. This is really wonderful. It smells great. What are you making?"

"Honey and soy chicken with stir-fry veggies and rice."

"I'm impressed. Seriously."

Mac blushed. "I have a confession to make. One morning a week, for the past couple of months, Maree and Terri have been taking turns trying to teach me how to make some basic dishes, so that I can help out with the cooking at home."

"You don't have to do that, honey. I'm happy to cook for you."

"I know. But I want to help out. I want to be able to put something nice on the table for you at the end of a long day, without burning the house down. I'm never going to be a whizz in the kitchen, but I want to be able to offer you more than a toasted cheese sandwich when you come home."

Sarah hugged her tight. "That is one of the nicest things anyone has ever done for me. Thank you, sweetheart."

Mac chuckled. "Don't thank me yet, you haven't tasted it."

"It looks and smells lovely. You've done a great job. I'm sure it will be fine."

Mac leaned over and snagged a glass of wine off the counter and handed it to her. Mac giggled. "I don't think I'll be any good in the kitchen long-term. I am so paranoid. I keep checking the clock so much that I think I'm bordering on OCD. But we have approximately seventeen minutes until the rice is done, so here is your wine m'lady. Come, sit, and tell me all about your day."

Sarah sat on the floor while Mac sat behind her on the couch and massaged her tired shoulders. "Oh, my word." Sarah leaned into Mac's hands. "If I had known this was waiting for me at home tonight, I'd have knocked off a lot sooner."

"Tough day?"

"Not really. Just a long one. How did you go today?"

"Not too bad." In addition to intensive physiotherapy, Mac had been working with a counsellor over the last couple of months, to help her deal with her nightmares. The last month, she'd reaped the benefits from her therapy, with the night terrors slowly beginning to recede. "We thought we might finish off today and see how things pan out. I can always go back if I need to. It's been good. I've learned how to deal with things a bit better, and I think I have a better skill set to work through other stuff. I'm certainly sleeping better. I only have the odd night now where I wake up, so I'm happy with that."

Sarah leaned her head back. "It's nice to have you in the bed all night. I love it when I wake up and roll over and you're still there. I love watching you sleep." Sarah shook her head and chuckled. "Who am I kidding? I just love watching you."

"And likewise, my love."

Smiling, Sarah watched as Nell sat in her bed, chewing happily on a rawhide bone. Terri and Maree had gifted Mac with Nell a few weeks after she had come home. During the day Mac took Nell on walks, which helped build up her stamina. At night, Nell retired to a soft bed beside the fireplace in the lounge room. Sarah always joked that she had the best room in the house.

Sitting on the floor with Mac's hands massaging her shoulders, life was slowly cruising towards a new groove of wonderful. Sarah couldn't remember ever feeling as happy and fulfilled as she did right now, despite the past harrowing few months as Mac fought for life and later battled valiantly through months of pain on to the road to recovery. It hadn't been easy, for either of them, but together they had grown stronger and closer than she ever could have imagined possible. Her heart was full.

Sarah finally understood and appreciated what Martha had talked about in the hospital. Smiling softly to herself she gave a small nod. It was time.

She reached up and patted Mac's hands. "Hold that thought. I just remembered something—be back in a minute." Quickly retrieving the jewellery box from her bedside table, she returned and sat on the couch next to Mac. She held the blue velvet box carefully in the palm of her hand. Mac looked on quietly. "Martha said this was Leonard's. She gave it to me when you were in the hospital and said that the next generation should have it." She reverently opened the tiny box and turned it around for Mac to see. "Martha said you would know what it meant."

As she looked into the box, a lump formed in Mac's throat as tears flowed down her face. She nodded. She knew exactly what it was, her tears duly honouring the gift.

Sarah lifted the chain from the box and put it around Mac's neck, gently smoothing it onto her chest. "What is it? That's the Maltese Cross isn't it?" Mac nodded and pressed the medal to her chest, closing her eyes for a few seconds, soaking in the enormity of the gift.

Mac opened her eyes. Her voice was husky as she tried to talk past her constricted throat muscles. "It's the medal of Saint Florian, the patron saint and protector of firefighters. Wives sometimes give it to their husbands, to protect them and bring them safely back home to them."

Sarah opened and shut her mouth a couple of times, but she seemed lost for words at what Martha had given them. Sarah shook her head and lovingly wiped the tears from Mac's face. "Martha really is amazing."

Mac grinned. "Don't I know it. Nothing but the best women in *my* life!"

Sarah laughed and slapped her on the arm. "You are too smooth for your own good, woman. Speaking of smooth, how did you get on at the physio today?"

"She's really happy with my progress. She said she might take me through a test next week to see if maybe I can go back to work full-time."

"Oh, hey, that's great, honey."

"Isn't it?"

"Well, you've certainly worked for it, babe. I never doubted you, but I have to say, you've certainly blown me away with how hard you've worked and how far you've come."

"The only thing left on my to-do list is to finish the piece for Maree and Terri." Mac ran slightly exasperated fingers through her hair. "I just want to get back to normal."

Sarah caressed Mac's face. "I know you do, love. But there's one more thing you forgot on the to-do list."

"Oh? What's that?"

"Your rice. I think it's cooked."

"Oh, crap!" Mac leaped up and ran to the kitchen with Sarah sedately following in tow.

❖

After working on light duties for a few weeks, the day had come for Mac to undergo her final tests with the physio. To everyone's delight, she had been given the green light to start back on active duty. She was under strict instructions to take it easy and was still required to check in with physio on occasion, but as of that afternoon, she was cleared to get back to normal duties.

As the anniversary day for Maree and Terri's refuge drew closer, Mac had spent long hours before and after work in the shed, sometimes only coming inside long enough to catch up with dinner and the happenings of Sarah's day before retreating back out again. The anniversary dinner was going to be on the weekend, and Mac raced against time in order to be ready.

There was a community open day planned at the refuge, with activities and education programs, but the dinner was going to be the family affair they'd been planning for what seemed like forever, just Mac, Sarah, Martha, John, Jean, and Thomas.

She had just finished checking the last coat of finish on the sculpture and was heading towards the house when she spied Sarah watching her through the kitchen window. They beamed at each other. Life was good, and they had seamlessly settled into a rhythm together, as if it had never been any different.

Sarah had given her place to Jean and had moved into Mac's house. They'd brought some of Sarah's furniture over and had enjoyed buying some new pieces together. Mac had used her recovery leave to paint a couple of rooms in the house. Now, while the shell of the house was still the same, the inside reflected a nice mix of them both.

Mac came inside and washed her hands at the kitchen sink as Sarah stood behind her and embraced her. "You're in early."

"Mm, just been checking on the last layer of finish. It's cured off nicely. It's all done." Mac turned around and faced Sarah.

"Are you happy with it?"

"I am. And happier still it's ready in time."

"Don't suppose I can get a sneak preview?"

Mac shook her head. "Nuh-uh. Just a couple more hours, honey."

Sarah chuckled and lightly kissed Mac on the nose. "I think you enjoy being a tease."

Mac kissed her and grinned wickedly. "Oh, you know I do." Her hands slid stealthily up the sides of Sarah's jumper, caressing bare flesh. She brushed Sarah's nipples with her thumbs.

Sarah groaned into Mac's mouth before pulling away laughing. "Okay, okay, you made your point."

Mac laughed and looked down at Sarah's front appreciatively. "I'd say I made a couple of good points."

Sarah spun her around and slapped her on the butt. "You better go and hit the shower, Casanova, or we'll be late for the festivities." Mac laughed as she headed down the hallway to the bathroom.

Sarah smiled as she watched her go. It had been a tough few months for them all. It was nice to be able to come out the other side and appreciate what they had. Mac had worked hard at getting her fitness and strength back. It hadn't been easy and there were times when she had nearly come to tears with the frustration of it all, but to her credit, she kept her head down and kept going until each challenge was met and eventually overcome. Sarah was both amazed and proud at how much Mac had achieved.

As for herself, she'd initially been worried how she would go, living with someone. She had never allowed a relationship to last long enough to test the boundaries before. She was surprised at how easy it had been. There had been differences of opinions and compromises that had to be made on both sides, but they operated like a well-oiled machine, complementing each other nicely, whilst still retaining their own identities.

Sarah loved her work, but she now loved coming home more than anything, to a wonderful and appreciative partner. As Sarah put the lid on the container of baked goods she'd made for the day's festivities, including Mac's favourite, chocolate brownies, she was humming in pure happiness. Life was good.

Mac padded out to the kitchen with a towel wrapped around her torso and another one wrapped around in her hands, drying her hair. "You nearly ready, then?"

Sarah packed the last container into a box and patted the top. "Absolutely. When's John due over to help with the sculpture?"

Mac looked at the clock on the wall. "About another twenty minutes. What time did you say you'd pick up Jean and Thomas?"

Sarah glanced at her watch. "I'll leave here shortly and be there in about ten. So I guess I'll meet you there."

"Okay. I'll text you and let you know when we're nearly there, so you can make sure Maree and Terri are away from the house, and we can drop the sculpture off and get it into position."

Sarah grinned. "That still leaves us with a couple of minutes to kill."

Mac froze, her hands in the towel bunched in her hair. "Huh?"

Sarah advanced across the room and backed her against the large wooden upright pole in the middle of the kitchen. Mac's towel quickly slipped off her torso and she put her hands above her head and hung on to the beam to stop herself from falling down, her knees turning to jelly as Sarah's hands and mouth scorched a relentless trail of fire across her body, lighting up every single one of Mac's erogenous zones until she was tuned to a high tension. Sarah kissed her one more time on the lips before stepping back, leaving Mac panting and trying to stand on shaky legs. Sarah chuckled and patted Mac on the cheek. "You might make the finest points, sweetheart, but I think I win this argument. Oh, by the way, you better eat up when you get there, lover, and conserve your strength, because you haven't heard my closing statement yet."

Mac groaned and whispered, "Touché."

Throwing her a cheeky wink, Sarah laughed and blew her a kiss as she grabbed the box of goodies. "See you at the party, gorgeous."

Shaking her head, Mac chuckled as Sarah breezed out the door. She contemplated going back into the shower and standing under cold water, but John would be here at any time and she needed to get changed. She quickly threw on some clothes and was doing up her boots when she heard John's tyres pull up on the gravel drive. Mac stuck her head out the door. "You can drive on round to the back."

Together they lifted the boxes into his vehicle, silently packing and tying them into place. John stood up and dusted his hands off. "We right to go?"

"Ready when you are, big fella. Thanks heaps for helping me with this. I really appreciate it."

"It's my pleasure, little mate. I must confess, I can't wait to see it."

"Well, the sooner we get it over there, the sooner we can join the party, huh?"

"Lock and load, Mouse."

After the boxes had been carried in and manoeuvred into place, Mac shooed John outside to join Jean and Thomas, so she could set up the pieces. Once she was satisfied, she wrapped it all in a blanket and tied it up with an enormous red ribbon.

She took the packaging back to John's ute and joined the tail end of the tour group. She walked up beside Sarah, wrapping her arm around her waist.

Sarah leaned in and whispered, "How'd it go?"

Mac kissed her on the cheek. "Smooth as. Thanks for the cover."

Sarah squeezed her hip. "Happy to play the wingman."

Several hours later the last of the guests had left and all the animals had been fed and put to bed for the night. The small party made their way back to the house and relaxed in the dining room. John did the rounds with a champagne bottle, and Maree and Terri stood together, facing the seated group.

Maree cleared her throat. "Well, we made it. We want to thank you all for today. We couldn't have done it without you. Thank you, girls, for all the cooking and to the boys for doing all the cleaning up. But more than that, thank you for all of your love and support over the years."

Maree looked at Terri to continue. "The refuge has been our dream for a very long time. It's been hard work, but every moment has been worth it. And we ended up with more than a dream come true, we ended up richer than we could ever have imagined. We found a family, and in that family, we found depths of love, support, and acceptance beyond our wildest dreams."

Maree raised her glass to the group. "Here's to five wonderful years, dreams that come true, and, most importantly, to family."

The group saluted with their charged glasses. "To family."

Sarah nudged Mac. Mac turned and looked at her and mouthed, "Now?"

Sarah smiled and nodded. Mac handed Sarah her glass, stood up, and walked over to Maree and Terri. "I was going to do this after dinner, but now is as good a time as any. If you will follow me, please?"

Maree and Terri looked at each other a bit perplexed but followed Mac into the lounge room, to the corner, where a blanket-covered object sat.

Mac suddenly felt nervous. She took a deep breath in and looked up to see Sarah beaming at her. It gave her the courage to continue. "I met you two not long after you got here, and I think it would be fair to say, we've been as thick as thieves ever since. We've seen good times and not so good times together. I've watched you both work, so hard, to build this place up and to make it into the success that it is today. We are all so proud of you. You guys are amazing beyond words. And you're right, we're all family. So to celebrate your anniversary, underneath this blanket is something that reflects a little bit of all of us. John lent me his muscle and his steadfastness, it incorporates a piece of Martha's favourite tree, and Jean, Thomas, and Sarah came into our lives and helped show me how to put into form and personify the magic that the two of you have made together, with the refuge." Mac took both of their glasses and kissed them on the cheek. "Happy anniversary, my friends." She stepped back and waved for them to unveil their present.

Together, they stepped forward. Terri undid the ribbon while Maree gently slid the blanket off. There were seven audible gasps in the room as the blanket fell to the floor, and the group stood frozen in awe at the sculpture before them. Rising out of the base of a tree stump stood a carved version of Thomas in the softest of maple hues.

In his arms lay a sleepy golden puppy, carved from Huon pine, and a soft muted grey piece of myrtle, that looked suspiciously like Henry, wrapped itself around Thomas's leg, looking up at him adoringly.

Thomas was the first to move. He turned to the group with a huge grin on his face. "That's me! You made *me*. And that's Henry and Nell."

Mac smiled. "Yes, it is."

He ran over and hugged Mac and then ran back to admire his likeness again.

Maree and Terri stood in front of the statue with their arms around each other's waists. Maree's hand covered her mouth as Terri shook her head in disbelief. Both had tears streaming down their cheeks. Terri pulled Maree in and kissed her, then walked over to Mac and threw her arms around her, weeping softly in her embrace. Maree joined the hug.

Terri's head finally emerged. "I don't have words. That is the most amazing, beautiful…" Terri shook her head as she lost the words. "Thank you." She kissed Mac right on the lips.

Mac cleared her throat and knew that she was blushing fiercely. "You're welcome."

Maree also kissed her. "Terri's right. It is amazing. I can't stop looking at it. It almost feels like it's alive. You've captured not only an incredible likeness, physically, but you've nailed the love aspect. It's perfect. Thank you."

"I'm glad you like it. Now if you'll excuse me, I'm just going to grab another drink."

Mac disappeared into the kitchen and snagged a drink from the fridge. She was leaning against the bench taking a sip when Sarah quietly walked in, drawing her in close to hold her in an embrace. "Thought I'd find you hiding out here."

Mac gave her a half-guilty smile.

Sarah leaned in, gifting her with a slow, gentle kiss on the lips.

Mac smiled. "Mm, what was that for?"

Sarah reached up and smoothed Mac's fringe from her eyes. "Everything. Your sculpture is breathtaking. You did a superb job. But more than that, it's the love you put in it. You made everyone feel a part of that special moment. That was beautiful. You're beautiful."

Mac shook her head.

Sarah gently took her face in her hands. "Yes, you are, sweetheart."

Mac rested her head against Sarah's forehead. "I am the luckiest person. I have the best family. And you—you showed me how to live and breathe again. You make my heart sing every day."

Sarah kissed Mac's eyes, cheeks, and mouth. "And you helped me find what I needed most. You gave me your love and you helped me find home. I'd say we're both pretty lucky."

Sarah gave Mac a quick hug and stepped back. "What say we make our way back out to the party before they come looking for us?" Mac nodded and gave Sarah a last quick kiss before holding her hand and walking back together to join the festivities.

They briefly stood behind the group revelling in the love and laughter the group radiated. Mac knew how lucky they both were.

The sound of two pagers squealing cut the air and rendered the group temporarily silent. Both Mac and John looked at their pagers and read the message.

Three car MVA, persons trapped. Cnr Ruthven and Nelson, Freyling Park. Turnout respond.

Mac looked at John. "Betts, that's just down the road."

His face broke out into a smile. "You up for a run, Mouse?"

Mac knew her grin mirrored his. "Never readier."

Sarah silently nodded and held out her hand to hold Mac's drink. Mac kissed Sarah on the cheek.

As they ran to the door, Mac threw over her shoulder, "Shotgun gets to drive!"

John could be heard laughing as he ran outside. "Then you better get your arse moving, Mouse."

About the Author

Mardi grew up on the Mid North Coast of Australia, with big rivers, sun, surf, and sand all within reach. Among Mardi's greatest loves are watching storms out to sea and sitting on a rock wall, fishing and watching the world go by.

She moved inland to study, where the mountains called to her and eventually stole her heart. It's where she now calls home, along with her partner, two dogs, two cats, and a couple of hundred sheep.

Easily bored, Mardi is always on the lookout for a new project of some sort or other, including, but not limited to, music, drawing, woodwork, and now writing.

When she's not working full-time, Mardi is also a volunteer firefighter, firefighting instructor, and a member of a local wildlife rescue service looking after orphaned, sick, and injured native animals.

Her love of storms has transferred from the ocean to the rolling fields and hillsides high in the New England.

Books Available from Bold Strokes Books

Twice Lucky by Mardi Alexander. For firefighter Mackenzie James and Dr. Sarah Macarthur, there's suddenly a whole lot more in life to understand, to consider, to risk…someone will need to fight for her life. (978-1-62639-325-7)

Shadow Hunt by L.L. Raand. With young to raise and her Pack under attack, Sylvan, Alpha of the wolf Weres, takes on her greatest challenge when she determines to uncover the faceless enemies known as the Shadow Lords. A Midnight Hunters novel. (978-1-62639-326-4)

Heart of the Game by Rachel Spangler. A baseball writer falls for a single mom, but can she ever love anything as much as she loves the game? (978-1-62639-327-1)

Getting Lost by Michelle Grubb. Twenty-eight days, thirteen European countries, a tour manager fighting attraction, and an accused murderer: Stella and Phoebe's journey of a lifetime begins here. (978-1-62639-328-8)

Prayer of the Handmaiden by Merry Shannon. Celibate priestess Kadrian must defend the kingdom of Ithyria from a dangerous enemy and ultimately choose between her duty to the Goddess and the love of her childhood sweetheart, Erinda. (978-1-62639-329-5)

The Witch of Stalingrad by Justine Saracen. A Soviet "night witch" pilot and American journalist meet on the Eastern Front in WW II and struggle through carnage, conflicting politics, and the deadly Russian winter. (978-1-62639-330-1)

Pedal to the Metal by Jesse J. Thoma. When unreformed thief Dubs Williams is released from prison to help Max Winters bust a car theft ring, Max learns that to catch a thief, get in bed with one. (978-1-62639-239-7)

Dragon Horse War by D. Jackson Leigh. A priestess of peace and a fiery warrior must defeat a vicious uprising that entwines their destinies and ultimately their hearts. (978-1-62639-240-3)

For the Love of Cake by Erin Dutton. When everything is on the line, and one taste can break a heart, will pastry chefs Maya and Shannon take a chance on reality? (978-1-62639-241-0)

Betting on Love by Alyssa Linn Palmer. A quiet country-girl-at-heart and a live-life-to-the-fullest biker take a risk at offering each other their hearts. (978-1-62639-242-7)

The Deadening by Yvonne Heidt. The lines between good and evil, right and wrong, have always been blurry for Shade. When Raven's actions force her to choose, which side will she come out on? (978-1-62639-243-4)

Ordinary Mayhem by Victoria A. Brownworth. Faye Blakemore has been taking photographs since she was ten, but those same photographs threaten to destroy everything she knows and everything she loves. (978-1-62639-315-8)

One Last Thing by Kim Baldwin & Xenia Alexiou. Blood is thicker than pride. The final book in the Elite Operative Series brings together foes, family, and friends to start a new order. (978-1-62639-230-4)

Songs Unfinished by Holly Stratimore. Two aspiring rock stars learn that falling in love while pursuing their dreams can be harmonious— if they can only keep their pasts from throwing them out of tune. (978-1-62639-231-1)

Beyond the Ridge by L.T. Marie. Will a contractor and a horse rancher overcome their family differences and find common ground to build a life together? (978-1-62639-232-8)

Swordfish by Andrea Bramhall. Four women battle the demons from their pasts. Will they learn to let go, or will happiness be forever beyond their grasp? (978-1-62639-233-5)

The Fiend Queen by Barbara Ann Wright. Princess Katya and her consort Starbride must turn evil against evil in order to banish Fiendish power from their kingdom, and only love will pull them back from the brink. (978-1-62639-234-2)

Up the Ante by PJ Trebelhorn. When Jordan Stryker and Ashley Noble meet again fifteen years after a short-lived affair, are either of them prepared to gamble on a chance at love? (978-1-62639-237-3)

Speakeasy by MJ Williamz. When mob leader Helen Byrne sets her sights on the girlfriend of Al Capone's right-hand man, passion and tempers flare on the streets of Chicago. (978-1-62639-238-0)

Venus in Love by Tina Michele. Morgan Blake can't afford any distractions and Ainsley Dencourt can't afford to lose control—but the beauty of life and art usually lies in the unpredictable strokes of the artist's brush. (978-1-62639-220-5)

Rules of Revenge by AJ Quinn. When a lethal operative on a collision course with her past agrees to help a CIA analyst on a critical assignment, the encounter proves explosive in ways neither woman anticipated. (978-1-62639-221-2)

The Romance Vote by Ali Vali. Chili Alexander is a sought-after campaign consultant who isn't prepared when her boss's daughter, Samantha Pellegrin, comes to work at the firm and shakes up Chili's life from the first day. (978-1-62639-222-9)

Advance: Exodus Book One by Gun Brooke. Admiral Dael Caydoc's mission to find a new homeworld for the Oconodian people is hazardous, but working with the infuriating Commander Aniwyn "Spinner" Seclan endangers her heart and soul. (978-1-62639-224-3)

UnCatholic Conduct by Stevie Mikayne. Jil Kidd goes undercover to investigate fraud at St. Marguerite's Catholic School, but life gets complicated when her student is killed—and she begins to fall for her prime target. (978-1-62639-304-2)

Season's Meetings by Amy Dunne. Catherine Birch reluctantly ventures on the festive road trip from hell with beautiful stranger Holly Daniels only to discover the road to true love has its own obstacles to maneuver. (978-1-62639-227-4)

Myth and Magic: Queer Fairy Tales edited by Radclyffe and Stacia Seaman. Myth, magic, and monsters—the stuff of childhood dreams (or nightmares) and adult fantasies. (978-1-62639-225-0)

Nine Nights on the Windy Tree by Martha Miller. Recovering drug addict, Bertha Brannon, is an attorney who is trying to stay clean when a murder sends her back to the bad end of town. (978-1-62639-179-6)

Driving Lessons by Annameekee Hesik. Dive into Abbey Brooks's sophomore year as she attempts to figure out the amazing, but sometimes complicated, life of a you-know-who girl at Gila High School. (978-1-62639-228-1)

Asher's Shot by Elizabeth Wheeler. Asher Price's candid photographs capture the truth, but when his success requires exposing an enemy, Asher discovers his only shot at happiness involves revealing secrets of his own. (978-1-62639-229-8)

Courtship by Carsen Taite. Love and justice—a lethal mix or a perfect match? (978-1-62639-210-6)

Against Doctor's Orders by Radclyffe. Corporate financier Presley Worth wants to shut down Argyle Community Hospital, but Dr. Harper Rivers will fight her every step of the way, if she can also fight their growing attraction. (978-1-62639-211-3)

A Spark of Heavenly Fire by Kathleen Knowles. Kerry and Beth are building their life together, but unexpected circumstances could destroy their happiness. (978-1-62639-212-0)

Never Too Late by Julie Blair. When Dr. Jamie Hammond is forced to hire a new office manager, she's shocked to come face to face with Carla Grant and memories from her past. (978-1-62639-213-7)

Widow by Martha Miller. Judge Bertha Brannon must solve the murder of her lover, a policewoman she thought she'd grow old with. As more bodies pile up, the murderer starts coming for her. (978-1-62639-214-4)

Twisted Echoes by Sheri Lewis Wohl. What's a woman to do when she realizes the voices in her head are real? (978-1-62639-215-1)

Criminal Gold by Ann Aptaker. Through a dangerous night in New York in 1949, Cantor Gold, dapper dyke-about-town, smuggler of fine art, is forced by a crime lord to be his instrument of vengeance. (978-1-62639-216-8)

The Melody of Light by M.L. Rice. After surviving abuse and loss, will Riley Gordon be able to navigate her first year of college and accept true love and family? (978-1-62639-219-9)

Because of You by Julie Cannon. What would you do for the woman you were forced to leave behind? (978-1-62639-199-4)

The Job by Jove Belle. Sera always dreamed that she would one day reunite with Tor. She just didn't think it would involve terrorists, firearms, and hostages. (978-1-62639-200-7)

Making Time by C.J. Harte. Two women going in different directions meet after fifteen years and struggle to reconnect in spite of the past that separated them. (978-1-62639-201-4)

Once The Clouds Have Gone by KE Payne. Overwhelmed by the dark clouds of her past, Tag Grainger is lost until the intriguing and spirited Freddie Metcalfe unexpectedly forces her to reevaluate her life. (978-1-62639-202-1)

The Acquittal by Anne Laughlin. Chicago private investigator Josie Harper searches for the real killer of a woman whose lover has been acquitted of the crime. (978-1-62639-203-8)

An American Queer: The Amazon Trail by Lee Lynch. Lee Lynch's heartening and heart-rending history of gay life from the turbulence of the late 1900s to the triumphs of the early 2000s are recorded in this selection of her columns. (978-1-62639-204-5)

Stick McLaughlin: The Prohibition Years by CF Frizzell. Corruption in 1918 cost Stick her lover, her freedom, and her identity, but a very special flapper and the family bond of her own gang could help win them back—even if it means outwitting the Boston Mob. (978-1-62639-205-2)

Edge of Awareness by C.A. Popovich. When Maria, a woman in the middle of her third divorce, meets Dana, an out lesbian, awareness of her feelings brings up reservations about the teachings of her church. (978-1-62639-188-8)

Taken by Storm by Kim Baldwin. Lives depend on two women when a train derails high in the remote Alps, but an unforgiving mountain, avalanches, crevasses, and other perils stand between them and safety. (978-1-62639-189-5)

The Common Thread by Jaime Maddox. Dr. Nicole Coussart's life is falling apart, but fortunately, DEA Attorney Rae Rhodes is there to pick up the pieces and help Nic put them back together. (978-1-62639-190-1)